The
Freedom Star

Jeff Andrews

Eiger Press
Virginia Beach, Virginia

To Mary Lou
When I doubted you still believed

DISCLAIMER

Although a work of fiction, *The Freedom Star* portrays several actual historical persons, including my great-great grandfather, James Coleman, a private in the 19th Mississippi Infantry. James died of typhoid fever at Chimborazo Hospital in Richmond, Virginia on June 13, 1862 (Chapter Thirty-three). One outcome of my research for this book was the discovery of his numbered but otherwise unmarked grave in Oakwood Cemetery where he was buried alongside casualties of the Seven Pines battle. After years of anonymity, James now rests beneath an appropriate headstone placed there by his descendants.

In addition to James Coleman, several other actual historical figures make appearances in my book. In Chapter Thirty-five, Henry mentions Reverend Jasper, a slave who routinely held services at Chimborazo Hospital for the wounded soldiers. As well, all the Union and Confederate officers mentioned by name were real people holding the billets as depicted.

By far, my favorite historical character in *The Freedom Star* is Thomas Day, the free black master carpenter. Thomas Day was a renowned artisan and an economic force in mid-nineteenth century North Carolina. He not only owned slaves, but also employed many whites—both examples of an antebellum reality far more complex than our twenty-first century perceptions of that time.

Without knowing the true personalities of any of these individuals, my only means for drawing out their characters was through my own imagination. I pray I haven't dishonored them in any way.

Jeff Andrews
July 2012

ACKNOWLEDGEMENTS

While I cannot begin to adequately recognize everyone who helped me bring this novel from a mere idea to the reality of publication, I do wish to thank all my friends in the Zoetrope writing community and the Hampton Roads Writers. I would especially like to thank Lauran Strait, Jean Hendrickson, Mike Owens, and Rick Taubold, each gifted writers who gave generously of their time and talents to provide me with the guidance, encouragement, feedback, and editorial insight needed to bring this work to completion. I also wish to thank Mildred Jackson for her willingness to provide feedback on all matters concerning African-American History and culture.

Chapter One
October 1860

Moonlight bathed the narrow wagon track separating the forest from harvested tobacco fields beyond. Isaac straightened and cautiously stepped from his hiding place behind a gnarled oak tree. "They's just shadows, Pa. Ain't nobody out there." He pointed toward the field. "Nobody, 'cepting that old cottontail over yonder."

"Sh-h-h." Abraham held up his hand and cocked an ear toward the dusty road.

Isaac peered along the path. "Pa, I done told you—"

"Down!" His father disappeared into the shadows.

Isaac dove behind a rotted stump as two horsemen rounded the corner of Johnston's cornfield, galloping straight toward them. Isaac pressed against the dank earth, burying his face in the rotting leaves. He held his breath as the pounding of hoofs grew louder, seeming to pass directly over him, before fading into the warm autumn night. He remained frozen, hidden from all but the swarm of red ants crawling up his calf. He bit down on his thumb, stifling a cry.

"P-s-s-t. They's gone." The evening sky silhouetted Abraham's towering, broad-shouldered frame and familiar wide brimmed slouch hat.

Isaac slapped at the burn on his leg as he stood. "One was Clancy, that boss man from over at the Johnston farm. He's a mean one, he is. Didn't recognize the other—the younger feller toting the scattergun."

"It don't matter none," Abraham said. "They's hunting runaways, that's for certain. Next, they'll be bringing out the dogs. We'd best get to the old smokehouse and warn them that's waiting."

Swatting the back of his leg with his hat, Isaac brushed away the last of the vicious little critters and then retrieved his gunnysack and followed.

Abraham edged closer to the road. Crouching, he scanned the distant shadows and then beckoned. Isaac quietly settled beside him. Other than the mournful cry of a barred owl in a distant woodlot, silence filled the darkness. No sign of the patrols that roamed the fields and roadways in search of runaways. On Abraham's signal, they dashed across the exposed path and ducked into the cornfield.

Sweat caught the corn dust on Abraham's forehead and drizzled yellow-gray rivulets through the dark stubble of his beard. Isaac's hand trembled as he wiped his own brow. Were those runaways shaking too, holed up like cornered rabbits? He curled his lip and blew at a bead of sweat trickling down his cheek. "You reckon we lost 'em, Pa?"

"Sh-h-h. Get down."

Isaac dropped between the cornrows and searched the tree line on the far side of the clearing. Where were those riders? Where'd they go? A feller could get himself killed running from those patrols. Them that were hiding out yonder must have wanted their freedom mighty bad.

Last summer they'd helped a family with three children, one a babe in arms. Word had it they'd made it as far as Petersburg before being caught. Some said they were split up and sold to different owners. Isaac shuddered. Could be the stories were wrong. Could be they found that Promised Land.

Abraham raised his hand and Isaac froze. Those two horsemen might be the only ones patrolling tonight, but men on horseback could cover a lot of ground.

"Knowing where they been ain't the same as knowing where they is," Abraham whispered. "The fox ain't eating no rabbit what can think like a fox and the whip ain't finding the nigra what can get in the heads of them pattyrollers."

"That's too much to think on, Pa. A body can get plum wore out chewing over all them possibilities."

"You pay heed, boy. The time's coming when you'll be out here alone."

* * *

The smokehouse sat in a small clearing surrounded by tall oaks and poplars. No more than a shell, it was the lone relic of a long-abandoned farm, burned out more years ago than Isaac could recall. Far from traveled paths, it served well as an overnight stop, longer on occasion.

Isaac crawled behind a tree and searched the glade. After a moment, he cupped his hands and imitated the call of a whippoorwill. An answer echoed from the darkened ruins, and then a young man stepped from the shadows.

"You the folks be taking us to Richmond?" The young man asked.

"We can't take you all that way," Abraham said, stepping into the clearing. "But we brung you vittles enough for three days, more if'n you's careful." He took the gunnysack from Isaac and handed it to the runaway. "They calls me Abraham. This here's my boy, Isaac."

As they spoke, a slender girl with short pigtails tied in cloth strips stole from the shadows of the crumbling chimney and slipped behind the young man, holding him by the waist as she peered at Isaac.

She was only a child—no more'n fifteen—no older than his own little sister. How'd she ever stay ahead of the dogs?

The man put his arm around the girl's shoulders and pulled her close. "This here's Rebecca. We was married last week. Soon as we jumped the broom we done skedaddled. Been running ever since."

Abraham nodded to the girl and then turned to her husband. "You got some idea where you's headed?"

"We hear there's jobs in New York. I has family there. We's praying we can make it that far."

"This here map will get you to the next station." Isaac held out a slip of paper. "Look for a small church on a rise above a creek about five miles past Richmond town. If it's safe to go in, there'll be three drinking gourds hanging beside the door."

"Bless you both," the young man said. "We been praying for deliverance and the Lord done provided."

"You'd best do a heap more praying," Isaac said. "There's trouble on them roads tonight. The white man's pattyrollers is out searching, so keep to the woods and streams."

The couple clung to one another. Their eyes widened and then the young man pointed toward the smokehouse. "Maybe we'd best stay another night."

"No." Abraham shook his head. "Dogs'll be on your scent

come morning. You keep to them streams. My Florence, she snuck you some black pepper." He handed the young man a small box. "If'n they gets close, you shake a mess of this on your track and hightail it out of there. Now get, and may the Lord be with you."

The young couple retrieved their belongings and resumed their northward journey.

* * *

Isaac and Abraham turned from the smokehouse clearing and slipped into the shadows, moving silently through the tangled forest. They paused when they reached a dirt road beside a harvested tobacco field. Abraham inched forward and scanned the dusty lane, then started across. As he reached the middle of the road, riders emerged from the shadows of Johnston's drying sheds. Abraham quickly turned and lunged back toward the dark woods, grabbing his ankle as he stumbled into the brush. "My ankle's twisted up something awful. I's done for, boy. They ain't seen you yet. Get on home best you can."

Isaac's stomach tightened. "I ain't leaving you, Pa—"

"They done seen me. You gotta go on alone. Now get!" He shooed Isaac away.

Reaching under his father's arms, Isaac dragged him deeper into the shadows.

"Boy, I done told you, get. I'll raise a ruckus and draw them over so's you can sneak away."

Was his pa figuring that Isaac didn't have the grit to run those trails ahead of the patrols? Isaac hitched his trousers. "They ain't seen but one darky tonight, and now they has to catch him!" He started for the road.

"Dammit, boy, don't—" Abraham grabbed, clutching only air.

Isaac flashed a smile. "Ain't no fox catching this rabbit." He darted into the open and paused for the horsemen to see him. Dust kicked up from the horses' hoofs as the riders dug in their heels. Isaac dashed into the forest, tearing through briar tangles and dodging trees. The horsemen stayed on his trail, cursing the low hanging branches as they turned off the road and charged into the stand of saplings at the edge of the woods.

A game trail led down to a stream. His lungs burned as he ran along the streambed, but he had to push on. Capture meant the whip—or worse. Images of scars on the backs of Johnston's slaves swirled in his mind. He splashed across the creek and clambered up the other side. Branches clawed at his face and arms.

Somewhere in the distance, a shotgun blast pierced the still air.

"Pa?" As Isaac turned toward the gunfire, he caught his foot on a tangled root and crashed headlong into a sapling. He tumbled to the ground clutching his shoulder and held his breath as he strained to hear.

Nothing.

Where had they gone? What about that gunshot . . . and Pa? Isaac grabbed his sides as he gulped the pine-scented air. White men weren't partial to running the woods at night. Those were Isaac's woods; no white man, except maybe Henry, knew the trails as well as he.

Reaching his arms above his head, Isaac straightened and took a deep breath. "Lordy, Henry," he whispered, "I sure do wish you was here right now." An unnatural quiet hung over the forest, as if the creatures of the night understood the life and death pursuit and were eager not to become involved. Isaac peered into the darkness. When they used to play down here, with Henry chasing and Isaac running, he'd slip over to Bennett's Creek and swim clear up to the old oak. Henry never could catch him. If it worked against Henry McConnell, it would sure enough work against those who chased him tonight.

Isaac pushed past a stand of pines and into an open field. A quarter-mile away on the far side of the clearing stood another woodlot. He dashed across the field and slipped into the shadows.

Silence.

Isaac breathed easier.

A narrow path meandered along the creek. Underbrush no longer clawed his legs. The shadows of the thicket concealed him; pine straw beneath his bare feet muffled his footfalls. Isaac slowed to a walk. After a while, the trail turned sharply. He ducked beneath an overhanging branch. As he straightened, a dark, broad-chested horse filled the path before him.

"Yo, Clancy! That nigger's over here!" The rider stood in his stirrups waggling the muzzle of his double-barreled shotgun toward Isaac. "Get out of them shadows, boy. Step over where I can see you."

Chills like icy spiders crawled up Isaac's neck. His mouth turned as dry as the pine needles beneath his feet. Trapped—what could he do? He gripped the low branch, shielding himself with the pine bough as he stepped back.

"Hold up, boy. Get your black ass over here before I fills you with buckshot."

The horse reared, pawing at the sky. Isaac released the branch as he turned and ran.

A scream pierced the woods.

Isaac glanced over his shoulder. The limb had swept the man from his saddle as cleanly as a corn broom through dry leaves. The rider lay motionless on the trail.

Isaac ducked into the forest and crashed through the underbrush. Had the rider remounted? Would the next sound be the roar of the shotgun? No matter, he had to keep running. Capture meant the whip for sure.

He pushed on until he reached a small clearing along the banks of Bennett's Creek. There he slipped into the dark water and swam against the slow current.

After a half-mile of swimming upstream, the clearing came into view. Isaac dragged himself up the muddy bank and dropped onto the cool grass under the old oak. Rolling on his side, he gasped for air. As he filled his lungs, his body finally released the burn, one muscle at a time. Exhausted, he stretched to his full length and covered his eyes.

* * *

Clouds drifted in front of the moon, draping a dark veil over the fields. Bats flitted about chasing invisible prey. Isaac breathed deeply. Finally, he was back on McConnell land. The patrols had no business there. Nevertheless, he searched his surroundings before struggling to his feet and heading home.

Isaac slipped past the drying sheds and along the white picket fence that enclosed Miss Ella's flowerbeds. He hesitated when he reached the big house. A motionless figure loomed in the shadows of the porch. A patroller? One of the McConnells? Too late for slaves to be about. What if he was challenged? Isaac bit his lip and continued to the cookhouse.

Florence met him at the door. "Boy, you's cut up to beat all. Get in here so's I can mend them scrapes. Where's your pa?"

Isaac peeled off his tattered shirt and slumped onto the wooden bench. "Mama, he done twisted his ankle something awful.

Last I seen him, he was holed up in them woods over by the Johnston place. I reckon them pattyrollers caught up to him."

"You hush. He'll be fine." She dabbed his wounds with a slab of fatback.

"Shots was fired."

Florence hesitated then continued treating his cuts.

Isaac winced when she touched a gash on his shoulder. "Them dogs'll be out come morning."

"Your pa's been running them woods since before you was born. White folk ain't never catched him and they never will. He's a ghost in them there trees. Ain't no dog, and surely no pattyroller, gonna be his undoing." Florence closed her eyes. Her lips moved silently and then she turned and prepared a bandage.

"Done—best I can, anyway." She tied the last bandage. "Now, off to bed."

"I ain't sleepy, Mama. I reckon I'll wait up in case Pa comes home tonight."

"There'll be no waiting up and no candles burning late to make them white folk curious. You get on now." She pointed to the loft.

He climbed the ladder halfway and paused. Florence stood at the foot of the ladder, still pointing.

Isaac reached the loft and slipped under the tattered blanket next to his younger sister and brother. Their soft breathing continued undisturbed. Shadows from his mama's candle danced on the ceiling, then the ropes supporting his parent's thin mattress creaked and darkness filled the room.

He fought to stay awake, but his worn body quickly surrendered to the exhaustion of the night's work.

* * *

Clattering pans intruded upon the early morning stillness. Isaac struggled to open his eyes. Golden hues crept through chinks in the cabin walls, spilling across the straw bedding. He stretched, then flinched at the awakening soreness from the previous evening's brush with the mounted patrols. What of his father? Was he safe? Had he made it home? Isaac eased himself down the ladder and slid into a chair at the rough-hewn table beside the hearth.

Florence busied herself preparing breakfast. A slender, handsome woman, she was worn less by age than the drudgery of keeping folks in the big house properly fed. Her dark hands told her story: boiling water, splattered grease, hot pans, careless knives, and rooster's spurs had all left their mark.

She filled a basket with biscuits as Tempie and Joseph scrambled down the ladder. Chattering and giggling, they took their seats at the table. The moment Florence set the biscuits down, six-year-old Joseph snatched one in each hand and raced out the door. His laughter trailed across the barnyard.

Tempie settled across from Isaac. Her smooth skin and delicate features mirrored their mama's. At fourteen, she already drew attention from the young men down at the slave quarters. Isaac stared at his sister. The runaway, Rebecca, she and Tempie could be twins.

The cabin door banged open and Abraham limped in, adjusting his trousers.

"Pa," Isaac called, "You's safe!"

Abraham glared as he settled into his seat. "Boy, you like to got yourself kilt last night. When I tells you to do something, you'd best listen."

"But I didn't get kilt, and you didn't get took up by them pattyrollers, neither." Isaac smiled.

"Don't sass me, boy." Abraham wagged a finger. "Your mule-brained doings is gonna bring trouble down on this house, just you see."

"But Pa, I had to keep them riders from finding you."

"Smart rabbit don't offer his self up to no fox." He pointed. "Pass them biscuits."

Isaac pushed the basket down the table. "How's your ankle?"

"A mite sore, but it weren't twisted bad as I thought."

"I heard a shot last night."

"That white boy was shooting at shadows." Abraham bit into the warm biscuit. "They give you trouble?"

Isaac rubbed his scarred forearm. "Just hard running."

"Pa," Tempie said. "That couple you was helping, they gonna make it to that freedom land?"

"They has a chance, baby, but they has hundreds of miles yet to go, and them pattyrollers and their dogs be on their scent. All we can do is pray that the good Lord will provide."

"They jumped the broom just last week." Isaac turned to his sister. "Said they knowed they'd be running. The girl, Rebecca was her name, she weren't no older than you—too young for marrying."

"I is too old enough for marrying." Tempie flipped her short pigtail with the back of her hand.

"No you ain't," Isaac said, "and I'll take a switch to any young buck what comes sniffing around here." He slashed the air with an imaginary stick.

"Mama . . ."

"Leave your sister be." Florence smacked Isaac's hand with a wooden spoon, then wagged the spoon at Tempie. "And any boy come sniffing around here, he'll be getting *my* switch."

Tempie folded her arms with a huff.

"I just can't think about being on the run," Florence said, resting her hands on Abraham's shoulders. "Dogs on your trail, that whip not far behind. That poor child sure enough must be running scared."

"She's with her man, Florence, and they's chasing that freedom star." He patted her hand. "For some, that's enough." Abraham turned to Isaac. "Boy, you sure they didn't get no good look at you?"

"No, Pa," Isaac said. "All they seen was a darky running them dark woods."

Abraham gripped Isaac's arm and lowered his voice. "Just the same, you lay low. Keep yourself busy with your chores, but don't be out where no white folk is noticing them scrapes."

Chapter Two
October 1860

Freezing rain stung Henry McConnell's cheeks. The late night storm transformed the rocky, tree-covered hillside into a quagmire. Henry grabbed a branch above his head and pulled himself over the ledge, and then turned and held out a hand to Edward Shepherd. As Edward grabbed hold he slipped and fell backward and both cadets tumbled to the ground.

"McConnell, you drunken bastard, you'll get us both thrown out, or killed."

"If you can't hold your grog any better than this, Shepherd, you deserve to be thrown out."

"Who puked?"

"Who puked first?" Henry looked at his roommate and laughed.

"Cadet McConnell, you're going to cost me my commission by process of demerit." Edward brushed mud off his woolen overcoat.

Henry shot his companion a look of mock surprise. "Are you telling me, Cadet Shepherd, that you have no faith in my ability to get us safely into the barracks? Sir, I am truly offended." Henry tried to stand, slipped, and landed hard on his backside. He grabbed the trunk of a small sapling and pulled himself upright.

"I've led three retrogrades from Benny Haven's Tavern back to West Point—all successful—and this too shall succeed. If you insist on sneaking out with me for a pint, then you, sir, must trust me to get you back without incident." Henry pointed toward the barracks. "Forward, at a route step, march!"

A mile separated the small tavern by Buttermilk Falls from the academy grounds. The rolling terrain provided cover from cadet sentries walking their posts. Sheets of cold rain sobered the two as they crept to the edge of the clearing and looked out at the gray stone barracks two hundred feet away.

Henry put his arm around Edward's shoulder and whispered, "I walked this post just last week. Sentry's coming around that corner yonder. He'll walk to the end of the building, then turn and come this way. When he turns the corner again we've got two minutes to get inside before he comes back."

The sentry came into view, walking the post precisely as Henry described. Henry whispered the drill commands as the sentry marched past, "Left . . . left . . . left, right, left. Column left, march!" He smiled and nudged Edward as the sentry disappeared behind the building.

"Follow me." Henry ran across the grassy field with Edward trailing. They dove through the barracks door just as the sentry turned the corner.

"McConnell, you'll make general one day. Brilliant tactics, sir." Edward rendered a mock salute.

Henry ignored the gesture. "Doesn't count for a can of army beans if we show for morning formation looking like drowned wharf rats." They dashed up the stairs to their room.

Henry sat on the edge of his bunk wiping mud from his boots. "We've been here four months—summer encampment and all them upperclassmen pranks—I'd say we've earned the right to partake of Benny Haven's hospitality every now and again."

Edward brushed his frock. "McConnell, you're the only plebe I know who actually enjoyed drilling under that stinking July sun."

Henry smiled. It had been an initiation, a challenge, an invitation to a quest—the one thing his older brother hadn't already done, nor ever would.

Edward shook out his coat. "Benny's a right decent fellow, don't you know?" He hung the coat on the back of the door, and then sat and pulled off his boots. "He's letting me carry a tab until my folks send me money."

"Should have done like I did."

"What's that?" Edward looked up from brushing his boot.

"I gave him an army blanket. Seemed like a fair trade for a night's drinking." Henry smiled, lay on his bunk, and closed his eyes.

* * *

A cacophony of drums shattered the predawn stillness of the

Sabbath. Henry bolted upright, rubbed his eyes, and looked around. West Point. Another day. His head throbbed. He staggered out of bed, splashed cold water on his face, and hurried into his uniform.

He raced down the stairs and found his place in the formation in front of the barracks. Mist added a surreal glow to the half-light of dawn. Henry studied his crumpled uniform. The darkness and drizzle would hide mud and wrinkles from the gaze of the cadet officers. He looked up and whispered, "Thank you, Lord."

"McConnell!"

"Present, Sir."

The roll call continued. When his name was called, Edward responded from the far end of the platoon. Henry smiled. Another Saturday night, another successful operation.

The cadet company commander issued the daily orders. "The company will fall in for morning chow in fifteen minutes. Now get those rooms ready for inspection. Company, dismissed!"

Henry took one step to the rear, executed an about face, then raced back up the steps to his billet on the third floor. He leaned against the doorway gasping for breath as he scanned the small room. Fifteen minutes to prepare for inspection. Fifteen minutes of house cleaning—a job that ought to be left to one's manservant.

Henry and Edward tore into the mess they'd left the night before. Henry recited the room inspection orders from memory. "Trunks—under foot of bedstead. Books—neatly arranged on shelf. Broom—hung behind door. Musket—in the gun rack with lock sprung. Bayonet—placed in scabbard. Accouterments—hung over musket. Saber—hung over musket. Clothes—neatly hung on pegs over bedsteads."

They were waiting at the bottom of the stairs when the drum roll sounded for chow.

Cadets marched in company formation to breakfast. The unit halted in front of the mess hall. Henry and his fellow plebes marched single file into the great stone hall. Inside, they stood at attention at their assigned tables awaiting the command, "Take seats!"

Henry piled his plate high with bacon and eggs, biscuits and flapjacks—none as good as Florence's cooking. As Henry shoveled in another forkful he longed for the leisurely meals he'd enjoyed back on the farm.

"Company, attention!"

Back in formation. Eyes straight ahead. No word or whisper. "Company, right face! Forward, march!" The long gray line responded as one.

Dismissed once more in front of the barracks, Henry found Edward and they walked to their room.

"Three demerits?" Edward waved the chit he'd found on his bunk. "Unclean accouterments. I'll be walking punishment tours forever."

"At least you won't be alone." Henry held up his own chit. "Soiled blanket. Should have taken my boots off last night before I laid down." Henry tilted back in his chair and rested his feet on the metal frame at the end of his bunk. "We'd best get that punishment tour done today. I'm not missing the cotillion next weekend. Miss Belinda Towers will be in attendance and I aim to thrill her with my grace on the dance floor."

"Henry, she might as well stick her dainty little toes under the wheels of a caisson as risk them on the dance floor with the likes of you."

"What do you mean? We've been practicing, haven't we?" Henry held out his hand. "Come here."

Edward recoiled.

"Come on." Henry grabbed his roommate by the shoulder. "And this time I'll lead."

Henry placed his arm around Edward's waist and scuffled across the floor to an imagined waltz. Together they counted, "One, two, three. One, two, three . . ."

Edward spun out of Henry's grip and onto his chair. "You're still a danger to all of civilization, McConnell."

Henry gave him a dismissive wave. "Miss Belinda will be so taken with my charm that she'll float across that ballroom like she's on a cloud. Trust me, Shepherd, she'll never give a worry to those dainty feet."

"McConnell, your arrogance is exceeded only by your exceptional good fortune, but heed my word; you'd best keep her close. A few cadets at the last social were taking more than a passing interest in that sweet young flower."

The drum roll once again called them to formation. As the company marched to chapel, Henry groaned inwardly. Two hours of sitting ramrod straight on a hard wooden bench, held prisoner by another long-winded oration. Back home in South Boston, Virginia young ladies in all their finery would add sweet soprano voices to every hymn and serve as pleasant distractions to the drone of a boring sermon.

The company halted in front of the gothic stone building. They marched single file into the chapel and lined up by squads in the pews. Henry stood at attention facing the pulpit. Redemption wouldn't come easily in this army's excuse for a worship service.

"Ready, seats!"

Chapter Three
October 1860

Isaac split the log cleanly and tossed both pieces on the woodpile behind the cookhouse. A swirl of dust far down the lane caught his eye as he reached for another log. He rubbed the scratches on his forearms, then set the log on the block and swung his ax. He'd best keep to working and not let on that he'd noticed the approaching horseman.

The rider reined his mount in front of the big house. Polly, Henry's little sister, sat in one of the rockers on the porch fanning herself. Patrick, Henry's older brother, came out to the porch and said something to the rider. With his back to Isaac, the rider made agitated, sweeping gestures, pointing in the direction of the Johnston farm. Whatever they might be saying, their voices didn't carry to the cookhouse. Patrick gave a quick wave of his hand and went back inside.

Isaac lowered the ax, rubbing the small of his back as he straightened.

The rider turned on his horse.

Clancy? Isaac covered his forearms as their eyes met.

The rider spurred his horse and the large stallion reared, then galloped down the lane.

Polly folded her fan, shielded her eyes, and stared at Isaac.

* * *

Isaac shoved a pitchfork under the straw, lifting another clod of manure into the wheelbarrow. When he'd filled the barrow, he pushed it outside behind the barn and upended it on a pile of rotting leaves. After Christmas he'd spread that compost and plant the tobacco seedlings but, for now, tobacco farming meant mucking stalls and turning compost, easy work and out of sight.

His cuts were healing, but Isaac still avoided places where the

McConnells or Sean O'Farrell, their overseer, might notice and ask questions.

He removed his hat and wiped his sleeve across his brow. The pungent sweetness of the compost filled the autumn air. Squinting, he gazed past the tobacco fields to the distant woods. Would they make it, that couple on the run? He leaned on the pitchfork. Soon, his day would come. Philadelphia would be his new home. Isaac righted the wheelbarrow and returned to the barn.

Footfalls crunched the dirt floor behind him as Isaac scooped another pile. He shoved the fork into the barrow and turned. Abraham stood in the doorway, satchel in hand.

"Morning, Pa."

"Anybody ask about them cuts?" He pointed to Isaac's arms.

"No. I been careful, like you said. What about them two we helped? You hear anything?"

"Massa Johnston's boy got kilt."

"He what?" Isaac dropped the pitchfork.

"One of Johnston's nigras come by the cabins last night with some corn squeezings. He said Johnston's oldest boy was with them pattyrollers the other night and got throwed off his horse."

"Getting throwed ain't getting killed . . ."

"Snapped his neck like a spring chicken." Abraham pointed to the wagon. "Hitch that jackass, boy."

"Dead? You sure?"

"Weren't none of your doing. He fell off'n his damned horse. That white boy never could ride no how."

Isaac slumped to the bench and rested his head in his hands. He'd killed a man, a white man. They'd hang him for sure.

"Boy, you pay heed. That Clancy fella is madder than a nest of copperheads. His whip comes out for no reason, none a' tall, and pray mercy for the poor soul what gets in his way." Abraham rocked the bench with his foot. "You hear me? Hitch that wagon."

"Sorry." Isaac reached for the harness. "Where's you headed?"

"Massa McConnell hired me out to fix some furniture for a fella over by Danville."

"You be gone long?"

"Week, maybe two." Abraham heaved his canvas tool bag into the wagon. "They done busted the leg off their breakfront, so I's making a replacement, then fixing some tools and such."

Isaac finished buckling the bellyband around the mule. He hesitated, then turned. "They'll be watching, Pa. Maybe it's time I headed north, followed that drinking gourd."

"Ain't nobody looking for you, boy, not as long as you keeps them cuts covered. Ain't nobody suspecting you was out there."

"Just the same, if'n I was free, I could head on up to Philadelphia now and get me a job."

Abraham looked him over then pointed to a wooden bench against the wall. "Set on down." He set a foot on the bench and rested on his knee. "Me and your mama, we been on this farm many a year, and Massa McConnell, mostly he done right by us—"

Isaac nodded. "He's a good owner, but—"

Abraham held up his hand. "Ain't no such thing as a good slave owner. We don't get no whippings, and Massa, he don't sell our children away, but any man what's keeping another in bondage be doing the devil's work."

"I reckon," Isaac said. "Still, whenever we's helping them that's running, I get to thinking on when it will be my turn."

"Your day's coming, boy. I has me a plan." Abraham bit off the end of a tobacco plug. "We'll all be getting to that Promised Land in good time—and we ain't needing no underground railroad."

"How's that?"

"In time, boy, you'll be learning in time." He spit a stream of brown juice into the corner of the stall.

"When I gets to Pennsylvania, I'm starting my own furniture business, and I'll get me a fancy coat too, one with pockets." Isaac hooked his thumbs in the front of his shirt and leaned back. "I'll be walking down that street free and proper, just like the white folk."

"White folk up north look at you and all they'll see is a nigger, same as old Clancy do."

"But, if'n I has me a shop—"

"Boy, nigras down here owns their own businesses, like that Mr. Day over the river there in Carolina." He spit, then wiped his chin. "White or black, he's the best carpenter south of Baltimore."

"But Pa, you once said folks down there, they treats him fine."

"The man makes good money, gives folk jobs. They respects him to his face, but they still calls him 'nigger' behind his back, and they'll call him the same up in Pennsylvania."

Isaac finished hitching the mule. "So how come Mr. Day gets

to keep his money, but you does the same work and Massa McConnell takes everything you earn?"

"Mr. Day was born to a free woman. Law says that makes him free." Abraham patted the mule's rump. "As for Massa McConnell, him and me, we has an understanding about the money I earns. Someday you'll be finding out about that, but for now, you just be patient and don't go crossing none of them white folks—not even Mr. Sean."

Isaac started to speak, but Abraham held up a hand and reached into his pocket. He pulled out a small rectangle of wood strung on a rawhide cord. "Your jubilation day's coming, boy, maybe soon. I made this here to remind you of that." He hung the medallion around Isaac's neck. "You wear this knowing that someday you'll be following that freedom star. Now hop up here and keep company with your old pa down to the post road."

Isaac climbed on board for the ride through harvested tobacco fields to the road connecting South Boston with Danville. The wagon bounced along the rutted path as Isaac studied the carved pine medallion. On one side, Abraham had burned in the seven stars of the Big Dipper. Isaac turned it over. Carved in relief was a single five-pointed star.

It had been a moonless winter night ten, possibly twelve years ago . . . Isaac could almost feel his pa's arm on his shoulder and hear the words he'd spoken. "Them two stars yonder on the end of that drinking gourd, them's the pointers. They points to the polar star. You follow that'n, you goes north, to freedom." Isaac squeezed the medallion, then tucked it under his shirt and rode on in silence.

Abraham reined the mule as they approached the junction. Another wagon headed down the old post road from the east carrying two white men. They were laughing and talking, but as they drew even, the nearest rider glanced at Isaac, then shifted a shotgun on his lap, pointing the barrels at Isaac.

Isaac froze. Did they know about the Johnston boy?

As the strangers passed, Isaac studied the bundle lashed in the rear of their wagon. "Look Pa," he whispered, "it's Rebecca."

The girl they had helped a few nights before sat bound and trussed like a hog on her way to market. Bruises covered her pretty young face. Her lips quivered as she stared at Isaac through tear filled eyes.

Chapter Four
October 1860

Henry pulled his chair next to the dormitory window and shook several drops of gun oil onto a rag. Working the rag over the lock plate of his musket, he removed the last vestiges of rust. "It was bad enough we had to walk our punishment tours in the rain. If these here muskets rust up, we'll be pulling guard duty forever."

Edward reached for the oil. "Hey, did you hear about the election?"

"What election?"

"Some boys from South Carolina hung a ballot box down on the first floor and passed the word for cadets to go and vote for the president, just like in the real election."

"What in tarnation for?" Henry asked, rubbing linseed oil into the musket's walnut stock.

"Not sure," Edward replied. "Some say it's just a civics exercise—"

"Civics be damned." Henry waved his cleaning rag. "We're soldiers, not politicians."

"Well, if you'd let me finish, McConnell, some was saying that the boys who've been talking up secession want to find out who's with them and who's against them. Word is, they'll be studying the handwriting on those ballots."

"Then they're fools. All they'll discover is that the entire corps of cadets is against them. No American is going to turn his back on the stars and stripes. If South Carolina secedes, she'll stand alone." Henry aimed his musket out the window and pulled the trigger. The hammer clicked on an empty breech.

"You been paying any mind to the world beyond these walls?" Edward pointed outside. "Mr. Lincoln's got your southern boys running scared. Hell, you're a slaveholder, how'd you feel if Lincoln was to be elected?"

"Last I heard, Mr. Lincoln said we can keep our slaves in Virginia, so I don't see that there's a problem, but my family's backing John Bell."

"McConnell, you're a fool." Edward ran a dry patch down the barrel. "Back in Wisconsin, we don't much hold with your notions of slavery, but at least I can abide our differences. But there's some around here," he said, shaking the ramrod at Henry, "they'd as soon hang you as not, and most of your southern boys are no better as to their affections for those Black Republicans."

Henry gave his roommate a dismissive wave and returned to cleaning his musket.

"Henry, you'd best start paying heed or you'll find yourself with a blanket thrown over your head and an abolitionist mob beating in your thick southern skull."

* * *

Henry awoke with a start at the first trumpeted note of reveille. The pre-dawn air held an icy chill. He stumbled out of bed, splashed cold water on his face, brushed off his uniform, and hurried to get dressed. Another tardy meant more demerits. Grabbing his books, he rushed to formation.

Morning classes began with algebra. Once in the classroom, Henry raced to his assigned desk and stood at attention. On command, he and the other students took their seats in the small room. Four large windows illuminated blackboards on the other three walls.

Many of his classmates were already pulling assignments from their notebooks. He glanced at his own scribbled notes. Although barely a month into the academic year, Henry was already behind.

The professor commanded, "Take boards."

All cadets rose and went to their assigned portion of the blackboard. Henry's heart raced as he copied the homework problem onto the blackboard. The instructor required all work to be shown, but Henry wasn't sure how he'd arrived at his answers. The cadet beside him finished with a confident flourish of his chalk.

"Mr. McConnell, recite the lesson, if you please." Professor Robertson, a distinguished gentleman with flowing white hair touching his shoulders, stood before Henry. He stroked his beard as he stared with apparent curiosity at Henry's solution.

Henry snapped to attention. "Sir, the cadet is not prepared." Beads of sweat moistened his brow.

"Very well." Professor Robertson nodded at Henry, then strolled between the desks and centered himself on another blackboard. "Mr. Wheatley, would you be so kind?"

"Yes sir!" Cadet Wheatley tapped his chalk on the boards as he explained each step in his solution. " . . . and finally, subtracting forty-five from each side leaves us with x equals minus twenty-two. Are there any questions?" The New York cadet turned toward Henry with a sneer.

"Very well, Mr. Wheatley." Professor Robertson nodded, then turned to the class. "Will everyone please continue with the next problem?" He glanced at Henry as he returned to his desk.

Henry slowly erased all evidence of his first problem, then turned a page in his composition book and pretended to study his notes. Eventually, he scratched the second equation on the board in handwriting so small as to make it undecipherable from more than a few feet away.

Finally, the minute hand on the clock above the door stood straight up. Professor Robertson rose from his chair, tapping the blackboard with a wooden pointer. "Copy the problems from the blackboard and come to class tomorrow prepared to recite your solutions. Dismissed."

The class snapped to attention, then rushed for the door. As Henry walked past the instructor's desk, Professor Robertson waved him aside. "Mr. McConnell, a moment, if you please."

"Sir?" Henry centered himself before the professor's desk as the last of the cadets left the room.

"At ease, McConnell." Professor Robertson sat on the corner of his desk. "Now, tell me, son, how do you intend to master geometry and trigonometry when you can't even solve a simple equation?"

Henry snapped to attention. "Sir, the cadet must . . . the cadet will . . ." Henry lowered his head. "Sir, the cadet does not know."

"McConnell, do you know where I'm from?"

Henry looked up. "No, sir."

"Shenandoah Valley, not more than a hundred miles or so from that tobacco farm you call home. Do you know what my most difficult subject was?" The professor didn't wait for a response.

"Algebra. I know what your upbringing gave you, same as most of the southern boys. Your momma served you heavy doses of Shakespeare, Homer, Byron, and Defoe, but you never had a need for higher numbers so you know little past the basic arithmetic. Am I correct?"

"Sir, the cadet can learn this, it . . . it just isn't anything he's ever studied before, least ways not anything he's paid any mind to."

Professor Robertson pointed to the blackboard that still held traces of Wheatley's homework. "The Cadet Wheatleys of the world would as soon see West Point become a northern academy. To them, Virginians and Carolinians are outsiders, throwbacks to a frontier lifestyle. It doesn't help that most of you southern boys come here ill-prepared for the rigors of the engineering curriculum."

Henry relaxed and looked at his instructor. "Professor Robertson, all of that may be true, but what does it have to do with me passing algebra?"

"Nothing, if all you're aiming to do is return to that Virginia farm and grow your tobacco."

"Papa's a long way from turning the farm over to me." Henry shook his head. "And when he does step aside, I reckon my brother's next in line to take over."

"Then you'd best pass your subjects or get used to the idea that you'll be working for your brother. Consider this, McConnell. Virginia needs strong cadets to represent her, both here at the academy, and later, in the army. When Lieutenant Colonel Robert Lee was superintendent there weren't issues with North-South politics. Now, the academy is being pulled apart by these elections and we cannot allow the genteel influences of our southern heritage to be lost to future generations of cadets. You and your southern friends must not only compete, you must excel."

Professor Robertson held out a small red book. "This primer is what most northern cadets would have seen in their preparatory schooling. Read it. Practice the problems. Come see me if you have any questions." The professor took his seat and pointed to Henry. "McConnell, you can learn this, just as I did, and it is important to Virginia that you do."

Henry quickly thumbed through the textbook and then he glanced at the clock and tucked the book under his arm. "Thank you, sir. I'll not disappoint you. By your leave, sir." Henry turned on his heel and raced out the doorway.

* * *

Henry held the reins and stroked the animal's muzzle as he stood in West Point's great riding hall. The horse nuzzled Henry's arm. The cavalry claimed the best riding stock. The nags that West Point used to train officers who would eventually lead that cavalry were leftovers. When not used for riding instruction, they were beasts of burden, harnessed to draw cannon and caissons about the Plain during weekly artillery drill.

"Forward, lean forward, man," The riding master, Sergeant Daniels of the dragoons, yelled at the hapless cadet whose turn it was to charge his steed through the saber course. "Extend your body, man. Make your saber sing through your enemy's hair." Sergeant Daniels threw up his arms and kicked at the dirt. "Mr. McConnell, kindly remount and demonstrate once again to this pathetic gaggle of mule drivers how the U.S. cavalry is supposed to attack."

Henry swung into the saddle, laid the reins across the horse's neck, and turned his mount. Nudging the horse with his boot, they galloped to the far end of the ring. Henry turned the animal and spurred it into a run straight for the ranks of straw figures staked out across the rink. He rose in his stirrups, flattened across the horse's neck and swung his saber left, then right, decapitating straw men on both sides.

"That, gentlemen, is a cavalry charge." Sergeant Daniels smiled and folded his arms.

Henry reined in his steed, slowing the animal to a trot as he rode to the center of the ring. Facing his classmates, he brought the hilt of his saber to his chin and, with a flourish, swept the blade down to his side in a flawless sword salute. As his classmates cheered, Henry bowed in feigned humility.

"Thank-you, Mr. McConnell. That will be all." Sergeant Daniels turned to the other cadets gathered in the riding hall. "Mr. Wheatley," he commanded. "Mount up and show us how they ride in the great metropolis of New York."

"They ride behind their horses, in the trolleys," someone called out in a southern drawl. The hall resounded with catcalls and whistles.

Sergeant Daniels ordered the class to attention. "Gentlemen, and I take great liberties in using such a term in reference to you hooligans, you will now remain at attention until every cadet has successfully ridden the course. Should you speak, waver, or drop we will begin again. Am I clear?"

"Yes, Sergeant Daniels!" The class responded in unison.

Cadet Wheatley mounted and rode to the far end of the rink. He brought his horse to a full gallop, leaned across the horse's neck and swung his blade. His aim was off. The impact of blade against the wooden post holding the straw figure unseated the cadet, sending him hard to the sawdust floor. Muted laughter echoed through the riding hall. Wheatley snatched his saber from the ground and sat, arms across his knees, his face twisted in an angry scowl.

Sergeant Daniels turned aside to Henry and muttered, "Never yet seen a New Yorker what could make a decent cavalry officer." He slapped his crop against the side of his leg. "Next."

Each cadet in turn ran the course. Several required more than one attempt before landing a killing blow on the dummies. When Sergeant Daniels finally appeared satisfied, he commanded, "At ease."

Cadets staggered, rubbing stiff necks and stretching tired legs.

"Gentlemen. Someday one or two of you might find yourselves leading dragoons, but most will be lucky to land in the infantry. For those who do make the cavalry, know this; you must ride better than the men you lead. You will be in front. Your troopers will observe how you set your mount. They will notice how you treat your mount. They will know which of you is in charge. Will it be you, or will it be the horse?"

Sergeant Daniels walked away, motioning the class to follow. "Over here, by the wall." He walked to the side of the riding hall and pointed to a mark on the wall above his head. "Look at that, gentlemen. Back in '43 we had us a cadet was the best-damned horseman to ever ride in this man's army. During a demonstration for General Winfield Scott himself that little cadet jumped a horse over a bar set at six foot, three inches. Never been done before or since. None of you have a prayer of ever riding that well, but that is what you all must strive for—excellence. Nothing less will do."

"Sergeant," a down east voice called from the rear of the group. "That cadet, where is he now?"

Sergeant Daniels rubbed his chin. "I hear tell he quit the army a few years back—grew tired of soldiering, I reckon . . . but to hear it from them that was here that day, why, it was something to see." He looked at the spot on the wall. "Some horseman, that fella. Name was Grant, if I recall; Ulysses Grant."

Henry touched the faded mark.

Chapter Five
October 1860

"You, boy, get over here." Morgan McConnell stood on the covered porch of the farmhouse and beckoned.

Isaac dropped the armload of firewood and hurried to the porch steps, brushing bits of tree bark from his frayed tunic. He bowed. "Yes sir, Massa McConnell?"

Morgan settled into his cane-backed rocker. He withdrew a match from his pocket, drew it across the tabletop, and relit his cigar. Drawing the smoke in slowly, he hooked a thumb into the corner of his coat pocket and studied his young bondsman. Tall, lean, muscular—a prime specimen of African manhood. On the market that buck could bring twelve hundred dollars or more.

"Boy, your daddy teach you all he knows about furniture?"

Isaac lowered his head. "Sir, Pa done taught me a lot, but he ain't taught me everything, least not yet. He knows more about working wood than most any man alive."

Morgan smiled. Boy's got a right to be proud of his ol' man. He tapped the ash from his cigar. "I reckon from where you stand old Abraham would be the best there is. Your daddy's sure enough a fine carpenter, and he earns me good money."

Morgan took another long draw on his cheroot, then leaned and pointed the cigar at Isaac. "You'll be worth more to me as a craftsman than you'll ever be as a field nigra. Your daddy ever tell you about that nigra down in Milton, name of Thomas Day?"

"Yes, sir. Pa said it was Mr. Day what taught him woodworking. He also says Mr. Day, he's the best there is, black or white." Isaac appeared startled at his own words and quickly looked away.

Morgan laughed, waving toward Isaac with the back of his hand. "It's all right, boy. Your daddy spoke the truth. Thomas Day is the finest carpenter this side of Philadelphia, and I haven't met any man, black or white, can hold a candle to him—but your daddy comes mighty close. Did you know that your daddy used to be one of Day's slaves?"

Isaac's eyes widened. He shook his head.

"More'n twenty years ago my pa bought your daddy from Thomas Day—and he's been making me good money ever since. Now I'm going to send Abraham's own son back to North Carolina to learn from that same master. What do you think of that, boy?"

Isaac snatched off his hat. He lowered his head, poking at the hard packed dirt with his toe. "Is . . . is Massa selling Isaac?"

Morgan chuckled. "No, boy, just loaning you out for a spell. Day has some big orders to fill and he asked if he could hire your daddy. Well, your daddy's too busy making me money, but I told him he could have you for no cost, except feeding and such, on the condition he sends you back with some marketable skills. So now what do you think?"

Isaac smiled. "I'll be doing carpenter work all the time, like Pa?"

"That's right, boy."

"I'll earn you plenty of money, Massa McConnell. Thank you, sir." Isaac clutched his hat in front of him and bowed.

"Good. I'll have Sean take you down to Milton next week. Now, pick up all that damned firewood and finish your chores." Morgan chuckled as Isaac scurried about, gathering logs scattered across the farmyard.

* * *

Sunlight warmed the green floorboards on the porch, bringing memories of summer to the late autumn afternoon. Morgan shielded his eyes as he surveyed his land. McConnell tobacco fields stretched to the horizon. He smiled and began to rock. Surely, they'd been blessed. Patrick, with a university degree in hand, would be running the farm soon enough, and now Henry, Lord, who'd of thought that boy would ever pass those entrance exams? He might turn into something yet.

"Massa care for a cool glass of sweet tea?"

Morgan turned. Tempie stood in the doorway holding a small tray containing a glass filled with amber liquid and a sprig of mint. Her bright calico dress complemented her innocent smile. In a few years she'd take a husband and bear offspring to work his fields, but today she was just sweet little Tempie, same age as his Polly.

"Thank you, Tempie. Set it there." Morgan pointed to the table. Tempie did as instructed, then curtsied and returned to the house.

Morgan took a sip and set the glass on the table. A moment later the door opened again. Ella McConnell stepped onto the porch wearing a silk day dress imprinted in a muted flower pattern. A crocheted shawl draped her shoulders.

"May I join you," she said, "or are you deep in your thoughts again and wishing not to be disturbed?"

"Ella, my dear, there are no thoughts worth holding if they would keep you from my side. Please, have a seat." Morgan stood and pulled the second rocker next to his.

Ella unfolded her fan and began rocking. "This is the first you've taken time to relax in weeks. Between finishing the harvest and worrying about those elections, I thought you would absolutely exhaust yourself."

Morgan nodded. "I'll go to South Boston next week and cast my vote, but I don't see much purpose to it. That Lincoln fella is going to win, and there's nothing any of us in Virginia can do to stop him."

"Now, Morgan, you said yourself that Mr. Bell was going to win. Has he fallen from favor?"

"John Bell's the right man, and Virginia will cast her votes for him, of that I'm sure, but the rabble in South Carolina and Mississippi won't, and with the South divided, no candidate will have enough votes to defeat Lincoln." Morgan rubbed his right forearm. "Besides, those radicals in Charlestown would just as soon follow that damned fool Breckenridge right out of the Union. They'll destroy us all." He stood and tossed the cigar stub into the yard.

"That arm still giving you trouble?" she asked. "You really should see Doc Blackman."

"Just tingling now and again, no need for concern." Morgan walked to the edge of the porch and surveyed fields that had just yielded another profitable crop of yellow leaf.

"Bell's an American first. Being from Tennessee, he understands the South, but he also stands squarely for the Union, and that's where Virginia must be."

"Well, I am sorry I mentioned politics. I surely did not mean to get you riled."

"Wasn't you got me riled." He leaned on the porch rail and lowered his voice. "Was that tomfool son of yours who'll be canceling my vote with his damned secessionist ballot. I don't know how we raised two boys so totally different from one another."

"Now, Morgan, Patrick takes after you in so many ways. You can't expect him to follow you in everything."

Morgan pounded a fist on the porch rail. "I just wish it wasn't my own flesh and blood waving those banners and calling for secession when I'm on the dais arguing to save the Union. It's not right, a son opposing his own kin like that."

* * *

Night air drifted through the pines, hinting at the changing season. Isaac pulled his rough tunic close around his neck and hurried toward the cluster of small cabins down the lane from the big house.

"You helping runaways tonight?"

Isaac stopped in his tracks at the soft voice. A figure in a hooped skirt stepped from the shadows, a bonnet covering her head.

"That you, Miss Polly? What's you doing out and about?"

"I know where you were, Isaac. I saw you."

Isaac snatched his hat from his head. "Don't know what you's talking about, Miss Polly."

"Tucker Johnston, it was you that killed him, wasn't it?"

"I didn't kill nobody." He searched the trail. They were alone. Should he run?

"Oh, Isaac," she said, grabbing his arm. "I know you wouldn't actually kill anyone—you aren't a violent man, but you were out there that night, weren't you?"

"Miss Polly, I needs to get on down to the quarters. It ain't right, me being out here at night talking to a white woman."

Polly circled around Isaac. She fingered the lace on her collar. "Take me with you next time."

He backed away, shaking his head. "Don't know what you's talking about, Miss Polly."

"I'm talking about when you sneak off to help the runaways." She twirled around. "It sounds absolutely dramatic—the dogs, the patrols, those poor, wretched slaves yearning for freedom—I could just die with all that excitement."

"Isaac'll be the one dying, them pattyrollers finds you out here talking to me."

"Oh, stop worrying. Your secret's safe with me." She started toward the big house, then paused. "But I'll be watching, and next time, I'll be dressed for running the woods."

* * *

He hopped the fence and stepped into a glowing ring of firelight.

"Isaac! Set on down and show us what you brung." Lilly, a large woman a few years older than his mama, patted an empty place beside her on the log.

Isaac settled beside her. "Got nothing tonight, Aunt Lilly. Mama says prices is high so she has to be careful buying her salts and sugars for the big house. Ain't no extra to share, but she'll try to save you some, if'n she can."

"That's all right, boy. We's glad to see you all the same. Ashcake?" Lilly poked a stick in the fire, retrieving a blackened loaf from the coals. She brushed off the ashes and held it out.

"Thank you, no. I's eaten."

"Say boy, when's your pa getting home?" Old July called from the far side of the fire. Snow-white hair crowned a dark, thin face as wrinkled as dried fruit. The top half of one ear was missing.

"Don't know for sure." Isaac poked at the fire. Sparks drifted skyward. "He's over by Danville doing some repairs, then he's heading up along the Roanoke to help trim out a new farmhouse. I reckon he'll be gone a few weeks."

"He sure enough be Massa McConnell's favorite nigger," a deep voice said from across the fire, "traveling with his fancy pass like he somebody special."

"Ain't so . . ." Isaac started to rise but Lilly blocked him with her arm, then shoved him down. She shook her fist at the hulking form on the far side of the fire ring. "Big Jim, I'm fixing to bust your fat mouth. You been fussing like an old woman ever since Massa McConnell sent your lazy ass back to the fields and brung Abraham in to work the carpentry."

"Why's you all the time taking up for them house niggers, woman?" Big Jim wagged his finger. "Ain't like they cares none about folks down here no how."

"Maybe she works at the big house now, but Florence is still my sister, and she and Abraham, they remembers their time in the fields. You speak poorly about them, you's talking about me."

Big Jim retreated into the shadows.

July tossed a stick in the fire. "Sure would be nice, traveling like old Abraham. These bones ain't never been no more 'n five miles from this farm since the day I was born. A body gets weary just planting and weeding, cutting tobacco, working them drying sheds." He sighed, gazing heavenward. "Old July would sure enough like to see them lights of Richmond town 'fore he passes."

"Maybe you'll get there yet," Isaac said. "Could be Massa McConnell will send you to help Pa."

July shook his head. "Reckon I'll settle for sneaking on down to the river every now and again and catching me some catfish."

"Old man, them pattyrollers gonna whip your ass down by the river just the same as if'n you was caught in Richmond." Banjo, a thin man with flecks of gray in his beard and a missing tooth that caused him to whistle when he spoke pointed toward the woods. "Why doesn't you just pack up your kit and skedaddle?"

"Too old for running them rivers and woods. Skedaddling's for young'ns, like this here boy." July pointed a crooked finger.

Isaac glanced at the other slaves around the fire. "The day's coming when I'll follow that North Star, but Pa says it ain't our time yet. And it ain't so bad here neither . . ."

"Sure ain't like yonder." Lilly jerked a thumb in the direction of the Johnston farm. "That Clancy, he's one to stay clear of since that Johnston boy died."

"Heard tell he was murdered," July said.

"Fell off his durned horse," Banjo replied. "That's all. Ain't that right, Isaac?"

"I reckon." Isaac lowered his voice. "Ain't nobody knows for sure."

"Well, maybe Massa McConnell don't whip us like Johnston do his niggers," Banjo said, wagging his finger at Isaac, "but you'll see the other side of that white man when his purse strings get tight. And you'd best watch out for Patrick, that boy of his."

"That's right," Lilly said. "He's a bad one."

"He sure enough is," Banjo replied. "He laid the butt of his crop against my skull last summer just 'cause I took me some rest time during the harvest. Split my scalp wide open, he did." Banjo pointed to the side of his head.

"He knock some sense into that old black noggin?" July steepled his fingers and pointed at Banjo. Laughter mixed with the crackle of burning logs.

Lilly wiped her mouth on her sleeve. "Yes sir, this here farm would be a whole lot different if'n Massa Patrick ever took charge. He ain't like Massa Henry. How can two brothers be so different?" Crumbs fell to her lap. She brushed them aside with the back of her hand.

Banjo looked at Isaac. "You and Massa Henry is tighter than stink on a polecat."

"Been friends ever since we been in long britches." Isaac smiled. "He's a mite crazy, but he ain't hard on folks."

"Yes, sir." Banjo chuckled. "He's crazy all right—like that time the two of you treed that bear over to Pittsylvania County and he clumb up after it. Said he couldn't get him a clear shot from the ground. Craziest white man I ever knowed." Banjo slapped his knee and laughed, whistling through his teeth.

Isaac leaned forward and lowered his voice. "I had to catch Massa Henry by his foot and drag him down from that tree. It was getting a mite too dangerous . . ." He gazed around the gathering. "For that poor ol' bear!" He slapped his hands on his knees and rocked back.

The clearing echoed with laughter.

"I got me some traveling soon," Isaac said after everyone settled.

Banjo tossed a log on the fire and looked at him. "Your pa taking you on one of his trips?"

"No, I'm going down to Milton to work for Mr. Day in his furniture business."

"That rich nigra with the big brick house?" July shook his head. "They say he owns his own slaves."

Mama Rose scowled. A stocky woman, she had been midwife to every birth on the McConnell farm, white or black, for the last thirty years. "The Lord don't look kindly on them white men buying and selling the African, what's he to think when he sees a brother putting his own kind in chains?"

35

"It ain't right, Mama Rose. That's for certain." July raised a trembling hand toward the heavens. "That nigra gots to get his self right with the Lord."

"Amen," the small group replied.

"It's a confusion, sure enough, a black man owning his own kind," Isaac said. "But I got no say in that, no more'n I got a say in what Massa McConnell tells me to do. All I knows is Mr. Day's gonna be teaching me furniture, then I'll be able to hire out on carpentry jobs, same as Pa."

Isaac turned to July. "Reckon I'll get up there to Richmond town one of these days. If'n I does, I'll fetch you one of them penny post cards so you can see Richmond for yourself."

"That'd be mighty nice." July poked the coals with his stick and watched as sparks drifted skyward.

Chapter Six
October 1860

Gaslights cast a pale glow across the quadrangle. Ten minutes until curfew. Henry hurried toward his dormitory. What an evening—the Napoleon Club—only the best students belonged. Professor Robertson said it was his riding that got him invited, but only this one time, so he could hear the discussion on Napoleon's tactics at the Battle of Eylau. Clever, using his dragoons that way to save the center of his line . . .

He turned the corner of the south barracks and leaned into a swirling wind. As he passed a row of bushes along the side of the building, someone grabbed him from behind. He struggled to pull away, but his attackers held him tightly. A figure emerged from the shadows and punched him in the midsection. Henry buckled. His captors yanked him to his feet. Another punch landed.

"I hear you southern boys like your slaves so much you sleep with them. Is that right, McConnell?"

A fist pounded his stomach. Henry gasped.

"Hey, secessh, you been poking your niggers? You buying your fun on the auction block? Maybe you cotton pickers think mounting horses and mounting pickaninnys is all the same."

A boot caught him below the belt. Henry doubled over.

"You're too stupid to make it in this man's army, McConnell. Stick to your plow horses and nigger women."

The hands let go. Henry dropped to the ground, drawing his knees to his chest as footfalls faded across the quad. He sucked in a deep breath and struggled to one knee. Ribs . . . broken? Standing on wobbly legs, he rested his hands on his knees. Finally, he straightened and limped to the barracks, staggering up to his third floor room. He opened the door, then slumped against the jam, clutching his side.

Edward looked up from his studies. "What in the hell happened to you?"

"Got jumped."

Grabbing Henry under his arms, Edward led him across the room and lowered him onto his bunk. "Who did this?"

"Some of your Republican friends, I reckon—caught me down by south barracks."

"You see any of them?"

Henry shook his head. " They wore hoods."

"And gave you a good whupping, I see." Edward pulled off Henry's shoes. "Must be the night for shenanigans. The word is, two boys from Vermont also got jumped by some of your South Carolina friends."

"They're not my friends."

"Just the same, Henry, I warned you."

Henry struggled to sit up. "Dammit, Shepherd, this isn't the West Point I signed on for. Damn the politicians. Damn the abolitionists." He threw his shoe against the door. "Damn those secessh bastards too."

* * *

The large dining hall filled with eager cadets. Henry ran a finger under his starched collar. "Never figured I'd be looking forward to some dandified dress ball. I wager Belinda will be first to arrive and she'll be looking for me." He elbowed Edward and pointed to the doors at the far end.

The rural Hudson River basin yielded few women of culture, so the belles of New York City came up river on a packet steamer for the monthly cotillion.

"Got your eye on that little blonde from New Jersey?" Henry said.

Edward brushed the front of his tunic. "Do you think she's sweet on me?"

"Calm yourself, Shepherd. Last month you were more nervous than a preacher caught with a jug of elderberry wine."

"You'd best worry about that Towers girl, McConnell. There's a mess of cadets who picture her on their arm. You'll be lucky if you get one dance." Edward nudged Henry. "Look, here they come."

A sea of pastel poured through the double doors. The corps of cadets let out a cheer as dozens of young ladies demurely gathered along the far wall.

Belinda's pale yellow dress set off her raven black hair and caused her to stand out from the crowd. Henry made his way behind the line of cadets, maneuvering as close as he could.

A captain, one of the tactical officers, marched to the center of the floor, snapped to attention, and faced the corps of cadets. "Gentlemen, these ladies have unselfishly consented to grace you with their company this evening. I trust you will repay their kindness with conduct befitting future officers of the United States Army." The captain nodded to the orchestra conductor.

The scuffling of feet drowned the opening notes of a waltz as cadets dashed across the floor in search of dance partners.

Henry raced too, sliding to a stop in front of Belinda, his left arm cocked behind his back and his right hand extended. Bowing, he gazed into her eyes. "May I have the honor of this dance?"

She blushed, accepting his hand with a curtsy. Henry twirled her onto the dance floor with a purposeful grace born of long evenings of secret practice with Edward.

"It's a pleasure to see you again, Belinda." His stomach tightened, reminding him of his recent beating.

"Why, Henry McConnell, I do believe you have found your talent for moving in three quarter time. The ladies present, and especially their feet, will be most appreciative of your newly discovered penchant for the waltz." Belinda squeezed his hand and gave Henry a teasing smile.

Henry floated across the dance floor, hoping she couldn't feel the pounding in his chest. They shared small talk. She returned his attentions with flirtatious laughs. When the music ended, a pattering of applause rose from the room.

A tall cadet strolled across the dance floor, heading straight for Belinda. Henry cut him off, stepping up to Belinda and extending his hand. "I would be honored to share the next waltz with you."

"Henry, you are quite forward, aren't you? But I would be delighted . . ." she curtsied and took his hand.

As they whirled to the music, Edward clumped past with the young blonde in tow. He appeared to be attempting some variation of the box step as he stared at his feet and counted, "One two three, one two three . . ."

When the music ended, Belinda turned to Henry. "I must

spend time with others. It would be improper for a lady to save all her dances for one gentleman." She batted her eyes.

"Would you care for some refreshment first?"

"Why, yes. Thank you." She fanned herself with her hand. "I am as dry as can be."

Henry went in search of the punch bowl, no doubt already spiked with a covert addition of rum. He found the table festooned with cups, plates and pastries. After ladling fruit punch into two cups, Henry maneuvered through the crowd to where he had left Belinda.

A rousing polka ended and Belinda and another cadet whirled off the dance floor, laughing as they high stepped together. Henry caught Belinda's eye. She rushed to him, pulling her dance partner by the hand. "Henry, you do know George, don't you? He dances a wonderful polka!"

Henry nodded at Cadet Wheatley. "We are acquainted." He turned away from the taller cadet and held a glass out to Belinda. "Here's your punch. I hope you find it refreshing after such vigorous exercise."

She gave Henry a reproving frown, then turned toward Cadet Wheatley. "George, I do thank you for a most enjoyable dance. Now don't be a stranger. I would be so disappointed if we could not share another polka." She tilted her head and curtsied. Cadet Wheatley returned the bow and stepped away.

"Now, Henry, I declare, you are exhibiting all the annoying symptoms of genuine green-eyed jealousy. You must allow me my polkas."

Henry drained his cup, then took Belinda's, setting both on a table along the wall. "Let's dance."

Henry whirled Belinda into the center of the swirling crowd. Silent and purposeful, he concentrated on matching his steps to the music.

"Henry, it is so warm in here. I must have some fresh air. May we go outside?"

"With pleasure." Henry guided Belinda around the dance floor until they reached the end of the long hall. There they exited through the double doors. A few couples danced on the flagstone patio. Others shared quiet conversation or talked in small groups. Laughter cut through the stillness of the cool evening.

"Is there no place without interruptions?" Belinda asked.

He pulled at his collar, swallowed hard, and pointed. "Yonder is Flirtation Walk."

"I suppose you must go there often?"

His face warmed. He wiped his damp palms on his coat. "Never been out there. The rule is, cadets aren't allowed on Flirtation Walk without a lady on their arm."

"Will I do?" She hooked her arm in Henry's.

He smiled. They walked in silence until they came to an overlook on the cliffs above the wide Hudson River. Moonlight painted a white swath across the dark waters below. Without the protection of the trees, the air turned cool.

Belinda shivered and snuggled against Henry. "Chilly . . ."

He put an arm around her shoulder.

"Like back there between you and George." She gave him a questioning look.

"That? Just a difference of opinion."

"Really?"

Henry took his arm from her shoulder and leaned against the stone wall. "Some don't care much for us southerners. All this political talk has folks riled."

"Henry, are you a Lincoln man?"

"I'm a soldier."

"And you are from Virginia." Belinda stepped back and seemed to study him. "You don't own slaves, do you?"

"My family's owned slaves for more than a hundred years," he said. "It's a natural and honorable economic system."

"It is so cruel . . ."

"Nothing cruel about it. We take good care of our nigras. We feed them, clothe them, give them homes. They're a right happy lot. Folks up here are making an issue out of simple property rights."

"But Henry, they're not just property. Those are people. They have rights too. Why, how'd you feel if you were sold off at some auction?"

"You ever meet a nigra?"

Belinda shook her head.

"They're different. Good folk, mind you, but most are a mite slow, like children."

"I read in *Harper's Weekly* that all they need is their freedom—"

41

"Do you know what would happen if all those slaves was to be set free?" Henry said. "They'd starve—that's what. They don't have the means of making a living on their own."

She folded her arms across her chest. "Last month you mentioned a friend back home, Isaac, I believe you called him. Is he one of your coloreds?"

Henry rubbed the back of his neck. "Sure, his mama's our cook, best cook east of the Mississippi."

"Is he a helpless child?"

"Huh? What are you talking about?"

"Well, is he smart?"

Henry leaned against the wall. A cloud drifted in front of the moon, momentarily darkening the overlook. "Isaac reads some, does figures too." Henry chuckled. "You should see him work long division. He figures numbers in his head faster than old man Crowley down at the mercantile can do with his pencil."

"He doesn't sound helpless, Henry McConnell."

Henry poked at a stone with his boot. "Isaac and his folks are different. They're like family and he's like a brother. Florence and Abraham, that's his mama and his pa, they've been with us since before I was born. They don't know any other way, and they don't want to be set free. Where would they go? Besides, they like it where they are."

Belinda tossed a pebble over the cliff. "Henry, have you ever asked Isaac what he thinks about that?"

"It's getting late." He took Belinda's arm. "I need to get you back before your ship sails."

Belinda stood fast. "Henry McConnell, you and your coloreds present me with a dilemma. Whatever will become of my standing in New York society if you don't change your prehistoric views?"

"New York society be damned." Henry turned and began walking back to the dining hall. Belinda ran to catch up, taking Henry by the arm. He looked straight ahead as they walked on in silence. Just before they reached the patio, Belinda pulled him to a stop. "This might be our last private moment until next month," she said. "I don't want to say 'good-bye' without giving you something to remember me by." She leaned forward and kissed his cheek.

Chapter Seven
November 1860

Morgan stared across the table. Please, Lord, no more battles . . . not tonight. He pointed at the chair. "Enough of this. Take your seat."

"But Father," Patrick said, "that Black Republican bastard will bring us to ruin!" His long red locks bounced as he pounded the table.

"Sit down, and you will keep a civil tongue while you're in this house." Morgan shook his fork.

"Father, you are ignoring the issue of property rights." Patrick dropped into his chair. "If Lincoln takes the presidency, slavery will be outlawed in the territories. The South will never again have a stronger voice than we have today. Breckenridge will open the territories to slavery, and with that we'll gain political allies to help fight off those abolitionist nigger lovers."

"I am not ignoring the issue of slavery, but the question of the Union is at the fore. John Bell understands the importance of the Union. I dare say, Abraham Lincoln understands it better than your Mr. Breckenridge. Without the Union, the South is nothing—a collection of farms with no markets, pitiful rail lines, and scarcely any manufacturing."

"We have Europe. Great Britain, the French . . ."

"Damn the French." Morgan shook his head in disgust.

"Morgan!" Ella tapped her finger on the table. "It is no wonder your sons behave in a manner so ill-suited to our more genteel expectations."

Morgan sighed. "Patrick, we need the North. We need the Union. Your secessionist rabble there in Charleston will tear this nation apart and we will be the poorer for it."

"Gentlemen, would one of you kindly pass the sweet potatoes?" Ella raised an eyebrow and locked her gaze on Morgan.

Morgan turned his head. "Tempie, come fetch the sweet potatoes for Miss Ella." He ignored Ella's frown and continued, "It is the responsibility of every son of our grand commonwealth that birthed the likes of Washington and Monroe to take a stand. We must ensure that the republic they founded is not torn asunder."

Patrick started to respond, but Ella shot him a stern glance and placed her finger to her lips.

Morgan took a deep breath. They'd had enough of politics. He must change the subject. Scanning the dining room, his gaze fell upon Polly. Sweet child. Takes after her mother—same delicate features.

"Polly, how are your studies?"

"I have mastered the romantic languages, Papa. Quel temps croyez-vous qu'il fera demain?" Polly raised both hands in a question and cocked her head.

Morgan looked at Polly, then Ella. He shrugged.

"I think the weather will be quite stormy if you don't eat your greens." Ella turned to Morgan. "And I hear from Sarah Johnston that one of their nigras ran off yesterday."

"Yes, spoke with Sam last evening. I sent Sean to help with the search. They'll be needing all their slaves when the planting starts next spring. It's important that we support Johnston, same as he would us."

"I hope this isn't the start of more trouble." Ella dabbed the corner of her mouth with her napkin. "Some northerners were in South Boston last week. Folks said they were Quakers. There's talk they were trying to stir up the nigras."

Morgan shook his head. "I wish those damned Quakers would mind their own business. Last thing we need is trouble with the darkies. Remember that uprising over to Southampton County, what was that, thirty years ago?"

You mean with that that nigra preacher, Turner?" Ella said.

"That's the one." Morgan slapped the table. "Got the darkies so worked up they went out butchering innocent white folks. We don't need any God almighty Philadelphia Quakers getting our nigras riled again."

Patrick took a bite of biscuit, chewing as he spoke. "I talked to

Clancy this morning. He said when they catch that nigger he'll be made an example of. If you ask me, a hundred lashes wouldn't be nearly enough."

Morgan shot Patrick a stern look. "And nobody asked you."

"But Father, Sam Johnston doesn't pamper his niggers. He understands the benefits of good discipline."

"What Sam does with his nigras is his business, but I won't hold with beating slaves on this farm. We sent you up there to Charlottesville so's they could learn you good business sense. They teach you anything at the university about husbanding your assets?"

"Whipping is training, no different than teaching a dog to fetch."

Morgan shook his head. "Why do you suppose Johnston's nigras are all the time running off, while ours are perfectly content?"

"They're content because life's too soft for McConnell slaves." Patrick rested his elbows on the table, his palms raised.

Morgan dismissed him with the wave. "As good Christians, we need to show the rest of the nation that slavery is a just, righteous institution. We have a duty to treat our nigras good, same as we treat our livestock, or any valuable property."

"But not coddle them, Father."

"God intended the black race to use the strength of their backs, not their child-like minds." Morgan wagged a finger. "It is our Christian duty to be caring stewards. If we treat our nigras well, they will repay us with their love, their loyalty, and the sweat of their brows. No nigra ever ran from a good master, nor would they want to."

"Well Father, the day's coming when we'll wish somebody around here had paid closer attention to those niggers." Patrick jerked his thumb toward the rear of the house. "Take that boy, Isaac. He spent so much time with Henry he's beginning to think he's white. There's one slave that surely needs a whipping."

"Enough, Patrick." Ella nodded at Morgan. "Your father has been dealing with the slaves since long before you were born. He is not only a smart businessman, but also a good Christian. You should heed his word."

Polly frowned. "Patrick McConnell, you lay a whip on Isaac, you'll answer to me . . . and Henry."

Patrick kicked his chair back as he stood. "Sometimes I think this family has turned into an abolitionist mob. Wouldn't surprise me to find all our nigras sitting around this very table come Christmas Day, sipping tea and eating cake—with y'all serving them!" He threw his napkin on his plate and stormed out.

Morgan caught Ella's worried look. He lowered his voice. "His passions are stirred by the goings on with the elections. Once the presidential race is decided, he'll settle back to learning tobacco. Give him time."

* * *

"Lincoln in a Landslide!" The headlines jumped off the front page of the *Richmond Daily Dispatch*. Morgan tossed the newspaper on the lamp table and looked at Patrick seated on the sofa across the parlor. "It's finished, son. Your Democrats did no better than John Bell and his Constitutional Unionists. The South must accept this result and move on."

"The Carolinas will not be accepting. Mississippi will not be accepting." Patrick pounded his fist into his open palm. "Word from Charleston is that South Carolina will leave the Union. Virginia must do likewise or we forfeit our rights as slave owners. Our way of life will end."

Morgan set his reading glasses on the newspaper. "Virginia is the birthplace of American democracy. She will never secede." He tapped his finger on the paper. "The Union cannot be ripped apart by the likes of Senator Chesnut and his Carolina cronies. When he speaks out against democracy and union, it's nothing short of treason."

"Treason? When the northern voters talk of taking away our rights and our means of a livelihood, as they did when they placed Lincoln on the throne, then it's high time we recognize that universal democracy is no friend to southern sovereignty. When the abolitionists can vote away our way of life we are no longer either safe or welcome in their union."

"Patrick, we solve nothing, you and I. You are my oldest. I'm relying on you to one day manage this farm for you and your brother. It is only important that we agree that the farm comes first. Without our tobacco we have no future."

Patrick grabbed his hat and walked to the door. He lifted the latch, then turned and faced Morgan. "Yes Father, and without our niggers we have no tobacco."

Chapter Eight
November 1860

Mist floated above the Dan River as the wagon approached. Isaac gazed absently at leaves swirling in the eddies around the bridge's large stone arches. Sean O'Farrell paid the toll, then flicked the reins. The muted plodding of the horse's hoofs on the dirt road gave way to echoed clops on the wooden planks within the darkness of the covered bridge.

Isaac had crossed that river years ago, in a time before the wide, two-lane bridge. Then he'd been in the back of the wagon, with Pa driving. The old Boyd's Ferry had carried them across to pick up a load of lumber from a mill in North Carolina. Now he rode up front.

Isaac glanced at the short, graying Irishman beside him. Mr. Sean was a good man. He got the work done, but he looked out for folks too. Isaac had sure enough seen worse.

Sean gave the horse the reins and rested his elbows on his knees. He turned to Isaac. "Well, me boy, yer off for a grand high adventure now, are ye?"

"I reckon, Mr. Sean. Never lived away from the farm before, except when me and Henry goes hunting up country. I expect I'll be learning right much from Mr. Day, but I reckon I'll be missing Mama's cooking some too."

Sean laughed. "Your ma give ye some vittles for the journey? Ye'd be wanting to share now with old Mr. Sean, would ye not?"

Isaac reached under the seat and produced a bundle wrapped in a bright red bandana. Sean's face beamed as he accepted one of the large golden biscuits.

The wagon rolled into the early morning sunlight at the far end of the bridge.

Jeff Andrews

Sean took a bite, talking as he chewed. "I don't never tire of Florence's biscuits. Your ma's the best cook in all of Virginia. Just wish ye'd thought to bring along some sorghum."

They rode on in silence. The rhythm of wheels on the dirt road and the warmth of the autumn sun lulled Isaac into a quiet melancholy. He placed his hand on his chest, touching the wooden star beneath his shirt. What kind of master would Mr. Day be? Would he abide whippings?

Sean broke the silence. "How long did Mr. McConnell say ye'd be staying down here?"

"Not sure, Mr. Sean, a few months, I reckon. I'll stay 'til he sends somebody to fetch me."

"Aye, and most likely that'll be me. You'll be missed around the farm, boy."

Isaac nodded. He'd miss that place too, especially Mama and Pa, and Henry . . .

The sun rose in the sky. Isaac dozed. Finally, Sean turned the horse. Isaac jerked awake as they entered the tiny village of Milton. A few wooden buildings dotted the main street. To the right sat a small red brick church with white columns and a pitched roof topped with a short steeple.

The wagon pulled in front of a large two-story brick building with three arched doorways. Sturdy brick chimneys anchored both ends of the structure. Smoke belched from a metal chimney protruding through the roof of a one-story wooden addition.

"Here ye go, Isaac. This here be Yellow Tavern, yer home until Mr. McConnell sends for ye."

Isaac clutched his wooden star, took a deep breath, and climbed down. Sean O'Farrell pulled the bell chain beside the door. After a few moments, the door opened and a tall man stepped into the late morning sunlight. He appeared to be older than Isaac by a dozen years or so, with light almond skin and a full, closely cropped beard. The man wore brown trousers and a pinstriped shirt. Black garters adorned each arm. He wore a green eyeshade similar to those worn by the merchants in South Boston.

"So, this is Isaac, son of Abraham!" The stranger crossed the cobblestone walk. "I am pleased to meet you. My name is Thomas Day." The man offered his hand.

White folks did that, but it wasn't anything Isaac had ever done. He hesitated, then took the man's hand. As they shook, Isaac studied his host.

"Is there a problem, Isaac? You seem puzzled."

"Mr. Day, sir, if you doesn't mind me saying, you looks a mite young to do all what my pa says you done . . ."

Thomas placed his hand on Isaac's shoulder. "Forgive me." He chuckled. "I did not intend to mislead you. I am Thomas Day." He paused, then added, "Junior. When your pa spoke, no doubt he was referring to my father."

* * *

"Feed the furnace like so." Thomas tossed a shovelful of Virginia anthracite coal into the flames. "Now bank the fire thusly, then adjust the grate. Too much air and she'll blow. Too little air and we have no steam to run the machinery."

Isaac stared at the steam engine in the long wooden shed. "I seen locomotives on the Danville to Richmond line, but a steam engine indoors? And doing the work of ten men? Pa won't never believe that."

A rhythmic pounding filled the room as leather belts and metal pulleys transferred power to lathes, drills, and saws, while heat from the engine circulated through a wood-drying kiln.

Thomas pointed to the lathe. "You done much turning?"

"Some. Mostly I cranked the great wheel for Pa while he worked the lathe. He don't have no steam engine."

Thomas laughed as he picked up a chisel. "Any experience you've had under Abraham's watchful eye will be good enough." He reached overhead, taking one of the wooden patterns that hung from the rafters. "Don't get greedy. The wood will give herself up to you a little at a time, much like a beautiful woman. You got yourself a woman, Isaac?"

Isaac shook his head.

"No matter. Now, if you move too quickly, try to take too much, she'll kick and bite with all the fury of a lady that's been misused. Do you know what I mean?"

Isaac shrugged.

Thomas tightened a piece of oak on the lathe and released the clutch. The wood spun into a blur. Thomas laid the chisel across the slide rest and eased the razor tip in until it met the stock. Wood chips flew and the squared piece began to take on a curve.

"Remember, slow and gentle and the lady will return your love. Move too quickly and she becomes a pile of matchsticks." Thomas handed Isaac the chisel. "Disengage the clutch and let the work come to a stop every so often, then check it against the pattern. You can always remove more stock, but if you take off too much, the piece is ruined, and ruined stock costs me money. You will pay for whatever you destroy with extra labor hours. Any questions?"

Isaac shook his head.

"Very well. If you need me, knock at the back door. I have invoices to finish." Thomas left Isaac alone at the lathe.

He'd watched his pa turn chair legs, table legs, spindles, and decorative columns. It had always looked easy. Now, as the whining of leather belts and flywheels filled the gas-lit shop, Isaac hesitated. Had he learned those skills simply by watching? Holding the pattern against the block of wood, Isaac penciled marks on the stock to guide his cuts. He shoved the clutch forward; the wood spun to life. Remembering Thomas's words, Isaac reached out to the "lady" before him and gave her his undivided attention.

* * *

Isaac unclamped the last of the chair legs. Running his hand over the smooth wooden curves, he examined his work, then placed it alongside the others. Not bad for his first afternoon. Pa would be pleased.

"Finally finished, are we?"

Isaac turned toward the unexpected voice. Thomas stood in the doorway.

"Yes sir, I done just like you told me."

Thomas glanced at his pocket watch. "If I were paying you a wage, I'd dock your pay for those." He pointed to a pair of shattered chair legs on the floor. "As it is, you'll reimburse me with your labor." He handed Isaac a broom. "When you're finished, get on over to the bunkroom and grab supper, then get some rest. Dawn comes early."

"Yes sir." Isaac gave a nod as Thomas left the shop, then he picked up the fractured spindles and propped them on a ledge above his machine. "Now, you fair ladies done told on old Isaac, but I forgives you 'cause you taught me a lesson. From now on, the both of you stand right there so's you can watch over me while I works. You'll be reminding me about how I needs to be more gentle." Isaac patted the wooden scraps. "Now you ladies set there and have yourselves a good night."

It was dark by the time he finished sweeping. Isaac turned off the lamps and shuffled wearily into the small bunkroom at the rear of the workshop. The room wasn't much, no bigger than two horse stalls put together. He pulled a small book from his pocket and tossed it on the table as he sat. On the far side of the room a Franklin stove hissed, flames licking through its grate. On top of the stove a blackened pot filled the room with a tempting aroma. Should he help himself?

Bunks three high lined one wall. Another three bunks were against the wall beside the window. Two of the bunks appeared to be occupied. Maybe he should just find an empty bed and catch some sleep. From the lower bunk closest to him, an old man suddenly rose and shambled across the bare floor.

"Sit," He gestured to Isaac, as he reached the stove. The man ladled what looked like stew onto a tin plate and set it in front of Isaac on the long pine table.

"What do they call you, boy?"

"Name's Isaac."

"Who'd Mr. Day buy you from?"

"Ain't bought."

"You free?"

Isaac shook his head. "Mr. Day borrowed me. My owner, Massa McConnell, he lives up in Virginia, there in Halifax County."

The old man pointed to the book. "He know you can read?"

"Was him what taught me, or least ways his son did." Isaac folded the tattered copy of *Peter Parley's Winter Evening Tales* and stuffed it back in his pocket.

"Don't be letting no white folk down here see you with that book. They'll think Mr. Day taught you to read and that'll bring trouble down on him."

The old man sat across from Isaac. "Gabriel's the name, except I ain't got no horn." He chuckled. "I been with Mr. Day most all my life. He owns me and old Mr. Jones over yonder there." He pointed toward the other old man, now sitting on the edge of his bunk, tapping out a rhythm on a pair of bones.

Mr. Jones raised his hand holding the dried goat's ribs above his head, then bought the bones down with a flourish of short clacks. "*George Washington* Jones." He winked. "But *Mr. Jones* be just fine."

"You all there is?" Isaac asked. "I heard tell Mr. Day owned a passel of slaves."

"Business been tough, boy," Gabriel said. "Mr. Day come close to losing everything. His boy, Thomas Junior, he had to come to his rescue. All the other slaves been sold to pay bills. Me and Mr. Jones, we's too old to draw top dollar, nor most any dollar at all, so Mr. Day had to keep us. We does what we can and he feeds us pretty good. We don't mind none a' tall."

Isaac took a bite. "Squirrel?"

"Yup. Throwed in some possum too. Mr. Jones there," Gabriel said, motioning with the wooden spoon, "he does most of the gathering and all the cooking. He's pretty good too, but . . ." Gabriel leaned closer and wagged his finger. "You watch him real close, you hear? He ain't always particular about how ripe a critter gets lying dead out there in the bushes. Mr. Jones reckons them maggots make for good eating too, says they put fat on a man's bones."

Isaac searched his stew, turning over lumps of meat—then he caught the gleam in Gabriel's eye. Isaac smiled and took another bite. "Where's the senior Mr. Day?"

"He done took sick—consumption, some folks say." Gabriel took in the room with a wave. "But you'll see him here by and by. He's a right fine gentleman."

Isaac leaned closer to Gabriel. "But he's black, same as us. How's a black man hold with owning slaves?"

"Business." Gabriel returned to the stove. "If'n a white man uses slaves to make his goods, how can a black man keep up, less'en he gets his own niggers? Mr. Day can't stay in business paying for labor what white folks is getting for free." Gabriel ladled another pile of stew on his plate and sat down again. "Truth be told, Mr. Day used to have whites working for him too, and nobody 'round these parts ever seemed bothered none by that. Ten years ago, this here business supported lots of folks, black and white."

Mr. Jones settled on his bunk and Isaac and Gabriel continued talking while Isaac finished his supper. No lights shone from the big brick house by the time Isaac went out back and washed his dinner plate under the pump. Returning to a quiet bunkhouse, Isaac grabbed a blanket from one of the empty bunks, blew out the oil lamp, and curled up on the lower bunk beneath the window.

* * *

Sunlight filtered through the dirty glass windowpane as Isaac ran his hand over the smooth maple. He measured the stock against the pattern. Close. Just a bit more off the end. He engaged the clutch. The leather belt hummed as it slipped around the pulley, then caught, spinning the lathe to life. Thomas had been a good teacher—no rejects for two days.

"Only Abraham's boy could turn such a piece."

Isaac pulled out the clutch and turned to face an old man, light-skinned, but African nonetheless. He was tall and thin, with short, curly hair that recessed at his temples to form a "V" of gray hair over the center of his forehead. Isaac looked into his tired, dark eyes.

"Mr. Day?"

The old man started to speak, then bent over, wracked by a violent cough. Finally, he straightened, pounding his fist on his chest. "At . . . at your service."

Mr. Day pumped Isaac's hand. His calloused grip still possessed incredible strength.

"Come. Sit." Mr. Day motioned toward two chairs beside a small table. "Your father was the best I ever taught. If I had five more with his skills today, I'd be competing with the best furniture houses in New York City." Mr. Day coughed again, then asked, "How is Abraham?"

"He's doing fine, sir." Isaac's throat tightened. Pa had said nobody could work wood as good as this man, and now, here he sat, talking to Isaac like he was somebody. Isaac took a deep breath. "He speaks highly of you."

"Good. Good." The elder Mr. Day reached below the table and produced a small desk drawer. He handed it to Isaac. "What can you tell me about this?"

Isaac turned the piece over. "Oak. Dovetailed." He pointed.

"Groove cut here, in the sides and front, and the bottom piece is glued in. Looks to be good workmanship, sir."

"Look at the front."

Isaac turned the piece over again. Beneath the brass drawer pull was an ornate relief carving showing an acorn surrounded by a cluster of oak leaves.

"Anyone can learn the craft of joinery, boy, and you will, but I also want to teach you the art of it all. Fine wood is like a fine woman . . ."

Isaac smiled to himself. Like father, like son . . .

Chapter Nine
November 1860

Isaac tapped the chisel with his mallet, carving a rabbet joint along the edge of a maple board that would overlap another board, similarly cut, to form one side of a china cabinet. He blew wood shavings out of the cut, then measured his work with the blade of his chisel.

"Hey boy, you got religion?"

Isaac turned at the sound of the voice.

The elder Mr. Day stood in the doorway. He coughed, then asked again, "You a church-goer?"

"Mama taught me religion, but we don't have no church—too far to walk."

"You ever been to a church?"

"Went to a camp meeting once," Isaac said. "Must have been eighty, maybe a hundred folks, all clapping and singing. We had us a fine time."

Mr. Day pointed out the window. "We worship up the street at the Presbyterian Church. Be sure you're ready first thing in the morning. We leave at quarter 'til eight, prompt." He turned and shuffled out the door.

Going to church with the boss man . . . Isaac smiled. What would folks say about that? He picked up his chisel and continued cutting the joint. He might be headed to church tomorrow, but that boss man still expected him to finish his work today.

* * *

Isaac entered the bunkroom, tossing his hat on his bed. A delicious aroma rose from the steaming pot on the Franklin.

"Hey, boy. Set on down." Mr. Jones pointed to the table. "One of Mr. Day's customers done kilt him a deer and gave it up as payment for his bill."

"Where's Gabriel?" Isaac pulled up a bench.

"Mr. Day sent him to deliver an envelope. Gabriel says it was billing for a table and chairs." Mr. Jones set a plate in front of Isaac. "I reckon he'll be back shortly, was only going two, three miles to the south."

Isaac pointed toward his plate. "You done good, Mr. Jones. This here is only a fistful of carrots away from being a real fine stew."

"Boy, you find me some good 'uns, I'll throw 'em in. Weather's been too dry, makes for small carrots—ain't proper for cooking." Mr. Jones stirred the pot, then took his plate and sat.

"You and Gabriel going to church tomorrow?" Isaac asked as he took a bite.

"Ain't set foot in a church for nigh on twenty years. "Mr. Jones shook his head. "Not since we built them pews."

"You built the pews?"

"The church folks asked Mr. Day could he make 'em, and Mr. Day said yes, they'd have themselves some fine pews and a right nice pulpit too, and all at no cost."

"He made 'em for free? How's that?"

Mr. Jones nodded. "Mr. Day said, if'n he builds 'em, him and Mrs. Day and their children, they all set down in the front of that church, just like the white folks."

"And the whites was okay with that?"

"You go look at them pews, boy. They's poplar wood with real nice curves on the end pieces. Pulpit's got fancy columns on each corner too, fine place for any preacher to set his Bible."

"Sounds right pretty." Isaac nodded. "So, is you going tomorrow?"

"Old Mr. Jones, he don't hold much with religion no more. If there is a god, he ain't hearing no nigra's prayers." Mr. Jones looked at his plate for a moment, then chuckled. "Ain't got no Sunday meeting clothes no how."

"Church clothes? All I has are these rags I wear for working." Isaac pulled his frayed, worn shirt away from his body.

Mr. Jones lowered his voice and leaned toward Isaac. "You'll be fine, boy. Ain't nobody gonna pay no mind to no nigger what's dressed like what he is."

Isaac glanced again at his shirt, stained with oil from the machines. "I reckon you's right." He clutched his wooden star and closed his eyes. It must really be something to have clean clothes to change into every Sunday.

A sudden commotion shook Isaac from his thoughts. Thomas pushed through the doorway half carrying, half dragging a bloodied Gabriel.

"Help me get him to his bunk," Thomas said. "Grab some bandages. Mr. Jones, get some water and fetch that whiskey I know you have hidden around here."

Isaac grabbed Gabriel's arm and helped guide him to the bunk.

"Lord Almighty," Mr. Jones cried out. "What happened?" He dug behind his blankets and handed Thomas a jug.

"Somebody jumped him coming home from the Benjamin place," Thomas said as he poured whiskey on a rag.

Isaac pulled off Gabriel's muddy shoes. He stared at the battered old man. "Why'd anybody do this to Gabriel? He never hurt nobody."

"Could have been highwaymen," Thomas said, "but I suspect it was something more." He daubed Gabriel's cuts with the whiskey soaked rag.

"What do you mean, 'something more'?" Isaac said.

Thomas put the jug to Gabriel's lips. Gabriel swallowed, then coughed and looked around. He laid his head down, covered his eyes with his forearm, and moaned.

Thomas looked at Isaac. "We can't collect on debt the way a white man does. Those that are paid to uphold the laws won't give us the backing. I suspect what happened to Gabriel was a warning from one of our customers to stop trying to collect on overdue accounts."

"There must be a sheriff or a magistrate? We got to tell somebody . . ." Isaac clenched his fists.

"Won't matter without a witness." Thomas pointed at Gabriel. "Right now it's just the word of one old slave."

Isaac studied Thomas. "So, what is you gonna do, Mr. Day?"

"All we can do is trust the good folks here in Milton to do right. Even now, with talk of secession, war, and slave uprisings, most still try to pay us as best they can."

"Folks what ain't got the cash, they still be paying in barter?" Mr. Jones seemed to be searching Thomas's face for an answer.

"Yes, my friend, we'll be eating like kings—until we go broke." Thomas smiled. "Chickens and pigs won't pay our New York creditors."

* * *

Gabriel's snoring filled the darkened room. Reflections from the Franklin stove danced across the ceiling. Gabriel was bruised a mite, but nothing broken. Isaac chuckled to himself. Gabriel said he didn't have a trumpet, but that nose of his sure sounded loud enough.

Isaac tossed restlessly on the narrow bunk. So many questions. Mr. Day wasn't free. Maybe he owned slaves, but he was a slave too—held captive by the color of his skin.

Closing his eyes, Isaac tried to push away the swirl of confusion in his mind. The fragrance of burning wood in the stove and the warmth of his blanket began to lull him to sleep, then he remembered church and Mr. Jones' words: "Nobody's gonna pay no never mind to no nigger what's dressed like what he is."

* * *

Somewhere in the woods behind the bunkroom, a rooster crowed. Isaac wearily awoke. He stumbled to the washstand and splashed cold water on his face. Mr. Jones had already stoked the fire and had corndodgers sizzling in hog fat.

"Morning Mr. Jones," Isaac said. "I need to speak with Mr. Day. Save me some breakfast." He dried his face and headed out the door.

Isaac paced by the back door steps of the of the large brick home searching for the right words. Finally, he climbed the steps and knocked. After a moment, the door opened and the elder Mr. Day looked down at him.

"Sir, I can't be going to church this morning," Isaac mumbled, staring at his feet.

"What seems to be the trouble?" Mr. Day raised an eyebrow. "You ill?"

"No sir, ain't ill." Isaac paused. He looked down at his shirt. "Ain't got no proper church clothes, just this rag I works in." He pulled the dirty cloth out from his body.

"A shirt is it?" Mr. Day smiled. "You need not miss the Good Word for want of a proper shirt. Wait here." The door closed.

In a few moments the door reopened and Thomas handed Isaac a small bundle. "This should suffice. It's yours to keep."

"Thank you, Mr. Day, thank you, sir." Isaac backed down the steps, then turned and ran to the bunkroom.

He cut the twine and spread the garment on his bunk. Seven oyster shell buttons lined the front of the white, finished cotton shirt. The full-length sleeves had cuffs that buttoned. Isaac touched the pocket on the left breast. He'd never owned a shirt with a pocket before. It had a stain, but it didn't show much, except when he held it up to the direct sunlight. He hung his new shirt on the peg above his bunk and sat down to breakfast.

* * *

Isaac caught his reflection in the window in front of the Yellow Tavern house as he waited for Mr. Day and his family. He turned, running his hand over the new shirt. Mighty fine, like how he'd look up in Philadelphia, meeting business folk or being admired by workers in his own shop . . .

"Boy, you ready?" Mr. Day stepped out the door followed by his wife, Acquilla, and Thomas. They proceeded up the street. Isaac fell in step behind.

A crowd gathered under the church portico while others shuffled through the arched doorway. White folks greeted the Days by name. Isaac smiled and nodded as he followed the Days into the church. They was just folks, friendly, too.

Inside, they entered a small foyer, then Isaac followed the Days into the sanctuary, gliding his hand across the smooth, curved armrests at the end of the pews. Mr. Day's handiwork? He inspected the craftsmanship.

"Isaac, come here," someone whispered.

He turned. Thomas motioned for him, then turned and walked toward the rear of the church. Isaac followed. When they reached the foyer, Thomas pointed to a narrow stairway in the back corner. "The slave balcony is up there."

Isaac could only nod. A fancy shirt didn't change what he was. He climbed the stairs.

The only seats were two long wooden benches. An old woman with a kerchief tied about her head sat on the far bench, her arm around a young child dressed in a plain white frock. Isaac nodded to the older woman and took a seat on the near bench. He gazed at the sanctuary below. Aisles on either side separated the pews along the walls from the wide middle section. In the front corners, pews faced inward, toward the raised wooden pulpit. Mr. Day and his family sat in the pew up front on the left.

A woman seated at a piano played a single chord and the entire congregation stood as one and began singing. Isaac recognized the hymn from the revival meeting he'd attended last summer. He joined in, trying to remember the words.

After the hymn, the minister raised his right hand. "And now, let us bow our heads and lift our hearts in prayer to the Lord Almighty.

"Dear Heavenly Father, Your humble servants come to You this day to confess our sins. We have not lived by Your word. We are unworthy of the blessings You have given us, and we ask Your forgiveness. We ask, Lord, that You give us a mild winter so's hungry mouths will be fed and, if it be Thy will, we humbly ask that those gathered here today be blessed with good health and prosperity. Finally, Lord, we ask that You heal the rift that is tearing our country apart. Touch the hearts of those in power and give them the wisdom to see the truth as You know it to be. Lord, as distant drums are sounding, we stand in humble assuredness that if war comes to this divided land, You will stand firmly with Your faithful servants here in North Carolina and bless our righteous cause. We ask these things in Your son's name—"

"Amen," the congregation responded in unison.

Isaac opened his eyes and took his seat. During the prayer, a young woman had found her place at the far end of his bench. Her black, closely cropped hair glistened. Smooth, dark skin reflected the warm glow of the morning light. She sat erect, her hands folded in her lap. Her simple dress was that of a house servant, pale blue, unadorned. Surveying the room as she settled into her seat, her gaze paused for a moment on Isaac, then, without acknowledgement, she turned her attention to the pulpit.

Isaac quickly looked away. Had she seen him staring? She had to be a slave girl, but she had—what was it Henry used to say? An air, she had an air about her. So, who owned her? Did she have a man? A pretty girl like that, she had to have a man . . .

In time, the drone of the minister's voice ended. The congregation stood, raising their voices in unison for the final hymn. Following the benediction, a buzz of conversation floated up from the sanctuary. Skirts rustled behind him. Isaac turned. Where had she gone? He rushed down the steps and into a throng of people. The old woman with the child came down from the balcony. Isaac followed them outside, searching up and down the street.

As he wandered back to the Days' house, Isaac carefully checked every passing carriage and scanned all the side streets. Nothing. Somehow, she'd vanished. He entered the bunkroom and took off his Sunday shirt, hanging it carefully on a peg over his bed. Without a word, Isaac slipped on his old work shirt.

Gabriel sat at the table, his left eye swollen and his cheek bruised, sipping a mug of sassafras tea. "You look snake bit, boy. Preacher put a scare in you with his fire and brimstone?"

Isaac flopped onto his bunk and folded his arms behind his head. "Gabriel, you know anything about women?"

"Ou-w-e-e-e. You got you some serious trouble, Gabriel can sure enough see that. Who is she?"

"Don't know. Don't know nothing about her. She came to church late and left before I could talk to her."

"Sounds to me like the good Lord has figured out how He's gonna get Isaac back to church to hear His word again next Sunday." Gabriel crowed with laughter.

Chapter Ten
December 1860

A shadow moved into the sunlight that poured through the open double doors and across the dusty floor. Isaac looked up from his work and smiled. "'Morning, sir. I've mostly finished that dresser. You done taught me well. Come see."

Thomas stood in the doorway. "Later," he said. "Grab your things. You have a visitor."

A visitor? Who would come to see him—and wouldn't Mr. Day be angry about interrupting his workday? "Yes, sir, be right there, soon as I cleans up." Isaac put away his tools and swept aside the wood shavings. He snatched his jacket from the peg on the wall and followed Thomas outside. Two familiar horses were hitched in front of the Day house. Isaac gave Thomas a questioning shrug. Thomas smiled and nodded toward the street.

Isaac followed his gaze. Suddenly, he clapped his hands and let out a laugh. "Lord almighty! Henry? Is that you, Henry McConnell?"

Henry crossed the street from the general store swinging a paper sack in one hand. He walked straight to the larger horse and swung into the saddle, then pointed to the smaller animal. "Get your tail up there. Time's a-wasting. There's critters afield and we're going hunting." Henry hooked one leg over the saddle horn and crossed his arms. A smile pulled at the corner of his mouth.

"Henry," Isaac said. "You tell me, did you up and quit that army school?"

Henry shrugged.

"Schooling don't suit this white boy." Isaac jerked a thumb toward Henry. "Never done a hard day's work in his life. Horses, hunting, and women, that's all he lives for."

Thomas raised an eyebrow and glanced at Henry.

Henry laughed. "He knows me well."

Thomas smiled and nodded.

"I'll have him back in a few weeks—unless the bears get him." Henry held the bridle of the smaller horse as Isaac mounted.

"Well then, good hunting." Thomas waved.

Isaac turned his horse and nudged it into a trot. "Fess up, Henry. What is you doing here? Your pa's gonna tan your hide if'n you got throwed out of that school."

Henry held out the paper sack. "Got you something."

Isaac smiled as he pulled out a handful of gumdrops. "You knowed they was my favorites."

"Henry, you in some kind of trouble again?" Isaac said, turning his horse toward the bridge. "You gonna tell me what happened?"

"I am a cadet in good standing." Henry straightened in the saddle. "I'm passing all my classes *and* I have the highest ranking of all the plebes in horsemanship!" He swept off his hat and bowed.

"So why ain't you up there at West Point?"

"Christmas. I got four weeks leave. Figured I'd came home for a visit, but I didn't figure on having to ride clear to North Carolina to rescue you from that chair factory. What in tarnation are you doing there?"

Isaac popped another gumdrop in his mouth. "Your pa sent me here to apprentice under Mr. Day."

Henry nodded. "I reckon it beats tobacco farming."

"It sure do. You serious about hunting bear?"

"Serious? Six months of book learning—never mind putting up with Yankee officers—I'm in need of some righteous distractions. Figured we'd head up along the Staunton River. You remember that cave we camped in last year?"

Isaac adjusted his hat. "The one they calls Injun Jim's?"

"That's the one. We'll camp there." Henry shot Isaac a quick glance, then leaned forward in the saddle. "Last one over the bridge is sleeping with a polecat!" He spurred his horse and disappeared in a cloud of dust.

* * *

Florence sat beside the hearth holding a squawking brown hen on her lap. She smoothed the bird's feathers. "There, there. Florence ain't gonna hurt you none, least not so's you'll notice." The hen settled, clucking softly. In a feathery blur, Florence snapped the bird's neck, then dunked the flailing carcass into a pot of just-boiled water. She held it under with a forked stick and began singing, "Swing Low, Sweet Chariot." Hot water loosened the feathers for plucking, but too long in the pot and the meat would begin cooking. One verse would be enough.

Winter chickens took more plucking. Pinfeathers grown for warmth didn't come out in clumps like the larger feathers. Each had to be plucked separately. Florence pulled her chair into the afternoon sun on the cookhouse porch and rocked back, humming as she pinched out the tiny feathers.

A breeze gathered dry leaves, tossing them against the side of the barn. Joseph ran past carrying a stick, followed close behind by one of the McConnell's dogs. Florence gave him a stern glance. "That boy disremembered the woodpile again . . ."

With Abraham and Isaac gone, firewood chores fell to Joseph. She should holler at the boy, but the respite offered by the quiet warmth of the December sun felt more precious right then than what few sticks of kindling the boy might split in the next hour. She let him pass.

To the southeast, a cloud of dust swirled near where the farm land met the post road. riders coming?

She sang quietly, plucking and watching. In time, a wagon came into view. Florence squinted, then sat back and smiled. "That ol' mule never could walk straight—always looking like he was gonna fall over in his tracks."

The driver sat tall and upright, his wide brimmed hat casting a shadow over his face. She shielded her eyes from the afternoon sun. Praise the Lord. Abraham was home.

The last plucked chicken hung with the others as Abraham strolled up from the barn. He stopped in front of the porch, placed his hands on his hips, and bent over, as if trying to get a better view. "I declare, you ain't my Florence, you's all young and pretty. What'd you do with my ol' woman?"

Florence folded her hands in her lap and looked into Abraham's eyes. "What is it about your time on that road that makes you all addle-brained? Don't you be playing no tricks with me, Abraham."

He stepped onto the porch and pulled her into his arms. "Been three weeks doing for others, sleeping in barns, eating hoe cake, or worse. All the time, I been thinking about my Florence and how I misses her cooking."

Florence buried her face in the familiar musk of the old woolen shirt. There had been too many nights alone. A sob caught in her breath.

"Hush, woman. Ain't no call for tears. I's home. We's together again."

She looked into his large brown eyes. "Every time you goes on one of them jobs, you takes my heart with you."

"And I always brings it back . . ."

"These is hard times, Abraham. Can't nobody know what the future holds."

He smiled, pulling her close again. "I always comes back, woman. I always has and I always will."

* * *

Isaac tossed his blanket over a pile of leaves, smoothed the lumps, then settled next to the fire and lifted the stewpot lid, sniffing the aroma as he stirred. "Near done. Be better if'n we had taters and carrots, but at least you remembered the onions."

Henry shrugged. "I can't think of everything." He fixed his blanket on a rock shelf dug into the side of the cave.

The cave's small and well-hidden opening belied a spacious interior with three large rooms. A natural spring bubbled into a basin carved in the rock that held the water before it spilled over and disappeared again through cracks in the floor.

Henry took a seat next to Isaac and held out his tin plate. "I'm sure grateful to Florence for teaching you to cook."

Isaac ladled a serving of rabbit and onions. "Was Pa what taught me. Critters ain't like farm stock. Critters need slow cooking, more seasoning." Isaac took a bite and wiped his mouth with his sleeve. "Tell me about West Point."

Henry laughed. "Army's different, that's for sure. They got more rules than ticks on a hound. They even have rules for what you can look at."

"Don't you be funning me."

"Honest," Henry said. "I got punished once just for looking at a pig."

"What's wrong with that?"

"We was on the parade grounds for inspection and this wild

hog come running out of the woods; he tears across right in front of us." Henry made a sweeping gesture with his fork. "I sure wanted to chase that porker. We don't get much fresh meat up there."

Isaac nodded. "Would have make for some good vittles, that's for sure. You catch him?"

"I done good, Isaac, honest. I stood my place, didn't move— not much anyway—though every muscle in my body was twitching. I figured I was demonstrating the absolute best in army discipline. Well, the captain comes over and hollers like I'd just dropped my musket in the mud." Henry held out his plate.

Isaac ladled out another serving. "If'n you was standing so still, how come he hollered?"

"He said my eyeballs were wandering. Don't that beat all? Two hours punishment tour for looking at a pig."

Isaac laughed. "Good thing it weren't no pretty girl, they'd a locked you up for sure." He paused, then looked at Henry. "You like it up there?"

Henry poked the fire, stirring a fountain of sparks. "The army's where I want to be, and West Point's going to get me there. I like the soldering part, it's the class work gets me to worrying, mathematics and such—"

"You still having trouble with them numbers? I thought I'd teached you good."

"Not talking about just adding and multiplying and such. They have something up north they calls algebra."

"Ain't never heard of no algebras."

"Shoot, you'd probably do good at it, the way you're all the time doing figures in your head. How'd you ever learn that, anyway?"

Isaac lifted a burning stick and traced a flaming figure eight in the air. "Ain't no learning, it just always been there—like with you and horses."

"I reckon," Henry said. "Still, it ain't natural. Don't be letting on you can do that. Folks might think you got the devil in you."

"No devil, just numbers . . ."

Henry tossed a stick on the fire. "It's not just the studying that's been worrying me, it's all the political talk. They're turning West Point into some kind of damned debating society."

"Isaac don't know nothing about politics."

"There's talk of war."

Isaac poked at the rabbit on his plate. "Don't want no war. Who you gonna fight?"

"There's Yankees figuring to come down here and take away our property rights." Henry pointed at Isaac. "But Virginia's got too many boys handy with a squirrel gun, like you and me."

"Isaac ain't shooting nobody. Ain't like putting a ball in this here rabbit." He tapped the cooking pot with his fork. "Besides, I got no fuss with the Yankees."

"If Yankee soldiers come to Virginia, you'll take up a rifle and stand with the rest of us. We'll defend our homeland, and we'll give the invaders hell."

Isaac stabbed at his food. McConnell land was white folk's land, wasn't his to die for. Besides, he'd done enough killing already.

"Hey, can you keep a secret?" Henry poked Isaac with his elbow.

Isaac nodded.

"I got me a girl."

"Shoot, when'd you ever *not* have a girl?" Isaac chuckled.

"This one's different." Henry smiled. "Belinda's her name. Belinda Towers. Most beautiful woman you ever saw; long black hair, green eyes . . . she's a true belle—except she's a Yankee, but best of all, she's totally taken with me."

"Like that girl over to South Boston you said was in love with you, the one what's marrying that store keeper?"

Henry rolled his eyes, then leaned back and folded his arms across his chest. "Right now, I bet Belinda's drowning her pillow in tears, just wishing Christmas would pass so's I'd come on back. When my army days are done, I reckon I'll marry her and we'll settle right here on the farm and raise us a proper family."

"Ain't that what you said last year about that girl over to Danville?"

Henry ignored the question. "How about you? Got yourself some sweet little thing?"

"No. Nobody." Isaac shook his head.

"Come on, not even one of those Johnston slaves?"

Isaac poked the fire. He looked up at Henry, then stared into the flames. "Seen a woman in church once down in Milton . . ."

"I knew it!" Henry clapped his hands. "What's her name?"

"Don't know."

"Well, how'd you meet her?"

"Seen her in church. Didn't talk to her, though."

"You know where she lives? Who's her owner?"

Isaac shook his head.

"So how you going to find this here 'mystery' woman? You want I should put the hounds on her? Maybe we can tree her like we did that bear."

Isaac smiled as he stared into the fire. "Don't rightly know how I finds her again. Guess Isaac'll be attending church more regular."

"How about that." Henry laughed. "Old Isaac's got religion! Well, if you're going to track bear come morning, you'd best forget that girl and get some sleep."

"Amen. Sleep's coming mighty easy tonight." Isaac stretched out on his pad of leaves and closed his eyes. Muscles that hadn't sat a horse for many months reminded him of the day's long ride.

Henry fussed with his blankets, then sat up. "Hey, Isaac . . ." He hesitated, "Belinda says I got to ask you something."

"What's that?"

There was a moment of silence. "Never mind. I'm reconsidering. Maybe this ain't the time." Henry wrapped up in his blanket. "Goodnight."

Isaac stared at the shadows dancing on the roof of the cave. So, who was she, and could there be any way that she was thinking about him too? What if she didn't come back to church?

Chapter Eleven
December 1860

"Florence, come quick!" An urgent voice called from the porch, followed by a flurry of sharp knocks on the cabin door.

"Lord, it ain't hardly dawn. Who's that making such a fuss?" Florence stumbled out of bed and flung open the door.

Banjo stood wide-eyed on the porch shaking a finger toward the quarters. "It's ol' July," he said. "He got himself busted up real bad, Florence. You gots to hurry." He turned and ran toward the slave cabins.

"I'll be along soon as I fetch my remedies," Florence replied. She lifted a goatskin pouch from a peg on the wall and stepped outside.

Abraham caught up with her in the barnyard, hobbling as he pulled on his trousers. Together they ran past the drying barns and down the lane to a small clearing where a half dozen rough-hewn cabins formed a semicircle around a blackened stone fire ring around which a dozen or more slaves gathered. The group parted as Florence approached, revealing one lone figure sitting on a log.

July's bowed head and tightly closed eyes suggested the countenance of a man at prayer, but his mouth turned up in a curious smile. A hand-woven straw hat sat jauntily on the back on his head. His bloodied arms rested on his knees. Dried blood caked the stubble on his cheek and stained his tattered shirt.

Florence glanced at Abraham. His knowing look told her what she already knew. She pressed her fingers against July's cold neck, then shook her head slowly, looking first at Banjo, then Lilly.

Banjo stepped forward. "Somebody beat him bad, real bad."

"He must a drug his self back here," Lilly said. "We'd all gone on to bed, but July said he was heading to the river to do some fishing. He don't have no pass. You reckon them pattyrollers done him like that?"

Florence shook her head. "Ain't no way of knowing."

"We come out this morning," Lilly said, "and there he be, all beat up and dead."

Banjo wrung his hands as he stared at the lifeless figure. "July said his old Negro soul was growing tired of this here life, but I reckon he never meant to go out this a-way. Least ways his days in them tobacco fields is over. It's time he took his rest with the Lord."

Abraham turned to the somber gathering. "I needs to make him a box. Y'all get to digging a proper grave so when we lays him out he'll see the angel Gabriel coming out of the east to take him home."

Florence placed her hand on Abraham's arm. "I best go tell Massa McConnell. He don't know yet that he don't own July no more." She turned and walked slowly toward the big house.

* * *

Slaves from neighboring farms, some with passes, others risking capture, joined the McConnell slaves as the torch lit procession wound through fields toward a small clearing in the woods overlooking Bennett's Creek.

The casket bounced lightly on the shoulders of the men as Florence followed a few steps behind holding a small basket. July had always been there, as much a part of life on the McConnell farm as the sun, the rain, and all the acres of yellow leaf tobacco. Her gaze turned heavenward. "Lord, July weren't no burden in life, can't be much of a burden now . . . I's sure gonna miss his laughter."

The trees surrounding the clearing reached their bare branches skyward, as though clutching at the fleeting clouds, while pine knot torches danced shadows across the flat boards and roughly hewn crosses that marked the final resting place for generations of McConnell slaves gone before. Florence noted her mother's tilted headboard at one end of the glade.

As mourners encircled the freshly dug grave, the pallbearers placed the casket on three ropes then, using the ropes, lifted July and lowered him gently into the ground.

The gathering grew quiet. Abraham removed his hat. Holding it to his heart, he gazed toward the heavens. "Lord, we ain't got us no preacher, so's this'll have to do 'til we gets us one. We brung you your servant, July."

"Amen," the mourners replied in unison.

"He was born right here on this land, before any of us here was alive, and he worked this land all his days."

"That's right, Lord." Banjo lifted a bony finger toward the sky.

"Now that he's dead, he be buried on this land." Abraham glanced around the gathering. Florence nodded for him to continue.

"Here on earth, July worked for Massa McConnell. Now he's in Heaven, he be working for you, Lord."

"Amen."

"Lord, come take your child on home. He been waiting on this day for a terrible long time." Abraham closed his eyes and bowed his head. "Amen."

"Amen," the mourners echoed.

Abraham tossed a handful of dirt on the casket. One by one, others did the same, then the men refilled the grave, tamping the dirt into a low mound with their shovels.

Florence opened her basket and removed several shards of broken pottery. She placed the pieces on the fresh grave. "July, this here's your body, broken by a hard life on this here earth. Now that you's in Heaven, the Lord'll be making you whole again."

"That's right," Lilly said. "You's with the Lord."

Florence smiled. "God bless you, July."

"God bless," the gathering echoed.

One by one they turned and began the walk back up the path toward the slave quarters. Once clear of the cemetery, someone began clapping softly. Others joined in. Soon, voices raised in song broke the stillness of the crisp December night. Florence fell in step beside Abraham, clapping in rhythm, listening to the deep voice she knew so well.

* * *

The crackling fire and an occasional cough from the sleeping loft were the only sounds as Florence and Abraham settled into their bed.

She rested her head on Abraham's chest. "Massa says he'll be asking the preacher from South Boston to come up next month and say some words over July."

"He'll sure enough be liking that," Abraham said. "Ol' July ain't never had no white man pay him no never mind, least of all a preacher. He'll know he's in Heaven when that happens."

"All he ever wanted was to see what lies beyond the river, past that next hill." She ran her hand across Abraham's cheek. "I's scared our children won't never see what's past that hill neither. I don't want them dying like July, wondering what's out there beyond them tobacco fields."

Abraham wrapped his arm around her. "Don't you be troubling yourself none about that."

"You and me, we's content where we is," she said. "But I wants better for our children. There's a whole world out there beyond South Boston."

"There sure enough is."

She raised up on one elbow. "Don't like to think on running, but I keeps wondering . . ."

"Sh-h-h." Abraham put a finger to her lips. "I been keeping a secret from you, woman."

She clutched his hand. "What secret?"

"A few years back I talked to Massa McConnell, asked him how can I buy my childrens. He said, 'Abraham, you works them jobs, you makes Massa McConnell the money, and we finds a way.' So I works them jobs, and I works hard. I makes Massa a passel of money and he holds out some from what I earns for payment for our childrens. I reckon by this summer coming I'll have enough to buy Isaac."

"For sure? You telling Florence the truth?"

"Sure enough. Be buying Tempie next, then Joseph. Should have money enough for each before they's all growed. Now hush, woman. Don't you be telling nobody. This'll be Abraham's surprise. Once our childrens is safe up north, you and me be getting on that freedom train too."

Florence wrapped her arms around Abraham and kissed his whiskered cheek. Her babies were really gonna see what was beyond that next mountain.

Chapter Twelve
December 1860

Henry glanced over his shoulder as he spurred his horse past the drying sheds. Isaac and the smaller pony were two lengths behind. He'd beat them easily. "Yee ha!" Henry waved his hat and galloped through the barnyard, kicking up dust and scattering chickens.

"You're slower'n a tobacco bug," Henry hollered as he reined his horse in front of the house. He turned in the saddle when Isaac pulled alongside. "Tarnation, I even gave you a head start . . ."

Isaac shook his head and smiled.

Morgan stepped onto the porch. He locked Henry in a stern gaze, then turned to Isaac. "Boy, you take those horses to the barn and rub 'em down real good, you hear? It'll be your hide if they catch a chill after being run so hard in this cold."

"Yes, sir." Isaac jumped from his mount, gathered the reins, and led both animals to the barn.

Morgan motioned to Henry. "Inside."

Henry followed him into the parlor. Greenery festooned the mantel and draped the chandeliers. Mistletoe hung in the doorway. The family had been busy in his absence, decorating for the holiday. Morgan faced the hearth holding his hands toward the fire. "Seven days you've been gone. Seven days with two of my best horses and a nigra that's supposed to be working." He turned toward Henry. "Where in blazes you been?"

"I told you I was going to do some hunting, and you was sitting right there when I said I was going down to North Carolina to fetch Isaac."

"For a two-day hunt. Your mother expected you home four, five days ago. So did I." He placed his hands on his hips.

"Papa, I—"

"I don't care to hear your excuses." Morgan glared. "Thank God your brother handles responsibility. This farm would fall to ruin if I had to leave it in your hands."

Henry clutched his hat in front of him, staring at the floor. No call for getting angry, he'd told him where he'd be. He wouldn't be pitching a fit if it had been Patrick that had gone hunting.

"Tomorrow's Christmas. Get yourself cleaned up—and you be on time for a change—don't go breaking your mother's heart by disappearing again."

"Yes, sir." Henry started up the stairs.

"Henry . . ."

He turned.

"I reckon Florence won't mind having Isaac here for a few days. You can take him back to Milton before you head up to West Point next week."

"Yes, sir. Thank you, Papa."

"Get on, now, and have Tempie pour you a bath." Morgan shooed him away. "You smell worse than a week old possum carcass."

* * *

Sunlight sparkled on the frost covered lawn. Henry dressed quickly and bounded down the stairs to the front parlor. The family was gathered around a Christmas tree bedecked with strings of popped corn, garlands of colored paper, and candied fruits. Polly, Tempie, and Joseph sat on the floor. Isaac, Abraham, and Florence stood in the archway leading to the dining room. Patrick took a seat on the sofa. Morgan was in his usual chair.

"Good morning, Henry. Merry Christmas!" Ella smiled from her rocker.

"Here, this is for you, Henry." Polly handed him a package.

He took a seat beside his brother and unwrapped the box.

"For the cold New York winter," Polly explained.

Henry smiled, holding up a pair of woolen stockings. "Thank you, sister. My toes will remember your kindness."

Morgan opened a present from Ella, a pair of chamois-skin riding gauntlets embroidered in red silk with his monogram.

Gifts passed from hand to hand. Tempie seemed delighted with a hand-me-down dress from Polly. She held it in front of her, turning for all to admire. Joseph excitedly accepted the wooden top that had passed from Patrick to Henry, then to Polly. Now it was his. The string had been replaced and the paint was faded, but otherwise it was in fine condition. Patrick got on the floor and showed him how to make it work. Everyone clapped when Joseph pulled the string, spinning the top across the wooden floor.

Henry offered Polly a small box. With a questioning look she opened the package. Inside was a pale yellow stationary with a single flower in the upper right corner of every sheet.

"So you can keep me posted on happenings around here while I'm out in the Indian territories with my cavalry troop," Henry said.

Polly smiled. "You always think of the nicest gifts. I'll write you every month 'til the stationary runs out. You'll know it's from me by these pretty yellow envelopes."

Abraham stepped forward, clearing his throat. "Uh, Miss Ella? I done fixed you up a shelf for your tea service." He reached behind the archway and pulled out a honey pine shelf with a plate groove cut across the top. "If'n you likes, it can be hanging in the dining room before dinner."

"Oh, Abraham, it is lovely!" Ella clasped her hands together. "Yes, yes, go put it up right now. I would dearly love to see my teacups and saucers on display when we sit down to our Christmas dinner."

"No university educated gentleman should be without a proper ledger set," Henry said, handing his brother a dark mahogany box with brass hinges. Patrick opened the lid, revealing styluses, an ink well, extra nibs, and a supply of paper.

"I'm not looking for letters, dear brother," Henry said with a smile, "just an accurate accounting of our tobacco sales."

"Like you'd know if the figures were close by even ten acres worth," Patrick chided him.

"That's a mighty fine gift," Morgan said, pointing to the lap desk. "Is the army giving you an extra allowance these days?"

Henry smiled. "A cadet from Boston wagered that desk against my riding boots that he could out-jump me on horseback. He figured himself a better horseman than any Yankee I've ever seen."

Morgan and Patrick laughed.

"Quiet! All of you!" Ella stared at Henry. "You know I don't hold with gambling. It's the devil's play."

Patrick slapped Henry on the shoulder. "It ain't gambling, Mother, not if there's no chance of losing."

Her face turned crimson as the room filled with laughter. "You hush, Patrick McConnell. You're encouraging your brother's bad habits. Now all of you, go get ready for breakfast." She turned to Florence. "We will be seated within the quarter hour. Kindly finish the preparations."

* * *

The afternoon sun caught the tops of the bare trees in its fading light. Slaves sang as they returned to the quarters carrying bundles of new clothes, shoes, and sacks of flour and sugar--all gifts from their owners. Henry stood in the doorway. "Good Christmas, don't you reckon?"

Isaac nodded as he sat, dangling his legs over the side of the porch. Being home had made it special.

"Got something for you," Henry said as he sat down beside Isaac. "Didn't want to give it to you this morning in front of everybody. Anyway, figured you were tired of those children's books, so . . ." He handed him a sack.

Isaac reached in the bag and withdrew a clothbound book. On its cover was a man dressed in rags wearing a broad-brimmed grass hat.

"Rob-robin . . ." Isaac's finger followed the letters as he tried to sound out the words. "Robinson, Robinson Crusoe?" He looked at Henry.

"Yes. It's about a fellow who gets kidnapped by pirates and then he's marooned on an island. He finds himself a native fellow he names 'Friday.' Reminded me of us. Now, don't let Papa or Patrick catch you with it."

"I'll be careful." Isaac tucked the book under his shirt. "I ain't got no present for you."

"Having you home for Christmas was present enough. Now get, before somebody sees you with that book."

* * *

Isaac set his foot in the stirrup and swung into the saddle.

"Go on down by the quarters and say your good byes," Henry said. "I'm going to see if your mama has some biscuits I can take along for the ride. I'll catch up."

Isaac waved and turned his horse. "I'll be waiting by the post road."

He rode slowly down the lane, turning into the clearing where a few slaves sat in the morning sun mending tools. Others were busy hanging wash or cooking in large cast iron pots over the campfire.

"Hey there, Banjo," Isaac called out. "Hey, Aunt Lilly. Y'all take care 'til I gets back this way."

"You stay safe down there in North Carolina, you hear?" Lilly shook out a quilt as she spoke and hung it across the top rail of the fence.

Isaac studied the quilt's pattern. Embroidered on a four-inch square of cloth toward the top was a star. Through the center a vine made of rags wound its way around the other squares, each with their own unique design. The outer squares added a colorful border. To the white folks, it was a simple bed rug, but to those on the run it was a map to the Promised Land.

Isaac cautiously scanned the grounds, then lowered his voice. "Freedom Train running tonight?"

"Sh-h-h. No telling what ears might be listening." Lilly stepped closer. "A feller from over Danville way is running. I's hanging the quilt in case he passes this way needing directions. Pattyrollers be out and about too, so you watch yourself."

"Thanks, Aunt Lilly. Henry's riding with me to Milton, so I'll be safe enough. You take care. I'll see you in a month or so."

Lilly patted his knee as Isaac turned his horse. He nudged the animal into a trot, turning to wave as the slave quarters faded into the pines. A short distance later Isaac laid the reins across the horse's neck and entered the grove of trees encircling the small cemetery. He dismounted next to the only fresh grave.

"July, wish I'd a been here for your burying. For me and Tempie and Joseph, you was the grandpa we ain't never had. We's sure gonna miss you. I been praying, asking the Lord to show you that world you ain't never seen when you was just a slave. I know you's in a better place now."

Isaac tossed a handful of dirt on the grave and remounted. He nudged the horse, guiding the animal back onto the trail that led to the post road and then glanced back at the cemetery. How could a man live out all his life on just one farm? Didn't he ever think about running? About freedom?

The lasso jerked Isaac from his saddle. He landed hard, knocking the wind out of him. When he struggled to sit up, a boot crashed into his side.

"You one of them McConnell niggers? What're you doing out here by your lonesome, boy? You stealing a horse? Let's see your pass."

Isaac cleared his head and looked up. Two men stood over him, one holding a shotgun. Isaac didn't know him. The other, whip in hand, was Clancy.

"Ain't got no pass. Me and Henry's riding to Milton—"

The butt of the shotgun caught Isaac on the side of his chin. Hands grabbed him. A hard slap landed across his face.

"I know you ain't speaking of Henry McConnell, 'cause that'd be '*Master* Henry' to you, boy. You don't talk about white folks disrespectful like that." Clancy grabbed Isaac by his collar and yanked him to his feet. "What do you know about that runaway from over Danville? You McConnell niggers got him hidden out somewhere?"

Clancy's fist landed hard to Isaac's stomach. He buckled. Clancy jerked him up by the collar, then flung him back to the ground. Isaac's head slammed against the packed dirt. The world swirled around him. His head pounded as he tried to focus. The pounding grew louder. *Hoofs? Horse's hoofs . . .*

A shot rang out.

"You! Hold fast or I'll put a ball through your hide."

Isaac rolled over. The sun silhouetted a rider looming above him. Isaac wiped dirt from his eyes. Henry?

Henry leaned forward in the saddle. Smoke curled from the barrel of the pistol in his hand.

"Mr. McConnell," Clancy said, "glad you come along. We just caught this here nigger trying to steal one of your horses. We was fixing to truss him up and bring him back to you."

"He wasn't stealing anything, and you got no business here on McConnell land. I'm counting to five, Clancy. If you're still here when I finish, I'll blow your head off."

"The word's out on you, McConnell." Clancy shook his fist. "Folks is talking. They's saying you's soft on your niggers. Fact is, they's calling you a nigger-lover behind your back."

"One . . ." The hammer on the Navy Colt clicked to full cock. "Two . . ."

Clancy and his partner clambered aboard their horses and disappeared in a cloud of dust.

"You all right?" Henry asked. He took the reins and steadied Isaac's horse.

"I . . . I's fine, just bruised a might." Isaac staggered to his feet and brushed himself off. He rubbed his neck. Something was missing. He felt again. The rawhide cord—his star. Isaac dropped to his knees, searching the weeds along the path.

"You lose something?"

Isaac clawed at the dried grass and catbriers.

"Hey, you need help? You want to go back and get some mending before we ride on?"

Isaac shook his head and climbed slowly into the saddle. His hand went to the place where the star had been. "Daylight's a-wasting. We'd best get on to Milton so's you can be back before dark. Them two might not treat you so good if'n they was to find you on the road at night."

"I reckon you're right," Henry said. "Here." He tossed over a small sack. "I was saving these for later, but I expect you could use 'em now."

Isaac caught the bag and looked inside.

Gumdrops.

Chapter Thirteen
February 1861

Sheets of freezing rain turned the road and surrounding fields into dark, formless shadows. Isaac pulled his slicker tightly around his shoulders and hunkered on the wooden seat. The horse plodded, as though in a trance. Isaac twitched the reins. "Hey there, wake up." He chuckled. "Shoot, I'd be sleeping too, if I wasn't so durned cold."

The road turned. Isaac reined to the left but a rear wheel caught the edge of the roadside ditch. He grabbed the seat with one hand while slapping the horse's rump with the slack of the reins. The wagon teetered, then slid sideways down the muddy bank and jarred to a stop.

"Tarnation! First time Mr. Day trusts Isaac to make a delivery and he busts up the wagon." He looped the reins around the brake handle and jumped down.

Rain stung his face as he examined the wheel. The axle looked fine. Nothing appeared broken, but a rear wheel was mired in mud clear to the hub.

Isaac turned to the horse. "We's stuck some. Getting us unstuck is all on you, ol' boy." He stood to the side of the wagon and slapped the horse's rump with the free end of the reins. "Ya-a."

The animal lurched forward. The wagon shuddered, then settled back into the mud.

Isaac put his shoulder against the rear of the wagon and pushed as he flicked the reins again.

Nothing.

"Got to pry that wheel loose. You hold on there." He searched under the tarps in the back of the wagon and retrieved a sturdy plank. Isaac wedged the board beneath the trapped wheel and flicked the reins again. "Hey! Get on there!" As the horse pulled,

Isaac leaned down on the board. The wheel did not budge.

He wedged the board further under the wheel and snapped the reins once more. "Get! Ha!" The horse dug into the slick mud, straining against the harness. Isaac threw his weight against the lever. The wagon shuddered, then suddenly pulled free, dropping Isaac face first into the ditch.

He wiped the mud from his face, grabbed his hat from the icy water, wrung it out, and then shoved it on his head. He then glared at the horse. The horse responded with a bemused look.

"Y'all just hold up on your funning there, mister. If'n you hadn't took that turn so close Isaac wouldn't be in this here mess." He scrambled up the bank and checked the pine dining table lashed in the back of the wagon.

"Ropes held good." Isaac yanked the lines that tied down the load. "Nothing broke. We ain't in no trouble if we gets it delivered tonight." He patted the horse's rump, then climbed back into the driver's seat. "Ain't just your problem, ol' boy. We both missed that turn. I'm hoping when we gets to the Patterson place they'll let ol' Isaac warm some by their fire before we head back to Mr. Day's."

Freezing winds swirled through his drenched clothing, chilling Isaac to the skin. He gripped the reins with frozen hands. He couldn't sleep now. If that horse wasn't gonna watch the road, Isaac had better.

"Mr. Day said the Patterson farm was halfway to Yanceyville, but Isaac ain't never been to Yanceyville, so how's he to know when he's halfway?" He shook the reins. "Hey horse, you know where halfway is?"

The night was late when the wagon rolled up the tree-lined lane to the large two-story farmhouse. A single light shone from a downstairs window. Isaac climbed from the wagon, stretching his tired, stiff body. He looped the reins twice around the hitching rail, then climbed the steps and knocked on the door. Shadows danced across the porch as a light inside moved. The door opened a crack. Light fell across Isaac's face, causing him to blink.

"What do you want this time a night, boy?"

"Sir, I come from Mr. Day's, up Milton way. I has a table for Mr. Patterson." Isaac couldn't control the tremble in his voice or the shake of his hands. He removed his hat and bowed slightly.

"Damn, boy, you're half frozen! Get in here." The door swung open. A short, gray haired gentleman with a full beard stood aside, his belly pressing against the buttons of his waistcoat. He waved toward the glowing fire. "What in tarnation is Day thinking, sending his nigras out on a night like this?" Mr. Patterson shook his head. "Here, set down on that stool and warm yourself."

Isaac hurried to the hearth.

Mr. Patterson walked to the darkened staircase and cupped his hand beside his mouth. "Raleigh," he called, "fetch a blanket and brew a pot of tea. We have us a boy here who like to froze himself to death."

Isaac pulled the stool close to the fire. Mr. Patterson stirred the ashes and added a log. Coals glowed red, then flames leapt around the newly added wood. Isaac scooted back as the heat brushed his face.

"Thank you, sir. Wagon went in a ditch. I fell in trying to unstuck a wheel."

"I can see that, boy."

Footsteps padded down the stairway as Isaac stared into the dancing flames. Mr. Patterson handed him a blanket. The footfalls trailed off toward the back of the house. Isaac wrapped the blanket around his shoulders.

"Where's your wagon, boy?"

"Out front, sir. I'll go fetch your table—" Isaac started to rise.

"You sit, boy." Mr. Patterson pointed to the stool, then walked to a door that led to a back room. "Raleigh, when you finish there, go wake Ezekiel and tell him to get that table off the wagon out front, and have him put that horse up in the barn too. Be sure he gives that poor beast a good rub down."

"Thank you, sir," Isaac said. "Mr. Day will be appreciating your kindness."

"No sense in letting a good animal die from exposure. No sense in you trying to get back to Milton tonight neither. You get warmed. I'll have my house girl bring you dry clothes." Mr. Patterson started up the stairs, then paused and turned toward Isaac. "You can sleep in the barn tonight."

A door creaked followed by soft footfalls. "Here, drink this." The voice was clear, like the song of a wood thrush. Isaac turned. She stood beside him holding a steaming cup of chamomile tea.

Isaac stumbled to his feet, dropping the blanket to the floor.

That same pale blue dress, now covered with a dark blue apron . . .

He gazed into large, almond eyes.

She smiled. "We have not been to church lately. Missus Patterson took ill, so we have not made the trip to Milton."

Isaac stepped away from the hearth, wiping sweat from his brow. "I . . . I been most every Sunday." He poked at the stool with his foot. "About gave up on seeing you again."

* * *

She faced away as Isaac peeled off the wet clothes and dropped them in a pile. He pulled on a pair of Ezekiel's trousers and slipped the borrowed shirt over his head. "They's a mite loose, but they's dry."

She turned around and looked him over, then motioned toward the fire. "You may sit a spell longer—just until the chill is gone. Do you have a name?"

"They calls me Isaac . . . 'cause I was the first son of Abraham. He's my pa."

"Nice to meet you, Isaac." She smiled and dipped in a mock curtsy. "My name is Raleigh, because that is where I was born." She sat on the sofa facing the hearth.

"Raleigh . . . that's a nice name." Isaac nodded. He took a sip of tea. "You been here long?"

"I have been in Mr. Patterson's employment for one year."

"He just bought you?"

"No. I am a free woman."

"How is you free? Was your mama free?"

"No, she died giving birth to me, but she died a slave. The Pattersons bought me when I was six years old. They raised me and taught me and, in return, I take care of their household needs."

"But you said you come here just last year?"

She rose and walked to the fireplace. "I said I came into Mr. Patterson's employment one year ago. When I was twelve, Mr. Patterson told me that if I worked hard he would pay me a small stipend to cover my needs. I told him my need was to be free, so he agreed to let me buy my freedom, one dollar at a time. A year ago he marked the debt paid and gave me my papers."

Isaac leaned toward her. "So, if you's free, why ain't you in New York, or Boston, or Philadelphia? Why's you here?"

"The Pattersons are the only family I've ever known. The Lord never blessed them with children, so they have no one to look after them in their old age. I guess I'm their family too." She sighed. "You'd best get out to the barn now. Take the blanket. You'll find saddle blankets in the tack room if you need more. I'll bring you coffee and biscuits in the morning."

"You be at church this Sabbath?"

Raleigh lowered her head. "I don't expect so." She wrung her hands, then looked up. "Now, go make your bed in the straw. And, Isaac . . ."

He turned as he headed toward the door.

"Stay warm." She smiled.

Isaac reached for his medallion. His hand wiped the front of his empty shirt.

Chapter Fourteen
April 1861

"War! They've fired on Fort Sumter!" The cadet raced down the hallway banging on doors, shattering the Saturday routine of cleaning rifles, polishing shoes, and tending to uniforms. Cadets in every manner of dress rushed into the hallway. Henry tossed his musket on the bed and ran to the door.

At the end of the hall, a cadet held up a page of newsprint. "The paper says Captain Beauregard commanded the southern cannon."

"Beauregard?" Edward said. "He didn't last five days when he was up here as superintendent, but it sure sounds like he's making up for it now." He nudged Henry with his elbow. Nervous laughter passed through the crowd.

"I hear tell West Point relieved him because of his secessionist leanings," a cadet called out in a down east accent.

The plebe with the newspaper held up his hand, silencing the crowd. "It says here *Brigadier General* P. G. T. Beauregard of the Confederate forces ordered his batteries to open fire on the U.S. fortress early Friday morning after negotiations between Beauregard and Major Anderson, United States Army, reached a stalemate concerning the surrender of Fort Sumter."

"Appears to me you make rank quickly in that rebel army," a Vermont cadet added. Several cadets laughed.

"Bet Sumter's guns showed them rebels what for," a lad from New Jersey said, waving his fist above the crowd.

"Did we take casualties?"

"Who won?"

"Where's the Navy?"

Questions flew at the self-appointed town crier as he appeared to try to make sense of the terse news story.

"Did *who* take casualties?" Henry glared at the gathering of cadets. The hallway became silent.

He studied his classmates. The sameness of their uniforms belied the differences in their hearts. Many wore confused, questioning expressions. The realization began to sink in; Americans had fired on fellow Americans.

"My God, what have they done?" Henry shook his head and walked away.

* * *

Henry avoided the cliques—southern cadets in one room, northerners in the next. Hushed discussions might be taking place behind closed doors, but the friction of earlier days appeared to have lifted. The weekend was cloaked in a surreal mantle of tense politeness.

Henry rose early Sunday morning and went to chapel. Many attended, but there seemed little agreement as to what their prayers should be. Afterward, Henry wandered back to the barracks, speaking to no one. He entered his room without a word, tossed his hat on the bed, and began unbuttoning his tunic.

"What will you do?" Edward asked. He had broken the rules by lying on his bed during daylight hours. In different times, cadet officers roaming the hallways would have been quick to issue demerits. On this Sunday, no one bothered. He crossed his feet and put his hands behind his head.

"Virginia is Union and she'll stay Union," Henry said as he hung his tunic on the wooden peg. "We had our election a week ago. Secession was soundly defeated. I stand with my country and I stand with Virginia."

"That might get you by for today, McConnell, but what about tomorrow? What about next week? Virginia is a slave state. She won't be staying."

"Then ask me again next week. I go where Virginia goes."

* * *

The rattle of drums woke Henry with a start. Rubbing his eyes, he climbed out of bed. Through the window, gray dawn heralded another Monday. He splashed cold water on his face and began preparing for morning muster when a commotion came suddenly from the hallway outside his room. He cracked open the door. A crowd filled the passageway.

"Sumter surrendered," a cadet shouted. "Anderson struck his flag."

"And Lincoln's calling for an invasion of the south," cried another plebe.

Politics and lies—a waste of his time. Henry slammed the door and finished dressing. He hurried down for morning formation.

Subdued requests replaced the normally sharp commands barked by the cadet officers. Henry took his place in formation. On command, the company covered down, filling gaps vacated by the cadets he'd seen packing their bags over the weekend. South Carolina, Mississippi, Florida, Alabama, Georgia, Louisiana, Texas—all gone.

As they marched to class, Henry reflected on the tensions created over the last several days. He'd have never guessed that he would look forward to algebra class. He smiled to himself. At least there were no politics in the classroom.

* * *

Henry strode to the blackboard and wrote out his solution in large block numbers.

"Mr. McConnell, please enlighten us with your solution to problem number three." Professor Robertson sat on the corner of his desk holding a wooden pointer across his shoulder.

Henry pointed to his solution, explaining each step.

"Precisely, Mr. McConnell, a worthy recitation. Are there questions?" The professor looked around the class.

"Just one." Cadet Wheatley rose from his seat. "How much longer are you seceshers going to linger here abouts? The true patriots among us are growing tired of having traitors in our midst."

Professor Robertson jumped to his feet. "Remove yourself at once, Mr. Wheatley." He swept the pointer toward the door. "I will tolerate no such outbursts in my classroom."

Cadet Wheatley picked up his books. He glared at Henry, then turned and marched out the door.

"Get back to work." The professor tapped his pointer on a desk. "Problem four. Are there any volunteers?"

* * *

Jeff Andrews

At the end of class cadets filed from the room. Professor Robertson motioned to Henry. "Cadet McConnell, a moment, if you please." The professor waited until all the other cadets had departed, then settled on the edge of his desk. "What's your decision, Henry?"

"There is no decision to make. Virginia stays with the Union; I remain with her."

"Did you hear the news?"

Henry shook his head.

Professor Robertson walked around behind his desk. "Word just came up from Washington—Lincoln is asking for volunteers. He's calling for seventy-five thousand men to invade the south and quell what he calls the rebellion. Virginia will never stand for northern troops passing through her to invade our neighbors. Virginia will have to secede, mark my word."

"I pray you are wrong, sir. I cannot envision lifting my sword against my country or putting a fellow cadet in my sights."

The professor smiled. "Not even Cadet Wheatley?"

Henry straightened. "Sir, in Virginia we are partial to our jackasses. They serve a useful, though often uninspiring, purpose."

"Touché, McConnell." The professor saluted with the pointer. "A word of advice. Keep an eye on Fitzhugh Lee. Follow his lead."

"Lee? Yes sir, Lieutenant Lee is well regarded by all cadets, north and south. Truly, a man to be followed."

"Good. Then watch Fitz.

* * *

The news arrived late Wednesday night, hitting the barracks like a flash of lightning: "Virginia secedes!"

Henry closed the door, leaning against the frame.

"What is it?" Edward asked, sitting up in his bed.

Henry waved him quiet, then blew out the lamp and dropped onto his bunk. An early spring breeze lifted the faint scent of honeysuckle and new grass through the open window. The familiar fragrances took him back to a simpler time—spring evenings in Virginia.

Somewhere down the hall a door slammed, followed by angry voices. Henry snapped back to the present. Gaslights outside cast the shadow of the window frame against the ceiling, forming a

92

cross. Secession? It couldn't be. The academy, the army, even the republic—now, all were his enemy? He closed his eyes, but sleep would not come.

Dawn brought no respite. Henry didn't bother preparing for class, but took extra time to ensure his uniform was inspection ready.

"Others will be watching, wondering what you Virginians will do." Edward stood before the mirror adjusting the line of his tunic.

"I know only what I must do. I spoke with Lieutenant Lee yesterday. We agreed. We must go with our state. Others may wait until they hear from home, but come Sunday, I will be on the packet boat returning to Virginia."

"And you will be missed," Edward said. "At least by this Yankee."

Henry hooked the last button on his frock coat, then turned to his roommate. "May God never place us on the same battlefield, but if he does, may he strike me down in all his fury if any harm comes to you by my hand." He placed his hand on Edward's shoulder.

"Likewise," Edward said, clasping Henry's shoulder. "The war will be over long before I graduate, but even if it isn't, there is no cause so just as to bring me to raise my sword against you, my friend."

"Enough of this pathos." Henry pushed Edward away. "Today is for social calls and farewells, and tomorrow . . . tomorrow I will see my Belinda." He checked the alignment of his tunic in the small mirror. "I dare say I will ask her to await my return, as I must fulfill my duty before I can ask for her hand."

"Why, you sly fox! Congratulations." Edward punched him on the shoulder.

"Hold on there. She still has to say 'yes.'"

"No chance she won't, Henry. That girl's stuck on you and all your southern charm."

"Well then, let's go warm up some of that charm. Come tomorrow night, it'll be flowing like hot apple butter on a buckwheat biscuit."

* * *

Henry surveyed the crowd surrounding the dance floor. The animosity of the past six months seemed forgotten as cadets, North and South, came together once more as brothers. Almost a third of the corps were Southern, and many had already departed. Tonight's dance was an occasion to bid farewell to the next group to leave— the Virginians.

Belinda should have been there by now. She always found a spot toward the front. The band opened with a polka and couples filled the dance floor.

"Good luck, McConnell. I'd stay close and provide support, but there's this little Jersey girl who needs my attention." Edward gave Henry a wink, then dashed away in search of his date.

Henry edged toward the band, searching the far end of the hall. It wasn't like her, she'd always attended, and she'd always made her presence known. He climbed onto a bench along one wall. The entire room came into view. Couples whirled past in blurs of pastel and gray. A familiar shade of yellow swept by, topped with raven black hair. Jumping from his perch, Henry kept pace with the couple, positioning himself to move in as soon as the dance ended.

A smattering of polite applause accompanied the final note. Henry leaped as high as he could, peering over the crowd. There she was, only a few feet away, surrounded by other cadets and their ladies. He pushed his way through the gathering.

"I thought you must have missed the packet boat," Henry said. "I was worried."

"Oh, hello, Henry."

The music slowed to a waltz. Henry bowed and offered his hand. "Shall we—?"

Belinda looked away.

He withdrew his gloved hand and straightened. "Is there a problem?"

She folded her arms. "The problem is your southern friends turning on our nation and attacking our flag. I can't abide a traitor, Henry, and I'll not be seen dancing with one."

"Is this cadet bothering you, Miss Belinda?" George Wheatley appeared, placing his hand on the small of her back.

"Come with me," Henry said, grabbing Belinda by the hand. He stormed through the double doors to the veranda. Outside, he spun her around. "Traitor is a powerful word. I swore my allegiance to Virginia and the United States, but when the government in

Washington saw fit to turn state against state, honor required that my sword be used to defend the oppressed, not aid the oppressor."

Belinda shoved her hands on her hips. "You can frame it any way you please, Henry McConnell, it's treason all the same, and I'll not have my reputation sullied by dallying one instant more with the likes of a man who is neither a patriot nor a gentleman."

"Belinda, wait—" He reached for her hand. From behind, a fist flew over his shoulder, crashing into his jaw. Henry crumpled to the flagstone patio. Clatter filled his ears like drumsticks on a tin pot. He shook his head and slowly pushed up on one elbow.

"You'd best leave our northern women alone, McConnell. Get back to your plow horses while you still can."

That voice . . . The night, back in November, returning to the barracks . . . .

Cadet George Wheatley towered over him, hands on his hips, his feet spread apart. Belinda peered from behind the swaggering cadet, her expression one more of curiosity than concern.

"Get back to your cotton," Wheatley said. "Your kind's no longer welcome here at the Point." He started to walk away with Belinda on his arm.

Henry struggled to his feet. "Wheatley . . ."

Cadet Wheatley turned.

"You're a damned coward." Henry balled his fists. "It took three of you to best me in November and tonight you sneak up behind me like the stinking polecat you are. Stand and fight or strike your colors. Either way, you'll learn a lesson tonight . . ."

A crowd of cadets and young ladies circled the two.

Wheatley sprang, unleashing a wild right punch. Henry dodged the haymaker and jabbed hard to Wheatley's midsection. Wheatley recovered, throwing two quick punches. Both missed. He came at Henry again with another violent lunge. Henry ducked, shifted his weight, and smashed an uppercut to Wheatley's chin. Teeth cracked against teeth. The tall New Yorker collapsed, blood gurgling from his mouth.

Belinda rushed to Wheatley's side. She cradled his head in her arms and glared at Henry. "You brute!"

Henry massaged the knuckles on his right hand, then pointed to the unconscious cadet. "Looks to be a long war for you Yankees if that's the best you can muster." He turned on his heel and marched to the barracks.

* * *

Henry lay on his bunk reading a letter penned on pale yellow stationary.

Edward entered the room and sat, straddling his chair. "I tried finding you after the ruckus, but you'd already left. You all right?"

Henry put down the letter. "Never better, my friend. Never better."

"You sure?"

"What use did I have for that little trollop anyway? In South Boston alone there must be a dozen girls who could best her."

Edward laughed. "One thing's for sure, Wheatley won't be bothering you anymore. Cadets were talking after you left. Even the northern boys liked what you did. He never had much of a following around here." Edward stood and shoved the chair under his desk. "The corps is gathering tonight to give Lieutenant Lee a proper sendoff. Come morning, he'll be on the packet boat with you. How about we head over to officers' row and join the activities?"

"Anything for Lieutenant Lee," Henry said. He hopped out of bed and buttoned his tunic.

They walked across the quadrangle, joining the growing procession of officers and cadets.

"Must be the entire corps here." Henry gestured toward the impromptu formation of gray gathered on the lawn in front of Lieutenant Lee's quarters. All of the cadets removed their covers, tucking them under their arms, as the officers led the serenade for their departing comrade.

The first song, a somber rendition of "Kathleen Mavourneen," was one of Henry's favorites. Two hundred male voices drew Lieutenant Lee to the small porch on the front of his quarters. He nodded and waved to the crowd, appearing hard pressed to resist the wave of nostalgia sweeping over those gathered in the commons. Next came a mournful rendition of "Auld Lang Syne." Finally, they bid the lieutenant adieu with the prayerful strains of "Dixie." As they sang the final verse, cadets and officers slowly broke ranks, drifting back to barracks and billets.

Chapter Fifteen
April 1861

"You may go on Saturday—*if* you get that chair finished." Thomas pulled the door closed behind him as he left the bunkroom.

Mr. Jones shot Isaac a quizzical look. "Where's you going Saturday, boy?"

"Eat your squirrel, old man." Isaac ladled stew onto the tin plate and took a seat at the table.

"But what's he talking about? You going somewhere and you can't tell Mr. Jones?"

Isaac poked at his food. "It ain't nothing. I just asked could I borrow the wagon after chores was done."

"What's you needing a wagon for?"

Isaac lowered his voice. "I's figuring to head down by Yanceyville, see if I might can have a visit with Raleigh."

Mr. Jones slapped his knee. "That girl sure enough got herself under your skin. You reckon she's partial to you too?"

A warmth rushed to Isaac's face. He stared at his plate. "Could be. She ain't said."

"I wager the two of you'll be jumping that broom before the corn's in the ground." Mr. Jones hopped up from the table and danced around the small room, laughing and clapping his hands.

Isaac pushed aside his plate. How would he know if she was partial to him? Did she lay awake nights thinking on Isaac like he did on her?

* * *

Isaac clutched his stomach as the wagon bounced over a rut. Years ago, he'd experienced similar queasiness. They'd been swimming down at Bennett's Creek and Henry and Patrick had held him under water. Then, a stomach full of creek water had forced him to lie on the bank until the nausea passed. Now, it wasn't creek water that turned his stomach in flips, but rather the prospect of a meeting with Raleigh.

"I ain't never called on a woman before," Isaac said to the horse. "Ain't certain what I should say. Shoot, I ain't even certain this is such a good idea. Well, too late to turn back." He tugged on the rein. The horse turned into the winding lane leading to the Patterson house. Isaac stopped the wagon beside the porch and hopped down, tying the reins around the hitching rail. He patted the horse as he studied the porch, then cautiously climbed the steps and crossed to the door. He lifted his hand, then hesitated.

She didn't know he was coming. What if she was off doing errands or tied up with chores? What if she didn't want to see him? His stomach tightened. He lowered his hand. This had been a bad idea. He turned toward the wagon.

The door opened.

"Yes?" Mr. Patterson stood in the doorway. "It is Isaac, isn't it? To what do we owe the pleasure? Was there something more from Mr. Day?"

Isaac snatched his hat from his head, clutching it in front of him. "No sir, Mr. Patterson, I don't have no business from Mr. Day. I . . . I come to see Raleigh. I was hoping for a short visit."

A smile crossed Mr. Patterson's face. He pointed to one of the straight-backed chairs. "Set on down, boy." He chuckled as he disappeared into the house.

The morning sun warmed Isaac as he sat, hat in hand. On the front lawn, daffodils encircled a thick, gnarled oak. Forsythia splashed yellow across the paddock fence. Isaac's knee bounced uncontrollably.

"Hey there."

Isaac turned quickly.

Ezekiel stood beside the porch. "You's that boy from up Milton way, ain't you? You bring us another table, maybe a new bed?"

"I . . . I come to see Raleigh."

Ezekiel glanced cautiously at the door. "She know you here?"

"Massa Patterson went to fetch her."

"Raleigh don't cotton none to men callers. Mighty particular, that woman, and she don't tolerate the attentions of no slaves."

Isaac's stomach tightened. She was free. What could she see in him, other than just another slave?

Ezekiel removed his hat and raked his fingers through his snowy hair. "Well, I has to go clean the barn. You take care, boy." He set his hat on the back of his head and whistled as he walked away.

Isaac started to wipe his sweaty palms on his shirt, then hesitated. That church shirt was all he had, not counting slave clothes. He rubbed his hands down the front of his britches.

The door creaked and Raleigh stepped onto the porch. She wore a plain gray dress with a white apron. "Good morning, Isaac. To what do I owe the pleasure?"

Isaac stumbled to his feet. "Morning." He poked at a board in the porch with the toe of his shoe. "I was hoping we might have us a visit." Isaac motioned to the other chair.

"I have chores."

"Won't take up much of your time." He twisted the brim of his hat. "Since you don't get up to church no more, I reckoned I'd come down here."

She brushed wrinkles from her apron. "Walk with me while I gather the eggs."

Raleigh took a basket from the back porch as they passed, hooking her arm through the wicker handle. "So, are you a city boy or a farmer?"

"Growed up on a farm," Isaac said. "My white folk, they has a place up by South Boston." He paused while his eyes adjusted to the darkness of the hen house. "We grows tobacco, corn, some wheat, plus vegetables for the table." He found a large brown egg under an old hen and handed it to Raleigh.

She turned the egg over and scowled. "That hen's too old for laying. Stew pot's where she needs to be." Raleigh placed the egg in the basket and continued down the row of nesting boxes. "Farming's all right for some, but I hope to live in the city one day. I can't see myself being a farmer's wife."

"I . . . I don't plan on farming. I makes furniture." Immediately, Isaac cringed. Why'd he say that?

Raleigh turned toward him. "Does Mr. Day intend to set you up in business?"

"I ain't ready for that, least ways, not yet." He searched for another egg.

"Someday?"

"I hopes to open my own shop, maybe in Philadelphia." He retrieved an egg from under a cackling hen and added it to the basket. "Pa and Mr. Day, they been teaching me all about making fine furniture. When the time comes, I'll be ready."

"Missus Patterson has a brother in Philadelphia," Raleigh said. "We visited there two years ago. It is certainly a fine city in which to open a carpenter's shop."

When they finished gathering the eggs they returned to the main house. Raleigh set the basket on a bench by the back door and turned toward Isaac. "Tell me about your family."

He leaned against the porch rail. Pink blossoms clung to the branches of an apple tree in the backyard. In the fields, slaves bent over, transplanting tobacco seedlings. Isaac faced Raleigh. "Pa, he goes off fixing furniture and Mama, she just keeps on cooking, but if I get tore up with cat briars or such, she knows all sorts of potions for healing. Joseph, he's my little brother, he got snake bit once and Mama sucked out the poison. She nursed him on back and cooked up that copperhead in a stew."

Raleigh laughed. "She sounds like quite a woman."

"She's as good as they come."

They wandered back to the front porch. Isaac pulled up his chair and sat.

Raleigh shook her head. "You must leave now. I have more chores that need tending to."

"Sorry," Isaac said as he stood. "It's been a pleasure." He glanced down. A toe protruded through a hole on the side of his shoe. He turned his foot away from Raleigh. "Maybe I can come back? Maybe next week?"

"Maybe." She smiled.

Isaac nodded as he stumbled down the steps. Raleigh waited until he climbed aboard the wagon, then she went inside. Isaac turned the horse toward the road. Was she watching from the window? He sat straight as the wagon rolled down the lane.

The horse hesitated at the juncture with the main road. Isaac flicked the reins and the wagon turned north. "So, she ain't gonna be no farmer's wife? Ain't taking up with no slave?" He snapped the reins again. "Horse, the day's coming when this slave will cross over from field hand to freedman, then he'll be paying her a proper visit."

* * *

To arms! Sons of Virginia, gather before the storm!

Henry tossed the handbill on the side table in the parlor. "Virginia's gone and joined the Confederacy, just like you wanted. They're raising a regiment in South Boston." He looked at his older brother, seated on the sofa. "I expect you'll be the first to enlist?"

Patrick crossed his legs and tapped the heel of his boot with his riding crop. "We all must serve, little brother, each in his own way. Should I be offered a commission in the home guard, I would gladly accept. It stands to reason, however, that one of us must remain here to help Father run the farm." He smiled. "You are trained in the ways of the military. I am educated in the business of tobacco."

Turning his back, Henry gazed out the window at the fields that produced the family wealth. "Papa managed fine while you was away at the university, besides, we have Sean O'Farrell now, and our nigras know what needs doing. Papa will be fine."

Patrick slapped the crop into the palm of his hand. "O'Farrell lets those niggers run all over him, and Father's no better. The rains have already set us back two weeks in getting the seedlings transplanted. Without a strong hand on the whip, this year's crop won't make it to market. The war will be over in a month or two anyway and one soldier, more or less, won't matter—but there'll be no tobacco harvest if I'm not here."

"Fine, then I'll have to fight your damned war for you." Henry snatched the handbill from the table, crumpling it and tossing it aside as he stormed out the door.

"Where you off to, Henry?" Polly's voice stopped him at the steps.

Polly and Tempie sat cross-legged on the porch, a pile of spring flowers between them. Each girl wore a colorful wreath as they twisted dandelions and crocuses into necklaces and bracelets.

"Morning Massa Henry." Tempie smiled, raising her hand in the air and turning it for Henry to see. On her wrist she wore a yellow band of forsythia. "Don't it look like pure gold?"

Henry studied the girls for a moment, then took off his hat and swept it across his waist, bowing deeply. "Yes, and befitting a royal princess of the Ivory Coast . . ."

Both girls giggled, then Polly shot him a quizzical look. "Where you headed in such an all fired hurry, Henry?"

"Got business in town. Tell Mother I'll be home by supper." He picked a sprig of azalea from the pile and slid it behind Polly's ear. "You beauties be careful or you'll get kidnapped by pirates and held for a queen's ransom."

The girls giggled again, then Tempie rose and retrieved the wadded paper. She smoothed it and handed it to Henry. "You dropped this, Massa Henry. Is it something important?"

He glanced at the handbill. "It might be. I'll know by tonight."

Chapter Sixteen
May 1861

"Corporal McConnell," the captain asked, "how do you plead?" Captain Claiborne, Commanding Officer, Company K, Fourteenth Virginia Infantry Volunteers, glared at him from across the table set in the shade of a white canvas tarpaulin. In all directions, rows of tents filled the green fields. The fairgrounds north of Richmond, now dubbed Camp Lee, were home to Virginia's fledgling army.

Henry snapped to attention. The midday sun burned Henry's neck as he stood between two sentries beyond the cool shade of the tarp. Lieutenant Bruce, the company first lieutenant, stood to one side of the captain, his hands clasped behind him.

Henry reeled. The din of shouted commands and thousands of marching feet carried from the parade grounds, echoing through a head still throbbing from the previous night's revelry in the Shockoe Bottom bars. A faint breeze tickled droplets of sweat running down his neck.

"Sir, the corporal pleads guilty, but with an explanation—"

The captain cut him off with a wave of his hand. "McConnell, we made you a noncommissioned officer because you had military training, West Point, no less. Did that training not include some discussion about the importance of actually showing up sober once in a while?"

"Sir, I—"

"Shut up. On the charge of absenting your unit without authority I find you guilty and I hereby reduce you to the rank of private—and you can forget your damned request to transfer to the cavalry." The captain ran a hand through his thinning hair, then leaned back and flicked open his pocketknife. He began digging dirt from under his fingernails. "Private McConnell, the Yankee army might let you get away with your chicanery, getting into God knows what trouble over there in Richmond, but in case you haven't noticed, this here ain't the Yankee army."

Henry stiffened, his knees weak, his mouth dry as corn dust.

"Maybe you West Pointers don't figure you need this here training." The captain jerked his thumb toward the ragged columns of gray receiving instruction from Virginia Military Institute cadets behind him. "But I can tell you this, the rest of us sure as hell would like a little more drilling before we go up against them Yankees. Time's growing short. If we don't get trained, there'll be a heap of dead Virginians when the shooting commences."

Henry stared straight ahead. His stomach churned.

"Now, keep your nose clean, McConnell, and help me turn these clod busters into fighting men," he pointed at Henry with the blade of the pocketknife, "and maybe you can earn back those stripes. You got that?"

"Yes sir."

"Very well. Dismissed."

Henry saluted and took one step to the rear.

"McConnell . . ." Captain Claiborne stood, leaning on the table with both hands.

"Sir?"

The captain glared. "You pull something like this once the shooting starts and I'll throw you in front of a firing squad." Captain Claiborne straightened and brushed the sleeve of his gray wool uniform. "Dismissed."

"Yes, sir." Henry saluted and marched away. He maintained his posture until out of the captain's sight, then doubled over, clutching his stomach. Not going to make it . . .

Henry braced against a tree, spewing what remained of a hard night's drinking onto the dry, packed dirt of the company street. When his head finally stopped spinning, he took a deep breath and wiped his mouth on the sleeve of his coat.

Company I, The Chester Grays, marched past. Old men and boys in a mixture of uniforms seemed to ignore the shouted commands of their NCO. They plodded on, each recruit marching to his own cadence. Some skipped awkwardly, trying to get back in step. A red-faced sergeant raced alongside the stumbling column, flailing his arms and pointing at their feet. "Dammit all, 'left' means the other un. Them's your right foots, you dagburned good for nothing bunch a dirt farmers."

Henry grimaced, fighting back another wave of nausea as well as an urge to laugh. Then his captain's words came back to him, "There'll be a heap of dead Virginians when the shooting commences."

Chapter Seventeen
July 1861

"Did you fetch yourself to church this morning?" Gabriel asked. He leaned over the sawbuck table working a whetstone across the blade of a spoke shave.

"I did," Isaac replied. He didn't much want to talk about it, though.

"Well, did she show?" Gabriel tested the blade on his thumbnail, then spit on the stone and continued rubbing in a circular motion against the steel.

Isaac shook his head. "She ain't been back since that first Sunday. I reckon Missus Patterson must be feeling poorly again." He rubbed the inside of the hot Dutch oven with a slab of fatback, then rolled corn dough into a ball and dropped it in the blackened pot. "Ain't had a pass to head down her way for a month or more, neither."

Isaac set the Dutch oven on the outdoor cooking fire and placed embers on the lid. Another pot held a chicken that had mysteriously appeared about the time Mr. Jones returned from one of his afternoon strolls.

"Why don't Mr. Day give you a pass?"

Isaac pulled a stool beside the fire. "He says the war talk is making folks skittish. Says this ain't the time for no darky to be wandering off where them pattyrollers can catch 'em, with or without a pass."

"I 'spect he be right, boy. Specially if that pass is signed by a black man." Gabriel ran a thumb across the blade and nodded in apparent satisfaction. "So what's you gonna do? You ain't sneaking off on your own, is ya? A body could get kilt doing a fool thing like that."

Isaac shook his head. "I ain't sneaking off, leastways not yet. I aim to ask Mr. Day again and hope he sees things different." Isaac poked the fire. A shower of sparks drifted into the evening sky, mixing with the flashes of a thousand darting fireflies.

Mr. Jones ambled up the hill from the 'necessary', adjusting the suspender fastened to one side of his trousers. He smiled at Isaac. "That there hen done yet?" He lifted the lid. The aroma of onions and chicken filled the evening air. "I swear, you's a better cook than ol' Mr. Jones." He laughed and replaced the lid, then pulled up a log.

After supper Isaac walked around the side of the large brick house. Most evenings Thomas could be found enjoying a cigar in his rocker on the side porch. Tonight was no different.

"'Evening, Mr. Day."

"Why, good evening, Isaac. Was that chicken I was smelling? I declare, you boys eat better than I do some nights." He smiled and flicked an ash on the lawn.

"Yes sir, chicken and onions, a passel of cornbread too. Mr. Jones, he has a gift for attracting lost critters. They come a looking for that stew pot."

Thomas laughed, then wagged his finger. "You tell Mr. Jones that he'd best be certain none of those poor lost critters are coming from the neighbors' coops . . ."

With a smile, Isaac looked away.

"So, to what do I owe this visit?"

Isaac snatched his hat from his head. "Sir, I been meaning to ask about one of them passes. I'd be much obliged if I could get on down to Yanceyville for a visit."

"That gal caught you heart, did she?" Thomas said. "But now's not a good time for colored folk to be wandering far from home. War's got everybody on edge, and you'd be putting yourself at risk, even with a signed pass."

"I'd be real careful, Mr. Day, and I'll only travel during daylight. Isaac won't cause no suspicion, just another darky going about his chores."

Thomas pursed his lips and blew, setting a circle of smoke adrift on the evening breeze. Finally, he looked at Isaac. "I haven't forgotten how hard a master the heart can be. If I don't give you a pass, I reckon you'll end up doing something stupid, then we'll both be in a pickle, you with dogs on your heels, and me with Mr.

McConnell demanding top dollar for a lost slave."

"Thank you, sir. Thank you." Isaac grabbed Thomas's hand and pumped it vigorously.

Thomas peered at their clasped hands, then at Isaac, his eyebrow raised.

"Oh, no . . ." Isaac released his grip and stepped back. "Sorry, Mr. Day, I didn't mean no—"

Thomas dismissed him with the back of his hand. "You throw some lumber in that wagon. If anyone asks, you were hauling it for me. I'll have a pass for you midday tomorrow. Stop by after chores—but you make sure you're back before dark, you hear?"

* * *

"Wait. Hold up," Thomas called, waving a yellow envelope.

Isaac pulled back on the reins. The wagon halted. Summer air hung heavily over the Carolina afternoon. He wiped his brow. "Yes sir?"

"I'm glad I caught you." Thomas stepped from the porch. "This came today." He handed Isaac the opened envelope.

Isaac turned it over, examining the writing, the broken wax seal, the tiny flowers along the top edge. "I ain't never had no letter before."

"Well, can you read it?"

Isaac pulled out the two sheets of yellow stationary, carefully unfolded them, then stared at the flowing, cursive handwriting.

"Do you know how to read?"

"Some, Mr. Day." Isaac shook his head, turning the sheets sideways. "But just book printing, I can't read no curly writing."

"Then allow me." Thomas held out his hand and Isaac passed him the letter. Thomas read aloud:

Dear Mr. Day,

I ask that you pass this letter on to our slave, Isaac, who is currently in your employ. My dear brother, Henry, recently of the military academy at West Point and now serving with the Fourteenth Virginia Volunteers, has written us of his wartime adventures. Henry asked that I pass along his news to Isaac, as I am able and so you will find enclosed my letter to Isaac. I trust you will not find it too much of an imposition to pass along Henry's news, as well as my own best wishes.

Sincerely,
Miss Polly McConnell

Thomas folded the first sheet under and continued:

Dear Isaac,

Henry says to tell you he's well. The army recognizes his leadership potential, and he says he should be seeing promotion soon. There was fighting last week by Bethel Church, near Fortress Monroe. Henry regrets that his regiment did not take part, arriving too late to the battlefield. However, he reports that Colonel Magruder sent the Yankees packing. He says next time, the Fourteenth will be there too, and then the Yankees will pay dearly for invading our home.

Your mama asks to be remembered to you. Florence said you are to work hard, not cause any trouble, and learn all you can from Mr. Day. She's rejoicing that my daddy gave you this fine opportunity.

Little Joseph and Tempie both say hello.

Take care and stay well,
Polly

Thomas handed the letter to Isaac. "Seems your white folks hold you in high regard."

"Yes sir, they's good people, mostly."

"Well, you're a lucky man then. Now, home before dusk, and stay to the main road. Put this where it will be safe." Thomas handed Isaac the written pass authorizing his travel to Yanceyville.

"Yes sir. Before dark. Thank you, Mr. Day." Isaac stuffed the pass and Polly's letter in his Sunday shirt pocket and flicked the reins. The horse stepped off in a spirited gait.

* * *

"I do think about us," Raleigh said. "I try not to, but I can't help myself." The long-stemmed dandelion she casually dangled in her fingers matched her pale yellow dress. White lace edged her bonnet.

Isaac took her by the hand. They strolled beneath the old oaks lining the lane to the Patterson house. In neighboring fields, green shoots reached for the sun after days of soaking rain. A shimmering haze edged the cobalt sky.

"But, you says we got no future—"

Raleigh stopped and turned toward him. "I mustn't lead you on. It isn't fair, not to either of us." She looked into his eyes. "You're a slave, I'm free. What does our future hold if you can be hired out or, heaven forbid, sold away at any moment? I can't live my days fearing that the man I marry will be torn from me at the whim of some owner who needs a few extra dollars."

"My white folk won't sell me. They's not slave traders, they's farmers, and Pa, sure, he travels some for Massa McConnell, but never no more'n a few weeks at a time."

Raleigh shifted her gaze to the fields.

"What if I was free?"

"What do you mean?" She turned, a questioning look on her face.

"What if I runs away, maybe up to Philadelphia? Then would it be different?"

"If you're up north and I'm in Carolina, and there's two armies fighting a war in between, how is that better?" She sighed. "Besides, you'll be hunted, and even if they don't catch you, you'll never be able to return to North Carolina."

"You can run with me, we'll go north together."

"No." She shook her head. "I'd slow you down. The dogs would be on us in no time. You'd get whipped, then sent back to Virginia, and likely as not I'd get sold at auction."

"They can't sell you. You got papers."

Raleigh tossed the dandelion toward a pair of geese. "I'm free because I have papers, and because the people who freed me are here to speak for me. Out there," she drew her hand across fields of new corn, "a black woman is a slave unless some important white man says otherwise. If I was to be caught with a runaway, no patroller would waste his time—or lose his profits—trying to prove me a free woman."

Isaac raised his hands in protest. "I can't be no slave, I can't be no runaway, I has to be free? What if I gets to that promised land and then I sends for you?"

"Isaac, I . . . maybe . . ."

He cut off her words with a kiss.

"Missy Raleigh? Missy Raleigh? You gots to come quick!" Ezekiel waved frantically as he hobbled down the lane. When he caught up to Isaac and Raleigh he bent over clutching his stomach and sucked in several deep breaths. Finally, he straightened. "Missy Raleigh, Missus Patterson took ill. Massa says she's having . . ." he took another deep breath and exhaled, "one of her spells. Massa says he needs you up to the house."

"Tell Mr. Patterson I will be along shortly, and tell him there is no need to worry."

Ezekiel hurried back up the lane.

Smiling, Raleigh turned to Isaac. "The missus has a weak constitution. When food becomes disagreeable she suffers a bilious attack. If Mr. Patterson is alone with her when it happens, he becomes overly excited. I must attend to her."

When they arrived at the farmhouse, Raleigh immediately went inside and Isaac took a seat on the top step. Soon, Ezekiel came out and settled next to him on the edge of the porch. He gazed at Isaac. "You ain't like them others."

"What others?" Isaac said. "What do you mean?"

"Many a buck's come by courting, but Miss Raleigh, she don't give 'em no never mind." Ezekiel dangled his feet beneath the porch. "She's sweet on you though."

"How do you know?" Isaac stared at Ezekiel. "She say so?"

"Boy, don't you know nothing about womens? It's in her eyes." Ezekiel pointed two fingers toward his own eyes. "I sees how she looks at you. She's thinking on them possibilities."

Isaac wrapped his arms around his knees and lowered his head. A toe protruded from a hole in the side of his shoe. "Maybe she's thinking on possibilities, but she ain't found none yet what suits her. She says I need papers, if'n I wants anything more'n a few hours of just sociable visiting. Can't be no slave, can't be no runaway, got to have papers . . ."

"So, how's you going to get you some papers?"

"Don't know. I ain't figured out nothing about that. Maybe I runs north, but Raleigh ain't much taken with that idea. Reckon I has some thinking to do."

"Ezekiel, come take this, please." Raleigh stood in the open door holding a white earthen washstand bowl.

Ezekiel sprang to his feet and crossed the porch.

Raleigh looked at Isaac. " The missus is feeling poorly. She'll want me close by. We'd best end our visit for today."

"I understands," Isaac said. "Maybe I'll come back in a week or so?"

Raleigh smiled. "Maybe . . ."

Ezekiel took the bowl, but stumbled as he turned, splashing the contents across Isaac's chest. Isaac jumped back, pulling the wet shirt away from his body with both hands. He glanced at Ezekiel, then at Raleigh.

She laughed. "You look like a scared chicken on the chopping block. It's only a little bile; it won't hurt you. Here, leave that shirt on the porch." She turned to Ezekiel. "Go fetch Isaac one of your fresh ones."

Ezekiel jumped from the porch and ran toward the barn.

"I'll launder that," Raleigh said, pointing to the soiled garment. She smiled. "I guess now you'll have to come back to get your shirt, maybe next week?"

Those beautiful eyes—what could they be saying?

Chapter Eighteen
July 1861

The sun hovered a hand's width above the horizon—daylight a plenty for the return journey to Milton. Isaac relaxed the reins, settling the horse into an easy gait. He rubbed a callus on his hand as he considered Raleigh's words. Freedom papers . . . sounds good, but how could he get them? She'd purchased hers, and Pa'd mentioned an arrangement with Massa McConnell—perhaps Isaac could make one too, work extra jobs and earn enough to buy his freedom.

A quarter mile up the road a rider on horseback appeared heading toward him. Isaac steered to one side, making room for the lone traveler to pass. Soon, the rider was upon him, a young man, more like a boy, his long, reddish-blond hair stuffed under a wide brimmed hat. His partially unbuttoned collarless red shirt exposed a sunburned neck. The cuffs of his frayed denim trousers hung over dirty ankle high boots. Freckles covered his face. Sixteen, seventeen at the most. Isaac nodded to the traveler.

The rider held up a hand as he drew alongside the wagon. A shotgun lay across his saddle. "W-where's you h-headed, boy?"

He didn't look like a patroller—he was just a boy. What could he want with Isaac? "Evening, sir. I's heading to Milton."

"Y-you running?" The boy stared at Isaac, then shot a nervous glance behind him. He pointed the shotgun at Isaac and asked again, "Y-you a r-runaway?"

"No sir, just hauling lumber for the man I works for." Isaac jerked a thumb toward the back of the wagon.

The boy peered behind him again and wiped his brow with the back of his hand. He lifted the shotgun to the crook of his arm. A finger slid inside the trigger guard. He thumbed back one of the hammers. "Sh-show me your p-pass."

Fear flashed in the boy's eyes as Isaac reached for his pass. His hand found a smooth shirtfront—no pocket. "I has a pass, it's in my other shirt. Shirt got spilled on, so's I left it to be laundered." Isaac patted his shirt and his britches, searching for the pass he knew wasn't there.

"T-that's b-bull." The boy spit a streak of tobacco juice on the wagon wheel. "W-what we g-got here is a r-runaway. Y-you probably stole that there w-wagon, the horse too."

"Didn't steal nothing. This here's Mr. Day's wagon, from up Milton. I works for him. Folks here abouts, they know me, you can ask down to the Patterson farm, they'll tell you."

"F-first day patrolling and I already c-catched me a nigger. Reckon I'll g-get me a nice reward." He spit again and wiped his mouth with his sleeve. "And y-you'll get a b-bullwhip across your b-black ass—or maybe a lynching."

The boy's just scared. He had to make him understand. "It ain't stolen, mister . . ." Isaac took in the wagon with a sweep of his hand. "This here is Mr. Day's wagon. He give me a pass."

"O-one more w-word outta you and I'll b-blow a hole clean through your lying hide. Now t-turn this here wagon around. We's going to Yanceyville."

They headed south, the boy riding beside the wagon, his shotgun resting on the saddle, pointing at Isaac.

Mr. Day was sure gonna be mad. He'd told him about being careful, but Isaac still forgot his pass.

His young captor spit, breaking the monotony of hoofs treading on packed dirt. Was his finger off that trigger? Maybe Isaac could jump him, take his gun? No, that would just get him in more trouble. He'd trust the people in Yanceyville to figure this out, then he'd be headed back to Milton.

The last rays of daylight reflected in the upper windows of the white clapboard homes as they entered Yanceyville. "Over there." The boy pointed. "That b-brick building."

Isaac did as instructed, reining the horse in front of a one-story structure. A faded sign above the door read, "Constable." Isaac formed the word on his lips, but made no sound.

"Get down." The boy poked Isaac with the barrel of the shotgun. "Set yourself yonder, by that wall. Y-you stir and you'll be p-picking buckshot out your ass."

Isaac squatted beside the brick wall. The boy knocked on the door. A short man with a gray beard appeared wearing a dark vest over a stained white shirt. Matted hair stuck up in the back as though he'd just awakened from a nap. The man rubbed his eyes, listening as the boy talked. Isaac couldn't hear what was said. Several times the boy motioned in Isaac's direction with the shotgun. Finally, the older man went inside. Isaac smiled to himself. The constable man would be setting things straight. He'd find out about Mr. Day and then he'd send Isaac back to Milton.

The constable reappeared with a set of iron shackles and a whip. He tossed the shackles at Isaac's feet. "You, lock those on your ankles and turn the key. Make 'em good and tight."

"Sir, I ain't no runaway. Isaac . . ."

The whip cracked against Isaac's arm. "Shut up and put on them irons."

Isaac's stomach churned. The man wasn't hearing Isaac—didn't want to hear him. He clamped the shackles onto his ankles.

"Test 'em." The constable pointed to the boy. "If he didn't lock 'em tight, you smack him and have him do it again."

The boy tugged at each shackle, then removed the key and handed it to the constable. "T-they's good. D-does I g-gets my reward now?"

"What you'll get is my boot up your ass if'n you don't get out of here—and if you go out patrolling again, you'd best partner up. You's lucky this here nigger didn't jump you and cut you wide open. They's savages, you know. He'd as soon cook you for supper as look at you. Now get. If there's any reward, I'll let you know."

The boy's shoulders slumped. He climbed on his horse and rode away.

"You, get up." The constable poked Isaac with his boot.

The shackles weighed on his ankles as he stood. "Sir, I ain't no runaway. I works for Mr. Day . . ."

"Shut up, nigger. This way." The constable pointed with the whip toward the open door.

The chains forced short steps. Isaac stumbled and caught himself on the doorframe. "Sir, Mr. Day, up in Milton . . ."

Like an angry barn cat, the whip raked across his back. Isaac fell to his knees. Another blow gashed his flesh, then another.

"When I tell you to shut up, that's exactly what I mean, boy.

Now, get in that cell. I ain't got time to stand here and give you what for."

Isaac pulled himself hand over hand up the doorframe. The constable jammed the butt of his whip into Isaac's bloodied back. Isaac stumbled into a small room illuminated by a single lantern on a wooden desk. Another shove forced him through a darkened doorway. He fell against a cold stone floor as a heavy door clanged shut, cutting off the lantern's light.

Chapter Nineteen
July 1861

Henry shoved the wheelbarrow up the earthen embankment and dumped another load of dirt in front of the logs supporting the breastworks. The mid-summer sun scorched his neck, already sunburned from weeks of preparing field fortifications. He'd known Virginia summers, but the dust of South Boston was nothing compared to the humidity of Virginia's Tidewater. In June the Fourteenth had moved from Camp Lee down the peninsula to Fort Allen, a small redoubt on Jamestown Island, south of Williamsburg. Fort Allen anchored the southern flank of Colonel Magruder's defensive line. Here they would halt, or at least impede, any Yankee advances up the peninsula against Richmond.

Work on the defensive positions filled every day from reveille until evening colors. For those still healthy, the workload increased as sunstroke and disease depleted the regiment's ranks.

Heat waves shimmered above the horizon in a cloudless sky. Henry wiped his brow. Next to him, a soldier leaned against his shovel, then staggered and collapsed.

"Townsend, quick, take his arm. Over there, to the shade." Henry pointed.

The other soldier grabbed the fallen rebel. Together, they dragged him to what little shade the redoubt provided. Henry splashed water from his canteen on the fallen soldier's face. Slowly, the man regained consciousness.

"Four more were taken to the hospital today," Henry said. He offered Townsend the canteen. "Water?"

"The colonel's a doctor, you know." Townsend took a drink. "He trained up in Pennsylvania. He's saying the regiment's having a touch of the typhoid fever."

"Then it seems like we ought to pull back to Richmond and leave all these skeeters and flies to the damned Yankees." Henry pulled a bandana out of his pocket and mopped his brow. "If Virginia boys can't tolerate this stinking place, think what it'd do to those blue bellies."

Townsend laughed. "Probably wipe 'em out within a month, but hell, let 'em come anyways. This here fort, and them four guns we're mounting, they'll stop durn near anything."

The breastworks rose above a ditch dug eight feet deep and fifteen feet wide on the enemy's side. Confederates could stand behind the embankment and fire down on any hapless attackers.

"I do believe you're right, Townsend. When I stand in front of Fort Allen and see what those Yankees will face, shucks, I can't imagine being ordered to attack such an obstacle. I sure hope the Yankees get that order soon, though, 'cause I'm itching for a good fight."

The Fourteenth had missed all the fighting so far: Big Bethel, a small Confederate victory just down the Peninsula, and Manassas, a grand rebel victory further north.

"McConnell, gather your boys and fall in for drill." The sergeant shaded his eyes as he looked up at the redoubt.

"Drill? Hell, all we do is drill, and if we ain't drilling we're shoveling dirt. We need us a shooting war." Henry brushed off his britches and straggled back to the tent area.

Muskets stood four to a stack, interlocked by their bayonets, teepee style, at "stack arms." The men formed two ranks behind their muskets. The sergeant centered himself on the platoon, looked up and down the files, then leaned back and bellowed, "Platoon, take-arms!"

At each stack, a soldier from the rear rank stepped forward, took his musket, and resumed his position. Two soldiers in the front rank then grasped the remaining weapons. They lifted the three muskets, raising the stack, and brought the butts of the muskets together, disengaging the interlocked bayonets. One of the soldiers passed the extra musket to the rear rank and then all four soldiers brought their weapons down to their right sides at the position, "ordered arms."

"Platoon, right-face. Shoulder-arms. Forward, march." The platoon stepped off smartly.

Drill lasted an hour and a half. Three soldiers fell out from the heat. At the end of the drill, the sergeant marched the platoon back to their tents and faced them to the front. On the command, "stack-arms," the muskets were returned to their stacks of four.

"Supper in ten minutes. Platoon, dismissed."

Henry turned to Townsend. "Do they think we can exist on that gruel they call soup? I was already lean when I joined up. I haven't cast a shadow now for more'n a month." Henry patted his flat stomach.

Townsend fanned the air in front of his face. "Course, the stench from the sinks, plus all that horse shit piling up in this little acre of paradise, that's enough to wipe any thought of food from a civilized mind."

"Maybe that's the plan." Henry slapped Townsend's back. "The shortage of rations won't be noticed, except on those rare days when a sympathetic breeze lifts the fragrance of this stinking hole from our midst."

Chapter Twenty
July 1861

Sweat stung the gashes left by the whip on Isaac's back. He rolled over. The cool brick floor momentarily soothed the burning.

Had he slept or passed out? Dank air held the stench of a summer outhouse. He struggled to his knees. The movement tore at fresh scabs. Lord, such pain. He'd best move slow or he'd reopen the wounds. Careful . . . . He reached into the darkness: cold, rough, a brick wall. He hit something that moved and rattled. He groped . . . . a tin cup? He set it against the wall and then crept forward again, brushing against an object covered in a rough cloth. A leg? Isaac jerked back his hand.

"I reckon it's past midnight," a deep voice spoke from the shadows.

Isaac recoiled.

"You gets used to the dark in time."

Isaac fled to the far side of the cell.

"Constable Branson, he locked up and headed home 'bout nine o'clock. Courthouse clock rings the hour, so's you knows the time. He returns most mornings around eight to feed us, if'n he remembers. They calls me Perkins, Moktar Perkins. Who is you?"

"They . . . they calls me Isaac."

"Got caught running, did ya?"

"I had me a pass, but I lost it. I been visiting my woman and this here pattyroller, he was just a young'un, he snatched me."

"Sounds like a heap of bad luck, sure enough."

"Come morning I'll be telling Massa Branson and he'll talk to Mr. Day—he's my boss man. Mr. Day, he'll get this fixed. I'll be heading up to Milton again real soon."

"You ever work cotton, boy?"

"Tobacco," Isaac said to the silhouette of a man across the cell.

"But I's learning carpentry. I might have my own place up in Philadelphia one of these days."

"Dreaming of that freedom land, are ya? I been running too. Left my whites in Mississippi during planting time. Got caught stealing chickens a few miles south of here 'bout a week ago." He shrugged. "A man gots to eat."

Isaac lowered his voice. "I thinks on running right often, but Pa says it ain't our time. He carved me a token to remind me about that journey to the freedom land. It had the North Star on one side, the drinking gourd on the other."

"Sounds real nice. Perkins would sure like to look on that."

"I lost it. Wish I had it now." Isaac rubbed his hand across his chest. "It brung me comfort."

"You keep looking, boy. That star's out there."

Isaac nodded. "What happens now? They telling our people we's here?"

"Don't reckon it works like that, boy. If'n he sells you, constable keeps the money. If'n he gives you to your massa, he just gets a small reward. Boy, you's headed south, sure enough. Now get some sleep. You'll be learning that cotton business soon enough."

Cotton? He didn't want to learn cotton, just wanted to get home to Mr. Day's—and see Raleigh again . . .

Isaac pulled his knees under him and dozed. When he awoke, a pale light cast shadows from the window bars onto the brick wall.

Isaac studied the small cell. No furnishings. A single tin plate lay in one corner. A wooden bucket rested beside the far wall. Flies swarmed above a narrow brick-lined trench built into the floor on the far end. No deeper than the span of a man's open hand, it ran to a hole in the outer wall.

Perkins curled in a ball, appearing hard asleep. From the gray of his whiskers he looked to be close to his pa's age. He wore nothing more than a pair of britches cut off and frayed below the knees. Dark welts, some festering, covered his back. Until yesterday, Isaac had never known the sting of a whip. Perkins's scars told a very different tale.

Isaac leaned against the wall, then recoiled as his wounds touched the coarse brick. He peeled his shirt away from his back, eased it over his head, and held it out. Slashes of dried blood stained the shredded fabric.

A grunt. Perkins stretched and groaned, then stood and hobbled to the trench. He lowered his britches and made water.

The cell door clanged open. "Back off or you get no grub." Constable Branson stood in the doorway, whip in hand. He set a bucket of water on the floor, then tossed two pieces of black bread in the direction of the tin plate. "Give me your empty."

Perkins tied up his trousers, then placed the empty bucket at the constable's feet.

The constable grabbed the bucket and slammed the door. Metal scraped against metal as a heavy bolt slid into place.

"Some days he forgets." Perkins tossed Isaac a piece of bread. "Some days we gets chitlings too, can't never tell. Water's for drinking, mostly. If you has to make a pile, wash it down the trench—but don't be wasting none—one bucket's all we get today, and maybe tomorrow too, if'n he forgets."

Isaac turned the bread over. The crust, soggy in places, crumbled in his hand. There was a sharp, bitter smell. "Bread's turning . . ."

"Eat. You ain't getting fed again today."

Isaac took a small bite. He gagged, then grabbed for the tin cup and washed another small bite down with water.

"Tell me about Isaac. You married? Has you any childrens?"

"Naw, no children." Isaac said. "I was visiting my girl yesterday. She's a free woman, working for the Pattersons up north of here. I lives in Virginia, but my massa loaned me to Mr. Day, up in Milton, to help get some furniture orders filled. You?"

"I jumped the broom twice," Perkins said. "Back in Louisiana I married a pretty young thing, '42 or '43 was the year. We had us a passel of childrens, seven last I counted, then I runned away. When they caught me, I got sold down to Mississippi. Didn't have no way to get over to Louisiana, so I found me another woman. She lived on the next plantation and her massa, I 'spect he took a liking to her, 'cause when he found out I jumped the broom with his little wench, he went all crazy, had me hung by my thumbs and whipped something terrible."

"You got whipped just for jumping the broom?"

"I 'spect I ruined his fun. He couldn't abide putting his little white pecker where my black'n had been. 'Bout that time was when I skedaddled."

The sound of chains clanking against paving stones echoed from beyond the barred window. Isaac raised on his toes and peered out. Three black men in shackles were being loaded into a wagon.

Perkins laughed. "Another freedom train done come to the end of the line. Best get used to it, boy. Them's the sounds of niggers heading south."

Chapter Twenty-one
August 1861

"Company, Fall in."

Henry snapped to attention.

Lieutenant Bruce saluted the company commander. "Sir, the company is formed."

Captain Claiborne returned the salute, then commanded, "At ease." He pulled off his gauntlets as he paced in front of the formation. "Gentlemen, pack haversacks with three day's rations and forty rounds per man. We move at dawn to meet the enemy at Newport News."

A wild cheer rose from the formation.

The captain raised both hands, silencing the company. "Cavalry will be on our flanks. We will demonstrate in front of the Yankee positions until they crawl from behind their barricades and fight. Let no man shirk his duty. Remember, we fight for the sovereignty of old Virginia."

The company erupted in another raucous cheer.

* * *

"Finally, we'll face the elephant." Henry rested against the trunk of a tree and wiped the barrel of his musket. He took aim at an imaginary target.

Townsend sat on a wooden crate, staring at the hardtack cracker in his hand. "Are we supposed to eat these or throw them at the Yankees?"

"I hear tell the Yankees have been eating high on the hog," Henry said. "Once we chase 'em back down to Fort Monroe, we'll toss all this southern hospitality and dig into some New York vittles—steaks, chicken, fresh greens. All we have to do is scare off a mess of blue bellies."

"You scared, McConnell?"

"Hell no. I've been training for this for the better part of a year. I'm ready."

"You ever kill anybody?"

"A bear once, and a mess of deer. It can't be much different." Henry checked his ammo pouch.

"Deer don't look like your brother." Townsend wagged the cracker in Henry's face. "And they don't shoot back."

"I swear, Townsend, you sound downright tentative."

"I'm just considering the possibilities. By this time tomorrow, some of us could be sleeping beneath the sod."

* * *

The pounding of hooves wrested Henry from a fitful sleep. Horse drawn cannons and caissons rumbled through camp, lending an air of excitement to the steamy predawn Tidewater morning. All around him, soldiers hurried to strike canvas, load wagons, and distribute ammunition. Henry gobbled a quick breakfast of cornmeal and sowbelly, washing it down with chicory coffee. Finally, they'd have the chance to show those Yankees how Virginians could fight. He tied his bedroll, shouldered his musket, and took his place in formation.

Six hours later, somewhere outside the city of Hampton on the eastern tip of the Tidewater peninsula, the captain commanded, "At ease."

Henry slumped to the ground and uncorked his canteen. He took a long swig, washing the dust from his throat, then wiped his mouth with the rough woolen sleeve of his gray shell jacket. "We've marched and counter-marched all the damned day," he said. "If the Yankees are up there over that bridge, they damned sure ain't looking for a fight."

Townsend nodded. "So tell me again why General Magruder wants to parade us in front of those guns yonder?" He removed his kepi and wiped his brow. Townsend looked as bedraggled as Henry felt. For that matter, the entire platoon showed the effects of the forced march and an afternoon of parading for no apparent purpose other than the entertainment of the enemy.

"Like the captain said, we aim to lure them out for a fight, but they seem disinclined to take up the invitation." Henry recorked his canteen.

"Okay, on your feet," the sergeant hollered. "Time to get

moving." He kicked the soles of their boots as he sauntered by.

Henry rolled his eyes. "One more time, for the sovereignty of old Virginia, right-face, shoulder–arms, forward, march . . ."

"Shut up, McConnell." The sergeant glared at Henry, then commanded, "Platoon, right-face, shoulder–arms, forward, march."

A faint breeze fluttered the stars and stripes above the Union ramparts on the far shore of Hampton Creek.

When evening came, Henry and Townsend took up residence on the porch of one of the hundreds of small, two-story wooden houses that dotted the city. Up and down the narrow street, the remainder of Company K spread out, enjoying the hospitality of their southern kin.

The door opened and an elderly woman toddled onto the porch with a pitcher of tea and two glasses. "Sorry I got no ice to cool you. What with this heat, I used the last of it back in June. My boy's a soldier too; he's with the Portsmouth Light Artillery. Are they here about?"

"I don't know ma'am." Henry accepted the tea and took a deep gulp. "We're the Fourteenth Virginia, from South Boston. We sure do appreciate you fixing us this here tea." He took off his kepi and fanned himself. "We're not used to this humidity. South Boston gets hot, but not like this."

"Folks here abouts take it for granted,' she said. "You boys hungry?"

Henry glanced at Townsend and smiled. "Yes ma'am," he replied.

The woman held up her hand as if to signal them to wait, then returned to her house. She reemerged a few moments later holding a platter piled high with fried chicken and bread still warm from the oven. "Help yourselves." She handed Henry the plate. "Maybe, somewhere tonight, some other mother is doing for my boy too. God bless all of you that's wearing the gray." A tear crossed her cheek as she went inside.

Henry pulled off his boots and rubbed his foot. "My dogs are howling tonight. I can't recall the last time I did that much marching."

"Me neither," Townsend said. "I aim to be asleep before that church over yonder chimes nine o'clock. I hope the sergeant will let us rise a mite late in the morning—I could sure use the rest."

Henry savored every morsel of the chicken, washing it down with sweet tea garnished with a sprig of mint. "Our first night campaigning," he said, gesturing with a drumstick, "tough duty, I'd say."

Townsend nodded as he bit into a slab of bread smeared with apple butter.

"You think the captain will let us stay here a few days," Henry said. "Just until we win this here battle with the chicken?"

"Hell, I'll reenlist right now if I can serve out the war on Mrs. Nelson's porch. She's a better cook than my mother." Townsend gulped his tea.

"Your mother cooks?" Henry asked. "Don't you have slaves?"

"We had one once. He died. Couldn't cook anyway. My father runs a small grocery. We don't have need for no slaves—couldn't afford to buy one no how."

Henry lay against the porch wall and fought back a belch. "Our Florence is the best cook this side of the Blue Ridge, but this here chicken comes mighty close." He patted his stomach. "Tell the sergeant I'll be ready for campaigning around noon." He curled on his blanket and covered his eyes with his hat.

* * *

"Up! Up! To your feet." The sergeant stormed down the street, banging a bayonet on a cooking pot.

"What in tarnation's going on?" Henry sat and rubbed his eyes. Darkness covered the street. "What time is it, anyway?"

Townsend rolled over and gave Henry a quizzical look. The sergeant came back and stood in front of Mrs. Nelson's house banging his pot. "Company formation, on the street, now."

One by one, soldiers pulled their kits together, rolled their bedrolls, and grabbed their muskets. They formed up facing the houses on the opposite side of the street. As the platoon gathered, a voice from the back rank called out, "It ain't dawn yet. What's going on?"

The sergeant centered himself on the platoon. "Captain said to brief everybody. We has us a mission." The clock tower chimed eleven.

"General says the Yankees aim to use Hampton to billet their troops this winter. There's talk they might be housing runaway slaves here too." The sergeant paused and rubbed his hand over his face as if he didn't want to continue. "Our orders is to burn the town."

A murmur rumbled through the formation.

"What about the folks what live here?" One soldier asked.

"Hey, they's been good to us . . ." said another.

"Hampton's a southern town," a soldier called from the rear rank. "What Yankee-loving peckerwood come up with that crazy idea?"

The sergeant waved his arms. "Hush up and listen. You go on back to them houses that put you up. You tell them folks living there they got one half hour to gather their belongings. One half hour—no more." He paused, then added, "Tell them General Magruder sends his deepest regrets. Dismissed."

The platoon stood in place. Not a soldier moved.

Captain Claiborne strolled up the street and stopped in front of the sergeant. "Is there a problem, sergeant?"

"No sir."

"Very well. Carry out your orders."

The sergeant saluted, then did an about face and again hollered, "Dismissed."

The platoon slowly dispersed and soldiers returned to their temporary homes. Henry glanced at Townsend. "You want to tell her?"

"Hell no. You were a corporal once, leadership material, I recall you saying. Sounds like a situation that calls for leadership."

"Thanks, buddy." Henry dropped his pack and climbed the steps. He knocked on the door and waited, then knocked again. The light of a candle flickered through the window.

Mrs. Nelson opened the door, holding her candle aloft. She wore a light floor length nightgown with full sleeves. Gray hair cascaded over her shoulders. "Yes? Do you boys need something? More tea, perhaps?"

Henry pulled off his kepi. "Ma'am, we've been ordered . . . I mean, well, I got some bad news." Her eyes filled with anticipation. "What I mean is, we've been ordered to evacuate the town. You have thirty minutes to get dressed and gather whatever you need."

"Them Yankees coming again?" She said. "I put up with 'em before, I'll manage."

"No, ma'am," Henry replied. "The town's to be burned. You

have to leave."

"No Yankee's going to burn our town as long as you sons of Virginia are here defending us. You boys give 'em hell." She smiled and shook her fist.

Henry ran a hand through his hair and shot a glance at Townsend. "Mrs. Nelson, ma'am, General Magruder has ordered the town burned so the Yankees can't use it for billeting. We'll be laying the torch to your home in thirty minutes."

Her chin dropped and her green eyes opened wide. She locked Henry in an icy stare and set her jaw, then stepped inside and slammed the door.

Henry gathered his belongings and scuffled to the street where the platoon would reform. He stared at Mrs. Nelson's tidy little home. It wasn't right, Virginia boys burning out their own folks. This wasn't how a war was to be fought. How could he write home about such terrible deeds? And when the news did reach South Boston, how could the Fourteenth ever march those streets again with flags unfurled and heads held high?

Mrs. Nelson stepped onto the porch wearing a tattered blue housecoat over her nightgown and carrying a small valise and a daguerreotype of a young man in uniform. She placed her belongings on the rocking chair, then turned and pulled the door closed, stooping to straighten the rug in front of the door. She gathered her belongings and walked to the street. Her gaze met Henry's; tossing back her head, she quickly looked away and stormed up the street.

By midnight the Fourteenth had shifted to the south side of the city to defend against Union interference from Newport News. With their backs to Hampton, the company manned the picket line, searching the darkness for Yankee activity, while to their rear, a diabolical firestorm roared through tinder-dry wooden structures. One by one, soldiers turned, as if drawn to the inferno, but Henry stood his post. If he refused to acknowledge the fiery maelstrom, perhaps he could deny the guilt that swelled within him. Yet, even as he looked away, he couldn't escape the conflagration reflected in the tears of his fellow soldiers.

Chapter Twenty-two
September 1861

Morgan reined in the dappled mare at the edge of a muddy field where slaves hunched over rows of yellow-green tobacco. The men split stalks and cut the plants while women and children hung the cut tobacco over six-foot long wooden sticks. When the sticks were full, slaves loaded them on wagons and drove them to the drying barns where they hung in the heat of hardwood curing fires.

"Sean, a moment of your time, please." Morgan motioned to his Irish immigrant overseer.

Sean straightened, rubbing the small of his back as he sheathed his knife. "Aye, Mr. McConnell?" He wiped his brow and made his way through the tobacco to Morgan.

"What's our progress, Sean?"

"Well, ye know, sir, the second barn's 'most half full. We've made up valuable time since the ending of the rains. With a wee bit o' luck, we should have the harvest under cover on the morrow, Friday at the latest."

"Look at that sky." Morgan pointed, then rubbed the tingling in his arm. "Weather's coming from the south. Set out torches and work them through the night. I can't afford to get caught with leaf in the fields if we get another storm like last year's—that hurricane cost me one fourth of my crop."

"Aye sir, that I'll do, and I'll have Florence make up some 'pone so's we can be feeding the nigras here in the fields—it'll save us some time, ye know. Don't ye be worrying none, Mr. McConnell."

"I know you'll pull us through, Sean. You always do." Morgan turned the horse toward the main house.

"Afternoon, Massa McConnell. The leaf be looking mighty fine this year." Mamma Rose smiled, revealing a gap where a front tooth used to be. She held a stick of tobacco.

"Yes, it is, Mamma Rose, mighty good, and you're looking right pretty yourself this fine day." He touched the brim of his hat and smiled at her laughter, then continued his ride up the lane.

Morgan dismounted by the side porch, handing the reins to Joseph. "Rub her down real good, boy, then turn her to pasture."

Joseph nodded and led the horse to the barn.

Ella looked up from her knitting when he entered the front parlor. "How is the harvest, dear?"

"Rain's coming. I told Sean to work them through the night. We have to get the leaf in the barns. Where's Patrick?"

"He rode out two hours ago; said he had business over at the Johnston place." Ella lay her knitting on her lap and folded her hands. "Is there a problem?"

"I'll need him this evening. Sean's been in the fields since before dawn and once the weather arrives, we'll be pushed to keep the fires burning in the drying barns." Morgan eased into his wing-backed chair and rubbed his arm.

"Sarah Johnston came by earlier," Ella said. "She'd been to town and picked up a letter for you at the post office. I left it there on your side table."

Morgan put on his spectacles and opened the envelope.

August 22, 1861

Dear Sir,

I trust this letter finds you in good health. Please forgive my intrusion. I am most embarrassed to have to bring to your attention a situation regarding your slave, Isaac. To be blunt, I must report that he is missing. I entrusted one of my horses and a wagon to Isaac two weeks past. I also provided him a pass for the afternoon. However, as the necessity of this letter attests, his return has been delayed. I have been in touch with the owner of the farm where he was visiting, and he assures me that Isaac departed his place on schedule to return to our home before the sun set. He also shared that Isaac seemed in a rational and sober state at the time.

As Isaac is a tireless, capable worker, and a bright young lad, this would appear to be very much out of his character. I cannot discern a reason for him to absent himself. He showed exceptional progress with his carpentry, and he appeared quite satisfied in these, his most recent surroundings.

Sir, as he was entrusted to my care, I must take full responsibility and will, of course, reimburse you for your loss, should he not return.

My fear is that Isaac has befallen some mishap not of his own doing. Please know that I will spare no effort in uncovering his fate. I will continue to correspond as events warrant.

Your humble servant,
Thomas Day, Jr.

Morgan lifted his glasses and pinched the bridge of his nose. He slowly shook his head.

"What seems to be the matter, dear?"

"Letter's from that Tom Day fella, down in Milton. He says Isaac's gone."

"Gone?" Ella covered her mouth as if to stifle a gasp. "Whatever do you mean?"

"Run off."

"Not our Isaac, he wouldn't run. He's such a good boy . . ."

"Day doesn't think he ran away. Could be he's fallen victim to some rogue or highwayman. Day will keep us informed."

* * *

"You's too young." Florence threw the rag on the table and stared at Tempie. She took a deep breath. This day had been coming for some time, but it might have waited another year. "I seen how you's filling out them dresses in a womanly way, but that don't mean you's old enough to be getting serious about no man."

"But Mama, he's sweet on me. Look, he brung me flowers." Tempie paused from the dough she was kneading and pointed to the jar by the window. Yellow buds opened toward the sun.

"If'n that boy wants to risk sneaking over here to meet you down by the quarters, that's fine, but if I hears of you sneaking over

135

to Johnston's farm again, I'll . . ." She wiped her hands on her apron and shook her head. "It's too dangerous, baby. Everybody knows them pattyrollers is out and about most nights now. Is you disremembering how your brother tangled with that Clancy fella last year?"

"Seems like Isaac come off pretty good. He weren't the one got kilt."

"You hush. Your brother didn't have nothing to do with that. The poor boy got throwed off his horse, and that's all."

"But I ain't helping no runaways, Mama, I'm just looking to spend some time with a fella."

"Then spend it on McConnell land," Florence said. "You's safe here. Can't say the same if'n you's sneaking off somewhere else." She pointed to the hearth. "Pull that oven out and check to see if'n it's hot enough."

Tempie wiped her hands, then grabbed an iron hook and swung the Dutch oven away from the fire. She lifted the lid and held her hand over the pot. The fat coating the inside of the oven glistened. Steam curled from the edges. "It's ready, Mama."

"Fine. Put them two birds in the pot and add that rice and sauce." Florence pointed to a bowl on the table.

Tempie added the chickens and rice, then swung the pot back over the fire and used tongs to place coals on the lid.

"Mama, mama," Joseph yelled, racing through the open doorway and knocking his sister aside. "Miss Ella says come quick. Massa's having fits."

Florence grabbed her youngest by the shoulders. "Slow down boy; now what's all this about Massa McConnell?"

"Miss Ella says he's dying, Mama, hurry . . ." Wide-eyed, Joseph pointed toward the big house.

"Tempie, pull that pot off the fire and come with me. Joseph, show me where."

They ran to the big house. Florence hurried down the center hall toward the parlor and Ella's wails. Morgan was slumped in his chair, his head tilted to one side. Ella knelt, hugging his knees.

"What happened, Miss Ella?" Florence grabbed Morgan's hand. Cold, damp. Eyes open, but not focused. One of his pupils appeared enlarged. He struggled to breathe.

She unbuttoned his shirt and placed a hand on his chest. "His heart's beating, Miss Ella, but he got something serious wrong. Somebody needs to fetch Doc Blackman. Where's Massa Patrick?"

Ella fought back a sob and shook her head. "I . . . I don't know. He went to the Johnston's. I don't know when he planned to return. Oh, God, don't take my Morgan."

"How about Miss Polly, she around?"

"On . . . on a buggy ride with some children from church." Ella sobbed again. "What ever shall we do?"

"Don't fret none, Miss Ella." Florence gently touched her shoulder. "Florence is gonna take good care of Massa McConnell." She turned to Joseph. "Boy, go fetch your pa and tell him we needs Doc Blackman. If he ain't down by the quarters, go to the creek. He took his pole when he headed out this morning."

Florence motioned to Tempie. "Fetch my remedy bag—it's hanging beside the chimney over in the cookhouse—and get some water boiling, then fetch garlic from the herb garden." She pointed to Morgan. "Miss Ella, you has to help me get him to the sofa." The two women tugged and pulled on his arms until they raised him, then, with one under each arm, they dragged him to the sofa and laid him down.

"Oh God, Florence, tell me he will be all right." Ella hovered, fanning her husband with her folding fan. "I can't imagine losing my Morgan. Whatever would I do?"

His eyes seemed to follow Florence as she propped his head with a pillow. "Miss Ella, don't you worry. Abraham done gone to fetch the doctor and Florence is right here to take care of both of you 'til he arrives."

Chapter Twenty-three
September 1861

"On your feet," Constable Branson hollered. "Get your black hides out here where a body can get a good look at you." He slapped the whip across the soles of Isaac's feet.

Isaac brought his hand up to shade his eyes as sunlight from the outer office filled the cell door. The whip snapped across his arm and face, slicing into his flesh.

"Don't you be raising no hand at me," the constable said. "What's wrong with you, boy?"

Isaac clutched his bloodied wrist.

Constable Branson cracked his whip and herded Isaac and Perkins to the street.

Two men waited by a carriage in front of the jail. The taller of the two had a thin, drawn face and wore a light blue suit. A gold chain dangled across his front from watch pocket to waistcoat. Boots, blackened and polished to a high shine, glistened under white gaiters. A blue top hat partially hid oil-slicked, coal black hair. The man stroked his waxed mustache with a pale, bony hand as he studied Isaac. Henry had spoken of such men once. Dandies, he'd called them.

The shorter man wore faded denim Kentucky jeans and a homespun brown jacket over a plaid cotton shirt. His scuffed brogans looked no better than those on Isaac's own feet. The butt of a pistol protruded from his belt.

The taller man paced, examining Isaac and Perkins. He placed the butt of his buggy whip under Isaac's jaw and tilted back Isaac's head. "Open your mouth, boy. Let me see those teeth."

Isaac obeyed.

"Very well, and you?" He tapped Perkins on the head with the handle of the whip. Perkins opened his mouth.

"I can move this merchandise. I have buyers in Mississippi. How much you asking?" the man said.

Constable Branson rubbed his chin, then pointed to Perkins. "This here nigger goes for three hundred dollars. That boy there," he said, pointing to Isaac, "will run you seven-fifty."

Isaac glimpsed Perkins twitching nervously beside him. He'd been right. This dandy was in the business of buying people, and Isaac was on the block. Raleigh feared that might happen. If he were sold south, who'd tell her? Would he ever see her again? Beads of sweat gathered on Isaac's brow. His heart pounded.

"Seven-fifty's too steep for my troubles. My buyers are looking for field niggers. If I can't get a decent price up here I can't make a profit down south."

"Six-fifty, but that's as low as I go. This young buck'll sell right fine on the local market."

"Then I'll purchase just the one." The man in the blue suit shook his head. "He'll bring a profit in Vicksburg. I have more merchandise to look at in Durham. I'll be by in the morning to pick him up."

* * *

The cell door clanged shut behind him. Isaac stumbled, catching himself as he fell against the wall. He eased to the floor and stretched on his side, his festering wounds still too raw to lean against the rough brick. Perkins sat across the cell.

"Looks like I'll be leaving ya come morning, boy."

"What's they gonna do with you in Mississippi?" Isaac said.

"Perkins can't go to Mississippi. Ain't traveling that road no more." What little light entered the high barred window painted Perkins in a warm glow.

"They's done bought you," Isaac said." Come morning, you's headed south whether you likes it or not."

"Boy," Perkins said, shaking his head. "I's been in them cotton fields too long. The blacksnake whip done cut me for the last time. Moktar Perkins ain't no white man's field nigger no more." He folded his arms across his chest and closed his eyes.

That man was talking nonsense. Isaac turned on his stomach, resting his cheek on his hand as he studied his cellmate.

Perkins sighed, then his breathing relaxed.

Was he sleeping? How could the man sleep knowing he'd been

sold south? At least Isaac hadn't been sold, not yet, anyway. He tried to nap, but visions of Raleigh, Mama, Pa, Tempie, Joseph, even Henry floated through his mind. If he was sold south, he'd never see any of them again. And what about Raleigh . . . how long would she wait? Would she find herself another man, one free to travel where he wanted and live wherever he chose?

* * *

The rattle of keys in the lock woke Isaac from a fitful sleep. He sat up and rubbed his eyes. Sunlight glowed through the window.

"The shackles stay here," the constable said from outside the cell. "You can tie him up, if you feel the need." The iron bolt scraped through the brackets, then the heavy door creaked open. Standing in the doorway with the Dandy behind him, Constable Branson tossed a key at Perkins's feet. "Get them shackles off, boy. You ain't taking my leg irons south. They cost me good money."

Perkins turned the key and freed his legs. He rubbed the raw skin where the iron cuffs had chafed his ankles, then he turned toward Isaac. "It's been real nice, boy. You finds that star you be searching for, you hear?" The other shackle clanged to the floor.

Isaac stood. Words would not come. He searched Perkins's eyes. They sparkled. Tears? No, joy. Where was the fear? Isaac held out his hand. Perkins grasped it in both of his leathery hands and smiled.

"Get a move on, nigger." The constable shoved Perkins with his whip, slamming the cell door closed behind him.

Isaac grasped the iron bars on the window above him. Sunlight warmed his hands. The voices outside grew faint. Isaac closed his eyes. Perkins's image was fresh in his mind. All those years of picking cotton, his back scarred from countless whips. The man lost his family—not once, but twice. Was that what awaited Isaac? He pressed his forehead against the cool brick.

"Hell, he's running!" The voice called from outside the window. "Stop him. Stop that damned nigger."

Two pistol shots echoed against the cell walls.

Isaac released the bars and slowly slid to the floor.

* * *

Florence tended to Morgan in the back parlor, eavesdropping on the doctor and Patrick as she worked.

"I gave your mother a potion to help her sleep," the doctor

141

said. "She's been through a lot, poor woman. Let her rest until the effects wear off." The doctor nodded toward Florence. "Your nigra woman there did a fine job.

"I apologize again for not getting out this way yesterday, but I was up country tending to a patient and the storm kept me there overnight. I didn't get your message until I returned this morning." Doctor Blackman closed his bag and folded his spectacles, placing them in his coat pocket. "It's apoplexy, there's no doubt in my mind."

"Will he recover?" Patrick glanced at his father, then back to the doctor.

"Hard to tell." The doctor put his hand on Patrick's shoulder. "Some have an almost complete recovery. Others may linger for years, never again speaking or walking on their own. Just no way of knowing."

"What will he need?"

The doctor bent over Morgan and examined his eyes. "The willow leaf tea your nigra concocted was helpful. I'd recommend continuing that. Also, after he gets some rest, regular stimulation will get blood to his limbs. Some patients respond well to vigorous exercise. Others remain backward, as unresponsive as any idiot."

"Thank you, doctor. I'll send for you if there's any change in his condition." Patrick walked the doctor to the door.

"Hope this rain hasn't damaged your crops, Patrick."

"The tobacco's already in the barns. We'll be fine, but thank you for asking."

The front door creaked open, then slammed shut.

"Florence," Patrick called. "Come here."

She hurried to the front parlor. Patrick was seated in Morgan's chair. "Yes, sir, Massa Patrick?"

"You may go back to your cooking now. I will tend to any needs my father might have."

"Yes, sir, Massa Patrick. You needs me to bring you some of my remedy? It'll fix him up real good."

"Father doesn't need any African potions. You just get back to cooking."

"Begging Massa's pardon, sir, they ain't African medicines—Indian woman up Roanoke way taught me . . ."

"I don't give a damn who taught you, keep your witch's brews out of this house. Your job is to cook, not sass white folks. I'll tend to my father's needs."

"Yes, sir. Thank you, Massa Patrick." Florence curtsied and left the room.

* * *

Florence set a platter of eggs on the table. Polly and Ella were already seated. Tempie poured coffee while Florence set china plates at each place. "Miss Ella, you want I should fix up something soft to feed Massa McConnell? He needs to be eating."

"That will not be necessary, Florence. Patrick says he's taking charge of Mr. McConnell's recuperation. You may leave a plate of eggs and sausage, maybe a biscuit. Patrick is in the back right now tending to his father."

"Florence . . ." A weak voice called from the parlor.

Patrick stood in the doorway, pale and shaken, his countenance a greenish pallor. "Get that cleaned up . . ." Patrick pointed to the rear parlor, then raced out the front door. Sounds of retching came from the direction of the porch.

Florence glanced at Ella. "Excuse me, ma'am." She curtsied, then hurried to the rear parlor.

Morgan lay on his back. A fetid stench filled the room. His eyes followed her as she lifted his blanket.

"Appears you done fouled yourself, Massa. It ain't nothing new for Florence, I treats lots of sick folk down to the quarters. I'll have you cleaned in no time." She pulled the blanket out of the way. "Tempie . . ."

"Yes, Mama." Tempie stood in the doorway, her face twisted in a frown.

"Fetch me a pitcher and a bowl—and some rags."

"Yes ma'am."

"First thing we has to do is get you out of these soiled clothes." Florence began to lift the nightshirt over Morgan's head. His gaze flashed from the doorway to Florence. She smiled and pulled the blanket up again just as Tempie returned.

"Set that over here," Florence said "Then pull them doors shut when you leaves."

Tempie set the pitcher and bowl on the side table and dropped the rags next to the bed. She reached for the brass latch and pulled the pocket doors closed across the wide doorway.

"Now we's private," Florence said. "It's just you and me." She placed a hand on Morgan's shoulder. "Massa, this here's gonna be hard on you, you being a proud man and all, but you knows Florence is gonna take good care of you, so you just make up your mind to stop fretting and trust ol' Florence." She smiled. His eyes welled, then closed tightly for a long moment. When he opened them again the fear was gone.

Chapter Twenty-four
November 1861

"Cato, you stop that." Tempie giggled and pulled away from the lanky boy.

"It's just a tickle to put a smile on your face. Come on, sit beside me." He dropped to the grass under a spreading oak and patted the ground next to him.

Tempie tucked her dress up under her knees as she sat. Moonlight danced on Cato's face, highlighting an impish smile. She and Polly had played make believe so many times, finding princes or handsome knights to marry, but play-acting never felt like that. What was he thinking? She peered at her chest. Wasn't all round yet, not like a grown woman's. She sighed. "Cato, Mama says I can't be coming here no more. She's fretting about them pattyrollers."

"Ain't nothing to worry about. They's out on the roads, not back up here in the fields. I been crossing this land from our farm to yours for better'n two years now, and I ain't never had no trouble."

"Just the same, if you wants to see me next Saturday, you'd best come on down by the McConnell's slave quarters. You runs faster than me, and if them whites is patrolling, you can run the creeks and jump the fences."

"I 'spect so, but I feel strange down there—like we's being watched. Your Aunt Lilly and that Mama Rose, they's all the time pointing at us and whispering . . ."

Tempie smiled. Her aunt sure enough teased that boy the last time he was there. Maybe he wanted some alone time, just the two of them. She snuggled against him. "Weather's turning. Winter'll be on us soon. Setting 'round that big fire will feel mighty good—better'n shivering out here like we's doing tonight."

Cato pulled Tempie's shawl tight around her. He smoothed the loose cotton wrap and settled his arm on her shoulder.

Tempie shivered, but not from the cold. It felt good, being close up like that. What if he tried to kiss her? Maybe she'd let him. What if he didn't try?

"Tell me about Isaac," Cato said. "You hear anything?"

There they were, alone, and all he wanted to talk about was Isaac? She glared. "Ain't heard none since Miss Ella said he'd gone missing."

"You think he's running?" Cato folded his arms over his knees.

"He talked some about running. He helps folks coming through on their way north, so he knows what to do, but this don't feel right—it ain't his time." Tempie pulled her shawl close around her, but it couldn't replace the warmth, or the excitement, of Cato's arm.

"You ever think about running?" Cato shoved a stalk of grass between his teeth.

Tempie stared into the distant sky. "I thinks about being up north, about being free, but some nights I lays awake, and I hears them dogs off in the woods—not knowing if they's chasing deer or tracking my kin—and I gets scared." She placed her hands on the damp grass, leaned back, and looked at Cato. "Still, being free has to be something special. Maybe someday, with the right fella . . ."

Cato tossed the grass stem aside and stood. "The hour's late." He held out his hand. "Pattyrollers or not, we'd best be getting home."

She took his hand and he pulled her up, holding her close. Their eyes met, then Cato stepped back and dropped his hands to his side. "Saturday night? How's about you meet me over by the old smokehouse? I know it's on Johnston land, but nobody ever goes there, and the white folk, they don't pay it no mind. If'n you likes, we can set a small fire in the fireplace, and we'll be alone."

She stared at him. Alone? So he could chew grass and talk about her brother? They could do that at the quarters. "No, don't think so."

Tempie flounced away, then slowed as she reconsidered. She turned toward Cato. "Same time?"

* * *

"Massa McConnell, you has to drink this here willow tea. I

146

done made it good and strong and it's gonna help get you back to rights." Florence slid her arm under Morgan's head and lifted, putting the cup to his lips.

Morgan shuddered. It felt as though his lips moved, but all he managed to utter was an agitated mumble. That was the most God-awful stuff he'd ever tasted. Willow bark tea? Pressed garlic? Was she trying to kill him? It had to be her revenge for not putting that new roof on the cookhouse.

"There, another big sip and you's all done, then I's going to change you. Good thing your insides is working proper. Now, don't you fret none, Massa. You'll be cleaned up and comfortable again in no time, then we begins your exercising, just like the doctor said." She smiled.

He wasn't some damned helpless infant. He didn't need a woman doing for him, especially a slave woman. Where was Patrick, or Ella? They should have known that wasn't right, some nigra woman tending to his private needs like that.

He couldn't move his head, but Morgan took in his surroundings as best he could by moving his eyes. Parlor . . . he was in the back parlor. His eyesight was no longer blurry—at least now he could see. Thank you, Lord. He'd thought he'd gone blind. Hell, there she was with those damned rags again. God, so humiliating. His face warmed. Could she see him blushing?

"There. Let Florence take care of these, then she'll be back and work them arms. They'll get strong again if'n you uses them." She lifted the pile of rags. Her footfalls trailed down the hall.

He must have blacked out, but he couldn't recall. He didn't remember Doc Blackman being there neither. Why wouldn't somebody tell him what was going on? Why couldn't he talk? He couldn't move his arms. My God, he couldn't even feel his arms. What had happened? God, he was scared . . .

"Give me that hand." Florence took his right hand. She massaged each finger, kneading them from the knuckles to the tips. Morgan closed his eyes and relaxed.

"Squeeze."

He looked up. Her focus was on his hand. Something laid across his palm—her fingers? He couldn't move his head to see.

"Squeeze, hard as you can."

Squeeze her fingers? He'd try . . .

147

"Massa McConnell, you has to squeeze. Ain't gonna get strong lessen you does like I tells you."

He was squeezing—squeezing hard as he could . . .

"That's good, Massa McConnell. I seen your fingers wiggle some. Try again."

Lord God, please . . . . He studied Florence's eyes as she watched his hand. Anger? No, more like disappointment. His fingers hadn't moved.

"Now, we's gonna work that arm, get them big muscles moving." Florence pushed his arm until it bent at the elbow, then pulled it fully extended. She repeated the motion again and again. "Gonna take some time, but you's gonna use this here hand. Ain't no apoplexy keeping you down."

Apoplexy? Oh God, was he going to die?

"Florence!"

Morgan turned his eyes toward the angry voice. Patrick stepped into view. Good, he'll tell him what happened. Had they gotten the crops in? What day was this, anyway?

"I told you, none of your potions or cures," Patrick said. "You just clean him up twice a day and feed him as best you can." Patrick looked down at Morgan as though studying a curiosity.

"But Massa Patrick, the doctor said exercising was good for your pa. It'll make him strong again, and—"

Patrick yanked Florence away from the bed. "For the last time, do as you're told. No doctoring, he's beyond that. His dying will be a mercy. Now, get out."

Her rapid footsteps faded down the center hall. The back door opened, then slammed closed.

What was wrong with that boy? Patrick knew they didn't treat their nigras that way. He'd have to have a talk with him . . .

Patrick stared at Morgan, then reached down and drew the blanket around Morgan's neck, tucking it under his shoulders. "You'd best stay warm, Father. Doc Blackman says there's a small chance you might recover, but I expect the farm is mine to run for now, and I plan on a few changes. For one, the slaves will learn what it is to do an honest day's work. Now get some rest." He smiled and turned away. The heavy clomp of boots trailed down the center hall.

Small chance he might recover? He'd show him. It was still his farm, and Patrick couldn't change that.

* * *

"Sir, sir . . ." Isaac banged on the thick wooden door with the tin cup. "Massa Branson, you out there? Isaac has to tell you something. I belongs to Massa McConnell, up South Boston way. He loaned me to Mr. Day, there in Milton. Isaac ain't no runaway. Isaac don't never run." He dropped the cup and slumped against the door. "Ain't nobody out there. Nobody listening. I beats on that door all the day long, gets nothing back but cussing and whipping. Dear God, don't let Isaac be sold south. I can't be working no cotton fields. I has a family to care for, Raleigh too, if'n she'll have me."

Isaac slid to the floor and clutched his knees, rocking to and fro. "Please, Lord, I been a sinner, I knows. I kilt me a man up there in Virginia. Didn't mean him no harm, but he's dead, just the same. And me and Henry, we stealed them pies off the sill last summer, and Lord, I doesn't pray near often as I should, but I's real sorry. Please, don't let Isaac be sold south to no Mississippi cotton farm."

He collapsed against the wall, leaning his head on his knees. Maybe Mr. Jones was right. Maybe God didn't hear slave prayers.

Voices in the outer office caused Isaac to press an ear against the door.

"I don't answer to no nigger," Constable Branson said. "I don't care who you is, and I ain't got your nigger boy in this here jail no how."

"Then you won't mind opening the cell . . ."

"I'll be goddamned if I'll open my jail for any damned nigger. You get on out of here right now or you'll see the inside of my cell, all right, and that's for sure."

"You are on notice, sir. My attorney shall be here within the day, and he will have an order from the county judge to open that door."

That voice—Thomas? Yes! "Mr. Day! Mr. Day!" Isaac banged on the cell door. "I's right here. This is Isaac. I's here, Mr. Day."

Isaac strained to listen. Had he heard?

The cell door flew open.

"I told you to be quiet, you goddamned nigger . . ."

The whip sliced Isaac's face and arm. He rolled away, but the leather cut into his back.

149

"I'll have you sold south before any damned lawyer can see a judge. This here's Friday. Court's closed 'til Monday. Come Sunday, I'll have folding money in my pocket and you'll be no more'n a bad memory headed to that land of tall cotton."

The cell door clanged shut.

Chapter Twenty-five
December 1861

Winter gusts rattled the brittle corn stalks. Tempie pulled her thin coat close. A tapestry of stars sparkled throughout the moonless sky. She hurried across the wagon path and slipped into the woods. Ahead lay the clearing and the stone chimney. She crept behind a large oak and watched. Without the moon, the clearing became a confusing pool of shadows. Was Cato there?

She waited.

Movement? Yes, there, near the chimney . . .

"Cato?" she whispered.

No answer.

She ducked behind the tree. Mama was right, she shouldn't be out there. The next time that boy wanted to see her, he'd best come on down to the quarters.

"Cato?" She called, peeking around the tree.

A dark, indistinct, figure stepped from the shadows.

"Cato, is that you?" Her voice trembled. Lord, it had better be—or she was fixing to take off running.

"Tempie?" Cato whispered. "Where was you? I been setting here most of the evening."

"Boy, you had me scared out of my wits," Tempie said, patting her heart as she walked toward him. "Why didn't you answer?"

"I wasn't sure it was you."

"Can't stay long," Tempie said. "Besides, it's cold out here. Didn't you say you was gonna light a fire?"

Cato put his arm around her shoulder and pulled her close. "Come over by the chimney, I set a small fire and I brung this here blanket to set on." He held up a threadbare cotton rag. "You'll be warm soon enough."

Tempie smiled. That arm around her shoulders was warming her just fine.

Cato spread the small blanket on a bed of pine straw, then knelt, striking a piece of flint with the back of his knife. Sparks caught in a nest of cedar bark shavings. He cupped the fuzzy ball of dried bark, held it close, and blew gently. A spark glowed, faint at first, then blossomed into a small flame. He set the burning wad under a teepee of dried twigs. The growing flames revealed Cato's broad smile.

"How you been, girl?"

Tempie nestled next to him, resting her head on his shoulder. It was sure better than fussing with Aunt Lilly or Mama Rose and all their carrying on down at the quarters. Here they had their own fire and no one watching.

"You mad or something?" Cato said.

"What?" Tempie responded. "'Course I ain't mad. Why'd you say that?" She lifted her head and looked at him.

"I asked you a question but you pretended like I weren't here."

"I was just enjoying the fire. Ask me again." She returned her head to his shoulder.

"I said, how is you? And Massa McConnell, how's he doing? He still having troubles? And what's they saying about Isaac?"

Tempie rolled her eyes. "Massa had a letter from Mr. Day, down North Carolina. I heard Polly reading it to him, even though Miss Ella says Massa McConnell can't hear none. Letter said he thinks Isaac was caught up by the pattyrollers. They's checking the jails and such, but no sign of him yet."

"You warm enough?" He pulled her closer.

"I'm doing right fine." Tempie smiled. Somewhere in the next woodlot, an owl's low, mournful cry drifted on the breeze. A warm glow flickered from the firebox. Was this the right time to ask how he felt? It seemed like he was all the time talking about everybody else. Maybe, just this once, he could put his mind on her.

"Cato, you ever think about me, I mean, when you's working the fields and such?"

"Course I does. I thinks on you all the time."

"It don't seem like you do. You only ever ask about Isaac, or Massa McConnell, or how does I like the weather . . ."

He scowled. "That ain't so. I asks about you all the time. I just now said how is you, but you wasn't listening."

Tempie cocked her head. "Ask me again."

He seemed to hesitate, then mumbled, "H-how is you?"

"I's pleased to be here. How about you?"

Cato smiled. "I 'spect I's pleased too." His arm tensed as he flexed the fingers resting on her shoulder. "Tempie, I . . . I doesn't know much about courting and such. Truth is, I gets . . . scared, well, maybe not scared, just shook up a mite. You know what I mean?"

"You ever kiss a girl?"

Cato stared at the ground and shook his head.

"I ain't never kissed no boy neither." Tempie searched his face. The muscles around his mouth quivered, as though he wasn't sure what to do. Tempie put her hand behind his neck and pulled him to her, closing her eyes. Their lips touched, then slowly he pulled away. She opened her eyes.

Cato lifted her face in his hands. "I . . . I 'spect I needs more practice." He smiled, closing his eyes again. They kissed once more, pulling each other close. Cato eased her to the ground.

She reclined, draping her arms around his neck. "You's a mighty fast learner, for a fella what never done that before."

"You ain't mad? I mean, for kissing you again and . . ."

Tempie pulled him beside her, silencing him with another kiss, then cuddled into the crook of his arm. The pounding of his heart through his shirt sounded like a runaway horse. So, was that what love really felt like? Nice.

They lay together watching the clear ebony sky.

"Tempie, you remember when I asked did you ever think about running?"

"I remember."

Cato raised up on one elbow. "You said it would have to be with the right fella . . ."

She placed a finger on his lips. "Ain't ready for that talk yet, but when I is, I 'spect you's one I'll be considering."

He settled back, apparently satisfied with her answer.

They lay together. The fire dwindled to a scattering of glowing coals. Tempie glanced at the stars. Orion, the great hunter, had moved a ways since their evening began, rotating around what Pa called the "Freedom" star.

"Evening's getting on. I best be on my way before Mama gets worried."

Cato sighed and stood, brushing leaves from his back. He helped Tempie to her feet, then pulled her into his arms. They kissed again. "I don't want to hear no nonsense about going down to the quarters no more," he said. "You meet me here next Saturday?"

Tempie tilted her head and gazed into his eyes. She'd never thought of Cato as tall, but now he seemed to tower over her. "Next Saturday? Maybe . . ." She smiled, taking a few steps toward the open field.

"No 'maybe.' You be here for sure."

She blew him a kiss, then sashayed into the woods. Once away from the warmth of the fire and Cato's arms, the air felt cold again. She walked faster, wishing his arm was still around her. Maybe he didn't know much about kissing, but she sure enough liked how he did it.

Tempie hurried through the broken corn stalks to the wagon path, then skipped, slapping her arms to fend off the damp chill. On the inside, a glow warmed her in a way she'd never before known. He wasn't ignoring her, he'd just been shy. Once he got past that shyness, he was a right fine catch. But did he like her as much as she liked him? Maybe, someday, they'd run away together to New York City, or perhaps Boston. That would sure be fine.

Tempie followed the trail into the forest. Down along the creek bottom it soon became black as chimney soot. How could she see? If only that old moon would come out.

She picked her way along the narrow trail, glancing skyward, following the open spaces where treetops stood apart and defined the trace of the path. At least it was too cold for snakes. Thank you Lord, for small blessings.

The path twisted, following the stream, then turned at a crossing. A row of stones served as a footbridge. She tried each stone with her foot, making certain of the hold before taking the next step. She lost her balance in mid-stream, thrust her arms to the side, then caught herself and hopped across the last two stones, dragging a foot in the frigid water, giggling as she found the dry ground on the far side.

"Well, well," a graveled voice snarled from the darkness. "What have we got here?"

She pulled up with a start.

"You a runaway?" A tall form appeared from the shadows. A match flickered, cupped in a large hand.

She shielded her eyes from the sudden glare. "Who's there?" She asked, trembling.

"I know you. You's the daughter of that cook on the McConnell place. I reckon you growed some since I last seen you." The match went out and a rough hand touched her shoulder. She brushed it away and pulled back.

"Hey, I ain't going to hurt you none. Just studying the merchandise. You's a fine young flower, ripe for the picking." He brushed the back of his hand across her breast.

"Leave me be." She slapped his hand. "I ain't no flower, and my massa ain't gonna allow nobody to get on with one of his slaves."

"You're a feisty one, that's for sure." The man grabbed her shoulders and held her tight. "Your master's dying. He can't do nothing. Besides, if you tell him, or anybody, your mama, your papa, maybe even that little pickaninny brother you got, they're all gonna feel my blade."

What was he talking about? Tempie sobbed. Her shoulders heaved uncontrollably. Lord, make him stop. This couldn't be happening . . .

He wrestled her to the ground, tugging at her dress. "I aim to have me some fun, so quit your fighting . . ."

Tempie clawed his face.

He slapped her with the back of his hand. "You little bitch, if you do that again I'll slice you up and feed you to the dogs—and I'll cut that little brother of yours too. Now, you settle back and just enjoy."

She struggled, but his weight pinned her against the damp leaves. She stifled her cries. He was talking crazy. Said he was gonna kill Joseph? Oh, God, make him stop . . . Cato? Where was Cato ?

He shoved a calloused hand down the front of her dress, fondling her small breast.

God, he smelled—cigars and . . . and whiskey?

"P-please, mister, please stop . . ."

Beard stubble scraped against her chest. A hand reached under her dress, groping, touching . . .

"No, stop . . . oh God, no . . ."

His weight dropped heavily on her. Something dangled in her face—a trinket around his neck?

He forced her legs apart and pushed into her.

"God, it hurts, hurts so bad . . ."

Bare branches overhead, fleeting clouds, stars dotting the winter sky—all faded into a swirling fog. His animal grunts became distant, no longer a part of her world. She floated above the forest.

* * *

A voice . . . calling her name?

"Mama . . . ?" Her eyes opened.

The night held only silence wrapped in a mottled blanket of shadows. She lay still. A wintery sky slowly came into focus above. Twigs and leaves pricked her bare legs. Why was she there? What had happened? Cato . . . ?

A dream? She moved her leg. "Oh God, hurts so bad . . ." The stench came back—sweat, tobacco, whiskey. "Lord, no . . ." Tempie rolled on her side and pulled her legs up, curling into a ball. Her sobs broke the silence.

"Mama? Please, Mama . . ." She touched the scrapes on her cheek from his rough beard. She couldn't tell her mama. Couldn't tell anyone. Lord, what had he done?

She reached down to where it hurt, then jerked her hand away. What was that? Tempie yanked a fern growing along the path. Ignoring the pain, she took the leaves and scrubbed herself dry, then pushed to her knees and took a deep breath. "I's clean now, won't nobody know." She stood on wobbly legs smoothing the wrinkles on the front of her dress. "Can't tell nobody . . ."

Tempie steadied herself against a tree. Slowly, the ringing in her ears faded. She brushed back her hair and stumbled down the path toward the McConnell farm.

Chapter Twenty-six
December 1861

"Massa McConnell," Florence said. "I has to talk with you. I been praying and asking the good Lord to tell Florence what to do."

Morgan opened his eyes. Shafts of sunlight filtered through the lace curtains, filling the room with a warm glow. Morning? Yes, and a good one. Coffee on the porch, then riding down by the creek. He had to get up . . .

His legs, his arms . . . nothing moved, and then the bed sagged. Florence was sitting beside him, brushing his hair.

"Massa McConnell, the Lord tells Florence she has to be a good woman, and the Lord knows she tries. You remembers that preacher man what come out from that white folk's church down South Boston to say words over poor ol' July?"

Sure. It was the least he could do for old July . . .

Florence turned down the blanket and began to change Morgan's diaper. "Well, he said the Lord expects us nigras to be obedient, and that's what Florence tries to be. Preachers all the time saying, 'Nigras, you has to obey your masters if'n you wants to go to heaven.'"

How he hated having others tending to his private needs—so damned humiliating . . . but what the hell was bothering her? He searched her eyes. Wasn't fear . . . what then? Get on with it, woman. Damn, he wished he could talk . . .

"Anyways, you remembers when Massa Patrick tells Florence no more remedies and no more exercising them ol' muscles? Well I goes to the Lord and I prays, 'cause Florence, she wants to be obedient, but she knows her remedies. Lord say, 'Florence, why you ask me this question? You know what's right.' I says, 'Lord, I's scared I makes you angry if'n I ain't obedient.' And you know what the Lord says?" She stopped her cleaning and looked into Morgan's eyes. "Lord says, 'Florence, you obey your heart.' Well, Florence's heart tells her Massa ain't getting no better, lessen he has remedies and exercise, so we's gonna keep that up. It'll be our secret."

Patrick had blocked his recuperation? Of course. Now it was beginning to make sense.

She pulled the blanket under his arms and began massaging the fingers on his left hand. Sunlight danced off her black hair, a glow encircled her head, silhouetting her face and hiding her expression. Morgan strained for a better look, but he couldn't move his head. Finally, she bent to adjust a pillow and her profile came into view. She wore a gentle, but determined smile.

Patrick had her scared to beat all, yet she was sticking her neck out for him. He'd have to work with her . . . he strained to push with the arm she pumped back and forth.

"That one side of your face still be drooping, Massa McConnell," Florence said as she touched his cheek. The doctor says one's got more damage than the other. We'd best exercise both sides. First, you drink this here."

No, not that snake oil . . .

She held a cup to his lips. "Florence mixed this special, just for you. Leaves from the maidenhair tree, a little garlic, a pinch of catnip . . . there, you drink it on down. It'll make you better." She poured the liquid into his mouth.

He gagged, fighting to swallow before he choked. A shiver ran through his body. Lord, that was the most God-awful concoction he'd ever imagined.

"That's good, Massa. You's making faces. Them muscles be finding theyselves again. Now, let Florence get back to working that arm."

Hands strong from a lifetime of kneading dough worked the muscles of his forearms. "I shouldn't be bothering you none with Florence's troubles, but you knows my boy, Isaac? He been missing now since before harvest. Ain't like him. He's a good boy. He wouldn't never run. I's worried, Massa, I truly is." Her hands massaged his bicep.

"Morning, Papa. Morning, Florence." Polly's cheerful voice filled the room. "You seen Tempie?"

Florence stopped massaging Morgan's arm but continued to

hold it in her grip. "She went off after breakfast. That child's been acting strange. I 'spect she's worrying about her brother, same as all of us."

"What's that you're doing, Florence?"

"The apoplexy done took your papa's muscles. This here exercising might just bring them back."

"Can I help?"

"You sure enough can, child. Just do like I shows you—up and down. There, that's good . . . now, tight, got to squeeze tight to get the blood moving."

"This is easy." She smiled at Florence, then Morgan. "Papa, can you feel this?"

Yes, he could, and God bless her.

"One thing, Missy Polly," Florence said. "Your brother, Massa Patrick, he don't hold none with Florence's remedies. He'll be getting angry, if'n he sees Florence—or Miss Polly—exercising on Massa McConnell."

"Patrick thinks he's the boss now, but he can't tell me what to do," Polly replied. "If I want to help Papa, he can't stop me."

"Just the same, child, you'd best keep this our secret. Morning and night, every day, even if Florence can't be here, you has to make him move—like this here." Florence took his jaw in her hand and opened and closed his mouth, rotating the jaw as she moved it.

"Don't worry, Florence. I won't tell a soul."

Greenery draped the mantle behind Polly. Could it be Christmas already? Where had the time gone? He didn't reckon he had much to celebrate.

* * *

Florence hung the pot on a blackened iron hook and swung it over the fire, then turned to Abraham, who was seated at the table. "I don't know what's wrong with that child, she's so quiet, 'cept this morning, when I hears her retching out back. You suppose she's taken ill?"

"Could be," Abraham said. "But I reckon she's just suffering from growing up worries. She still seeing that boy from over at the Johnston's place?"

"Cato? She ain't said nothing about him for days. Might be that child's just worrying herself sick over love."

Abraham walked behind Florence and wrapped his arm around

her waist. "I 'spect you's right, Flo. It could be our baby's feeling her first broken heart. In time, she'll be back to her ol' self—playing with Polly, filling up this here cabin with all her laughter. . ."

She turned into the shelter of his arms. "Lord, I prays it ain't nothing more. That child just ain't been herself." Florence gazed into Abraham's eyes. "I worries more about Isaac. You hearing any news down by the quarters?"

"Nobody's heard nothing," Abraham said. "If he was running, we'd a known by now."

"Lord," she whispered. "I prays the Lord will watch over that boy. I can't be having two of my childrens in trouble all at once." She buried her face in Abraham's chest. He held her close and smoothed her hair.

* * *

"Morgan, dear," Ella said. "We have a letter from Henry." She pulled a chair beside his bed and leaned forward. "I feel silly, talking like this to an invalid. I don't even know if you can hear me, and if you do, that you understand anything I'm saying. Patrick said the doctor doesn't think you're in control of your faculties, but I expect that reading to you can't do any harm." She patted his shoulder and gave a small laugh.

Morgan stared into his wife's face. Lord, Patrick had her believing too. She figured him for an idiot, nothing more than a potted plant that required occasional watering.

"Oh, Morgan, Henry's doing so well. They're still down by Newport News. Listen:

Dearest Family,

We are in winter quarters on Mulberry Island. The awful storms of this past autumn destroyed most of our tents, so we have taken to building small cabins of lumber and mud. I would dearly enjoy a winter in any of our slaves' quarters, as it would be quite an improvement over what our noble army has provided.

Mail service has been approximate. Tell Polly I received her letter of October 27th only last week. It had been delivered in error to someone in the Boydton Calvary. At least the fellow was kind enough to send it over by courier. I do look forward to your letters and packages, so please do not hesitate to write, even though results are not always as we would hope from the postal service. Maybe if you sent my mail via New York? I hear tell the Yankees get theirs delivered quite regularly.

Food continues to be a problem, as is disease. We have lost more good Virginia boys to fever and dyspepsia than could ever be accounted for by Yankee bullets. I am doing well, however, and I hope to be home for a few days this winter. The colonel has authorized seven days' leave for everyone, in their turn. The officers received the Christmas holiday. My time will be later. I hope you had a fine holiday celebration.

Yankee gunboats came up the Warwick River the other day and lobbed some shells at our pickets. A terrible waste of ammunition, as they had no effect, other than to provide some much needed entertainment. All's quiet now, and looks to remain so. The Yankees do not appear eager for a fight.

Give my regards to Isaac. Tell him we'll do some hunting while I'm home on leave.

Your obedient son,
Henry

"I suppose he hasn't received any of our letters with all the latest news. Poor boy's living in squalor. We ought to write President Davis—southern boys oughtn't be treated that way." Ella placed a hand on his shoulder as she stood to leave. "You need your rest. You look peaked."

Henry was coming home? Thank God. Patrick didn't give a damn that he was laid up—he seemed down right pleased to finally have control of the farm. Maybe Henry would sit and visit some. Polly was always good about that . . .

"Joseph! Abraham! Where's all our niggers?" Patrick stormed up the center hall, doors slamming behind him. "Mother, where's Joseph?"

The voice reverberated in the hallway. Morgan strained to understand.

"Did you check the barn, or out by the woodpile? What seems to be the matter?" Ella replied.

"This letter here from that Day fella. Did you read it?"

"You know I don't read business mail. That's for you or your father."

"Day says his attorney has ascertained that the damned constable down in Yanceyville is holding Isaac and trying to sell him south. I have to send someone down there before that tin badge sells my slave and pockets the money. If you see Abraham or Joseph, tell them to get my horse saddled." Boots echoed on the hard floor. The back door slammed.

Chapter Twenty-seven
December 1861

The cell door clanged open. "Get out here, boy. It's time you made me some money." Constable Branson kicked the sole of Isaac's boot.

Isaac crawled to his feet. The constable poked him with the butt of his whip, shoving him through the door. Outside, the bright winter sun was blinding. Isaac winced and closed his eyes, but was careful not to raise his hands.

"Four hundred, and that's my last offer."

A familiar voice . . . Isaac blinked and turned to face the man who was speaking. Tall, skinny, light blue suit . . . the dandy.

"You know damned well this here nigger could sell for twice that amount in Alabama or Mississippi and nobody'd give it a thought," Constable Branson said.

"So take him to Mississippi," the dandy replied. "My offer is four hundred dollars in North Carolina, and I happen to know there's been a lawyer fella snooping around, so you can sell him to me or you can give him back to his owner."

"Dornhoffer, you ain't no better'n a damned crook. Why I ought to lock you—"

The dandy raised his hands in protest. "You, sir, have no room to be accusing anyone of larceny. You, who steal from your neighbors and sell their slaves on the secondary market. I am merely a businessman; it is you, sir, who are the thief."

Constable Branson tossed a key to the dandy. "Give me my money, then get my leg irons off that nigger."

The dandy reached inside his coat and withdrew a smooth, dark leather billfold. Isaac silently counted as the man peeled off bills: three hundred and eighty dollars.

"Four hundred. Done." He slammed the wad of money into the constable's hand. "It has been a pleasure, sir." The dandy unlocked the leg irons around Isaac's right ankle and reached for the left foot.

"Put them irons on his wrists, then stand aside."

Isaac turned at the gruff, familiar voice. Clancy sat atop a tall horse, a double-barreled shotgun resting on his saddle horn. What was he doing there?

"This nigra belongs to me, sir," the dandy said. "You have no right—"

"This here scattergun and Mr. Patrick McConnell of South Boston, Virginia says differently," Clancy replied. "Now, put them irons on his wrists before this thing goes off and sets you to bleeding all over that purty suit."

Clancy was taking him home? That was one man Isaac never figured he'd be happy to see.

"Them irons is mine." Constable Branson pocketed the money and stepped forward. "You can have the nigger, but the irons is part of my law enforcement apparatus."

Clancy swung the shotgun toward the constable. "Them irons was yours. Now they's mine. You go stealing other people's niggers, you's lucky I don't kill you right here. Now, you can shut up and go back in that hole you call a jail, or you can enjoy the right barrel while your purty friend here gets his fill of the left."

The constable wagged a finger at Clancy. "This is preposterous. I shall swear out a warrant . . ."

Clancy cocked the hammer.

The constable scurried into the jail and slammed the door. Metal scraped metal as the bolt on the door slid shut.

"After you gets them irons on him, tie my rope securely about them so's I have a rein on this pup."

The dandy placed the irons on Isaac and tied the end of Clancy's rope around the chain that joined them.

"Now, get." An explosion of buckshot ripped the sign above the jailhouse door. The gangly man raced down the alley like a blue crane with hounds on his trail.

"Don't need to be tying me, Mr. Clancy. Isaac ain't running. . ."

"Shut up, nigger." Clancy jerked the rope.

Isaac stumbled, then caught himself, straightened, and fell in step behind the horse.

* * *

The horse plodded at an easy gait, but weeks with neither sustenance nor exercise had left Isaac weakened. With wrists chained, he hung his head and staggered behind the animal, glancing up only once—when they passed the Patterson farm. He stumbled and fell as he searched the familiar house. The horse dragged Isaac by his arms until he was able to regain his footing.

Was Raleigh there? What if she was watching? If she saw him in chains, would she ever want to marry him?

Clancy yanked the rope. Isaac focused again on the rutted road.

"We camp here." Clancy reined his mount in a small grove two miles above the Patterson farm. Twilight settled over the fields.

"Over by that tree." Clancy waved the shotgun at a sturdy maple. "Set on down so's I can tie you good. You ain't running on me like you done on that Day fella. Serves him right, trusting a nigger . . ."

"I didn't run. Is you taking me back to Mr. Day?"

"Shut up. You belong to the McConnells and that's where you're going. Patrick—that's *Master* Patrick to you—he's in charge now, and he hired me bring back his property."

Clancy tied Isaac to the tree, then gathered wood and lit a fire. He unsaddled his horse and pulled a small sack from his saddlebags. Settling by the fire, Clancy popped a corndodger in his mouth, washing it down with what looked to be whiskey.

"Y'all got some food for Isaac? I's right hungry too."

Clancy tossed down the sack and stormed toward him. "I ain't listening to you flap your gums, so shut up." He smacked Isaac with the back of his hand.

Blood trickled from Isaac's nose. He shook his head. The ringing slowly cleared. Clancy towered above him, hands on his hips. Dark, ragged hair and a scraggly beard encircled the man's pocked face. A scar ran from his lip to his right ear. Something dangled from around his neck. A star? His wooden star? It wasn't lost; Clancy must have taken it during their last scuffle. Isaac strained against his ropes.

Clancy's eyes darted suddenly to his right. He put a finger to his lips. "Shut up, boy, or I'll cut you wide open." He snatched his shotgun and slipped into the bushes.

Isaac turned. To his left, someone, or something, was sneaking up on the camp. A bush parted, then a short man in a homespun brown jacket slipped into the clearing holding a pistol.

"Looks to be all clear, Mr. Dornhoffer," the little man whispered. "He must be off answering nature's call. Hurry." The little man crept to where Isaac was tied and began working on the knots. "Boy, you keep quiet or you'll get what your friend back there in Yanceyville got." He raised up, peering into the bushes. "Mr. Dornhoffer, will you please hurry?"

The gangly man in the blue suit looked all around before he stepped into the clearing. He held a pepperbox derringer in one hand. "Just cut the damned ropes and let's get out of here. I paid for that nigger fair and square. Nobody's going to steal him from me."

"Evening, gents." Clancy entered the clearing from the same direction the other two had come. He leveled his shotgun at the intruders.

Panic gripped the little man's face. A scattergun wouldn't be particular at that range. If Clancy pulled the trigger, they were all dead.

"Get over there, away from my nigger," Clancy said. "Step easy now." He motioned with the gun barrel. The two men complied, but neither had dropped their pistols. The little man's back was still to Clancy. As he moved, his thumb cocked the hammer on the short-barreled Colt and his expression turned to glee, as though he were about to reveal a delicious secret. He spun around and raised his pistol.

An orange flame and a deafening roar leap from the shotgun. The little man folded as a wet, dark mass flew out of his back.

Isaac turned away, overcome with nausea. Lord, Clancy had sure enough killed him dead, and that was one hard way to die . . .

The blue crane dandy dropped his pepperbox and danced with his hands in the air, a wet stain covering the front of his fancy store-bought trousers.

"You. Stop your damned hopping about and stand still." Clancy motioned to the dandy.

The dandy froze in mid-dance. Trembling, he began to sob.

"Aw, ain't nothing to be upset about, mister." Clancy tilted his head and smiled.

"I got money," the dandy said, beseechingly. "I'll pay you good for that nigger." He reached for his wallet.

A blast from the second barrel lifted the blue crane from his perch and threw him backward. A dark, gaping hole exploded beneath his collar.

Clancy leaned his shotgun against a tree, then yanked at the knot that held Isaac. "Get up. We're heading back to the McConnell place now. I ain't hanging around to clean up this mess."

After he untied Isaac, Clancy reached into the coat pocket of the man in blue. He removed a wallet, pocketed the contents, and tossed the empty wallet on the corpse. "We'll make the Dan River by sunup. If'n anybody asks, this here was purely self-defense. You got ideas otherwise, that little sister of yours will be the one paying."

Chapter Twenty-eight
January 1862

"Damn it," Henry said. "You can't treat our slaves like that. It's pure meanness." He pounded his fist on the dining room table and glared at his brother. "Isaac didn't run off, he was stolen."

"Yes, perhaps it was a bit unorthodox," Patrick said. "Nonetheless, I am in charge of the farm now and from what I heard, he did run off. He deserved worse than he got."

"Worse? That son of a bitch Clancy mutilated him—he notched his damn ear! And speaking of Clancy, what about those two men Isaac says he killed down in North Carolina? Did you hire him to commit murder too?"

"Little brother, that's all been settled. The constable in South Boston squared it with the constable in Yanceyville. Self-defense, pure and simple." Patrick sat at the head of the table—Morgan's seat—and tilted his chair. "So you tell Isaac that the constable has no need for his testimony."

Henry stabbed the air with his finger. "If you, or that bastard, Clancy, lay a hand on Isaac, you'll both answer to me."

Patrick tapped the palm of his hand with his riding crop and smiled.

"What else has changed since I left for the army?" Henry straightened, shoving his hands on his hips. "Are we still growing tobacco, or did you turn this into a cotton farm? Next, you'll be selling our slaves to save a few dollars until the crops go to market."

Patrick rested his elbows on the table. "Dear brother, I shall do whatever is necessary to protect our investments while you laze away down there in Tidewater with your soldier friends."

Henry started for the door, then turned and faced his brother again. He pointed toward the back parlor. "Pa said this farm will belong to both of us when he's gone, so I have equal say in whatever decisions must be made until he's back on his feet."

"He's not going to recover," Patrick said. "That apoplexy has taken his mind. He's been reduced to an idiot, anyone can see that. So unless you're going to take off that uniform and help me run this farm, the decisions will have to be left to me."

"You're the caretaker," Henry said. "Not the owner, not the sole proprietor, you're only the caretaker, and don't you forget it." He grabbed his hat and stormed out.

* * *

"How's the ear?" Henry said, pointing to Isaac's head.

"It's mending, I reckon." Isaac strolled along the old creek road with a single barrel twenty gauge shotgun over his shoulder.

"Looks like you'll have a scar where that whip caught your cheek" Henry cradled a twelve gauge double in the crook of his arm.

"That constable, he found plenty of use for his whip, that's for sure." Isaac carefully touched his cheek. "How's your pa these days? He mending?"

"I'll tell you," Henry said, "seeing Pa that way, it's downright unsettling. He used to be as strong as those old oaks yonder by the creek . . ." His shoulders sagged. "Now, he's as helpless as a child."

"He gonna die?"

"Patrick thinks so. Mother does too, though she doesn't talk about it, but your mama said he's showing some improvement. She and Polly showed me how he can move his fingers when they tell him, and he can make sounds—not words, mind you, but sounds. Don't you be telling anyone though, Patrick doesn't want them messing with Papa. He sees it as a waste of time."

"He won't be hearing nothing from my mouth."

Henry paused and shifted the gun to his other arm. "So, what was it like? You know, when Clancy done in those two slavers?"

"That man's got no soul."

Henry raised an eyebrow.

"He busted a cap on that second fella after he'd dropped his pistol and surrendered. I seen his eyes." Isaac formed a 'V' with two fingers and pointed at his own eyes. "Clancy found pleasure in pulling that trigger."

"It ain't right. I'm the one goes off to war and you see more action back here than I did on the front."

"I seen too much already," Isaac said. "I don't want no more killing." What if Henry knew what he'd done to that Johnston boy? Would he consider Isaac no better than Clancy—just another murderer?

A rabbit darted across their path. Henry pointed. "Guess we're not hunting so good."

Isaac laughed. "I reckon my mind ain't on it today, but Mama's got chicken in the pot. We'll still be eating fine."

"Well, you watch out for Clancy," Henry said. "I talked to Patrick about how the slaves are to be treated—like how Papa would want—but I got no control once I'm gone, and I don't like that he's using Clancy for work Sean ought to be doing."

"I'll be fine. I just wish I could get back to Mr. Day's. He's been teaching me real good."

"I'll talk to Patrick, see what I can do. By the way, how's that girl? You fixing to jump the broom any time soon?"

Isaac kicked at a dirt clod, sending a puff of dust in the air. "Ain't gonna be no marrying. She's a free woman, not looking for no slave husband."

Henry looked away. "There's some fine slave girls over at the Johnston place. You talk to Patrick, see if he'll give you a pass one Saturday night."

Isaac stopped in his tracks. He stared at Henry.

"Yeah, you're right." Henry shook his head. "Patrick ain't real big on giving out passes. Well, maybe they'll come down to the quarters one night for the campfire. Anyway, something will come up."

"Isaac ain't just looking for *something*. Raleigh's my woman, not some slave girl from over to the Johnston place."

Henry studied Isaac, as though searching for some secret meaning. Suddenly, his face seemed twisted in fear. "Oh hell, you're not going to do anything dumb, are you?"

"Henry McConnell," Isaac said, "you ain't never been no slave." He snapped off a stalk of grass and shoved it between his teeth, then glared at Henry. "You chases women all over New York, up to Charlottesville, over by Richmond town, and there ain't nobody saying, 'Henry McConnell, you stop that, you ain't got the right.' But Isaac finds him a woman and it's, 'Isaac, get a pass, Isaac, you can't go to visit, Isaac, try one of them Johnston nigras.' Nobody says, 'Isaac, what's going to make you happy'?"

Henry walked on in silence. Finally, he stopped and faced Isaac. "Look," he said, rubbing his neck. "It's not always that simple." He tossed a pebble at a crow perched on a low hanging branch. The bird took flight, winging toward the far woods. "Damn, there's so much I don't understand. I thought I did, but . . ." His eyes seemed to plead with Isaac. "I have to return to my regiment tomorrow. Don't do anything stupid, okay?"

Chapter Twenty-nine
April 1862

"Hand me that spoke shave, boy." Abraham pointed to the bench. Wagon wheels, shutters, tables, and wood scraps filled the workshop beside the barn.

Isaac handed him the tool. Abraham pulled the shave over the stock, shaping it to fit the rounded hole in the wheel.

"Has Mr. Day been teaching you about fixing wheels?"

"Some," Isaac said. "Mostly he learned me how to work the lathe and do fancy work, relief carvings and such."

"You doing that?" Abraham gave a low whistle as he straightened. "He must think you're mighty good. That's work that takes a keen eye and a steady hand." He brushed away shavings and held the spoke to the hole. "Needs just a mite bit more." Abraham clamped the spoke in the vice and trimmed off the excess wood.

Isaac returned to the dovetail joint he was cutting for a drawer front. The chest of drawers had come from Danville in need of repair, work Massa McConnell had arranged for before he took ill. "Pa," he said, nudging the chisel into the board, "do you recollect last summer, you said something about having a deal with Massa McConnell?"

"I remembers." Abraham spit a stream of tobacco juice into the dirt.

"Well, Massa McConnell, he's laid up now. Henry says maybe he'll get better, or maybe he won't. What will that do to your deal?"

"Hadn't thought none about that." Abraham tapped the workbench with the handle of the spoke shave. "Guess I needs to have me a talk with Massa Patrick."

"You gonna tell me?"

"Tell you what?" He spit again.

"About the deal, Pa."

"Been saving that part." Abraham set the shave on his workbench. "It was to be a surprise, but I 'spect, what with all that's going on, it's time you knew." He flipped over a wooden bucket with his boot. "Set on down." He lowered his voice. "Deal's just this; I gets paid for the work I do and Massa McConnell, he keeps that money, 'cept he sets aside some so's I can buy your freedom."

"My freedom? You mean papers, I'll be having papers?" Isaac sat on the edge of his seat. "How soon, Pa?"

"Best I can figure, you's about paid for. Just need to finish up this here job and I has what me and Massa agreed to. Tempie comes next—"

"For certain?" Isaac jumped to his feet. "Pa, you know what that means? I can go to Philadelphia. Raleigh, she'll look at me and she won't be seeing no slave." He grabbed Abraham's shirtsleeve. "When's you gonna talk to Massa Patrick?"

"I expects I ought to be having that talk real soon," Abraham said, "seeing's how Massa McConnell is laid up. I'll let you know. Now, get that drawer finished—it's your ticket on that freedom train."

* * *

"Do tell? Well then, come in, Abraham. Have a seat here next to the bed and tell my father all about that."

Morgan stirred at the commotion. First Patrick's voice, then Abraham came into view beside the bed. He seemed confused.

"I insist," Patrick said. "Have a seat."

Abraham disappeared from sight as he sat.

"Go on, tell him," Patrick said. "Tell him just like you told me."

"Uh, Massa McConnell, sir, this here's Abraham. I come to speak with you about our deal. You know, about the money?"

Yes, he remembered. Morgan strained to turn his head.

"Well, sir, after I finishes this last job, I figures I has the money to be buying Isaac's freedom, like we agreed."

Yes, Abraham had been close, very close. But what was Patrick up to?

"Did he answer you?" Patrick said. "Well? Did he say anything about a deal?"

"Massa Patrick, he can't . . ."

"Because there is no deal and there never was. See for yourself,

Father doesn't acknowledge any such thing. Sounds like you're trying to take advantage of a helpless invalid. Now go finish that job, and be neat about it, and maybe you'll avoid a whipping—this time."

"Massa, please, four years I been saving . . ."

"This discussion is over. Get back to work."

No . . . wait. Morgan strained to raise his hand in protest. His fingers bent. The arm trembled. Patrick was wrong . . . What was Abraham to think? He'd given his word, and now his own son mocked the honor of that word. Lord, give him the strength to answer . . .

"And, Abraham, we will not speak of this to anyone. Am I quite clear?"

Sweat beaded on Morgan's brow. His quivering right hand moved slowly across his chest.

* * *

Florence dropped the bread dough on the table and punched it down, her hands cloaked in floury white gloves.

Isaac pulled a stool beside the fire. He lifted the lid on the blackened iron pot and poked at the ribs simmering within. Their aroma filled the cabin. "They're near done, Mama. Might could use a bit more garlic, though. You got any?"

"There, on the table." She pointed with her elbow. "You seen your pa?"

"He mentioned something about talking to Massa Patrick on business. Ain't seen him since."

Joseph scurried through the open door, followed by one of the field slaves, a boy around seven. "We caught us a green snake, Mama." He held up the slender green reptile for her to examine.

"Not now, Joseph," Florence said. "I has dinner to fix—and I done told you, don't be bringing critters in here where I'm fixing food, lessen you wants me to cook 'em."

Joseph gave Isaac a sly smile, then turned to his companion. "We can find Tempie, or maybe your sister, and scare 'em good." The boys disappeared into the barnyard.

"Mama," Isaac said. "Is something bothering Tempie? She's been mighty quiet."

"That child's fine, but you seen how she's filling out? I 'spect she's coming of age. That can start a girl to acting peculiar."

Jeff Andrews

Florence smiled. "Could be she's working on a heartbreak, too. She ain't seen that Cato boy for many a week."

Heartbreak? Isaac winced. That sure sounded familiar . . .

Abraham walked through the doorway and tossed his hat on the table. He glanced at Isaac.

"Supper be ready in a bit," Florence said. "Did you get your business straightened out with Massa Patrick?" She wiped her hands on her apron.

"Some." He turned to Isaac and lowered his voice. "Word is, there's runners coming through tonight."

"How many, Pa?"

"Looks to be two. After supper I'll mosey down by the quarters and round up some vittles for them."

"Anything you need me to get?"

"Gather what you can from here, foodstuffs, mostly—and don't forget the pepper. I'll have Lilly cook up some dodgers."

"Pa," Isaac asked. "Did you talk to Massa Patrick?"

Abraham's shoulders sagged. "Come along, I need some help in the barn." Abraham gave Florence a quick kiss and headed out the door. Isaac hurried to catch up. Abraham didn't speak until they rounded the barn.

"I didn't want to say nothing where your mama could hear, she's worried enough about that sister of yours . . ." He pulled Isaac around the corner, then peered into the barnyard, as if to see if they had been followed. Apparently satisfied, Abraham turned Isaac to face him. "There ain't no easy way to say this, boy, so I reckon I gots to tell you straight. Massa Patrick said there weren't no deal, never was. I can't prove nothing different since Massa McConnell took ill and can't talk no more." He sighed. "It breaks my heart, son. I been praying on your jubilation day from the time you was born. That Massa Patrick, he sure enough ain't the man his papa is."

His deal . . . gone? Isaac steadied himself. What about dreams of Raleigh and Philadelphia? He slammed his fist against the barn. "He can't do that, Pa, it ain't fair . . ." He started toward the big house.

Abraham grabbed him by the shoulders. "Boy, ain't nothing fair when you's a slave."

"Henry won't let this happen. He'll fix it." Isaac struggled in his father's grasp.

176

"Henry ain't here," Abraham said. "It's done. Let it be." He slowly released his grip.

Isaac closed his eyes. His pa was right. Henry couldn't help—and Patrick wouldn't. He took a deep breath. "Guess I'll speak to Henry next time he's home from the war."

"You do that," Abraham said. "And you keep quiet about this—don't be upsetting your mama none. Now, get on and fetch them vittles."

* * *

The moon cast a shimmering veil over the barnyard as Isaac crouched beside the cookhouse. Even the McConnells would look suspiciously on anyone out and about at that hour. He waited for a cloud to drift in front of the moon, then darted to the shadows along the path leading to the slave quarters. Once away from the main house, he hurried down the path until he reached the semicircle of small cabins. The glow of the campfire danced against the rough-hewn walls.

Lilly looked up from her cooking and waved. "Isaac, come set next to your Aunt Lilly." She patted the log.

Isaac settled beside his aunt, tucking his gunnysack between his feet.

"Not so fast, boy. You hold that open. Lilly's got herself a mess of dodgers for them that's running." She pulled a cast iron pot from the fire and dumped its contents into the sack.

The aroma of the freshly baked corn bread filled the air. "My mouth's watering just smelling them," Isaac said, then he pointed toward the river. "Any word?"

She leaned close and whispered, "Wind's from the south. You watch yourself. There's riders down by the creek—pattyrollers, most likely."

"Is Pa around?"

"He come by. Said you's to meet him by the bridge on the post road."

"He say when?"

"Midnight, so it's time you be leaving. You want some 'pone?" Lilly pulled a skillet from the fire. She poked at the cornbread, then dropped one of the steaming biscuits into Isaac's outstretched hand. He tossed the bread from hand to hand, letting it cool.

"You hear anything about them runners, Aunt Lilly?"

"Word from Johnston's slaves is there's two, a father and son. They's coming up from North Carolina."

Banjo slipped in beside Isaac, whistling through his teeth as he tried to catch his breath. "Clancy and another one been riding the post road. I seen 'em go by twice. Ain't no mistake, they's looking."

"I'd best get out there and warn Pa. He'll be waiting. You figure it's midnight?"

Banjo studied the sky. "Moon's moved a fair piece. I reckon it's close enough."

Isaac grabbed his sack, kissed Lilly on the cheek, then slipped through the fence and headed down the lane.

* * *

"You're helping those runaways, aren't you?" A soft voice whispered from the darkened tree line.

Isaac stepped back and crouched, facing the intruder.

She stepped from the shadows, her head covered in a floppy slouch hat. She wore trousers with the cuffs rolled up above her ankles.

"Miss Polly? Is that you? You oughtn't be out here."

"Hush," she replied. "I'm dressed for the woodlands and I aim to help those who are running."

"What makes you think anybody's running?"

Polly pointed to the gunnysack. "Are you going out to feed the hogs?"

"They's just vittles," Isaac said. "Aunt Lilly fixed 'em for me."

"So, your mama's the cook, yet you wander down to the slave quarters in the middle of the night to fetch a sack of vittles?"

"Miss Polly, there's danger here about. You don't know nothing about what's going on. If'n you was to get hurt, Massa McConnell, he'd most likely lay the whip on Isaac, maybe worse."

"Papa doesn't hold with whipping our slaves," she said.

"That might be true, Miss Polly," Isaac replied, glancing about for signs of danger. "But his daughter never runned off in the middle of the night before to shepherd no runaways."

"You have to let me help." Polly tugged at Isaac's sleeves. "Please."

"This ain't no game, Miss Polly. Besides, you's a white woman, and a slave owner. Ain't no place for your kind out here."

"I am a white woman, but I do not own slaves, nor do I hold with that practice." She placed her hands on her hips. "I've read the abolitionist pamphlets, and they're correct. No man has the right to own another."

"That's all well and good, Miss Polly," Isaac held up his hands, "but this here is different. There ain't no pamphlets out here and death's waiting on them what ain't careful."

"I insist, and that's that." She folded her arms across her chest.

* * *

Isaac ducked into the woods as two riders galloped past on the farm lane. Cautiously, he peered around the trunk of the tree that shielded them, then held up his hand. "This here's as far as you go, Miss Polly. Can you make like a night owl?"

She lay beside him, dirt smeared across her cheek. "You mean like this?" She cupped her hands. A plaintive moan drifted across the fields.

Isaac recoiled. "Where'd you learn that?"

"You and Henry would be surprised at what I've learned from watching the two of you."

Isaac shook his head. "For sure, you done a heap more sneaking around in these woods than we knowed about. What else you seen?"

Polly smiled and looked away.

Isaac stared at her a moment, then shrugged. "Listen, you stay here and keep hidden. You see them riders, you give that owl call, but not so's you bring no attention to yourself, hear?"

"Yes, just like a sentry." Polly smiled. "I will do that."

"You be careful, Miss Polly."

"And you, Isaac. I'll not let you down."

* * *

Isaac crawled to the edge of the field. No sign of the riders. He cradled the gunny sack in the crook of his arm, took a deep breath, and dashed across the moonlit pasture to the forest on the far side. Safely within the shadows once more, he stopped and caught his breath, then snuck through the tangled thicket to a small stream. He followed the stream to a bridge that crossed the post road, ducked behind a tree, and listened. Then he cupped his hands and whistled. Somewhere to his front, a whippoorwill's call answered. Isaac grabbed his sack and crept to the meeting spot.

"Any trouble, boy?" Abraham asked.

"There was pattyrollers on the post road headed west," Isaac replied. "Banjo says they been riding back and forth all night."

"That they has," Abraham said. "I seen 'em twice. Is that the foodstuff?" He pointed to the sack.

Isaac nodded. "Where's them runners?"

"Right here." Abraham lifted a pine bough that leaned against the small wooden bridge. A man and a small boy peered out.

"Hey there." Isaac held out his hand. "Where's you headed?"

"Petersburg," the man replied. He glanced at Isaac's extended hand, but didn't take it. "We has relatives there. They's free and they says they can hide us, maybe get us down river behind them Yankee lines. Folks is saying, you gets to Hampton, it'll be jubilation time."

Isaac dropped his hand. "Where's you coming from?"

"North Carolina, down by Yanceyville."

"Yanceyville?" A sudden shiver ran up Isaac's neck. "Did you happen to know a girl by the name of Raleigh? She works for Mr. Patterson."

"Sure," the man replied. "Everybody down that way knows Raleigh. She teached our children a Bible class last summer, out behind the white folk's church. But some of them whites, they didn't hanker none to nigras getting the book learning, so they made her stop."

Isaac's stomach knotted.

"You best be moving along," Abraham said. "Them pattyrollers will be back this way before long, so you needs to put some distance between you and that road. These here supplies will last you four, five days." He hefted the bag, then cocked an eyebrow and turned toward Isaac.

Isaac straightened and faced his father. He cleared his throat. "Pa, there's food there for three. Tell Mama I loves her. Tell Joseph and Tempie too."

Abraham slowly shook his head. "Boy, it ain't your time . . ."

"It weren't yesterday," Isaac said, "but things done changed."

"You's gonna break you mama's heart."

"Life ain't getting no easier on that farm. She'll understand."

"There be danger out there: dogs, pattyrollers, bad folks to do you harm . . ."

"Pa, I knows what to do." Isaac smiled. "You done taught me."

Abraham grabbed Isaac by the shoulders. "Are you sure, boy?"

Isaac nodded. "It's time I be chasing my own dream. When I gets to Philadelphia, I'll write. Miss Polly, she'll read it for you."

A distant owl called out across the woodlot.

"Down!" Isaac pushed Abraham to the ground. In a moment, horse's hoofs pounded the packed dirt road, then crossed the bridge and faded in the distance.

"That was too close, boy. How'd you know?"

Isaac stood, brushing off the leaves. "We has us a friend."

Abraham raised his eyebrow.

Isaac shook his head and smiled. "Best you don't know."

Abraham held him at arm's length. "Lord be with you, boy. That freedom star will guide you true." He squeezed Isaac's arms, then let go and slipped across the bridge.

Placing a finger to his lips, Isaac turned to the other runaways. "We needs to be real quiet."

Moving slowly so as not to splash, they walked down the middle of the creek for an hour or more, until they arrived at a stand of pines. "We's past where them pattyrollers will be looking," Isaac whispered, "least ways tonight. If we gets under them pines, we'll be well hidden." He pointed to the stream. "Staying in the creek like we done, them dogs'll have trouble picking up our scent."

"Much obliged," the man said. "Me and the boy, we can use some rest."

"Make your beds from that there pine straw," Isaac replied. "I'll keep watch."

"Bless you," the man said. He took his young boy by the hand and started up the draw.

"Hey," Isaac whispered, "What does they call you?"

"I's Moses," the man replied. "This here's my boy, Carter Louis."

Isaac nodded as he settled against a tree where he had a clear view upstream.

Chapter Thirty
April 1862

The cookhouse door flew open. "Outside now," an angry voice demanded.

Was that Massa Patrick yelling? Florence bolted upright in bed and shook Abraham. "Wake up. There's trouble brewing."

Abraham grunted and rolled over. Florence poked him again then climbed out of bed. "Isaac, Joseph, Tempie, y'all get down here," she called to the loft. "Massa Patrick wants us all outside."

Florence wrapped a shawl around her shoulders and stepped onto the porch. Abraham joined her, tying his britches with a rope belt and rubbing his eyes. A hint of pink sliced the eastern sky.

Slaves filled the barnyard, some still in nightshirts. Lilly and Banjo stumbled past. Their faces reflected fear and confusion. Crying children clung tightly to their mothers. Sean O'Farrell held a lantern and directed people to their places.

Patrick paced like a bantam rooster. He drew a pistol and fired into the air. "Get over here. All of you, line up now."

Florence flinched. What had him all riled? Must be something terrible bad. She gathered Tempie and Joseph and they took their place in the back row beside Abraham. "Where's Isaac?" She whispered to Tempie.

Abraham put a finger to his lips and hushed her.

"Appears we have us a problem," Patrick said, pacing in front of the gathering. "Seems like some runaways crossed our land, and rumor has it, McConnell slaves were out giving them aid. O'Farrell, do you have a count?"

"Aye, that I do, sir."

"Well . . . ?"

"We'd be missing but one slave, sir."

"And who would that be?"

Sean hesitated. His glanced at Florence, then quickly looked away. "That would be Isaac, sir."

"Isaac?" Florence cried. She turned to Abraham. "Where's my boy? Where's he at?" She grabbed his shirt. Abraham pulled her close. Joseph clutched her skirts.

"So, he's a good boy, he'll never run?" Patrick gazed at the dawn sky. "O'Farrell, send them to the fields. Looks like we'll get an extra hour's work today."

Slaves drifted quietly toward the tobacco fields.

Patrick approached Abraham. "Where were you last night?"

Abraham eased Florence behind him.

Patrick holstered his pistol and yanked Joseph from Florence's side. He turned the boy's face toward him. "This cuffy could fetch three hundred dollars, maybe more . . ."

Florence gasped.

Abraham looked at her, his eyes filled with terror. "I was in the woods, sir."

"Helping the runaways?"

"Y-yes sir."

"And Isaac?"

"He was there too, Massa Patrick."

Patrick released Joseph. He wagged a finger in Abraham's face. "I'll deal with you later." He pointed to Florence. "Breakfast in thirty minutes." He turned on his heel and marched toward the house.

Florence grabbed Abraham by his shirt. "Why didn't you tell me my boy was running?"

"He done surprised me with that last night. I was gonna tell you this morning soon as you woke."

Joseph tightly clutched his mother. "Mama, Them dogs ain't gonna get Isaac, is they?"

"He'll be fine." Florence wiped her tears. "Ain't no dog, nor no pattyroller, can catch him in them woods." She put her arm around Joseph and leaned into Abraham. Tempie hesitated, then slowly slipped her arms around Florence too.

* * *

"See them railroad tracks?" Isaac lay next to Moses, pointing to a slight rise across the open field. "They's the Richmond and Danville line. If we stays to the woods and follows them tracks, in two days we'll be at Burkeville."

"Then is we safe?" Moses said.

"Nigras ain't safe nowhere," Isaac replied, "'cepting up north. These rails cross the Petersburg line in Burkeville. We follows that and, Lord willing, we'll be to Petersburg in three, four days."

"Me and Carter Louis, we's mighty beholding to ya, Isaac."

"Never mind that," Isaac said. "Soon as it's dark, we needs to get a move on. There's clouds rolling up from the south—could mean rain. That'll be good for hiding."

Isaac waved for Moses to follow as he slipped back into the forest to the stand of pines where Carter Louis waited with their supplies. Isaac sat beside a tree and fished a corndodger out of his sack. He popped it in his mouth, chewing slowly. A soft rain rustled the treetops.

"How much longer?" Moses hunkered next to Isaac and ate as well.

"Another hour. Remember, we stay close, move together. If we runs separate, them pattyrollers has three chances to see us. We runs together, they ain't got but one."

"How'd you learn so much about this here underground railroading?" Moses stared at Isaac. "You ever run before?"

Isaac shook his head. "No, but I listened good when Pa told others what to do. How's that boy of yours holding up?"

"Oh, he'll make it," Moses said. "He's scared, but I reckon we all is."

Along with the rain came a chill. Isaac pulled his shirt tight. It was going to be a cold night. Moses was scared. Isaac was too; he had been ever since the Yanceyville jail, but there was no turning back . . .

"What's that?" Moses pointed toward the tracks.

Isaac strained to hear. "Train's coming."

"How about we hops one them boxcars and save some walking?" Moses said.

Isaac shook his head. "Too dangerous. If that brakeman sees you, he'll stop the train. There could be poor whites riding them boxcars too, and they'll turn you in for a free meal. We'd best stick to the woods."

They followed a creek, pushing through brambles and undergrowth, pausing to listen, then trudging on again. The patter of rain masked their noise. After what seemed like an hour, Isaac stopped and held up his hand. "This here creek's bending south. Rest, then we need to head north, back toward them tracks." The three sat beside a large tree and shared a few dodgers.

"My feet's hurting." Carter Louis said, rubbing his foot.

"Them shoes is all wet," Isaac whispered to Moses. "See if they's rubbing. He might be better off barefoot."

Moses removed the shoes and checked the boy's feet.

After they had rested, Isaac crawled to the edge of the forest and peered across an open field. Nothing stirred. He motioned for Moses and the boy. "You see them woods yonder? Run hard, stay low, and don't make no sound. You ready?"

Moses nodded.

"Be quick about it." Crouching low, Isaac took off running. Mud clung to his feet as he slogged across the plowed field. Carter Louis stumbled, landing on his face in the muck. Moses yanked him to his feet and hurried him along. Once they reached the tree line, Isaac held up his hand. "Rest here. I'll be right back."

He crept to the far end of the field, straining to hear any sound. Off to his right, telegraph poles silhouetted against the gray sky traced the railroad tracks they would follow. Silently, Isaac retreated into the shadows and rejoined Moses and the boy. He knelt, pointing toward the tracks. "Them tracks is running to the north. We's right where we needs to be." Isaac forced a smile as he reached for his wooden star. His hand brushed across a wet, empty shirt. He turned to Moses. "Is that boy all right?"

"I reckon," Moses replied.

"Good. We'd best head north by east, up through them woods," Isaac said. "I can't see no stars, but we'll be fine following them tracks. We'll bed down on the other side."

They moved silently, except for the occasional whimpers when Carter Louis stubbed his bare feet on roots or sharp twigs.

* * *

"It's been two days," Florence said. "Do you think he's safe?" She chopped off a chicken leg, rolled it in corn batter, and set it in the skillet. The oil sizzled.

"That boy knows them woods," Abraham replied. "He knows about running too—I learned him good." Abraham set his elbows on the table and rested his head in his hands.

Florence studied her husband. The man was tired. Those eyes, they'd lost their sparkle. Was he blaming himself? It wasn't his doing. Isaac had made his own decision.

"The boy'll be fine," she said. She wiped her hands on her apron, then kneaded Abraham's shoulders. "Let it go. He's off to Petersburg, or Hampton, maybe even Philadelphia. We'll get word by and by."

Tempie wandered in and took a seat by the fire. "Any word, Mama?" She poked the coals.

"No word," Florence said. "It means he's safe. The Lord will provide." That poor child wasn't back to her old self, at least not all the way, but she was coming around. Florence smiled. She must be over that Cato boy by now. It was about time.

"Pa?" Joseph dragged a stick behind him as he entered. He swatted the side of the door, then tapped the edge of the table before settling onto the bench. "Is dinner ready, Mama?"

"In a bit. You looking for you Pa?"

"Massa Patrick, he said could Pa come see him. Something about business."

"Must be he's hired me out again," Abraham said. "He's been mighty quiet. You reckon he's over that fit he tied his self into?"

Florence shrugged and returned to her cooking.

Abraham stretched. "Well, I'd best go see what he wants, but I'll be thinking hard on that fried chicken." He pointed to the skillet and smiled. "I'm feeling mighty hungry."

That smile was the first she'd seen from him since their son departed.

"I'll be back shortly." He closed the door behind him.

"Joseph," Florence said, pointing to the bucket beside the door. "Take that pail and fetch me some water, then get more firewood."

Joseph grabbed the pail and skipped out the door.

"Tempie, you finish getting everything cleaned up at the big house?"

"Yes, Mama."

"Good, then check that 'pone and tell me if'n it's done."

Something crashed on the porch, then Joseph rushed through the door, waving his arms. "Mama, Mama they has Pa, they has Pa!"

"Who has Pa? What's you talking about?" Florence wiped her hands on her apron as she raced out the door. Two horses hitched to a buckboard wagon stood beside the big house. Near the rear of the wagon, Abraham struggled with two men who were trying to hold him down. His hands were tied and Big Jim knelt trussing his feet. Patrick stood on the porch, hands on his hips.

Florence ran to her husband, grabbing at the men who held him. "Leave my man be."

One of the men turned and shoved her hard to the ground.

Clancy?

Abraham struggled, but he couldn't escape.

Joseph and Tempie rushed to Florence's side and huddled with her on the ground. She glared at Patrick. "What's this you's doing, Patrick McConnell?"

"Your husband has become what we refer to in business as a liability. It's time I cut my losses."

"Y-you's selling my Abraham? You can't do that, he belongs to Massa McConnell." Florence started to rise, then Clancy cocked his fist as though to strike her. She retreated, clutching her children as she dropped onto the hard-packed dirt.

"I'm sorry, Florence, but Abraham has caused me too many problems. I can put an end to those problems now, or later I might need to find buyers for these two." Patrick pointed at Joseph and Tempie.

"Florence, I's coming back, I's coming back . . . ." Abraham called as the two men heaved him into the wagon.

"Sure, you'll be back," Patrick said. "After you've picked all the cotton in Mississippi. Give my regards to Natchez." He saluted with his riding crop, then turned and strolled into the house.

"I loves you, Florence. Don't you fret," Abraham called. "I'll be back."

She rose to her knees as the wagon lurched forward. "I loves you, Abraham. I'll be here waiting."

Chapter Thirty-one
April 1862

"Stay close and keep to the shadows." Isaac surveyed the clearing, then signaled Moses and Carter Louis to follow him. He darted across the muddy field to a split rail fence that wormed along the crest of the open ground. Crouching beside the fence, Isaac motioned for the others to get down.

"The moon's too bright; we's casting shadows. This is a bad night for running." Isaac pointed. "Them tracks bend to the east and into them woods yonder. Once we's in the woods we'd best hold up for the night." He slowly shook his head. "I ain't got good feelings about us being out here tonight."

The field appeared to be a half-mile across. At the north end they came to a gully that ran into the forest and toward the tracks. "We'll follow this," Isaac said.

"The boy's feet is real bad," Moses said, "and he's cut up all over from last night. I don't reckon he can go much further."

Isaac glanced at the boy. "Another hour, then we'll bed down. Can you make it?"

Carter Louis nodded.

"Come on, then." Isaac stayed low and stepped carefully to keep from snapping twigs. The gully ran along a dirt road, parallel to the railroad tracks. Isaac held up a hand. They crouched and listened. He pointed in the direction they had come. "Train. It's running east. Be here within the quarter hour. We'd best keep moving."

"I can't." Carter Louis sat and grabbed his foot. He began to cry.

"The boy's done for tonight, Isaac. Can't we hold up?" Moses' face showed a mix of frustration and fear.

"Stay here," Isaac said. "I's gonna scout ahead, maybe find us a hiding place away from that road." He slipped away. After a quarter mile, the ditch turned and cut under the road. Logs supported a double bridge, wagon road on one side, railroad on the other—a good hideout. The train drew closer as he scurried back to Moses and his son.

"I can't make it, Isaac. Can't walk none." Tears streaked Carter Louis's cheeks.

Isaac tugged the boy's sleeve. "A quarter mile—you can make it."

"I can't . . ."

Moses placed his hand on Isaac's arm. "You go on ahead. We'll catch up tomorrow."

"No." Isaac replied. "We stick together. Come on, we'll take the road. It ain't that far. We'll take turns carrying the boy." Isaac scooped Carter Louis into his arms and clambered up the bank. Moses followed close behind.

The two men walked side by side along the dirt road, Carter Louis in Isaac's arms. The chugging of the approaching steam engine drowned out all other sounds. Isaac and Moses crouched in the ditch as the train rounded a bend and its headlamp swept the road with a wide beam of yellow light. The engine throttled down for the curved track ahead, spewing smoke and sparks from its stack. Boxcars clattered and swayed, many with doors open on both sides.

Isaac pointed toward the cars rumbling past. "You still want to ride that train?"

"You said it was too dangerous—"

"The boy ain't walking none for a few days no how. Better risking the train than risking them woods and pattyrollers. Get on up in that boxcar. I'll pass him to you."

Moses raced to the track. He paced himself and jumped, landing easily in the open doorway. Isaac trotted alongside carrying the boy. His stride placed him beside the open door.

"Riders!" Moses pointed at the road behind Isaac.

Barking dogs broke the monotony of wheels clattering on the tracks. The train began to pick up speed. Isaac ran harder.

Moses reached out with one hand, holding the door handle with the other. "Run. They sees you. Hurry!" Moses leaned out as far as his arms would allow.

A stone bridge loomed ahead. It had to be now! "Moses!" Isaac lunged, tossing the boy forward. Moses caught Carter Louis by the arm and swung him into the open door as Isaac stumbled and collapsed beside the tracks.

* * *

Florence sat in her rocker on the porch, the sewing in her lap untouched. Tears moistened her eyes. Spring air carried a scent of honeysuckle and newly turned earth. She sighed. Abraham would commence to speechifying on such a pretty day, but words never came as easily to her. Still, it was sure enough a day the Lord had made, and Abraham would be expecting her to find the joy. She closed her eyes. In her mind, his tall, angular frame ambled across the barnyard, broad-brimmed hat cocked to one side. Clasping her arms, Florence hugged herself tightly. "Lord, I prays You'll watch over my man, keep him safe, and when it be Your time, You bring him on home to Florence . . . and Lord, don't mean to be taking up all Your time, but if it ain't no bother, could You watch over that boy, Isaac too? Thank you Lord."

She took a deep breath and opened her eyes. Time to get the supper on. Florence rolled up her mending and went inside.

Tempie sat by the fire, poking at the coals.

"Girl, you cooking or dreaming?"

"Sorry Mama. You ready for me to put on that ham roast?"

"This be as good a time as any, but first you rinse it down real good and get off all that salt, you hear?"

Something different caught Florence's eye as Tempie began preparing the meat. What had changed? Was she getting thick around the middle? Yes, and not like a little girl what's growing up. Oh Lord, she has her a baby in there—and she don't want her mama to know. It must be Cato's. Florence looked up and whispered, "Lord, I got one more for You to keep an eye on . . ."

She laid scallions on the chopping board. This early in the season, choices for greens were few.

"Miss Florence? You in there?" Banjo had taken over chores around the barns after the departure of Isaac and Abraham. He usually found his way to the cookhouse around suppertime.

"Evening, Banjo. You staying for supper? Be ready once the big house gets fed."

He stood in the doorway, twisting his hat in his hand.

"If'n it's food you's wanting, you's gonna have to wait."

"Y-your boy, Florence." Banjo nodded toward the yard. "He's home."

She dropped the knife and ran to the porch, pushing Banjo aside. A man on a tall black mare rode slowly into the barnyard. Stumbling behind him was a bloodied figure bound at the wrists and dragged by a rope.

"Tie him to that tree yonder." Patrick walked across the porch, pointing with his riding crop. "O'Farrell, bring the whip."

Florence ran to Isaac's side, catching him as he staggered. "Massa, please, don't be whipping my boy. He ain't gonna run no more, he'll be good . . ."

Patrick pushed Florence aside and grabbed the rope that bound Isaac's wrists. He tossed the free end over a limb and pulled hard. Isaac rose up on his toes. Patrick tied off the line, then ripped the shirt from Isaac's back. "O'Farrell, twenty lashes, hard and slow."

Sean O'Farrell looked quickly at Florence, then turned to Patrick. "The boy don't need a whipping, sir. Look at him, he's all used up."

"It's for his own good, O'Farrell. Lay them on."

"I'll not do it." Sean threw the whip to the ground. "'Tis the devil's work. I'll not take part."

"Damn it, O'Farrell, the devil's got no play here. That slave needs the lesson. Get out of my way . . ." Patrick pushed Sean aside and grabbed the whip. He drew back and cracked the lash across Isaac's back. Isaac twisted in pain, but did not cry out. Patrick landed another blow on the bare, bleeding back. Isaac slumped, his weight hanging on his bound and outstretched arms.

Florence lunged, grabbing Patrick's arm. "You sells my man, then you whips my boy? What's got hold of you, Patrick McConnell?"

Patrick pushed her aside. "I don't expect you to understand, but good discipline is a necessary part of business."

"I understands this, Massa Patrick, when you was a baby, was me that cleaned your bottom and was my teat you suckled. When you cried out, was me rocked you back to sleep."

Patrick hesitated. Finally, he said, "I need him in the fields tomorrow. He'll pay me back for the days I lost." He tossed the whip down, turned on his heel, and retreated into the house.

"Help me carry him to the cookhouse, will you, Mr. Sean?" Florence supported Isaac while Sean cut the ropes. Together, they carried Isaac to the cookhouse and laid him face down on the bed. "Thank you, Mr. Sean, and don't you fret none, he'll be in the fields come morning."

"I'll do my best to go easy on him," Sean said as he started out the door.

Florence tended to the lashes across Isaac's back and the rope burns on his wrists. Isaac soon drifted to sleep. After several hours he stirred, then slowly pulled himself around and sat on the edge of the bed rubbing his face. He stretched, then flinched at the apparent pain.

"Soup?" Florence held out a bowl.

Isaac accepted the vessel without speaking. He appeared groggy, unsure of his surroundings. As he sipped, he looked at Florence. "You said something about Pa?"

She sat beside him and took the bowl, setting it on the floor, then grasped his hand. "After you left, Massa Patrick said your pa was a troublemaker. He sold him to slave traders what took him south to Mississippi."

Isaac stared at her as though trying to comprehend what he'd just heard, then he slumped forward, leaned his elbows on his knees, and rested his head in his hands. "I shouldn't a run. It's my fault." His shoulders heaved as a sob escaped him. "If'n I'd stayed put, Pa'd still be here."

"Hush. Don't be troubling yourself with that nonsense," Florence said. "Your pa, he'll be back, he promised. We just has to be patient."

Isaac wiped his eyes with the sleeve of his tattered shirt, then looked straight at Florence and smiled. "I'll be right here with you, Mama." He squeezed her hand. "I ain't running no more."

Chapter Thirty-two
May 1862

Iron wheels clacked a monotonous rhythm as the train chugged across the narrow James River bridge. Henry stood in the boxcar's open doorway, fighting clouds of thick smoke from the engine's stack. To the west, crimson streaks painted the evening horizon. "I'm beginning to think this whole war's nothing but a rumor," he said. "We've been soldiering better than a year and we haven't fought one damned battle."

"We're in Armistead's brigade now," Townsend replied, swaying with the motion of the train. "Folks is saying he's one of Longstreet's favorites. If anybody can find the action, he can."

"I sure hope you're right," Henry said. "We've been from Richmond to Jamestown, across to Hampton, down to North Carolina, over to Petersburg, and now back to Richmond. I figured by now we'd be laying siege to Washington." He pointed out the right side of the car. "Look yonder. There's the Tredegar Iron Works. They're the ones who forged our cannons."

Two short blasts from the train's whistle announced their arrival in Richmond. Henry braced against the door. The car lurched. Soldiers tumbled over one another as the engine came to a halt and a blast of steam marked the end of their journey.

"Everybody out. Let's go," the lieutenant yelled. "Sergeants, form your platoons."

Inside the crowded boxcars, men in butternut and gray pushed, cursed, and fought to reach the open doors. Henry grabbed his bedroll and musket and jumped from the car. Sergeants barked commands, gradually bringing order out of the chaotic mob that gathered along the siding.

Captain Claiborne stepped to the front of the formation. "At ease, gentlemen. We've been a long time waiting to mix it up with the Yankee invaders, but that's fixing to change." He pointed toward the northeast. "McClellan has two corps facing us south of the Chickahominy, perhaps more troops north of the river. I can't give you particulars, least ways not yet, but I can tell you this; we come to Richmond to fight, and we'll be up to our necks in Yankees soon enough."

A raucous cheer rose from the formation as the soldiers pumped their fists and waved their caps.

The captain raised his hands, silencing the men. "There's a storm coming," he said. "Keep your powder dry. Lieutenant, take charge and move the men to the bivouac."

"Yes sir." The lieutenant saluted, then turned and faced the company. "Right face. Shoulder, arms. At the route step, march."

Company K turned east on Cary Street. Henry poked Townsend, pointing as they marched past the capital building. "Seems strange seeing those stars and bars flying where the old flag used to be."

Townsend nodded.

"Down there," Henry whispered, nudging Townsend as they marched past the Shockoe section of town. "Toward the river there's the best little tavern you'll ever see."

"You'd best forget that," Townsend said. "Didn't the Captain promise to put you in front of a firing squad next time?"

Henry laughed.

They marched east, following the James River until they reached a clearing along Gillies Creek. There, the lieutenant halted the company. "Fall out. Set up your fixings as best you can. We don't have any tenting, so get into them pines over yonder and build yourself some shelters. Try to stay dry."

Henry and Townsend followed their platoon into the stand of pines and dropped their bedrolls beside a tree. Henry glanced at the gray sky. "We'll be okay. The clouds appear to be breaking. I do believe we'll miss the rains."

* * *

Townsend held the rubber blanket over the small fire, protecting it from the downpour. "Glad we missed that rain, McConnell."

"That was yesterday. I don't recollect making any such predictions for this morning," Henry said. "Keep that fire lit while I get this cooking. At least we can enjoy some 'pone until we float away." He molded the corn meal into a ball and dropped it in the pan. The dough sounded a wet "plop" when it hit.

"Get some wood on that fire, Townsend, it ain't hot enough to warm soup."

"You want to show me where that dry wood might be, McConnell?"

"To hell with it." With a sigh, Henry dropped the pan in the mud. "I never seen such rains. You got any hardtack?"

Townsend passed Henry a cracker. The two huddled under the poncho while the downpour extinguished their small fire and filled the cold frying pan.

"Townsend, come morning this field will be a river. Maybe it's time we consider joining the navy."

* * *

Henry rolled into a puddle and awoke with a start. He flung caked mud from his face and scowled at the gray, rain-filled sky. "Tarnation. When's it going to end?" He poked Townsend. "Hey, wake up."

Groggily, Townsend peered from under the poncho. "You'd best be saying there's coffee on and bacon cooking."

"Our chances of finding a cup of coffee are about as good as our chances of getting a two week furlough," Henry replied. "How are we fixed for hardtack?"

"Got two left," Townsend said, handing Henry one of the rock hard crackers. "But we don't have so much as a pan of hot bacon grease to soften it in, so watch your grinders."

"Fourteenth Virginia, rise and shine. Formation in ten minutes." The sergeant wandered the camp, kicking at piles of wet blankets.

"Looks like we're moving out. It's about time." Henry said. "Maybe we'll finally have us a go at them Yankees." He rolled his blanket and grabbed his musket.

The Fourteenth marched to Gillies Creek, then stood in formation in the rain while another unit crossed the single narrow bridge.

Henry grabbed the sleeve of a passing noncommissioned officer. "Hey sergeant, can't we get moving? What's that outfit we're waiting on?"

"Longstreet's division. The general says his boys go first."

The Fourteenth waited. Some spread their ponchos and sat. Others leaned on their muskets or milled about, cursing the weather, cursing the Yankees, and quietly cursing the division ahead of them. Finally, word came to move out, followed by a muted grumble from the troops. Soldiers grabbed their gear and slogged across the narrow bridge to the Charles City Road, where they turned south and marched another mile or so, then halted. After several minutes, the colonel gave the order to stand easy. They would be waiting again. A groan went up from the formation.

Henry and the rest of the regiment settled beside the road. Some wrapped themselves in ponchos and attempted to sleep. Others gathered in clusters talking quietly. A few tried to write letters home or read. Henry and Townsend pulled out the poncho they shared, spread it on the ground, and sat.

As the day passed the rain slackened. Distant echoes of musketry and the thunder of artillery rumbled across the fields.

"Waiting, that's all we've been doing all the day long." Henry tossed a stone into a nearby puddle. "Ain't war grand?"

"From the sound of the guns, the Yankees can't be far." Townsend pointed toward the noise. "You think we'll be called up today?"

Henry shrugged. "I reckon General Armistead figures we haven't been tested in battle, so he's afraid to use us. All I want is one chance . . ."

"Hey, you scared, Henry?"

Henry looked at his friend, but didn't respond.

Twilight faded as the lieutenant finally called Company K to formation.

Henry grabbed his Enfield and joined the march through a stand of pines and into an open field. Mud tugged at his feet, sucking off his shoe as he raised his foot. He stopped to retrieve the shoe. Through the gathering darkness he could make out rows of tents. He nudged Townsend and pointed. "Look there, that outfit knows how to travel. We ain't seen a tent since Jamestown."

"Company, halt. Order, arms. Left, face," Lieutenant Bruce commanded. "Platoon sergeants take charge of your platoons and set the company in bivouac. Dismissed."

"You heard him," the sergeant said. "Time to bed down, and it appears we have us some tents tonight, so make yourselves to home. Reveille at four thirty. Dismissed."

Henry raced to the nearest tent, tossed his gear inside, and crawled in. Townsend threw his bedroll on the other side and clambered in beside him. "Who do you reckon set up all these tents?" Henry said. "It's not like the army to be so thoughtful."

"I expect it weren't our army what done it." Townsend held up a haversack he'd found in the tent. "Looky here." Stenciled across the flap were the words, "11ᵗʰ Maine USA."

"Now don't that beat all?" Henry said. "We're sleeping under canvas tonight, courtesy of Uncle Sam." He chuckled as he unrolled his blanket.

"Hey, would ya look at this," Townsend said. He pulled a bag of coffee from the haversack, followed by cans of meat and beans and a box of hardtack. "Tonight we'll eat like Billy Yanks, then we can sleep like 'em too."

They shared the cold rations, then Henry settled in for what promised to be a comfortable night. The occasional pop of musketry on the picket lines would not keep him from a sound sleep. He pulled his blanket around his shoulders, closed his eyes, and dreamed of hot coffee.

Several hours later, Henry awoke. He stretched and drew back the tent flap. Fog hung over the muddy field, while above, stars flickered in the blackness. To the east, hues of pink and pale blue painted the dawning sky. As he gazed upon the new day, something out in the field caught his eye. Long, dark—a pile of equipment, perhaps? Henry pulled on his brogans and crawled out of the tent.

The dark mound lay no more than fifteen feet away. Henry moved closer. A soldier? Must be he couldn't find a tent. Since Henry was already awake, perhaps the soldier would appreciate spending the hour or so before revelry under his blanket in the tent. He poked the man with his boot. "Hey, fella . . ." Suddenly, Henry gagged and turned away. Dawn's first glimmer revealed a bloated Yankee, most of his face blown away, festering in the muck of yesterday's battlefield.

He must go tell somebody. Shouldn't they dig a grave?

Henry started to call out, then caught himself as the early light revealed other forms through the mist. A wave of nausea swept over him. The field where he had enjoyed his night's rest held in its muddy furrows scores of enemy, now resting forever.

"Dead, all dead—and left to rot." He shook his head. "I don't reckon I have the stomach for this side of glory." Henry turned away.

* * *

A clutch of officers raced through the camp on horseback. The call went out to form for battle. It was impossible to ignore the now visible corpses half buried in the ooze of the plowed field. Henry took his post in the formation just as Colonel Hodges, the regimental commander, reined his horse in front of the unit.

The colonel raised his hat in the air. "Sons and patriots of Virginia, General Armistead sends his regards."

The regiment cheered.

The colonel put on his hat, then held up one hand, signaling for silence. "The general asks that we steel ourselves for the task at hand." Colonel Hodges pointed. "To the east, the enemy awaits. It is there our swords will quench their thirst for Yankee blood." He drew his sword and held it above him.

The soldiers cheered again, eagerly waving their muskets and kepis.

The colonel rested the blade of his sword on his shoulder until the cheering subsided, then continued. "We will not put out skirmishers. The undergrowth is too thick. Maintain your alignment and be certain of your targets before you fire. Companies F through K, form a line of battle from left to right. Companies A through E follow in column and be prepared to deploy on line and respond as required."

The officers saluted.

Henry leaned toward Townsend and whispered, "We're to the front . . ."

Captain Claiborne faced Company K and drew his sword. "Load in four times, do not prime, load," he commanded.

The company went through the manual by rote—charge cartridge, ram cartridge, shoulder arms.

The captain faced the colonel and saluted with his sword. "Company K formed and ready, sir."

Colonel Hodges returned his salute. When all companies had reported, the colonel stood in his stirrups and raised his sword. "Regiment, at the carry, route step, forward, march." On command, the drummers sounded a cadence and the front line companies stepped off.

"This is it, Henry." Townsend nodded toward their front. "That elephant's waiting up yonder. Come tonight, we'll still be eating Yankee food, but this time it'll be spoils we took in battle." He marched beside Henry. His eyes seemed to dart from tree to bush, as though searching for rattlesnakes in the dense undergrowth.

Henry's stomach twisted in knots. Was Townsend scared too?

The Fourteenth pushed into the thicket, clawing through tangles of vines and cat briars. The early morning light had yet to penetrate the dense canopy above, adding to the difficulty of keeping the formations aligned. To the right, the battle line bent toward their front. Henry poked Townsend and pointed. "If they stray out any further, they'll be masking our fires."

Muskets popped suddenly to their front. Someone had made contact. Smoke drifted through the dense forest.

"Halt!" The captain ordered. "Order, arms. Prime your weapons." The rattle of musketry mixed with the distant thunder of battle. Henry capped his Enfield and thumbed the hammer to full cock.

"First rank, take aim . . ."

Henry peered out to the front. Nothing but trees and thick underbrush. Aim at what? The captain must be getting edgy. He's seeing things . . .

"Fire!" A wall of flame belched from the line of muskets. "Second rank . . ." The soldiers in the rear hurried through the front rank and took aim. "Fire!"

The roar of muskets echoed through the dense thicket; a blanket of blue smoke spread throughout the forest. Bits of leaves sheared by the volleys fluttered to earth as an eerie stillness settled over the woods. Henry stood agape, the pounding of his heart drowning out any other sounds. Then, without warning, the forest to their direct front erupted in a thunderous blast. A line of jagged flames lashed out from the hazy underbrush. A soldier to Henry's left grabbed his face, blood spurting between his fingers, and crumpled to the ground. Another soldier down the line cried out and fell.

"Reload, fire at will!" The captain yelled.

Henry pulled a paper cartridge from his pouch and bit off the end, struggling to steady his trembling hand as he poured powder down the muzzle. He rammed the bullet home and tapped it twice with his ramrod, seating it tightly against the powder. Primer . . . don't forget the damned primer. He pulled a brass cap from his pouch and pushed it over the nipple under the hammer. Full cock. Can't see . . . nothing but smoke and brush . . .

Without aiming, he pointed his musket in the direction of the enemy and fired.

The captain stepped in front of their line, waving his sword. "Forward! Follow me." He pointed his sword at the enemy. The Yankees greeted their advance with a smattering of uncoordinated fire, then withdrew.

"Push them. Push forward, men." Captain Claiborne stepped over a wounded Yankee and fought his way through the mesh of wiry vines.

Henry ducked beneath a low branch, turning to pull his arm free of a tangle. When he faced to the front again the fallen soldier was at his feet. He was just a boy, couldn't be no more than sixteen. The wounded soldier stared at a dark puddle spreading across the front of his blue uniform, then looked up at Henry with pleading eyes. Henry hesitated, then looked away and pushed on.

They drove the Yankees through the thicket. Ahead, musket fire cracked sporadically.

"Halt!" Captain Claiborne ordered. "Hold and reform your line." The captain stood in front of the company, holding his sword by the hilt and the tip of the blade, indicating where the front rank should form.

"Fix bayonets."

"Prepare to charge."

Movement to the front. Henry strained to make it out.

"Gray . . . gray. They's Confederates," someone hollered. Nobody fired.

More commotion, clattering of equipment. Bayonets became visible through the brush. Henry nudged Townsend and pointed. "We're in for it now . . ."

Townsend rolled his eyes. "There's gonna be hell to pay, that's for sure." He wiped a hand across his sweat-stained face.

Captain Claiborne held the company at the ready, his sword in the air. "On my command . . ."

To their front, branches snapped as hundreds of footfalls trampled the undergrowth. Sweat dripped from Henry's cheeks. He held his musket at the ready. Leaves rustled with movement. Suddenly, the forest in front of them filled with Union blue.

"Fire!" The captain ordered.

The Yankee line disappeared in a cloud of smoke.

"Reload. Fire at will."

Henry grinned at Townsend as he fumbled for another round in his cartridge box. "Looks like those blue bellies got more than they bargained for."

Townsend tore the end of a paper cartridge with his teeth. He nodded and smiled, his face smeared with black powder. "We seen the elephant, Henry McConnell, we sure enough did, and now we's whupping them Yankees. We's whupping 'em good." He turned to load, then spun back toward Henry, the smile still pasted on his face. A wet, dark hole appeared above his right eye.

Henry dropped his musket, catching Townsend as he crumpled.

"Forward, men. Push them." The captain entreated the company to move.

Gently, Henry lowered his ashen friend to the ground. Townsend stared into the forest canopy above, his smile locked in death. Henry placed his fingers over Townsend's eyes and pulled them closed. "Goodbye, friend . . ."

"Let him go, McConnell, there's a war a-waiting." The sergeant prodded Henry with the butt of his musket.

A final glance, then Henry hefted his musket and ran to catch up with the company, now halted fifty yards ahead. The sulfurous stench of gunpowder hung in the air. The company formed on line again, firing at movement to their left front.

"Reload. Fire at will."

The staccato popping of muskets filled the woods.

A figure broke through the brush to their front waving frantically. He pointed behind him as he hollered, "Cease fire! Cease fire—53d Virginia . . ." The rebel soldier collapsed, his gray frock soaked in blood.

"Cease fire!" The captain yelled. He jumped in front of the line waving his sword, a horrified look on his face. The muskets went silent. Captain Claiborne stared at the fallen soldier, then faced his own men, his eyes seeming to plead for forgiveness.

Henry gritted his teeth and nodded to the captain. Smoke. Confusion. How was he to know?

A blast of musketry from their right flank tore into the Fourteenth. Soldiers cried out as they dropped. Henry spun around. A line of Union troops, their muskets at charge bayonet, pushed straight at them through the undergrowth. A soldier to Henry's right turned and ran, then another dropped his musket and took flight. Behind him, the company was breaking ranks and racing to the rear.

"Wait . . . hold the line . . ." Henry glanced at the Yankee charge. "Damn!" He turned and joined the rout.

Hurdling deadfalls and tearing through briar tangles, Henry raced past other soldiers, slowing only when the forest finally thinned and the ground rose to form a low ridge. "We . . . we can hold here," He hollered. "Form a line. Defend."

Henry grabbed a soldier running past. "Make a stand. Turn and fight. We can hold." He spun the soldier around to face the retreating company and then grabbed another. Some kept running, but many stopped and reloaded.

Captain Claiborne broke through the tangles, sword in hand, and climbed the rise. "Good work, McConnell. Set them on line. We'll hold here."

The troops gathered in the semblance of a formation. "There, to the right front. Hold your fire until they break clear," the captain called. He paced nervously, then glanced at Henry, nodding in silent acknowledgement, and commanded, "Fire!"

The long blue line wavered, but kept coming.

"We can't hold," Captain Claiborne yelled. "Fall back, fall back." He waved his sword. The small band of butternut and gray again raced to the rear.

Henry fired his musket at the on-rushing Yankees, then joined the retreat. Racing through the forest, his foot caught on a fallen limb. He stumbled forward, gashing his forearm on a broken branch, and scrambled back to his feet. He had to keep running.

Briars ripped at his legs.

Ahead, through the underbrush, the reserves formed in double ranks on a slight rise. There they guarded the Fourteenth Virginia's withdrawal. The soldiers manning the reserve position waved and shouted encouragement to Henry and the others who were racing for the safety of the rear. Henry reached the small embankment and grabbed the hand held out to him. A bearded, weather-beaten face grinned down at him from under a floppy slouch hat. Suddenly, his forehead seemed to explode in pain. A high-pitched ringing filled his ears, blocking the sounds of battle. The friendly rebel disappeared, replaced by swirling, unfocused shapes of green and gray . . . then darkness.

Chapter Thirty-three
June 1862

"You holding up, boy?" Banjo pulled a worm from the tobacco leaf and pinched it in half.

Isaac straightened, shielding his eyes from the midday sun. From one end of the field to the other, slaves slowly walked the rows, picking juicy bugs from the leaves. "I seen worse," he said, biting the head off a worm.

"I reckon I don't hear much from your mama no more," Banjo said, "not since Abraham been sold away. Come suppertime, she sets a plate for ol' Banjo, but she ain't much on talking."

Isaac reached for another worm. "Mama's been aching right much for Pa—I ain't never seen her all broke up like that—and Tempie, she's having a troubling time too; she's been real quiet and Mama worries."

Banjo lowered his voice. "Is that why you's still here?"

"Lord knows, I ain't staying for long, but I can't be running right now, not with Mama needing a man around."

"You, get back to work," Patrick hollered as he spurred his mount and galloped to the edge of the field closest to Isaac. "Damn it, O'Farrell, do you job. Those lazy nigras are costing me money." He shook his whip at Sean O'Farrell, then slapped the horse's flank and took off at a gallop toward the big house.

Sean picked his way through the tobacco to the row Isaac was working. He smiled and shook his head. "Patrick, meaning Mr. McConnell now, he's been pushing hard lately, so you boys best be saving your socializing for the evening campfire."

"Sorry, Mr. Sean. We didn't mean to get you in no trouble." Isaac lowered his head.

"Nah, 'tis no trouble." Sean smiled and rested his hand on Isaac's shoulder. "Don't you be worrying yourself. I'll not be around much longer anyway."

"Is you leaving?" Isaac looked into the green eyes of their overseer.

"Things are changing, Isaac. It's not like before. I can't abide Mr. McConnell's new ways, and I'll not be taking the whip to any one of ye—and that's what he be asking."

"Boss," Banjo whistled through his teeth. "Don't you worry none, we'll have this here field cleared of worms by sundown."

* * *

A piercing scream jarred him awake. Henry bolted upright, instinctively reaching for his musket. Yankees? Sunlight streamed through an open window. He blinked and looked around. What was this place? He tried to stand, but the motion sent a throbbing pain through his forehead.

"You'd best lay back and rest." Strong hands lowered him to the bed. "You're one lucky young man."

He opened his eyes again. A woman close in age to his mother leaned over him, her dark hair pulled back and tucked inside a lace bonnet. She wore a starched white apron smeared with blood.

"I heard a scream . . ."

"Yes," she said, "'tis unfortunate that war brings so much pain." She straightened the small pillow beneath his head. "Many here suffer wounds far more serious than yours."

"Where am I?" Henry cautiously touched the bandage on his forehead.

"You're in Richmond. This is Chimborazo Hospital. A musket ball creased your skull. You bled quite freely and you were unconscious for a day or so, but the doctor says you should recover fully. You'll be back on your feet in about a week. As I said, you're one of the lucky ones."

"If you don't mind my asking, ma'am, who are you?"

"You may call me Mrs. Templeton. I've been nursing here since the hospital opened last October."

Henry surveyed the room. "It seems strange to see a woman working, a white woman, that is, and especially tending to the wounded."

"I do what I can to ease the suffering," she said.

"And that slave?" Henry pointed to a black woman at the far end of the room.

Mrs. Templeton turned her head. "Oh, that's Sally. She's a free woman. She works here for wages, just as I do."

"Wages?" Henry said. "Your husband lets you work for wages?"

"My husband, may God rest his soul, was killed at Manassas Junction last summer. I either work or I take charity. Now get some rest and stop worrying yourself about things that aren't your concern." She daubed his cheek with a damp cloth.

Henry studied the long, low clapboard room. Six open windows on each side let in what little breeze the humid day might offer, while daylight splashed off the whitewashed walls. Outside, a large yellow flag dangled limply from a pole. Thirty or forty beds, most occupied. Flies buzzed piles of bloodied rags that littered the floor.

"Well, did we whip 'em?" Henry asked. "Did we push those blue bellies?"

She patted his hand and stood to leave. "General Joe Johnston's been wounded. General Lee commands the army now, and he's pushing the Yankees down the peninsula. Now, get some rest."

The stench of festering wounds and bodily waste hung in the air. Henry fought an urge to gag. He eased onto his pillow and stared at the bare rafters. He'd only been wounded in battle, but Townsend . . . Henry closed his eyes, trying to push the image away. He'd fought a good fight, died a soldier's death. At least he hadn't suffered. And a free black woman . . . working for wages . . . ? Henry drifted.

A whimper from the next bed pulled him back to consciousness.

The soldier didn't look much older than Henry. Curled in a ball, he clutched his stomach. "Ma'am, you there? Help me. I's burning up. Help, please . . ."

With great effort, Henry raised on one elbow. Mrs. Templeton was tending to a patient on the far side of the room. "Ma'am? Mrs. Templeton?" Henry called. "This here soldier needs help. He's in terrible pain."

Mrs. Templeton tossed the bandage she was rolling onto an empty bed and crossed the room, placing her hand on the soldier's brow. "He has the fever. There's nothing we can do for him. I'll try

209

to come back later and cool him, but there are other patients that need me more—some that might still live."

"Maybe one of the other nurses," Henry asked, "or that nigra woman, Sally?"

"We're all busy, young man. Look around. All these boys are in pain. Each gets tended to in his own time."

"Wait, ma'am . . . can I help? How . . . how do I cool him?"

She smiled. "See those rags?" She pointed at a pile on the floor. "Soak one in water and hold it to his forehead. It won't cure him, but it will help with his pain." She turned and resumed her rounds.

Henry sat up and swung his feet to the floor. The room seemed to spin. He tucked his head on his chest and waited for the motion to stop, then slowly picked up a rag and dipped it in the washbowl on the stand between their beds. Two wobbly steps and he eased himself onto the stranger's bed. He held the wet rag to man's forehead. Light hair, blue eyes, hands used to hard work—had the look of a farmer. The stranger's face softened as the cooling water seeped the pain from his burning head.

"The name's Henry . . . Henry McConnell. Fourteenth Virginia. I got shot over at Seven Pines."

The man raised a hand slowly and placed it on top of Henry's, holding the wet cloth. He licked his lips. Henry moved the rag over his mouth and squeezed. Drops fell to the soldier's tongue. The man swallowed, then whispered, "Coleman, James . . . James Coleman. Nineteenth Mississippi." He struggled to get out the words. "My . . . my boy, Tommy . . ."

"You'd best rest, mister. Don't be wasting your strength." Henry wet the cloth and returned it to Coleman's forehead.

"Bless you, Henry McConnell. Tell my Nancy I been thinking on her . . ." The soldier closed his eyes.

Henry changed the cloth again, then journeyed to his own bed and laid down. Seemed like a mess of suffering for a fellow that hadn't even been shot. Maybe, if his fever was to break, he'd get himself a furlough and visit his Nancy.

* * *

Stifling heat greeted the dawn. Henry slowly opened his eyes. Stagnant air clung to the rafters and blanketed the wounded in its foul stench. His bedclothes were soaked in sweat and his head still hurt, however, the throbbing had eased. It seemed like days since he'd eaten—three or four eggs and a slab of bacon would sure taste good. Would they have real coffee? That Coleman fella was probably hungry too—had he gotten any rest? Henry rolled over and faced his neighbor's bunk. Stripped of bed sheets, the straw mattress was rolled at the foot of the empty bed.

Chapter Thirty-four
June 1862

Morgan lay face down while Florence rubbed oil on his back. Ella fanned herself in a rocking chair beside the bed. A breeze wafting through the open parlor windows brushed his bare skin, bringing merciful relief from the humid afternoon.

"Miss Ella," Florence said. "It ain't rightly none of my business, but last year when I was down to South Boston buying foodstuffs I seen a slave pushing his mistress in a chair what had wheels."

"Yes," Ella replied, "I've read of them. Are you suggesting that my Morgan needs such a chair?"

"That he do, ma'am."

"No, it's out of the question," Ella said. "He's not ready for such a contraption. The poor dear's bedridden."

"Begging you pardon ma'am, but Massa's all laid out 'cause he got no place else to be, but even now he sits up some and he can move his hands, his arms too. Watch." Florence stopped massaging. "Massa McConnell, Miss Ella's setting right here. She wants to see you move that hand."

Ella? Sure was nice of her to stop by. If she was home, that meant she'd already bought out all the shops in Richmond. Could he move his hand for her? Sure . . .

"Florence, look," Ella said. "It is moving! He's moving his hand. Can he hear me?"

"Miss Ella, I been telling you for months, ain't nothing wrong with that man's ears. He don't miss a thing."

Damned right. And there'll be some explaining to do, once his faculties returned—and they would, thanks to Florence.

"But what could he do in a wheelchair? He needs constant watching."

"Miss Ella, you set him out on that porch in the evening or

early morning, you brings him to the table when the family gathers, you might even push him down by the paddock. I reckon that dapple mare's been missing him something awful."

"But Patrick does not want his father doing anything that might cause a strain. Patrick says rest will do him best."

"Miss Ella, ain't meaning no disrespect, but I been healing folks nigh on thirty years, and I can tell you, rest only helps them what's tired. Massa McConnell ain't tired, 'cept he's tired of laying around this here bed all the day long."

Damn right! Morgan lifted his hand and thumped the mattress. Twice.

"Very well. I'll be in South Boston tomorrow. There's a new hat in the millinery that I wish to try on—it came all the way from New York. While I'm there, I will see about having one of those wheeled devices delivered, if one is available."

"It's too warm in here." Ella waved her paper fan. "I shall be on the porch if you need me." Her footsteps crossed the carpet to the wooden floor.

Morgan waited until the footfalls had faded, then whispered almost inaudibly, "Thank you . . ."

Florence spoke in his ear. "Again, Massa, slowly . . ."

"Thank you."

She resumed his massage. "Florence is gonna get you in that wheelchair, then she'll be hitching that contraption behind a plow mule and hanging an ear of corn to his front, just to see you go."

Morgan's chest heaved in a silent laugh. Florence rubbed oil into his shoulders. He closed his eyes, imagining that he was sitting on the porch, looking over his fields again—what a joy that would be. God bless her. A mockingbird called from a tree outside the window. He dozed.

"Massa McConnell."

Florence? He opened one eye.

"I don't mean to trouble you none, but I sure misses that time before you was taken ill. I reckon I can speak my mind—least ways you don't complain none when I do. Things is different these days. I've been missing my Abraham something terrible, and folks down at the quarters is saying how they's feeling the whip. It ain't like before . . ."

Morgan struggled, but could not form the words. She was right, and it wasn't how he wanted his slaves treated . . . He lifted his hand and dropped it to the mattress. Things would change, Florence, they would . . .

"I can see you's trying to talk, Massa, but you oughtn't push yourself. I declare, you keep straining like that, you's gonna pop out your eyeballs. You'd best stick to one or two little words 'til you gets your health back. Miss Ella's gonna be surprised when I tells her how you can talk some."

He banged his hand on the mattress and strained as he whispered, "Don't tell her . . ."

* * *

Isaac straightened and wiped his brow. Picking bugs from the tobacco had been early morning or cool of the evening work before Massa McConnell fell sick. Now, there was no escaping the searing midday sun. "This heat's a misery, little brother. You'd best drink you some water." He pointed to the bucket in the back of the wagon.

Joseph squashed the tobacco worm he'd just picked off the leaf, then walked to the wagon and scooped a dipper of the warm liquid. "How about you, Isaac? You thirsty?"

Two horsemen came into view from the direction of the big house. "Never mind that water," Isaac called. "There's riders coming. Get back to work."

Joseph dropped the dipper in the bucket and started walking through the tobacco rows when the riders turned off the road and came straight at him.

Patrick trotted his horse alongside Joseph and reached down, grabbing him by the back of his shirt and lifting him until his bare feet dangled helplessly. "This is what you must deal with—lazy nigras." Patrick glanced at Big Jim, who was mounted on the other horse, then he dropped Joseph to the ground.

"There weren't no call for that, Patrick." Isaac took a step toward the riders. "That boy's been doing a man's work. He just stopped to fetch me a drink."

The tip of the blacksnake whip cracked like a pistol as it caught Isaac's bare shoulder. "That's '*Massa* McConnell' to you, boy." Big Jim pointed the butt of the whip at Isaac. "This here is one uppity nigger, but he'll be learning his place soon enough."

Isaac grimaced, but did not cry out. Instead, he stared at the ground and braced for the next blow. The whip cracked again, ripping his flesh. Others in the field stopped what they were doing and watched.

"The rest of you lazy niggers get on back to work or you'll be feeling the same," Big Jim hollered. He snapped the whip across Isaac's back again, driving Isaac to his knees. "And you'd best be calling me *'Mister* Jim' from now on." Big Jim grinned, then turned his horse and followed Patrick across the field toward the big house.

Isaac stumbled to his feet.

Joseph rushed to his side. "How come Big Jim's setting up on that horse and cracking that whip like he was somebody?"

Isaac brushed the dirt from his knees. "I reckon we has us a new overseer, little brother."

Chapter Thirty-five
June 1862

"Lift your foot, Papa." Polly helped Morgan into the wooden wheelchair that Banjo had picked up at the mercantile the day before. His head rested against the chair's rattan back. Arm and leg rests held him in position. Lord, it felt good to sit upright again. Would Polly notice the smile welling within him, or would facial muscles that were no longer under his control mask his delight?

"It took two weeks to get this shipped from Richmond," Polly said, "and Mother says we were fortunate to get it at all. With all our wounded boys, most chairs go to the army now." She cinched a leather strap around his chest, then carefully pushed the chair forward. The wheels bounced over the edge of the carpet. They moved slowly into the hallway, pausing at the side door.

"I need to get help, Papa. I don't want to spill you all over the porch on your first outing. Wait here."

Morgan nodded. Wait there . . . of course.

In a moment, Polly returned with Banjo.

Banjo tipped his hat and smiled. "Morning, Massa McConnell, you's looking well this fine summer morning." He scratched his head as he studied first the chair and then the step down. "Miss Polly, I do believe we has to back into this. Like so."

Banjo turned the chair, facing Morgan into the hallway, then pulled. Morgan rolled backward, bouncing as the rear wheels dropped from the door's threshold to the porch.

"Now, Miss Polly, you gives Banjo a holler when you needs to get Massa back up off'n that porch. Maybe I comes by later and builds you a ramp. You has a good day, now." Banjo tipped his hat and returned to his chores.

Polly turned the chair around and faced Morgan toward his barns and fields.

Jeff Andrews

Nothing much had changed. A few of the outbuildings showed fresh coats of whitewash. The tobacco looked good; should yield twelve hundred pounds per acre.

"Papa," Polly said, "enjoy the breeze while I fetch us something to drink." Her footsteps trailed into the house and down the hall.

The mid-summer heat trickled sweat across his brow, but the sun was an elixir for his spirits. Morgan turned slowly, stretching muscles weakened by months of bed rest. The farm appeared well-tended. Patrick must have been finding success, but at what cost? Poor Florence—Patrick never should have sold Abraham . . .

"Here's a drink for you, Massa McConnell." Tempie stood beside him holding a glass filled with a green liquid. "Mama fixed it special."

Oh God, not more of her potions. Their healing powers didn't matter—they tasted awful.

"Open up, Papa." Polly lifted the glass to his lips.

He sipped, then gagged. Lord, it was worse than sourweed . . .

"Once more." She tipped the glass.

Polly smiled, handing the glass back to Tempie.

With effort, Morgan turned toward them. The girls were the same age, but now Tempie seemed older, different . . . like she'd lost her sunshine.

"There's a wagon coming, Papa." Polly bounced on her toes and pointed. A wagon pulled over at the end of the long lane, let off a passenger, then turned and continued on its way.

Tempie's soft footfalls faded into the house as a lone figure sauntered up the lane in a familiar gait. The lane disappeared into a swale, hiding the visitor from sight. Morgan remained focused. The lane eventually lifted the traveler back into view, closer now. Gray jacket. Butternut pants. Something white wrapped around his head? He swung his arms in a jaunty stride. Morgan strained against the leather straps, grabbing Polly's hand. The name formed, first in his heart, then on his lips. He forced a raspy whisper. "Henry . . ."

* * *

Dust swirled around Henry's boots as he ambled up the lane. He gazed across the green tobacco fields. Thank goodness the rains hadn't washed them out, at least not yet. Slaves were busy pulling tobacco bugs—Lord, how he'd hated that job. Hey, there was Isaac. "Isaac! Hello, Isaac." Henry smiled and waved as he strolled toward

218

the cluster of slaves.

Isaac straightened and leaned on his hoe. "Morning, Massa McConnell."

Henry backed away, glancing over his shoulder as though expecting to see someone behind him. He turned and studied his friend. "'Morning, *Master* McConnell'? I get shot up in the war and all you can say is, 'Morning, *Master* McConnell'? Have you been in the sun too long, or are you trying to get me riled?" He landed a playful punch on Isaac's shoulder.

Isaac's gaze met Henry's for a moment, then he looked away.

"Hey," Henry said. "Who stuck a burr under your saddle?"

"I reckon things has changed since you been gone," Isaac replied, slowly shaking his head. "Ain't like before." He pointed to the main house. "I 'spect that be your pa setting up there on the porch. Best not keep him waiting."

Henry searched for a sign, a clue, anything. Finally, he stepped away. "I don't know what's stuck in your craw, but we need to talk—and soon."

* * *

Pain throbbed behind his eyes as Henry shuffled along the lane toward the house. Was it the glaring midday sun, his wound, or Isaac's curious greeting that triggered this latest relapse? Never mind, it would pass quickly—they usually did.

Morgan appeared to be seated in a chair set on wheels. Ella stood beside him, the sun warming her smile. Polly was behind, her hands on Morgan's shoulders. She bounced on her toes as though she would take off running if given the slightest encouragement. Tempie stood behind his family, her hands folded in front of her, her expression revealing no emotion.

"Mother . . ." Henry climbed the steps and gathered Ella in his arms.

"Your head." She gently touched his bandage. "Henry, dear, what happened?"

"The bullet just grazed me." Henry laughed. "Them Yankees can't shoot straight."

Ella smiled tightly, tears welling in her eyes.

"You get any of them?" Polly asked. "Did you make 'em pay?"

He studied his sister for a moment. "Land sakes, girl. I'd a never recognized you. You look all growed up. Must be time to get

219

out that shotgun and start scaring away the suitors."

"Oh, Henry. Don't be silly . . ." Polly giggled, throwing her arms around his neck, then she stepped back and pointed to his sleeve. "What are these?"

"Didn't my letter arrive? Captain Bruce came by the hospital a couple of weeks ago and promoted me all the way to sergeant—he said it was for heroism there at Seven Pines. Ain't that something?"

"*Isn't* that something," Ella said. "And I thought Captain Claiborne was your commanding officer."

Henry grinned. "*Isn't* that something." He winked at Polly. "We held elections in May. Captain Claiborne wasn't reelected." Morgan sat stiffly, his gaze transfixed on some distant field. Henry knelt, taking Morgan's hand. Morgan turned, his moist eyes now fixed on Henry. His grip tightened. He gave Henry an almost imperceptible nod.

"Come tell us all about the war and how you received those awful wounds." Ella took Henry's arm and led him across the porch. When they reached the door, she turned to Tempie. "Tell Florence we require a special dinner tonight. Our Henry's come home."

* * *

Henry tossed the dusty wool uniform in the corner. Florence could clean it later. He put on a fresh suit and studied himself in the mirror, then tugged at the civilian clothes hanging on his lanky frame. Army life had cost him a few pounds.

As he descended the stairway, Henry was greeted by the familiar aroma of Florence's fried chicken. Ella and Polly were already seated in the dining room. Florence wheeled Morgan to his place at the head of the table.

Ella smiled. "Your father wanted to join us." She extended a hand toward the far end of the table. "He takes his meals privately in the back parlor, but he will enjoy our mealtime chatter." She motioned to a vacant chair. "Please, take your seat." She turned to Polly. "Would you ask the blessing?"

"Certainly, Mother." Polly folded her hands and bowed her head. "Lord, bless this food which we are about to partake, and thank you for bringing Henry home safe. Amen." She looked at Henry and smiled. "Tell us all about the war, Henry. How many Yankees did you kill?"

"Hush," Ella said. "Let your brother enjoy his dinner."

"Aw, it's all right, Mother." He winked at Polly and reached for a drumstick.

"They feed you like this in the army?" Ella pointed to the fried chicken and biscuits.

Henry shook his head. "Not likely. We were almost out of food last winter. No greens at all. Fresh meat was scarce. We lived on corn meal and whatever fish we could pull from the James River. Where's Patrick?"

"Tending to some business in South Boston," Ella replied. "He'll be along shortly." She pointed to his bandage. "How did you receive that terrible wound?"

Henry took a bite of chicken and rested his gaze on Morgan. "Seven Pines Crossroads, it was the first of June," he said as he chewed. "We'd pushed the Yankees and all was looking good, then suddenly they hit our flank and all hell broke loose—" He quickly covered his mouth. "Sorry, Mother."

"Continue . . ." She smiled.

"Anyway, the Yankees had us on the run. Those woods were thick as anything—like down there by the creek, only stretching for miles. The reserves pulled up on this rise and tried to make a stand. I was climbing up the embankment to join them when, wham!" Henry slapped his fist into the palm of his hand. "It felt worse than getting kicked by a plow mule."

Morgan flinched.

"I awoke in the hospital—most God-awful place you'd ever lay eyes on. Blood everywhere, and piles of arms and legs just festering in the sun—"

"Henry, *not* during dinner." Ella tapped the table and covered her mouth with her napkin.

"Sorry, Mother." He smiled at Polly, who appeared to be hanging on his every word. "Chimborazo Hospital sets on a hill overlooking the James there in Richmond. There must be forty acres of buildings, all set in these neat rows. They say it's the largest military hospital ever there was."

"Did they take good care of you?" Polly set her biscuit on her plate and focused on her brother.

"Never saw a doctor but once. They was all the time doing surgery and such, so they don't have time for tending to the less serious wounds, but don't you know, they had *women* working there."

"Well, of course, you ninny," Polly said. "We have Florence and Tempie right here."

"*White* women," Henry said. He turned to Ella. "Mother, there were white *southern* women working jobs side by side with free blacks. I never thought I'd see the day . . ."

"White women, you say?" Ella dabbed the corner of her mouth with her napkin. "Well, there's no accounting for those with no social standing."

"One was a Richmond society woman. Her husband had been an officer, killed up there at Manassas Junction." Henry paused while his mother considered this new reality.

Ella took a deep breath but remained silent.

"They had a preacher man too," Henry said, "a Reverend Jasper. He come around and held services every Sunday. Most everybody attended."

Polly pulled back in mock surprise. "Imagine that, a preacher holding church services. Whatever will they think of next?"

"He was a slave." Henry gave Polly a satisfied smile.

"This war's a terrible thing," Ella said. "It's simply tearing apart our institutions and our fine Commonwealth. Tempie, clear these dishes and bring us some of Florence's peach cobbler." She smoothed the tablecloth beside her plate and looked across at Morgan.

A horse galloped to a halt outside and a voice yelled for Joseph to come tend to the animal. Shortly, boots clumped across the wooden floors.

"Florence, I'm starving," Patrick shouted. He rounded the corner, halting in the doorway as he surveyed the gathering, then he pointed to their father. "He should be in bed, and I thought I told you not to be wasting our money on those useless contraptions."

"We will discuss that later," Ella replied, glaring at Patrick. "Have you not noticed? Your brother has returned from the war."

"Henry? Yes, of course." Patrick looked surprised. "Welcome home, brother." In two strides he was beside Henry's chair, clasping him by the shoulders. "Good to see you in one piece." He pointed to the bandage. "More or less . . ."

"A minor wound," Henry said. "Just a few headaches every

now and again. Jeff Davis says I should be back to winning the war in a few weeks—as soon as I've checked up on things here. The tobacco's looking good . . ."

Patrick slid into his chair and unfolded his napkin. "If the weather holds, we'll cut better than eleven hundred pounds an acre. Prices are steady, though the federal blockade is putting pressure on. I hear rumors the English are looking to buy foreign tobacco. If they do, it will destroy our profits."

"Patrick, we were just finishing, but I'm sure Florence has saved some for you." Ella turned and called to the rear of the house. "Florence, have Tempie bring Patrick his supper."

Tempie set a plate in front of Patrick loaded with chicken, snap beans, and biscuits. He took a bite, wagging the drumstick as he spoke. "You know that nigra of yours run off."

"What are you talking about?" Henry said. "Who?"

"That boy of yours, Isaac. You said he wasn't a runner. Well, about a month ago he took off. I had to pay forty-five dollars to the fellas that captured him up by Richmond."

The strange reunion with Isaac flashed through Henry's mind.

"And Abraham's been sold too," Polly blurted.

"I believe Patrick described it as a means of reducing our financial risk." Ella folded her hands in her lap and smiled at Patrick.

"He was helping runaways," Patrick said, "so was Isaac. I needed to teach all of them a lesson." He spoke matter-of-factly between bites of chicken. "I plan to sell Isaac too, if he doesn't settle down."

Henry's fist tightened. The pounding suddenly flared inside his head. Morgan's gaze met his. Was that a nod, some recognition? He seemed to be saying what Henry had already decided—this wasn't the time, not now. "Mother, dinner was wonderful. Please excuse me. I have some things to tend to." He folded his napkin and placed it beside his plate.

Chapter Thirty-six
June 1862

From beyond the horizon, the sun's lingering rays gilded evening clouds as Isaac settled on a log beside the crackling fire. On the far side of the fire ring, Lilly basted a catfish that was nailed to a plank and propped up facing the fire. Banjo wandered over and pulled up a stump. He sat and began quietly strumming the rough-hewn instrument for which he'd been named. He was soon joined by a slave named Jacob.

"I seen Massa Henry today," Jacob said. "Did he go and get his self shot in that war?"

"I reckon," Isaac replied, stirring the coals. "He ain't said."

"Boy, you's mighty quiet tonight," Lilly said. "Something bothering you?" She pointed to the planked fish. "How's about some of this here catfish?"

Isaac shook his head. "I ain't all that hungry, Aunt Lilly."

He looked up as a figure stumbled through the brush next to the lane and stepped into the firelight. Slaves stopped whatever they were doing. A few pointed. The clearing grew silent, then Mamma Rose stepped from her cabin doorway and waved. "Massa Henry! Welcome home, sir. You's coming to visit?"

"'Evening, Mamma Rose," Henry said. "I'm looking for Isaac."

She nodded toward the fire ring.

"Isaac, grab your pole," Henry called. "We need to catch us some fish."

"You want a taste of this'n?" Lilly pointed to the catfish tacked on the board in front of the fire. "It's good as you's gonna find in these parts." Her broad smile reflected the glow of the campfire.

"Not tonight, Lilly," Henry said. "Me and Isaac have some catching to do on our own." He motioned for Isaac to join him.

Isaac hesitated. Why should he spend time fishing with the boss man? Wasn't it enough that he had to work his fields, mend his tools, and chop his wood?

"Come on," Henry said. "What's keeping you?"

Isaac turned to Lilly. "Appears the massa be needing me." He rose slowly from his seat by the fire and took up a cane pole that leaned against one of the cabins.

They walked in silence past the slave cemetery, along the edge of the tobacco fields, and down to the creek where the limbs of the old oak stretched over the dark water.

Isaac brushed aside leaves and sat on the bank. He glanced at Henry. "Where's your pole?"

"I didn't bring one," Henry said, settling on the ground beside Isaac. "You do the fishing—but I want some talking too."

"Talking 'bout what?"

"How about begin by telling me what the hell's going on?"

"Don't know what you mean . . ."

"I mean, this afternoon—that 'Master McConnell' stuff—and you running off, and helping other slaves to run away."

"I caught the whip for not saying 'massa.'"

"We don't whip our slaves. Sean doesn't even carry a whip—"

"And he ain't working here no more, neither."

"What? When—"

"Been a few weeks. Massa Patrick sent him packing. Big Jim's your man now."

"Big Jim?" Henry stared into the dark waters as he chewed on a grass stalk. "That doesn't make any sense . . ." He bit off a nib, spit it out, and tossed the stalk aside.

"You ain't got to pay a nigra like you does Mr. Sean, and if Big Jim ain't hard on us slaves, he'll be back working the fields. Do it make sense now?"

"Did you run away?"

Isaac threaded a grub onto the hook and dropped the line in the creek. He let the bait sink to the bottom, then turned to Henry. "Your pa ever tell you about the deal he had with my pa?"

"No, what deal?" Henry said.

"Your papa, Massa McConnell, he held back money from every job Pa worked. He set it aside so's Pa could buy his children, buy us our freedoms."

"Sure sounds like Papa." Henry smiled. "He was partial to Abraham, that's for certain . . ."

"Now Massa Patrick's the boss, he says there weren't no deal."

"Figures." Henry nodded. "I'll speak to him. But that ain't reason enough for running, you have all you need right here—"

"Don't have no freedom."

"Freedom? Hell, you have a good home, we keep you well fed, we give you clothes—"

Isaac jiggled the pole, dancing the bait along the creek bottom. It was time Henry faced the truth, but how to tell him—what were the right words? Isaac took a deep breath and looked at him. "You remember when we was hunting up country and you talked about Virginia boys fighting for their land?"

"Sure," Henry said. "That night in the cave. We enjoyed some of your good possum stew . . ."

"Was rabbit," Isaac replied. "And you's fighting now 'cause you has land, you has a home, you has your freedom. Isaac ain't got none of them."

"Sure you do. Your home's here, on McConnell land." Henry took in the landscape with a sweep of his hand. "You're a part of all this, a part of our family."

"Pa's home ain't here. He's off to Mississippi, working the white man's cotton. I won't never see him again." Isaac stared at Henry.

Henry lowered his voice. "That was wrong, sure enough, but it weren't my doing." He clutched his knees to his chest.

"You's a McConnell, right?" Isaac didn't wait for an answer. "You want to know why Isaac runned? I runned 'cause I doesn't want to be sold south. 'Cause up north I'd be free, free to own my own business, marry the woman I loves, have babies what can't be sold."

"Is that was this is all about?" Henry said. "You want to get down to North Carolina and see that girl of yours? Hell, I'll write you a pass—"

Isaac slammed down the fishing pole and jumped to his feet. "Who writes you a pass, Henry McConnell? Who writes you a pass when you goes sparking one of your lady friends?"

"What?"

"Who writes you a pass?" Isaac poked Henry in the chest.

Henry searched Isaac's face. "You're talking crazy. I don't need a damn pass—"

"'Cause you's white? You don't need no pass 'cause you's better than Isaac?"

"No . . .not better, just . . . different. It's how things are supposed to be."

"Ain't how black folk think it's supposed to be."

"Damn it, Isaac. You're pushing me . . ."

"You's the ones in charge 'cause white folks is smarter, right? Seven times thirteen . . ."

"What?"

"Seven times thirteen." Isaac pointed at Henry. "If you's so smart, Henry McConnell, seven times thirteen."

Henry shook his head and shrugged. "You know I ain't good at numbers . . ."

"Ninety-one. You ain't no smarter than me, Henry McConnell, you just holds the power. You say 'marry this one, work that job, sleep here, and if'n you runs away to be free, you'll be feeling the whip.'"

Henry jumped to his feet. "Stop this right now. You got no right—"

"No right?" Isaac stared, his face inches from Henry's. "No right, 'cause a nigger's just property. Isaac ain't got no right—no more'n pigs in the sty nor mules behind your plow. Isaac got no right 'cause you and all your white kin is scared—scared that if'n the black man gets rights, you can't be stealing from us no more. If'n the black man gets rights, you can't be laying that whip across our backs."

"Damn it, Isaac, we don't use the whip—"

Isaac glared, then turned away, pulling his shirt up over his back.

"My God," Henry whispered, "who did that to you?"

"I's a slave, Henry McConnell." He lowered his shirt and faced Henry again. "I's a McConnell slave."

"I . . . I didn't know." Henry bowed his head. "Things will change . . ."

Isaac started to walk away, then hesitated. He turned and pointed at Henry. "You's a big toad in a little puddle. You thinks you knows everything, but you's just seeing your own little mud hole. It ain't a problem no McConnell is gonna fix. The problem ain't how you white folks is managing your property, the problem is that we *is* your property."

"Isaac, damn it, I . . . I don't have the answers." Henry rubbed the back of his neck. "When Papa used to explain it, it always made sense. Now, I'm not so sure.

"You know what you need?" Henry said. "You need to get away from here, put some miles between you and this farm. Why don't you come with me when I go back to the army? Food's not so good, but you could doctor it a mite—the fellas would sure appreciate that."

"Isaac don't want your army."

Henry stepped forward, his hands extended. "You're more like me than my own brother. I don't know how we got in this mess, not just you and me, I mean all of us, we're all stuck in that same little puddle, and I don't know how to fix what's wrong, but I know this, you're still my friend—"

"Friend?" Isaac spit. "You mean your man Friday kneeling in the dirt with your foot on his black head? Is you disremembering about how you owns me? Isaac ain't no friend, Massa McConnell, Isaac's just your property."

Chapter Thirty-seven
July 1862

"Boy, you's fixing to catch yourself a whupping." Banjo pitched a clod of manure into the wheelbarrow, then leaned on his pitchfork.

"I won't catch nothing," Isaac said, "long as you keeps this barn clean and that woodpile full." He wrapped Lilly's ashcake in his bandanna. "I'll be back before anybody knows I been gone."

Banjo pushed his straw hat back on his head and wiped his brow. "Florence gonna be mad if you runs off. She's still working on Abraham being gone."

Isaac leaned against the barn door and gazed at the paddock. Massa McConnell's dapple mare pranced around a puddle, pawing at a gray and white barn cat. What if he had a horse? It was a full day's walk to Milton, then another day or more getting over to see Raleigh. Probably not a good idea. If a horse was missing, someone would notice, but if a nigra was missing, nobody would pay no mind—as long as chores got done. He reckoned he'd walk.

He turned to Banjo. "You tell her tonight, but you wait 'til after dark, and you tell her not to fret none. I'll be back soon enough. I ain't running, just visiting."

* * *

Tempie's plain cotton dress pulled tightly against her stomach as she bent and lifted the large Dutch oven from the fireplace and struggled to carry it to the table.

Florence wiped her eye. Lord, that child's been hiding it good up to now, but not even a loose dress could cover that tummy no more. She couldn't put off talking with her any longer.

Tempie set the iron kettle on the table and began ladling black-eyed peas and pork knuckles into tin plates. Isaac and Joseph would be in from the fields soon, and Banjo always appeared whenever food was served.

Florence wiped flour from her hands and faced her daughter. "Getting close?"

Tempie looked up, her eyebrows raised in a question.

Florence pointed at her stomach. "Be time for birthing soon, by the looks of things."

Tempie slid her hand across her stomach, slowly smoothing her dress. She held her gaze with Florence for only a moment, then dropped onto the wooden bench beside the table and lowered her head, covering her eyes. "Mama," she sobbed, "I don't know what's happening to me. I's scared . . ."

Florence knelt and wrapped her arms around her baby's shoulders, pulling her close. "Now child, don't you fret none. Everything's gonna be just fine, your mama will see to that."

Tempie buried her face in Florence's shoulder and clung tightly. "Oh, Mama, I's so scared . . ."

Florence stroked her hair and rocked her slowly, trying to hush Tempie's sobs. "You ain't the first girl to find herself in a family way, child. Everything's gonna turn out just fine, you'll see. Does Cato know?"

Tempie sat back and took in a deep breath, wiping her eyes with the palm of her hand. "Ain't his baby."

Not Cato's? Florence held her at arm's length and studied her little girl. "Who then . . . ?"

Tempie shook her head slowly, then burrowed into her mother's arms. The tears began anew. Florence held her tightly, patting her shoulder. "Everything be fine, child. Don't you fret. When you's ready, we'll talk."

* * *

Thunder rumbled through the night, chasing a pair of doves from the treetops along the creek. Rain began to fall, splashing against Isaac's uplifted face and splattering against the dry, dusty road. "Thank you, Lord," he whispered. A good storm might keep those pattyrollers in their homes, not out looking.

Heading south, Isaac crossed rolling tobacco fields, finally pausing along the muddy banks of the slow moving Dan River. If he followed the river upstream, he'd be in Milton come daybreak. In the distance, a dog's bark pierced the quiet pattering of raindrops on the leaves overhead. Most likely it was just some cur treeing a possum. Still, he'd best be careful. Tonight, Isaac needed to think like a pattyroller.

He followed the river, dashing across open fields and picking his way through dense thickets, always listening for the patrols. Finally, as the rain eased, a pink glow touched the eastern sky. Directly across the river lay the town of Milton. Mr. Jones would be awake and cooking breakfast. Isaac could grab some food and hide out until nightfall. He slid down the muddy bank and slipped into the cool water.

* * *

The glow of an oil lamp cast shadows through the bunkhouse window onto the wet grass. Isaac eased the latch open and poked his head inside the door. "Hey, does you have some bacon for a poor, hungry soul?"

"Lordy! Gabriel, wake up!" Mr. Jones hollered. "Look at this here river rat what's come a-begging at our door."

Gabriel hopped out of bed and grabbed Isaac by the shoulders. "Boy, you gave us a scare. We took you for dead, then Mr. Day told us you got caught by that pattyroller. Is you back with us again?"

Isaac closed the door behind him and took a seat at the table. "Not here for long, I just need a place to hide."

"Lord, you's in trouble, ain't ya, boy?" Gabriel scowled. "You running?"

"Not north," Isaac said. "I sneaked off to see Raleigh. Last I seen her was before I was put in that jail."

Mr. Jones set a plate of eggs and squirrel in front of Isaac, then took a plate for himself and sat across the table. "Mr. Day said that constable down Yanceyville tried to sell you south."

"Sure enough," Isaac replied. "Perkins, the fella what was locked up with me, he got sold, then the men what bought him shot him down when he tried to run. He said he weren't never going back to them cotton fields." Isaac poked at his food, glancing up as Gabriel took a seat next to Mr. Jones. "Pa got sold south too."

Gabriel rested his elbows the table. "Thought you said your white folks didn't sell their nigras."

"Everything's done changed," Isaac said. "Massa McConnell

got took with the apoplexy and now Massa Patrick's running the farm. He favors whipping and selling."

"So, what's you gonna do?" Gabriel asked.

Isaac wiped his mouth on his sleeve. "I can't be staying on that farm much longer. Henry's off fighting the war, and that Patrick, he's no good. I 'spect I'll visit Raleigh some, then get on back before I's missed—but I'll be running again, and soon."

"North?"

"I been thinking some on that," Isaac said. He pointed at Gabriel with his fork. "I hear tell there's a passel of runaways hiding over in that Dismal Swamp. I 'spect it'll be easier to get there than to go north, what with all that fighting going on."

Gabriel nodded. "I heard about them maroons over in the swamps. Knew a fella two years ago, he lit out for there. Ain't heard if'n he made it, but he never showed up 'round these parts no more."

"Get some rest while I cleans up." Mr. Jones gathered the plates. "What's Raleigh gonna say about you running? I thought she don't want no runaway for her man."

"Don't know what she'll say, but I can't be staying at that McConnell farm no more and take the chance of being sold." Isaac climbed into the same bunk he used when he worked for Mr. Day. "That Dismal Swamp is a whole lot closer to the Promised Land than Mississippi is. Maybe I'll find my way north, get behind them Yankee lines." He rested his forearm over his eyes. "If I's sleeping, will you wake me come evening?"

* * *

"Isaac, whatever am I to do with you?"

The familiar voice shook Isaac from his slumber. A lantern bathed the bunkroom in light. He rubbed his eyes and sat up.

"Hello, Isaac." Thomas stood by the table holding a cigar.

Isaac glanced quickly at Gabriel, seated across the table.

"No," Thomas said, "they didn't tell me you were here. I stumbled upon you quite by accident. So, to what do we owe the pleasure?"

Isaac rubbed the back of his neck. "I come to see Raleigh."

Thomas smiled. "Ah, yes. 'Pains of love be sweeter far than all other pleasures are.'"

Isaac shrugged and shook his head.

"Never mind." Thomas waved his hand. "Just a verse from long ago. But your quest, I fear, is for naught. She no longer lives here."

"She don't?" Isaac jumped to his feet.

"No," Thomas said. "Mr. Patterson passed away six months ago. Mrs. Patterson's brother came down from Philadelphia and took her north. He stopped by to settle the Patterson's account and told me they were sailing out of Wilmington on a blockade-runner, and that Raleigh was going with them."

Isaac walked to the window. The reflection of the lamp in the glass hid the evening sky outside. Philadelphia? He pondered the news for a moment before turning back to Thomas. "I'd best be getting back to the farm before I's missed."

"What about that swamp?" Mr. Jones asked. He leaned on one elbow and looked up from his bunk.

Should they talk about such things in front of Thomas? It wouldn't matter— Thomas wasn't calling out any patrollers. "I reckon I needs to be finding my way to Philadelphia."

"That could be quite risky," Thomas said, gesturing with his cigar. "Do be careful."

"I ain't worked out the particulars on traveling north," Isaac said, "but I's becoming downright gifted when it comes to fooling them pattyrollers."

"Just the same, use caution," Thomas said, placing his hand on Isaac's shoulder. "For your sake as well as Raleigh's." He looked Isaac in the eye and smiled.

* * *

Clouds softened the night shadows, blending trees and bushes into dark, indistinct forms. Ground still wet from the previous day's rain muted Isaac's footfalls as he followed the river toward South Boston.

After several hours, Isaac reached the covered bridge, its arch looming above the dark river. Creeping as close as he dared, he eyed the small hut on the far side. Was the bridge keeper sleeping? A patchwork of planks, cross beams, and shadows crisscrossed the inside of the bridge. Isaac stepped carefully, masking his footsteps. He was almost halfway across when the loud "clop" of horse's hoofs suddenly echoed through the cavernous structure. Behind him, the silhouette of a carriage filled the far opening. He couldn't run—too much noise—and he'd be seen. Isaac slid over the low fence dividing the two lanes and lay prone, pressing himself against the fence. Lie still—become another shadow.

The sound of hoofs grew louder. Soon, the carriage was beside him. Then, just as quickly, it rolled on toward the far end of the bridge. Isaac remained frozen against the fence as the carriage stopped for its driver to pay the toll. No question, the bridge keeper was now awake for sure. Isaac had best stay put until he'd settled back to sleep. A lantern flickered near the keeper's shack, then darkness.

Isaac lay on the hard boards, staring at traces of sky visible through cracks in the roof. What about Pa? Would he ever return? Isaac's chances of getting to Philadelphia were better than the odds of Pa escaping those cotton fields. Was that bridge keeper back to sleeping? Isaac pushed to his hands and knees, watching the far end. Finally, in a crouch, he slipped quietly across the remainder of the bridge.

A shortcut across fields brought him to the post road, then a few more miles of easy walking placed him at the end of the lane leading to the McConnell farm. The glow of dawn warmed the eastern sky.

Home. Isaac relaxed and strolled up the familiar lane. Field hands stirred as he passed the slave quarters.

"Morning Isaac. What's you doing down these parts so early? You in the fields today?"

"Just passing, Aunt Lilly. I 'spect I'll be down to the fields soon enough." He waved and continued walking. Rounding the corner at the drying sheds, he met Henry coming down the lane on horseback.

Henry reined his horse. "Where you been?"

"Down to the quarters," Isaac said.

"And last night?"

"Been around."

"You run off?" Henry said. "'Cause if you did, I could have you whipped, you know that?"

"Now you's sounding like a real McConnell," Isaac said. "Just like your brother. Go ahead, fetch your whip."

Henry lowered his voice. "Damn you, Isaac, I could—and he would. How am I going to keep him off your back if you go and run off? You know he was asking about you yesterday?" Henry pointed a gloved finger. "You know that?"

"What did Massa Patrick want with Isaac?"

"Big Jim couldn't find you when it was time to go to the fields, so he reported you missing. Patrick came to me and I told him I had you running an errand."

"Isaac don't need nobody making up stories for him . . ."

Henry raised his hands. "Damn it, shut up and listen. McConnells have been protecting you and yours for better than a hundred years. Lately you've been throwing about ideas that have me thinking hard. We may be slave owners, but we're *not* the evil tyrants that you make us out to be. You and me have been friends for as long as I can remember, and because we're friends I spend nights worrying about what you've been saying. Maybe things do need changing, but maybe you just need to sit tight until this damn war's done with. I leave tomorrow to rejoin my unit and I won't be able to change anything between now and then."

"Take me with you."

"What?"

"You said Isaac could go with you, cook your food. Take me with you."

* * *

"You don't want me selling that troublemaker? Fine, go ahead, take him. It'll be one less headache." Patrick leaned from the saddle and cut off a top leaf, rolling the tobacco between his palms. He cupped the balled leaf in his hands and sniffed.

Henry's head pounded. Nausea swept over him as the sun beat down on the back of his neck. He was still weak, maybe too weak for this confrontation, but after Patrick raised the question of selling Isaac, he couldn't simply let the comment pass. "I will. He's mine anyway, Papa said so back on my sixteenth birthday."

"Fine. Go." Patrick waved dismissively with the back of his hand.

Henry reined his horse as it shied away from the sudden motion. "And what of Big Jim?"

"What about him?"

"What gives you the authority to let Sean go? He's been a fine overseer for better'n eight years and he was Papa's choice. You had no right to turn him out without my say so."

"You want a say in things," Patrick said, "stop playing soldier and start helping around here. See those bugs?" He pointed to a stalk next to Henry's boot. "You want to take part in managing this farm, how about you start by gathering up all the women and children who are loafing down there at the slave quarters and get their lazy asses out here pulling tobacco bugs."

Henry wiped his brow with his sleeve. "You tell Big Jim if he lays a hand—or a whip—on any more McConnell slaves, he'll answer to me, and he'll be the one being sold."

* * *

"It ain't our war," Florence said.

"Ain't gonna fight, Mama, just cook, and when the time's right, I'll be slipping behind them Yankees and heading on up to Pennsylvania."

Isaac continued gobbling his eggs and ham. Of course he was right. Nothing held him there, not now. She'd be running too, except when Abraham escaped—and he would—he'd be coming back there. She had to wait. "You's right, boy. Your mama just worries—all that shooting and killing, some bullet might find you, even if you's hiding real good."

Isaac wiped his mouth on his sleeve. "Cooking, Mama. Not fighting, cooking. Isaac ain't gonna be nowhere near the battle. I'll be back in the camps."

"How will you know when to cross over, when to head north?" She asked.

"Ain't certain, but I reckon the good Lord will give me a sign," Isaac replied. "For sure, I'll be a whole lot safer traveling north with Massa Lee's army than on that underground railroad. I don't need no pass if I's with Massa Lee."

Florence smiled. "You'll be in freedom's land come Christmas, I just knows you will. How you gonna find Raleigh?"

"Mr. Day gave me an address. I has it memorized." Isaac frowned. "Will you and Tempie be all right?"

"Your sister will be having her baby most any time. She still ain't talking none about it. I reckon she's just feeling shamed. Me and Joseph, we'll take good care of her. Here, these is for your trip." She handed him several warm biscuits wrapped in a bandanna. "Massa Henry said you'd be riding a train. I ain't never rode no train before . . ."

"Ain't never rode no train, neither, Mama, but I come close one time." Isaac smiled and put his arms around Florence.

She held him close, burying her face in his chest. Lord, he was almost as tall as his pa. She squeezed tightly, then stepped back, still holding him as she fought back the tears. "You be careful, Isaac, you be real careful, and I prays the Lord be with you."

Chapter Thirty-eight
August 1862

"Get on there," Isaac said, flicking the reins. The mare kicked, then settled to the task of pulling the wagon down the dusty post road toward South Boston. "So, tell me again how we's gonna find that regiment of yours?" Isaac said. "I hear Richmond's a big town."

"Not that many places to hide an army," Henry replied. He sat ramrod straight on the wagon seat with his kepi squared on his head and newly sewn sergeant's chevrons adorning the sleeves of his gray tunic.

If finding Massa Lee's army was so durned easy, how come those Yankees had such a time of it? Isaac bit his tongue, then pointed to the horse. "When we gets to South Boston, what are we doing with this here rig?"

"Mr. Throckmorton at the livery will watch over it until Banjo can come and claim them." Henry rested his elbows on his knees. "How's that sister of yours doing?"

"Mama says she'll be birthing real soon." Isaac shook his head. "It don't seem right, a child like that having babies."

"I know what you mean," Henry said. "It's hard to believe she and Polly are the same age. Who's the daddy?"

"Tempie ain't talking, except to say it ain't Cato." Isaac gazed at the cobalt sky and sighed. "She's holding in a mighty sadness."

Henry seemed to consider his next words. "It's been hard on you and yours this past year. I can't say I blame you for getting angry the other day."

Isaac shuffled in his seat. "I ain't worrying none about what's past, we has a war waiting for us up yonder." Isaac pointed ahead. "We'd best consider that some."

Henry nodded.

The sun rose above the trees, warming the tobacco fields and burning off the morning mist. Isaac smiled to himself. He wouldn't be working those fields again. A pair of turkey buzzards circled high above. They knew about being free. When the time was right, he'd slip behind those Yankee lines and he'd know freedom too.

Isaac wiped his brow. The fields shimmered in the August heat as they rode on in silence past mile after endless mile of corn, cotton, and tobacco. Finally, almost as a mirage, buildings hazily came into view along the horizon. Isaac snapped the reins. The horse picked up her gait. Soon, they rolled into South Boston, along streets lined with one and two-story clapboard storefronts dwarfed by large brick tobacco warehouses.

Henry pointed. "Over yonder."

Isaac turned up a broad street filled with wagons, horses, and people going about their daily errands.

A man stepped from the covered porch of a small tavern and waved. "Henry, Henry McConnell. Can that be ye?"

Isaac reined the horse as the man stepped into the sunlight.

"Sean? I'll be damned." Henry slapped his knee. "Sean O'Farrell. What mischief are you up to?"

"Ain't had the money for much mischief since that brother of yours terminated my employment."

"Sorry about that, Sean." Henry shrugged. "Weren't none of my doing, you know that, and he was a fool for doing it."

"Aye, on that we agree. Where ye be off to, Henry?"

"Me and Isaac's heading up to Richmond to find the Fourteenth Virginia. General Lee believes our war of Southern independence once again requires my presence. How about you?"

Sean shrugged. "There's not a soul here about that's hiring, and me beer money is growing mighty scarce. I've not a decent plan stewing in this lovely head of mine, beyond drinking up my last two dollars."

"How about throwing in with us?" Henry said. "The army will pay you eleven dollars a month, plus all the moldy cornmeal you can eat. You'll walk twenty miles a day, get shot at more than you'll like, and sleep under the stars—or the rain—whichever the good Lord provides, but you'll have fine company."

Sean laughed. "Sure and it sounds lovely. Truth be told, I've been thinking on your grand war of southern independence." He placed his hands on his hips and leaned back. "Me own dear father, God rest his soul, filled me with tales of the uprising of '98, he being an unfortunate patriot of that glorious cause. Now, 'tis not that I have such an abiding love for your fair state mind you—your fine tobacco, aye, but I'll not be missing your stinking summers— still, I can't be thinking of a reason not to take up me sword against them that would be setting the boot of tyranny on you freedom- loving Virginians."

"Well then, climb aboard." Henry waved.

Sean glanced around, then lowered his voice. "It appears your Yankees would be having a wee bit in common with that bonnie Prince of Wales, God damn his royal arse. Besides, eleven dollars a month buys more beer than Sean O'Farrell is buying on his present wages."

"So you'll join us?"

"Isaac, you'll be holding that animal still whilst old Sean O'Farrell comes aboard." He stepped onto the wheel hub and dropped hard onto the bed of the wagon. "Me bones are a wee bit old for such nonsense, so I'm certain I'll be regretting this decision, should I ever again be cursed with clear-headed sobriety."

* * *

"You, back there with the horses." The station agent pointed Isaac toward the open door of a boxcar.

"We'll see you in Richmond." Henry waved, then he and Sean climbed the steps of the passenger car.

Isaac scrambled into the boxcar. Two horses were tethered in the front of the car. An old slave in a dusty bowler sat in a corner chewing a piece of straw.

"Morning, pilgrim." The man touched two fingers to the brim of his hat.

"Morning," Isaac replied, pulling a pile of straw under him as he sat.

"What's your business in Richmond town?" The man asked.

"Me and Henry, I mean my massa, we be soldiering. We's gonna catch up with Massa Lee's army. How about you?"

"My massa, Doctor Pritchard, he owns these here nags." The stranger pointed to the horses. "I's taking them to his brother in Ashland to be sold to that same army. You seen much fighting?"

Isaac shook his head. "Been down on the farm. I's just now

going off to find the war."

"Well, you be careful, boy. I hear tell them Yankees is a mean lot. Massa Pritchard says if they catches a nigger, they cooks 'em up and feeds 'em to their dogs." The old man winked.

Isaac looked away and smiled, then lowered his voice. "You going back after you delivers them horses?"

The man took the straw out of his mouth and squinted. "What's you talking about?"

Isaac shifted his seat in the straw. "Richmond's a big town. A nigra could get lost, might not find his way home . . ."

The old man turned his head, pointing to a notch cut deeply into his right ear. "You see that? I got the mark of the whips too. Ol' Jeremiah's run too many times, been caught every one. I 'spect a man needs to know when he ain't cut out for running."

Isaac put a hand to his own ear and nodded.

"You?" The old man raised his eyebrows.

"Reckon the army will be finding them Yankees soon enough," Isaac said. "When they does, I's looking to get to the other side, then make for the north."

"Whu-e-e-e!" The old man slapped his knee. "That Confederate Army be taking the nigra all the way to the Freedom land." He chuckled, then pulled his hat down over his eyes and lay back on the straw. "I sure enough likes that."

The whistle sounded a long blast, followed by a rumble that grew louder as it rolled from the front of the train. Isaac's car jerked forward with the clanging of couplings then, as quickly, the clatter of iron against iron faded down the track. The train began to roll. Brick tobacco warehouses passed in front of the open doorway. Isaac closed his eyes and pictured Raleigh standing by the fireplace in her pale blue dress, a steaming cup of tea in her hand.

* * *

"Sergeant McConnell," the lieutenant said, "I know you boys is tired and all, but we need pickets out in them woods yonder, across the river."

"Yes sir." Henry saluted and turned away. The company bivouacked in a wheat field south of the Rappahannock River. Discarded muskets and scraps of equipment littered the ground below Waterloo Bridge where Brigadier General Jones's division had skirmished Union forces the day before. Somewhere across the river, maybe up near Warrenton, General Pope and the entire Yankee army were said to be waiting.

"Henry, will we be moving out?" Sean asked. "We've only just arrived." He was accompanied by two younger soldiers, their bare feet and torn britches a testament to their length of service in the Fourteenth Virginia.

"No, we ain't moving. We're setting up yonder." Henry pointed.

"But Longstreet's moving, why ain't we?" One of the privates asked, pointing to the formation plodding along the distant road.

"Our orders are to hold the Rappahannock line," Henry said. "I don't know what Longstreet's up to, but we're staying put. I need you three to get on across that river and set up with the picket line in the woods." He pointed to the two young veterans. "You fellas show O'Farrell here what to do."

"Aye, that we'll do, Henry. You can count on us. " Sean and his young comrades gathered their muskets and took off for the river.

Henry wandered toward the company area. Soldiers gathered in small groups, some busily setting up lean-tos, others cooking or working on gear. Three men sat in the shade of a sycamore tree joking and playing cards. They looked up and waved as Henry passed. A circle of slaves gathered behind the wagons, laughing and talking amongst themselves as they cleaned equipment and mended uniforms.

"How do, Massa McConnell." One of the slaves tipped his hat and smiled as Henry walked past. Isaac looked up from his work and simply nodded. Henry continued on until he reached a gathering of soldiers huddled over maps laid on a table under a white canvas tarp.

Henry saluted, then pointed to the trees beyond the Waterloo Bridge. "Sir, I placed pickets in the woods watching that road up to Warrenton. Is there anything more you need, Lieutenant?"

"Not at the moment, McConnell." The lieutenant rubbed the back of his neck as he gazed at the troops moving up the road. "I wish to hell they'd let us go with Longstreet. Word is, he's swinging around to catch up with Jackson, and they'll be giving the Yankees what for while we set here on our asses guarding this damned river."

"I know what you mean," Henry said. "It appears the generals keep pushing us to the back of the line. Do you suppose they're still fussing over that little skedaddle back at Seven Pines?"

"It's hard to say, but it ain't like we haven't made up for that one ten times over. Hell, we lost a passel of good men back there on Malvern Hill, including Captain Bruce. You remember that, Henry?"

Henry bit off a chaw of tobacco. "I missed that one. I was in Richmond tending to my wounds from Seven Pines."

Lieutenant Sternberger nodded. "The Fourteenth fights as good as any regiment, and Armistead's brigade is as good as any in Lee's army. Our time will come." The lieutenant pointed across the river. "That Irishman, is he going to work out? He looks a might used up."

Henry laughed. "Sean? He'll do just fine. He ain't ornery, but when the time comes, he'll stand and fight."

* * *

Isaac fell in step with the rest of the slaves plodding along at the end of the long column. A cloud of fine yellow dust stirred by artillery caissons, supply wagons, and thousands of marching feet hovered over the lumbering army. Somewhere ahead, Henry marched too.

"You reckon we'll find them Yankees today?" Jebediah asked. The short, rotund slave sweated profusely as he struggled to keep pace with Isaac. "I ought to be riding in that there cook wagon." He pointed and wiped his brow.

Isaac scowled at the pudgy man. "So why ain't you? I ain't never seen you down here with us common nigras."

"Massa said I burnt his coffee. He said Jebediah has to walk today for his punishment. That coffee weren't burnt, it just tasted bad. Tarnation, we ain't had real coffee in better'n a year. How's he know burnt coffee from chicory?"

"We been walking for three days." Isaac spit. Dust lingered on his dry lips. "I expect them Yankees is lost. I heard two officers talking last night and they said we's pushing to catch up with General Longstreet, but nobody knows where he is." Isaac held out his canteen. Jebediah took a long drink.

Exhausted soldiers dotted the sides of the road. A skinny young man with sandy hair and reddened cheeks staggered between the columns. He gazed vacantly at Isaac, then stumbled to the ground. Isaac wiped his brow and marched on. If he thought that was hot, he should spend a day in the tobacco fields.

The column halted late in the afternoon. Soldiers quickly staked their claims to what little shade they could find while slaves built fires and began cooking the evening meal. Isaac rummaged through his haversack, retrieving a slab of salted pork wrapped in cheesecloth. He started a fire and heated two slices, then searched for Henry. He found him near the company headquarters.

"Damnation, McConnell, where's your nigra finding that pork?" The Lieutenant pointed at Isaac. "where'd you get fresh bread?"

"I've been home, Lieutenant, remember?" Henry said. "We brung all we could carry. Bread won't keep, but the pork'll be good for a month or so. You care for a taste?" Henry offered a slice of sourdough and a piece of pork to the officer, who accepted it gratefully. "You should see what Isaac does with venison."

"Will that be all, Massa?" Isaac waited for Henry's nod, then returned to the back of the column. Henry was sure quick to give away Isaac's share, and there wasn't time to cook any more. His meal would have to be cold.

"Column of fours, on the road," one of the officers shouted.

Isaac stumbled to his feet. "We's moving out again, Jebediah, you able to walk?" Isaac tugged on the heavy man's arm.

Jebediah refused to budge. "I's plumb wore out. This here nigra's waiting on the wagons."

"For sure? What if they pass you by?"

"Then I sleeps by the roadside and you can fetch me after the war's done. These old bones ain't moving no more tonight." Jebediah rested his head on a clump of grass and pulled his hat over his eyes. "No sir, can't move no more . . ."

Isaac joined the others, falling into the mechanical shuffle of a tired army on the move.

Darkness enveloped the column. One foot in front of the other, eat dust, hurry up, stop for no apparent reason, then hurry again. Isaac gazed at the heavens. There was the drinking gourd, and yonder, the Freedom Star. They were headed north by east. Would Pa be looking on those same stars tonight? Would he be thinking that now was his time for running? Isaac stumbled over a fallen soldier and caught himself.

Chatter died with the darkness, leaving the rattling of equipment against exhausted bodies and the shuffling of feet through the dry Virginia dust the only sounds of the night. Isaac fought to stay awake. On either side, men appeared to be sleeping as they walked. Did they even know they were walking?

The column halted. An officer hurried down the line, hushing the regiment. "We're lost, boys. Some jackass took us plum past Groveton and we're behind the Yankee lines. Now, y'all stay real quiet like and turn yourselves around." He spoke with a frustrated urgency. "We're going back the way we come."

The sleeping, walking ghosts awoke, intent on escaping a possible enemy trap. Other than an occasional whispered curse, the column moved silently. The march took on a sense of urgency. Soldiers continually glanced over their shoulders. Would the enemy close in and make them pay for violating the northern lines? Yankee campfires flickered in the woods beyond the road.

After what seemed like an hour, the column halted again.

"Local pickets only," the lieutenant called. "We're in reserve. Bivouac north of the road over there, the Warrenton Turnpike." His voice didn't hold a fear of detection.

Isaac glanced at the stars. It had to be two, three in the morning. He was ready for some sleep. He moved off the road and rolled out his blanket close to Henry's. "You expect we'll be fighting tomorrow?"

"I can't say," Henry replied, "but if we do, you come along with me and see it for yourself. Once you've faced the elephant— been through a battle—nothing else will ever seem near as frightening again."

"I expect you's right, Massa Henry, but Isaac don't need no fighting."

"You won't have a choice. Once the shooting starts, you'll be drawn to it, just like a honeybee to clover."

Chapter Thirty-nine
August 1862

Isaac bolted upright as the distant pop of musketry shattered the early morning calm.

"Just skirmishers," Henry mumbled. "Go back to sleep." He rolled over, pulling a corner of his blanket over his face.

But Isaac couldn't sleep—the war was close, closer than it had ever been. Was today his day? Would he be bedding down on freedom's soil come evening? He stretched, then wandered across the dirt road and made water. In the eastern sky, grays and pinks streaked the dawning horizon. The sporadic musket fire continued, then a deep "boom," more violent than the thunder of any summer storm, shook the ground. Smoke rose from the hillside a mile away. The musketry ceased. It was too early for serious fighting. He'd best get some coffee going. Isaac drifted back to the camp, gathering firewood along the way.

The morning passed quietly. The sun was directly overhead when Henry finally rolled over and gave a sniff to Isaac's cooking. "Sowbelly again?"

"Ain't got no chickens. Ain't got no eggs, neither. You wants dinner, you eats sowbelly and corn or, if'n you'd rather, you's welcome to corn and sowbelly." Isaac tilted the cast iron skillet, displaying the sizzling meat.

"Corn? Where'd you find corn?"

Isaac pointed to the fields across the road. "Good harvest there going to waste."

Henry scratched his head with both hands and walked to the fire.

"Them guns up north," Isaac said, pointing to the ridge where the earlier cannon fire had originated, "is they Yankee?"

Henry nodded and stuffed a piece of cornmeal bread into his

mouth. "The lieutenant was saying Jackson's somewhere up yonder."

"Jackson," Isaac said, "he one of your Confederates?"

"Boy, don't you follow the war?" Henry smiled. "Thomas Jackson, from over at V.M.I. They call him 'Stonewall' now, after he stood up to the Yankees last summer at Manassas."

Isaac raised an eyebrow. "We don't get no newspapers down at the slave quarters."

Henry started to speak, but his words were cut off by cannon fire and musketry from the direction of Jackson's forces. Smoke rose from the woods. The firing quickened.

"I reckon it's begun." Henry stood, gazing toward the spectacle unfolding before them. "General Longstreet will be calling on us for sure. Best get ready to move." Henry dropped his plate and rolled his blanket.

* * *

Isaac paced. The eerie calm throughout their small encampment seemed in stark contrast to the brutal destruction taking place no more than a mile to the northeast. If today was his day to escape he'd have a lot of shooting to get through first. Maybe he should reconsider.

"Ye're wearing a bloody path in that bloody meadow," Sean said with a smile. "Yer more nervous than a Rhode Island Red stretched across the chopping block. A wee bit o' the barley might settle your nerves." He held out a bottle. "And besides, the afternoon's late, they'd not be bringing us to the battle so close to the ending."

Isaac shook his head. "Mama don't hold with drinking. If she caught the devil's brew on my breath, she'd do me a whole lot worse'n any of them Yankees could."

"Devil's brew, indeed. 'Tis the sweet nectar of the high holy saints of Erin." Sean raised the bottle, then took a swig.

"Put it away, Sean. We're forming up." Henry pointed toward the gathering troops as he returned from a meeting under the company tarp. "Longstreet's pushing the Yankees to our front. We have a chance to turn their flank and General Anderson is sending us in to do just that."

The sun was high in the western sky. Isaac took off his hat and shielded his face. Late afternoon. Smoke, dust, sun beating down—

he might as well be back home pulling tobacco bugs.

Drums beat a staccato urgency. "Company, fall in." The lieutenant drew his sword.

"Stay close to me." Henry pulled Isaac by the sleeve as they found their position to the rear of the company.

The regiment formed in two ranks, with sergeants and corporals to the rear as file closers, responsible for pushing stragglers forward and closing gaps in the line caused by enemy fire. Several slaves behind the regiment carried muskets. Isaac nudged Henry and whispered. "I won't carry no musket."

"You'll change your tune when the shooting commences—and if it comes to pass that you need one, there'll be plenty to choose from." Henry put a finger to his lips and pointed as Colonel Hodges drew his sword and faced the Fourteenth Virginia.

"Men of Virginia. General Jackson holds on our left. General Longstreet is attacking to our front. Yonder is the enemy." He pointed his sword toward the smoke covered high ground to the northeast. "The Yankees hold the very field where, last summer, General Jackson stood like a stone wall. They defile sacred ground stained by the blood of brave Virginians. We are the army's right flank. We will drive the invaders from our state. You carry the honor of Virginia with you today. Do not fail her."

The men gave a rousing cheer. As the celebration subsided drummers beat out the quick step and the regiment marched off, bayonets fixed and muskets at the carry. Isaac glanced around, waiting for orders. When none came, he fell in step behind Henry.

The regiment moved in line, colors unfurled. To either side, other regiments joined the attack. A shell burst overhead. Isaac's heart pounded faster. His stomach twisted in a knot—would he puke? Was Henry also scared?

Another unit pushed up a grassy slope to their front. Smoke rose from the distant heights, mixing with clouds that now enveloped the battlefield. The Fourteenth Virginia waded a stream, then struggled to realign itself as it climbed the next hill. The roll of drums continued the cadence.

Muskets, haversacks, canteens, and bedrolls dropped or abandoned by men in a rush to save their lives littered the ground. The regiment halted at the top of the hill. Soldiers rushed forward to pull down a rail fence, then the drummers struck up a beat and the unit moved again.

As Isaac stepped over a winding fence his gaze fell upon a solder in blue. The boy lay over the bottom rail, hugging the fence post. He stared straight at Isaac, a curious, frightened expression on his young face. A dark pool spread on the dry grass beneath him.

He couldn't be more than sixteen. Isaac turned away, fighting a wave of nausea.

The regiment held at the crest of the hill while units ahead pushed the Yankees. A swath of bodies in blue along a dusty lane marked what must have been the final, fateful stand for some brave but unlucky regiment. The Yankees were skedaddling with great urgency. Isaac wouldn't find his way behind their lines today.

The lieutenant passed the word to stand easy.

"Looks to be closing on supper time," Henry said. He pointed to the overcast sky. "You reckon it'll rain?"

Isaac studied the clouds. "A good soaking will settle the dust, wash away that terrible stench too." He waved his hand in front of his face. "What in tarnation is that?"

"Death," Henry said. "I smelled it some at Seven Pines, more at the hospital. It sticks to the inside of your nostrils."

Isaac wrinkled his nose. "It don't seem right, all that killing."

The long roll of the drums called the regiment back to attention. They moved out, swinging to the right and climbing another ridge, then down onto a well-worn road. They turned to the west and climbed a low rise. Suddenly, a chaotic sea of blue swirled to their front. The colonel gave the order to fire by companies. The lieutenant stepped to a position to the side of the company and issued the command. Isaac shuddered as the line of muskets roared. The field of blue disappeared behind a curtain of white smoke.

"They're running!" Henry pointed to the field below them filled with Union soldiers, some running, others limping, all struggling to find a path away from the battle. "We've got 'em, Lieutenant," Henry hollered above the din. "We can roll them up. We must attack."

Before them the entire Union flank lay exposed and undefended. The lieutenant looked toward the fleeing enemy, then to Colonel Hodges. The colonel responded with a frustrated shrug. Rain began falling as evening settled around the Fourteenth Virginia. The Yankees withdrew across the creek bordering the northern edge of the battlefield. Apparently, the Confederate generals were not interested in pursuing.

The burned out shell of a house stood in the center of the hill, surrounded by broken wagons, dead animals, and hundreds of dead and dying boys in blue. Isaac stared at the carnage. Across that creek somewhere, Raleigh waited, but the Yankees were running too hard. He wouldn't be crossing any lines tonight.

Chapter Forty
September 1862

Tempie slipped out to the porch of the main house. The pain was constant now. Could she sneak a few minutes of rest between chores? She rubbed the knotted muscles in the small of her back, then dropped into one of the rocking chairs. Humid morning air closed around her. Sweat and tears moistened her cheeks. She clutched her stomach. She didn't want no baby. All that bleeding and hurting all the time—why couldn't it be like it was before?

"Girl, what's you doing up there?" A gruff voice called to her from behind.

Tempie jumped.

Standing beside the porch, Big Jim gazed up at her as he wiped his brow.

"Shouldn't be sneaking up on folks." Tempie folded her arms with a huff. "Breakfast's done and Mama ain't got chores for me again 'til noon."

"Tobacco needs cutting," Big Jim said. "With your brother gone, we's shorthanded. Get on down to the fields and help with the harvest."

"But Mr. Jim, I's feeling poorly," Tempie said. "This here baby's making me terribly discomfortable."

"That's what you get for spreading them legs. Now get on down to the fields before I takes my rawhide to your sassy little tail." Big Jim snapped the whip above his head.

Tempie glared at the large man. Was he's thinking he's top rooster? He wouldn't be acting so high and mighty if her pa was there. "Your whip don't scare me none." Tempie pushed up from the chair and grabbed her stomach. Clutching the rail to steady herself, she slowly straightened. "I'll be there shortly, Mister Jim. No cause for your fussing."

"See you does, girl." Big Jim shook the coiled whip at her. "You people is all the time thinking you's too good for working them fields. You be learning, you's just another darky on this here farm."

Tempie eased down the steps and walked around back to the cook shack.

Florence sat on the small porch plucking a chicken. She glanced up as Tempie approached. "You's looking peaked, child. Go rest a spell on my bed until dinner."

"I can't, Mama. Big Jim says I has to go on down and work the fields."

"Land sakes," Florence said. "Can't that man see your condition? I declare, he's getting too full of his self. Somebody needs to set him straight."

"Don't be getting riled, Mama. I'll be fine." Tempie dipped a ladle in the bucket on the bench and drank the cool spring water. She poured another dipper over her bandana and dabbed it on the back of her neck. "I'll be back in time to help with dinner."

"No bother, child. Just fixing this here bird for Banjo and Jim. Massa Patrick is off to South Boston and Miss Ella, she and Polly is up to Richmond again. Said she's visiting her brother's family. Maybe Polly will bring you back a bolt of cloth so's we can make some clothes for that baby." Florence smiled, patting Tempie's stomach.

"That'd be nice, Mama." Tempie forced a smile as she tied the bandana on her head and started toward the tobacco fields.

* * *

"Here, you drink this." Florence lifted the glass to Morgan's tightened lips. "Don't you be fussing with me." He was always difficult at medicine time. She pinched his nostrils. His mouth opened. She poured in the potion. His eyes flared. He gagged, then swallowed.

Florence wiped his chin, then rolled the wheelchair next to the open window. "There ain't no sense in you fighting me every day. You knows them medicinals is fixing you up—and real good, too." She took his hand in hers. "Now, it's time for your exercising. The horse don't win no race except he be run hard in practice." She held her hand on top of his. "Push."

Morgan pushed against her hand until his arm straightened

above his head. He turned slightly and faced her with a twinkle in his eye. "I win . . ." The raspy whisper posed a playful air.

"Sure enough, Massa, you be winning most every time now." She placed a knotted stocking in his hand. "Squeeze this." He worked his fingers around the large knot, squeezing, then releasing.

"Pulling teats . . ."

Florence leaned closer, placing her ear next to his mouth. "What'd you say, Massa? Florence ain't but barely hearing you."

He coughed, then tried again. "Like milking . . ."

Florence laughed. "Maybe I'd best roll you out to the barn and shove you upside that ol' milk cow. Least ways then we'd get some work out of you, instead of all this here lazing around."

He held his hands in front of him, appearing to pull at imaginary teats, then glanced at Florence with a twinkle in his eye.

She shooed him with the back of her hand. "You'd best be behaving or I'll give you another dose of my special medicines." Florence peered out the window, running her fingers along the sill, then turned and faced him. "I ain't heard none from Miss Polly. You get any letters from Massa Henry?"

He shook his head. The movement was almost imperceptible.

"Been worrying on my Isaac, Massa Henry too. They's both good boys. Shouldn't be off fighting no war. I prays they's safe." She adjusted the crocheted lap robe covering his legs. "I prays on my Abraham too . . ." Florence turned and looked out the window, hiding a sudden tear.

"Tempie . . . ?" He whispered.

Florence turned. "She's doing fine. Be birthing that baby most any day. She ain't saying who the daddy is, but I reckon it's that Cato boy over to the Johnston place."

"Child . . ."

Florence leaned closer. "Yes, sir, her baby be coming real soon."

He scowled and shook his head, struggling to form the words. "No, Tempie . . . she's just a child."

* * *

Tempie dropped the stick filled with tobacco on the back of the wagon, then grabbed an empty pole and returned to the row where Lilly and Mama Rose worked at cutting the plants.

Lilly glanced at Tempie, then straightened and placed her hand on Tempie's forehead. "Child, you'd best take some rest."

Tempie stuck the pole in the ground and leaned against it. "Every time I stop working, Big Jim hollers. If'n he sees me resting, he'll put that whip to me."

"You been going most all day, child." Lilly put her hand on Tempie's stomach. "You set on down and don't be worrying none about Big Jim." She peered down the long row. Across the field, Big Jim was yelling at one of the other slaves, then he smacked the man on the side of his head with a coiled whip.

Tempie turned toward Lilly. "But—"

"Hush." Lilly pointed to the ground. "You sit."

Tempie settled cross-legged in the dirt between the rows of yellow tobacco, folding her arms across her tummy and blowing out through pursed lips. "Be mighty hot, Aunt Lilly."

"Sure enough, child. You set there and rest. I's gonna fetch me some water. You want I should bring you some?"

Tempie nodded.

Lilly tossed aside the stalk of tobacco she'd just cut and walked to the bucket hanging on the back of the wagon. She took a long, slow drink from the dipper, then poured water over the back of her neck. She refilled the dipper and headed toward Tempie.

Tempie stretched her legs and leaned back, twisting to work out a crick in her back. Something poked against her stomach. An elbow? A foot? She patted her tummy. "You be still, child. It ain't your time. I's feeling too poorly for your kicking and playing."

A crack like the shot of a rifle sliced the heavy air. Tempie jerked upright, yelping as the end of the whip seared her shoulder.

"I done told you, girl, Mister Jim don't tolerate no lazy house niggers in his field." Big Jim coiled his whip, preparing for another strike. "You'd best get off your ass and get back to work or I'll . . ."

"Or you what?" Lilly stepped between Tempie and Big Jim.

"The girl's lazy," Big Jim said. "And this is what lazy gets you in this field." He shook his whip.

Tempie rolled onto her side, then struggled to get to her feet. Mama Rose stooped to help her.

"Can't you see this girl's close to birthing?" Lilly took a step toward Big Jim. "You lay your whip on that child again and you'll answer to me."

"I's in charge now," Big Jim said as he retreated. "And I'll be whipping any nigger what I choose." He glanced at Lilly, then Mama Rose. "And the two of you got no say."

"Mama Rose," Lilly said, wagging her knife in front of her, "does you be remembering last spring, when Massa McConnell bought him that young bull?"

"I sure enough does, Miss Lilly." Mama Rose stepped around to Big Jim's side, flashing her knife as well.

"And you be remembering what Massa tells Miss Lilly?"

Mama Rose smiled. "I sure do. He tells Miss Lilly, 'You cut the balls off'n that young bull, geld him proper like.'"

"And Miss Lilly, she done right for that poor beast—tied them balls off tight so's they be numb to the knife." Lilly stepped forward again. "I ain't tying no balls today, just cutting."

"You's crazy, woman." Big Jim stumbled as he backed away.

"Crazy enough." Lilly nodded. "And I'll be cutting all your hanging down things, you ever touch this child again." She sliced the air with her knife.

Big Jim crabbed backward through the dirt, distancing himself from the two women, then rolled over and regained his feet. "You's both crazy." He pointed at Lilly with his whip. "You's gonna pay for this . . ."

"And you'd best be sleeping with one eye open," Lilly shouted. "You hurt this child, you'll wake one morning to find that little thing you likes to play with been hacked off and fed to the hogs." She wagged her knife.

Big Jim grabbed his crotch and took off across the field.

Lilly motioned to Mama Rose. "Help me lift this poor child to the wagon."

* * *

"That baby ain't coming just yet," Mama Rose said, seated on the far side of the bed. "Go get you some air."

Florence nodded. She placed Tempie's hand on her round tummy, giving it a gentle pat. "I'll be back shortly, child. You rest. Mama Rose is right here, if'n you needs anything." Tempie looked at her and seemed to force a weak smile.

Florence stepped onto the small porch and gazed skyward. The full moon cast a silver hue over the barnyard. "Abraham, I don't know where you is tonight, but I's sure needing them strong arms 'round me right about now. Our baby, she's trying to birth her own child, and she's in a bad way." Wrapping her arms around herself, she leaned against the cook shack wall as tears welled in her eyes. She took a deep breath. "My boy's off to war, where Abraham is only you knows, Lord, and my baby's in there struggling with labor. Lord, you don't never ask Florence to take on no more'n what she can bear, so I knows you'll be finding a way to give your servant the strength she'll be needing to endure all this here pain. Be with my baby, Lord. She's so young . . ."

"Florence," Mama Rose called out, "the baby's coming." Tempie moaned, followed by Mama Rose's soothing murmur.

As Florence hurried into the cabin, Mama Rose moved to the foot of the bed and pushed the covers aside. Tempie lay there, small and scared, her knees raised, tears streaming down her cheeks as she clutched her stomach.

Florence took her station at the head of the bed and held Tempie's hand. "Mama's right here. Everything's gonna be just fine."

Tempie tightened in pain.

"Wait," Mama Rose said. "Don't be pushing just yet." She moved the lantern so it cast light over her shoulder. "You puff, like what I showed you. Now, child. Puff."

"Mama, it hurts . . ." Tempie cried out, squeezing Florence's hand.

"I know, baby. I know. It'll be over shortly. Listen to Mama Rose." Florence wiped Tempie's forehead with a damp cloth.

"Head's showing," Mama Rose said. "Next pain, you takes a deep breath and push."

Tempie tensed, then groaned and pushed. And pushed. And pushed.

Florence studied the worry on Mama Rose's face. Been taking too long. That child had to be worn out. Florence leaned close and looked into Tempie's eyes, forcing a smile. "You's doing just fine, child. You's doing just fine."

"Again. Breath deep and push," Mama Rose said.

Tempie rose up on her elbows as she strained.

"Push again. Push. Push."

Tempie fell back against the pillow.

Mama Rose shook her head. "Ain't so good."

Florence stroked Tempie's forehead. "It'll be all right, baby.

Mama Rose is gonna fix you up."

"Cord's wrapped," Mama Rose whispered. "Stop your pushing, child." She worked on the baby, then glanced at Florence and nodded.

"Now, like before. Do like Mama, come on . . ." Florence began blowing short, quick puffs.

"All right, Tempie, give Mama Rose a big push . . ."

Florence supported Tempie as she rose up and strained.

"There's your baby, Tempie, there's your baby boy." Mama Rose paused, staring at the newborn child; she gave Florence a grim look, then lifted the baby by his ankles and slapped his backside.

Florence cradled her exhausted daughter and stared at the quiet baby, its wet skin a bluish hue.

Mama Rose wiped the baby's face then draped him across her forearm and pounded on his back. "You breathe, child, you hear me?" She wiped a finger through the baby's mouth, then massaged his tiny chest. "Come on, boy, you's gonna make it." She slapped his bottom once again. The baby hung limp in her hands.

Tempie drifted in and out of sleep, unaware. Florence placed her hand on Mama Rose's shoulder. "It's the Lord's will, weren't nothing you could do."

Mama Rose laid the baby in the cradle of Tempie's arm. "I's sorry, child."

"M-mama?"

"Sh-h-h. It's all right, child." Florence held Tempie's face in her hands and leaned close. "The good Lord knows best."

"My baby?"

"The Lord, he decided Tempie needed more time before she was a mama. This was his will."

Tempie looked at Florence. "I hurts so bad . . ."

"You rest." Florence patted her hand. "Everything be all right now. I's right here."

Tempie sighed and closed her eyes.

Florence wiped her daughter's forehead with a damp cloth, then kissed her on her cheek. "Sh-h-h. You sleep now, child."

Mama Rose pulled aside the blanket. "She's bleeding some."

Florence stared into Mama Rose's eyes. "Can you make it stop?"

"I prays I can." Mama Rose massaged Tempie's stomach. "The

afterbirth needs to be coming out."

Florence lifted the baby from the bed and wrapped him in a small blanket, then hesitated. Finally, she placed the tiny bundle on the table and turned back to Tempie. "That baby done wore her out. She'll be sleeping good."

Tempie groaned.

"Praise the Lord, the afterbirth delivered." Mama Rose grabbed for rags as the flow came. "All we can do now is wait and pray."

* * *

"You seen that baby?" Mama Rose stood on the porch, her thumb pointing toward the cook shack door.

Florence nodded. "Don't be telling nobody, hear?"

"I won't, but why you wanting to keep that a secret?"

"Folks don't have no need knowing her dead baby was white. That'll just bring trouble."

"Been trouble enough, for sure." Mama Rose put a hand on Florence's shoulder. "I needs to check on her."

Florence followed Mama Rose into the cabin. Tempie appeared to be in a deep sleep, her breathing shallow but regular. Florence took Tempie's hand as she turned to Mama Rose. "It's the Lord's will. You done all you could. Now get on back to the quarters and get you some sleep. Morning will be here soon enough."

Mama Rose nodded. "I'll be back to check on her come dawn."

* * *

A pale glow filtered through the cabin window. Florence lifted her head with a start. Was she late? The big house would be wanting breakfast. She eased away from the bed where Tempie lay quietly and rubbed her eyes.

"You's had a rough night, child." Florence touched Tempie's forehead, then drew her hand back quickly and placed her ear next to Tempie's mouth. Slowly she shook her head as she straightened. With trembling hands, she lifted the blanket. A dark stain covered the bedding. "No, Lord . . ."

Florence gathered Tempie in her arms. Her tears fell onto the sweet, lifeless face. "Not my baby. Lord. Not my baby . . ."

Chapter Forty-one
September 1862

"Off the road. Step aside," the sergeant yelled. "Clear the way for the artillery." He directed the regiment into an open field. Ahead, predawn fog silhouetted the rooftops of a small village.

"We been marching all night," Isaac said. "My feets is wore out. Is we in Maryland yet?"

"Been in Maryland since we left Harper's Ferry last night." Henry pointed north, toward the sound of sporadic musketry already rupturing the early morning quiet. "By the sounds of it, we're fixing to go straight into battle."

"Ain't much shooting," Isaac said. "Least ways, not yet. Maybe today will be quiet." He adjusted the satchel hanging over his shoulder as he stepped off the road. Philadelphia wasn't but a few days' walk from Maryland. What would Raleigh think if she opened her door and found him standing on her step?

The Fourteenth Virginia followed the rest of the brigade across the field, halting along a road that led out of town toward the west. Tents filled an orchard on the far side of the road. A rider galloped in from the east, dismounted, and ran to a table set under a large tarpaulin. Men in gray huddled over what must have been a map.

"General Lee's headquarters." Henry pointed to the flag hanging limply beside the tarp. "Reckon we'll be safe enough here."

"Company, fall out," the company commander ordered. "Food and sleep. We're in reserve."

Henry spread his blanket, tossed his haversack on one end, and dropped to the ground. "I've been marching since before midnight. Don't any of you wake me—unless the Yankees start coming down that pike." He jerked a thumb toward the town.

"Aye, and I'll be more'n happy to join ye, lad," Sean said. "I don't know how you talked me into this here infantry. Me thinks a mature condition such as my own would earn a fellow a fine little wagon." He spread his blanket beside Henry's and lay down, tipping his kepi over his eyes.

To the north, cannons answered volley with volley, drowning the crackle of musketry. Smoke drifted above the trees. "The fighting's commencing. Appears to be a might heavy up yonder," Isaac said. He sat on his blanket staring at flashes of artillery exploding in the distance.

"Ain't our problem," Henry replied. "Catch some sleep while you can." He rolled to his side, pulling a corner of the blanket over his head.

* * *

"McConnell, wake up."

Isaac opened one eye. The first sergeant stood over Henry, poking him with his boot. The sun, high in a bright blue sky, warmed the plowed field. Mid-morning? Cannon fire and musketry filled the air. The fighting had grown heavier. Isaac sat up and rubbed his eyes.

"Wake up, McConnell. I need you to get a detail together, gather up the canteens and head on into Sharpsburg village yonder and fetch us some water." The first sergeant pointed in the direction of the small hamlet. "We'll be moving out soon, so get your tails back here quick as you can."

"Tarnation." Henry sat up, scratching his head. He squinted at the bright daylight, then turned toward town. "Battle's shifting some, listen."

"North and east o' town, if yer asking me." Sean rolled his blanket.

"Isaac, gather up as many canteens as you can carry. You too, Sean." Henry poked two soldiers asleep beside him. "Fraley, Akers, on your feet. You're coming too. Maybe we'll get lucky and one of those fine Maryland ladies we've been hearing about will invite us to breakfast."

"That's the least they can do after we liberates 'em from them damned Yankees." Akers was on his feet, canteens already draped across both shoulders.

"Come on, move out." Henry grabbed his rifle and headed

toward the town. Isaac, Sean, and the others trailed behind.

They entered the village of clapboard one- and two-story buildings set on gently rolling hills. A few houses bore evidence of the battle, plaster knocked off walls or broken panes of window glass. A large house on the south side of the road displayed trappings of wealth. A half circle window high on one end separated two large chimneys. Henry walked to the front door and knocked.

A middle-aged gentleman answered.

"Begging your pardon, sir. We're looking for a well to fill our canteens, and a taste of breakfast too, if it's no trouble."

"Well's around back. Won't deny water to anyone." The man waved toward the side of the house. "I've been a Union man all my life. I'll be damned if I'll break bread with you rebels. Fetch your water and be gone." The man stepped inside and slammed the door.

"I expect he ain't partial to being liberated, Henry." Akers grinned at Isaac and Sean.

Henry waved his small patrol onward. "That damned Yankee most likely poisoned his own well, just for spite. We'll move on."

They walked through the village, stopping at a house on the eastern side of town. A mile to the north, smoke blanketed lines of gray and blue blazing at one another across newly harvested fields.

Once again Henry knocked on the door. No one answered. He tried the latch. The door swung open into a parlor. Henry peeked inside, then motioned the others to follow.

Isaac brought up the rear, stepping into the front parlor as Fraley came around the corner with his mouth full of food.

"Biscuits. Still warm." Fraley motioned toward the back of the house. "Best get you some, boy. There's plenty."

Henry sat at a table in the small dining room with Akers to his left and Sean to his right. They busied themselves with a ham roast in the center of the table.

"Folks must of got scared off by the shooting." Henry waved his knife toward the din of battle echoing through the open window. "Cut some ham and have one of these here biscuits. Not as good as your mama's, but right tolerable for Yankee fare."

Isaac sliced off a thick piece of ham and placed it inside a biscuit. As he ate he studied a tapestry hanging on the wall. A large animal, not a deer, but similar, standing on a snowy mountain peak, his head tilted as if braying to all within earshot. Beneath the tapestry, a book set on a small table. Isaac flipped open the cover. The printed page was senseless gibberish. "Massa Henry, can you read this?" He handed the book to Henry.

Henry opened the cover of the leather-bound volume and studied the title page. "German. Looks to be a Bible." He handed it back to Isaac.

A thump sounded in the floor beneath them. Akers jumped from his seat, grabbing his musket. Henry studied the floor, then lifted a corner of the tattered blue rug under the table. "It's a trap door. Cover me." He drew back the carpet.

Akers and Fraley aimed their muskets at the opening in the floor.

"Out. Come on, we ain't going to hurt you." Henry motioned to someone below. In a moment, an old woman, her head wrapped in a scarf, appeared in the trap door. She climbed out, followed by a young girl, possibly nine or ten years old. The girl cowered behind the old woman, her wide eyes darting first to Henry, then Akers. Her gaze fell upon Isaac and her mouth dropped open.

"We won't hurt you, ma'am," Henry said. "We're just looking for food and water—we need to fill these." He pointed to the pile of canteens in the corner.

"Ya, ve have vater out back in da vell. Help yourself, just please, don't be hurting mien kleindochter." The woman placed a hand on the little girl's head. The child hugged her, hiding behind pleats in her plain black dress.

"We won't be hurting anyone, ma'am." Henry tipped his hat. "Fraley, take them canteens out back and fill 'em."

Fraley looked at Isaac and pointed to the canteens. "Boy, fetch them up and follow me."

* * *

"Thank you, ma'am. Your gracious hospitality has been more than kind." Henry tipped his hat as he backed out the door clutching a leg of fried chicken. The old woman smiled and waved.

"Nice folks," Akers said as he wiped crumbs from his beard. "For Yankees, that is." The patrol turned west on the dirt road, heading toward the center of town.

"We shouldn't have stayed so long," Henry said. "The First

Sergeant's going to have my hide."

"Quit your belly aching," Akers said. He slapped Henry on the shoulder. "We got the water. Besides, it ain't your fault the locals wanted to share their food with us. First Sergeant would agree, ain't that right, Fraley?"

Fraley nodded.

Isaac stumbled under the load of canteens. Akers reached back. "Here, boy, give me a few of them." He took two. Fraley turned and grabbed a couple as well.

Isaac followed the others, the straps of the filled canteens digging into his shoulders. Sounds of battle grew closer. A shell burst above the street, shattering a brick chimney. Debris rained on the road.

"Hold up." Henry raised a hand. The intersection ahead was filled with troops on the move. He called out, "What outfit?"

"Nineteenth Mississippi, Featherston's Brigade," one of the marching soldiers answered.

"They're Anderson's division. That's ours," Henry said. Henry turned back to the marching troops and hollered, "Where's Armistead? Where's the Fourteenth Virginia?"

The rebel cupped a hand to his mouth. "The whole division's moving. The Virginians must be somewhere up ahead. Hop on in here and join us. You'll catch up to your outfit soon enough."

"I knew a fella in the Nineteenth Mississippi once . . ." Henry motioned to Isaac and the others. "Step lively. Looks like we're marching with Mississippi this morning."

* * *

The long gray column snaked along narrow streets, then climbed a gentle rise toward smoke-filled fields north of town. The crackle of musketry punctuated the warm air. An artillery shell exploded overhead. Isaac ducked. Tarnation—bombs weren't bursting overhead back in Manassas when they'd marched up Henry House Hill, but they'd won that one. Must be the Yankees were doing the winning this day. Maybe they'd give him his chance to skedaddle on up to Pennsylvania . . .

Columns of soldiers peeled off to the left and took positions in an orchard. The Nineteenth Mississippi halted. Drums began the long roll and the column shifted into battle line. Ahead, harvested fields sloped toward a sunken lane lined on both sides with wooden fences and crowded with men in gray. Past the dirt road, the fields rose again, revealing row after row of soldiers in Union blue.

"Henry," Fraley called with a questioning look. "Shouldn't we find our own outfit now?"

Henry pointed to the troops in the orchard. "None of them appear to be ours. We'd best stick with Mississippi. Maybe we'll find the Fourteenth up yonder in that cut." He nodded toward the road.

Isaac fell in line with the file closers behind the formation and smiled to himself. Maybe he wouldn't close any ranks, but he'd sure enough be jumping fences and heading to Philadelphia—if the blue bellies out yonder gave him the chance.

"Forward . . ." An arm clad in gray lifted a sword in front of the formation. The sword swung down. "March!"

Drummers beat out a quick step. The regiment hurried down the slope, pulling Isaac along. The roar of musketry rolled across the fields. A man beside Isaac fell, then another. Someone ahead shouted a command. The line broke into a trot. Canteens banged against his side. Isaac shrugged. Canteens dropped. A soldier in front tossed his musket in the air as he stumbled, a dark stain spreading across the back of his shell jacket. Isaac stepped over the dying rebel. He dropped canteens from his other shoulder. Running became easier.

The formation halted on the near side of the lane while soldiers tore down the fence blocking their way. Once cleared, the regiment hurried into the narrow road and continued up the far side, knocking down another fence as they attacked. Rebels who had taken cover inside the sunken lane cheered as the Mississippians slammed into the exposed flank of a Yankee regiment.

"Look yonder," and officer called. "They's flying the traitor's flag of West Virginia. Drive them, men. Show no mercy."

Fraley screamed, then dropped to one knee and stared at Isaac, his face twisted in pain. "I's hit, boy. Get me on back to that road."

Isaac eased him to the ground and examined the wound in his thigh. "Henry, he's bleeding something awful."

Henry glanced at Fraley and jerked a thumb toward the rear.

Back to the cover of that sunken road? Yes, thank you, Lord. Isaac took a bandana from his pocket and tied it tightly over the spurting wound, then hoisted the heavyset soldier to his feet. Fraley flung an arm over Isaac's shoulder, using his musket as a crutch. Together, they hobbled down the hill. Once within the sunken road, Isaac lowered Fraley to the ground and propped him against the embankment.

"Bless you, boy." Fraley placed his hand on Isaac's arm. "You done saved my life." He pointed to the canteen. "Got any left?"

Isaac handed him his last canteen.

Muskets roared from high ground to their right. A fresh Yankee formation came over the rise, bayonets gleaming in the midday sun. Green flags crested the hill alongside the familiar red, white, and blue banners. Isaac peered over the fence rail. The new unit crashed into the flank of the Mississippi brigade. Boys in gray fell by the dozens. Regimental formations crumbled as Confederates fled to the safety of the sunken road. The farmer's field, once plowed for winter wheat, was strewn with the human residue of battle.

Henry dove over the fence, landing face down in the sunken lane. Sean tumbled in close behind. Henry glanced at Isaac. "You okay?"

Isaac nodded.

Henry bit off the end of a paper cartridge. "Akers is dead. How's Fraley?" He spit out the paper and poured powder into the muzzle of his musket.

"Bleeding's mostly stopped." Isaac nodded toward the crumpled figure at the bottom of the lane.

"Good. Stay low." Henry shoved Isaac down. Bullets splattered against the fence rails and splashed dirt up from the forward embankment.

Isaac burrowed into the side of the swale. The Mississippians seemed confused. To their left, a regiment from North Carolina stood from behind the embankment and fired in unison. A second rank followed, their muskets barking out another volley. The first rank then stepped forward again and fired at the Union lines on the crest of the rise.

"Dearest mother in heaven, will ye look at that?" Sean O'Farrell stretched to his full height with his kepi shoved back on his head.

Isaac peeked over the fence. Yankees stood before them in a

perfect line, not fifty yards away. Green flags snapped in the midday breeze. The Yankees held their ground as devastation rained upon them. With each new volley, dozens of Union soldiers dropped, but as quickly as one fell, another stepped in to take his place.

"Sons of Erin, they be. There boy, see that harp upon that green banner? They's Irish lads all, and may God bless 'em." Sean removed his cap. "They's standing tall, like the boys of '98, spilling their blood upon Vinegar Hill . . ."

"Get down you damned fool." Henry yanked on Sean's shirt, jerking him into the protection of the sunken road. "Those Irish lads would just as soon splash that Gaelic blood of yours all over this damned road."

Confederates in the road to their left poured deadly fire into the exposed Union lines. Smoke filled the lane. Sean leaned forward again, staring over the fence. He turned to Henry with a tear in his eye. "Murder it be. Proud, noble murder. A thousand Irish mothers will be weeping tonight." Sean focused again on the battle, waving his cap above his head. "God bless ye, lads. God bless ye, every . . ."

The bullet slammed into his neck, cutting off his words as it threw him to the ground. Blood gurgled from a dark hole in his throat. Isaac knelt and lifted Sean's head, cradling it in his lap. Sean looked up and smiled, then stiffened. The light drained from his eyes.

Isaac lowered him gently to the ground. "You was a good man, Sean O'Farrell . . ."

"Here they come, boys." An officer waved his sword, pointing toward the rise to their right. A swarm of blue crested the hill, filling the void left by the dead and dying Irish. The front rank of Yankees knelt as one. Smoke and flame belched from a hundred muzzles, then from a hundred more.

"They have our flank!" Henry hollered. He pushed the soldiers closest to him toward the enemy on their right. "Fire at will. Load and fire at will." He reached beneath a fallen soldier and pulled out a musket, thrusting it at Isaac. "Now's your time. Load and shoot."

Isaac stared at the musket with its long bayonet, then looked at Henry, who was straddling a wounded rebel and taking aim at the advancing Yankees. Isaac shook his head. He'd already killed that Johnston boy back home. Maybe, if Henry knew about that, he'd understand why he couldn't raise a musket against those Yanks. "It ain't my war, Henry. I ain't killing nobody . . ."

Confederates scrambled to retreat from the sunken road, only to be cut down by Yankee bullets as they clambered up the rear embankment. Dead and dying tumbled into the blood-filled trench.

A searing pain sliced Isaac's shoulder, spinning him around. He tore away the shredded cloth and looked. Just a scratch. Henry? Where was Henry? There, to the front. He climbed over bodies, dragging the musket he had yet to fire. A boy in gray fell against him. Isaac caught the soldier, staring into eyes filled with terror. The rebel shuddered, then collapsed. Isaac brought his musket to the ready and called up to Henry. "Ain't healthy here, Henry. It's time we be finding our own regiment."

Henry looked over his shoulder and smiled. "You gonna shoot that thing?"

"I ain't fighting your war, Henry McConnell . . ."

A Yankee raised his bayonet, thrusting toward Henry's back. Isaac leveled his musket and fired. The dead soldier tumbled against Henry's leg.

"Thanks. I reckon now it's your war too." Henry winked.

Isaac nodded and reached for another cartridge. The Confederate line to their right dissolved. Yankees poured over the fences and into the sunken road. Henry aimed and fired. A man in blue fell. Henry bit off the end of a cartridge and turned to pour the powder down the barrel when another Yankee lunged, bayonet at the ready.

Isaac's musket wasn't loaded. He dove, thrusting his musket like a spear. The Yankee bayonet entered Henry's shoulder as Isaac's bayonet gored the attacker.

The startled soldier dropped his weapon, peering at the dark blood pouring from the wound in his stomach. His eyes rolled back and he collapsed on top of Henry.

Isaac pushed the soldier off and lifted Henry in his arms. "Henry, Henry McConnell, you listen to me. Don't you die." Tears streaked Isaac's face. "It ain't your time, Henry. This ain't how it's supposed to be . . ." He cradled Henry in his arms.

A blur of movement—Isaac turned.

The rifle butt smashed into the side of his head.

271

Chapter Forty-two
September 1862

The annoying buzz grew louder as Isaac drifted toward consciousness. He rolled over and grabbed his head. "Lord, I's hurting . . ." Easing himself into a sitting position, he shooed the swarm of flies around his face. Where was he? Scattered clouds drifted across a midnight sky. Beyond the flies, only muffled groans and an awful stench interrupted the silent darkness. Rotted deer meat? No, worse.

He steadied himself. Beneath him, something protruded wrapped in a wet cloth. Rough woolen fabric—uniform? He felt again—the bloodied trouser of a soldier. Isaac recoiled. His eyes slowly adjusted. Bloated, festering mounds of gray filled the sunken road for as far as he could see, piled randomly atop one another, rotting where they fell.

Lanterns carried by dark silhouettes dotted the fields, drifting from body to body, pausing, apparently in search of a familiar face.

Henry? Where was Henry? His head throbbing, Isaac struggled to pull the top body from the pile of soldiers. A Yankee. The corpse tumbled to the road as Isaac searched the darkness for gray. There . . . . a leg. He tugged. The long dark hair and full beard weren't familiar. Suddenly, a hand grabbed his arm. Isaac recoiled. Alive? Frantically, he pushed aside another body and pulled the wounded soldier from under his tomb of rotting flesh.

"Water . . ."

He found a full canteen on a body wearing a blue uniform and held the water to the wounded soldier's lips, drizzling measured drops to keep the man from choking. The soldier sipped, then lay back in the crook of Isaac's arm and looked up. "Mississippi?"

"Virginia."

"I'm mighty grateful, boy." The soldier smiled and closed his eyes.

"I reckon you'll be sleeping a good while, Mississippi." Isaac eased him to the ground and pulled another Yankee from the pile, this one still impaled on the bayonet that killed him. Isaac brushed aside the light blond hair. Was he the one, the soldier who tried to kill Henry? He studied the young face. "I didn't mean you no harm, mister . . ." He eased him aside, then tugged at more bodies, uncovering old and young, blue and gray, but no sign of Henry. Exhausted, Isaac slumped against the roadbed cut. He wet his bandanna and dabbed at the throbbing knot on the side of his head. Henry wasn't there. Maybe he wasn't hurt so bad. Had he escaped? It would soon be daylight. There was time enough to search then. Isaac closed his eyes and surrendered to the exhaustion.

* * *

"He's still breathing. Grab him by the feet—and be careful."

The voice was near. Isaac opened an eye. Daylight, but the sun had not yet crested the trees lining the far field. A short, ruddy-faced man in a blue uniform with a rusty beard stood in the roadway pointing toward a body. Another soldier lifted the wounded man's feet as the one who had apparently spoken grabbed the fellow under his arms. Together, the two men placed the wounded soldier on a stretcher and carried him up the embankment.

Isaac stretched. His head still hurt, but the fog of dizziness had cleared. The battle appeared to be over. The only rebels around him looked to be dead. He stared at the pile of bodies in the sunken road. The long line of corpses filled the trench as far as he could see in both directions. Up and down the road and in the fields to the north and east, Union soldiers gathered their wounded. Isaac turned toward the town. Gray bodies dotted the field they'd crossed yesterday. Most lay facing the town, felled by Yankee bullets as they ran from the Union assault. Lord, such a terrible sight.

Isaac approached a soldier in blue who was tending to a fallen comrade. "Sir? Sir, begging your pardon, but is we behind the Yankee lines?"

The soldier straightened, wiping his hands on his trousers. "You a slave?"

"Yes sir." Isaac snatched his black slouch hat from his head and twisted it in front of him.

The soldier paused while he looked Isaac over. "You been fighting for them rebels?"

"No sir. Ain't no soldier. Isaac just do the cooking. I be looking for that freedom road now."

"North's yonder." The soldier jerked a thumb over his shoulder. "You's in a slave state 'til you gets to Pennsylvania, maybe two day's walk." He returned to his fallen comrade.

"Thank you, sir. Thank you." Isaac bowed slightly. Apparently it went unnoticed. He started up the lane. "Yes sir, get behind them Yankee lines and I'll be free at last. Free, and walking to Philadelphia."

The pain drained from his forehead. His legs forgot the weariness of all-night marches. Isaac headed for the bend in the road where yesterday the Yankee assault had rolled up the rebel flank.

"Raleigh's sure enough gonna be surprised when she opens her door and there's Isaac, free as a man can be." He stepped around a rebel body whose legs were cocked as if crawling along the bloody lane. The soldier's arm reached forward. Isaac stopped. That hair . . . . He rolled the soldier onto his back and gasped, then dropped to his knees. "Henry—Henry McConnell?" He cradled Henry's head in his lap. "What did you figure on doing, crawling all the way back to Virginia?"

Squinting, Henry partially opened his eyes. "Isaac?" He grabbed Isaac's shirt. "Did we beat 'em?"

"You got your asses whupped is what you got."

Henry groaned and clutched his bloody shoulder.

"A Yankee run you through with his bayonet."

Henry closed his eyes again, moaning softly.

"I'd best find you some doctoring." Isaac scanned the battlefield. Union soldiers were helping wounded comrades climb the rise through the break in the fence. "The Yankees must be fixing their wounded up yonder. I has to get you to their hospital." He stood, then looked down. "This is gonna hurt some."

Pulling Henry to his feet, Isaac shoved his shoulder into Henry's stomach and straightened. Henry groaned as Isaac lifted him from the ground, staggering under the limp weight. He struggled up the grassy rise, following Union soldiers who were carrying their own casualties. They crossed a wide creek and came to an encampment. Wounded soldiers, mostly Union, lay on the grass under the shade of large trees. Rows of tents stretched across a field. Gently, Isaac lowered Henry to the ground, propping him against a tree next to an old, bearded Yankee who helplessly clutched a stump where his arm used to be. "You set right there. I'll be back."

Henry opened his eyes, but didn't answer. His face reflected the pain of his wound and the agony of being jostled across a mile of farmland on Isaac's shoulder.

Isaac approached a cluster of tables outside a row of tents. Men in bloodied smocks gathered around each table, working over injured soldiers. Cries and whimpers accompanied the sounds of saws cutting through bone. A tall man in a top hat at the first table turned around with the mangled lower half of a man's leg in his hands. He tossed the useless limb onto a growing pile of discarded appendages. Isaac gagged and turned away.

A pretty young woman dressed in black, her hair covered by a simple white bonnet, hurried past with an armful of rags. Several rags fell to the ground in front of Isaac. He scooped them up. "Ma'am? Ma'am, you dropped these."

The girl stopped and turned. She gave Isaac a startled look. "Thee is a Negro."

Isaac brushed his hand across his jacket self-consciously. "Y-yes ma'am. I reckon I is." He remembered the rags. Bowing slightly, he held out the cloth. "You . . . you dropped these."

"Thank thee. Bandages are in short supply." She stared at Isaac. "Thee wears the garb of the rebellion. Is thee Confederate?"

Isaac shook his head. "Just a slave looking to find the road to the Promised Land, but first I has a friend what needs doctoring."

"Where is thy friend? Has he been tended to?"

"No ma'am. I just now brung him over. He got stuck with a bayonet—run him clean through."

"See that copse of trees?" She pointed to a grassy area in the shade of three large trees. "If thee will fetch thy friend, I shall look at him there."

"Thank you, ma'am." Isaac bowed, then raced back to find Henry.

"Henry, I has to take you over yonder. There's a white woman who talks funny, she says she's gonna mend you. Help me get you up." Henry didn't respond. Isaac tugged on Henry's jacket, pulling him to his feet, then scooped him up in his arms and carried him to the trees.

"Place thy companion over there." The young lady pointed to an open spot between two Yankees.

Isaac gently laid Henry on the ground and stepped aside. The girl knelt, unbuttoned Henry's jacket, and lifted his blouse. "Thee said a bayonet? This wound appears severe. Has he lost much blood?"

Isaac nodded. "Bleeding most all night, I reckon."

"Hand me a bandage, there." She pointed to the bundle of rags. Isaac gave her a bandage.

She dipped the rag in a bucket of water and cleaned Henry's wound. "Thy friend has been blessed." She tossed the bloodied rag aside and bound the wound.

"Ma'am?" Isaac knelt beside her, offering another bandage.

"The wound is high in his shoulder, above his vitals. With prayer and rest, he has a chance."

"Doctors be fixing him soon?"

"The doctors are much too busy operating on the gunshot wounds, they will not see him today. Be thankful thy friend was not shot." She nodded toward the operating tables. "Those who manage to survive the surgeons do so at the cost of a limb. Thy friend's wound is serious, but I pray it will not be mortal." She studied Isaac for a moment. "Thee appears to be wounded as well. Come."

She cleaned and bandaged Isaac's shoulder. "What shall I call thy friend?" Her freckled face peered intently behind wisps of blonde hair.

Isaac stammered, "H-Henry, Henry McConnell."

"And what is thee to be called?"

"Isaac, I's to be called Isaac." He placed his hand on his chest and nodded.

"Yes." she smiled. "Son of Abraham . . . and thy surname?"

"Ma'am?"

"What is thy last name?"

Isaac shook his head. "I . . . I ain't got one of them, least not that I knows. Folks just call me Isaac."

"Well, Isaac, you have a fine first name. That should do for any man. And you may call me Hannah, Hannah Bunting. Will thee be remaining with thy friend, I mean, with Henry?" She placed a hand on Henry's good shoulder.

"Reckon I'll stay 'til he's on the mend, then I'll be off to Philadelphia. I has a woman waiting there." Isaac settled against a tree.

"And a most fortunate woman, I would suppose. What is she called?"

"They calls her Raleigh, 'cause that's where she was born."

Hannah glanced at Henry. "And thy friend, I suppose he has a girl waiting somewhere too?" Her cheeks flushed.

"Henry? He don't have no woman, not since the war. Used to be, he liked chasing them girls, but I reckon this here fighting is getting in his way."

Hannah pursed her lips, then quickly looked away. "I have never met a slave before. Thee must tell me of all the horrors. Is it as Harriet Stowe has written?"

"Don't know about no Harriet Stowe, nor nothing she been writing, but it's just living, same as anything else, 'cept somebody's all the time telling you what for and cracking the whip if'n you doesn't do right."

"Sounds absolutely inhumane." she gazed at Henry. "Does he own thee?"

"Me and Henry, we growed up together. I expect now that Massa McConnell, that's Henry's pa, now that he's laid up with his apoplexy, must be Henry is my massa." Isaac took off his hat and fanned it in front of his face. "Don't matter none though, 'cause I's heading north."

"And well thee should. 'Tis an evil thing, one man believing he can own another. Thee must never go back where thee will again be placed in bondage."

"No ma'am, I ain't going back. I reckon I's done with slavery."

"Good." She stood and brushed the grass from her dress. "I must tend to the others. Will thee be here to watch over Henry?"

"Yes ma'am. I expect I'll be right here just resting up against this here tree."

Chapter Forty-three
September 1862

"Where am I?" Henry opened his eyes, blinking at the waning daylight. Pain coursed through his chest.

"Hush," Isaac said. "You been hurt real bad. Lie still." He adjusted a frayed blanket around Henry's shoulders.

"Are we in Virginia?"

"Maryland," Isaac said. "You's in a Yankee hospital. Miss Hannah, she been taking good care of you."

"Who?"

"Miss Hannah," Isaac said. "A Yankee woman what tends to the wounded."

"How . . . how long have I been here?"

Isaac gazed skyward. "Going on four days. You took a bayonet in that shoulder. I brung you over here to get you mended."

Henry tried to raise up on one elbow. Pain drove him back down. "Yankees? You brought me to a Yankee hospital?"

Isaac plucked a stalk of grass and shoved it between his teeth. "All your Johnny Rebs skedaddled across the Potomac. This here is the only doctoring you's gonna get."

"How is thy patient, Isaac?" A young woman in plain garb nodded to Isaac as she approached, then turned to Henry and smiled. "Good evening, Henry. 'Tis nice to finally meet thee." Even in the fading light her deep blue eyes sparkled.

"I . . . I . . ." Henry shot Isaac a quick glance.

Isaac gestured toward the woman. "Massa Henry, this here be Miss Hannah Bunting."

"We have neither porridge nor meat," she said. "Fill up as best thee can on this hardtack." She handed each a hard, thick cracker. "The Union soldiers fare only slightly better. I will try to find something more tomorrow."

"Isaac says you've been tending to me," Henry whispered in a raspy voice. "Thank you."

"'Tis the kindness one of God's children offers another," she replied. "I should expect no less of thee, were the circumstances reversed."

"Meaning no disrespect, ma'am," Henry said. "But you's speaking in a curious tongue. Are . . . are you American?"

She smiled. "Pennsylvanian. Germantown Monthly Meeting, Society of Friends. Perhaps thee has heard of our work in the abolition movement?"

Henry scowled. "Quaker?"

"Yes. I came here with the Sanitary Commission to help relieve the suffering of all victims of this terrible war, blue or gray—even slave owners." She cocked her head to one side and smiled.

Henry laid back on the blanket, clutching at the sharp pain in his chest. Even slave owners? She was a testy one . . .

"Here's another over here." Two Union soldiers approached the copse of trees. One pointed at Henry.

"What is thy need, sir?" Hannah looked at the taller soldier.

"Begging your pardon, ma'am." The taller soldier touched the brim of his cap. "The provost marshal ordered us to gather up all these here rebels and take em' yonder where they can be guarded."

"Can't thee see this man is injured?" Hannah stepped in front of the provost guards. "To move him now could prove fatal."

"Sorry ma'am, orders is orders."

"And what then? Will thee see to it he gets proper medical attention?" She placed her hands on her hips.

"I don't rightly know, ma'am. They ain't promising our own boys will get looked at. I can't say what this here Reb can expect. Reckon they'll give him a bandage before they send him off to Fort Delaware, but that ain't none of my concern."

"Fort Delaware? Does thee know the horrid stories that are told of that place?"

The soldiers looked at one another. The shorter of the two shrugged.

"Our monthly meeting has written a letter to President Lincoln demanding that he close that wicked prison at once. God frowns on such inhumanity."

"I expect he do, ma'am." The taller soldier pointed at Isaac. "Is this here nigger a rebel too?"

"Certainly not." Hannah gestured toward Isaac. "This poor man has spent a lifetime in bondage. Now, he has found sanctuary behind the Union lines. Finally, he is free."

The taller soldier glanced at his companion and smiled. "Good. Then he's free to pick up this here rebel and haul him yonder with the rest of them prisoners, lessen you'd rather we just drag him over."

"He has a severe wound. Will thee allow me to visit him and tend to his needs?"

"Shouldn't be no problem, ma'am. There's a passel of Johnny Rebs over yonder. You can tend to them all."

She turned to Isaac. "Does thee mind?"

Pain shot through Henry's shoulder as Isaac carried him to the plowed field filled with wounded men in gray. No fences separated prisoners from the other wounded and what few guards were posted appeared disinterested in their duties. Isaac placed Henry on the blanket Hannah spread for him.

"Ain't no difference, here or where we was," Isaac said as he gazed toward the evening sky. "Either way, you's wet when it rains and hot with the sun."

"I must take care of others before I turn in for the night." Hannah knelt beside Henry, checking his bandage. "Will thee be all right until morning?"

Henry opened one eye. "I reckon so, ma'am. You've done some fine doctoring. Thank you."

Hannah smiled as she stood. "Until tomorrow, then. Sleep in peace, Henry McConnell."

* * *

Campfires flickered across the vast battlefield. Isaac rose on one elbow. Beside him, Henry appeared to be sleeping comfortably. Miss Hannah had him on the mend. This was his time . . .

He rose quietly and wandered toward a group of Yankees seated on boxes around the nearest fire.

"You has coffee?" Isaac asked.

One of the soldiers glanced up. "You say something, boy?"

Isaac quickly snatched his hat from his head. "Begging your pardon, sir. Was wondering if'n I could get me a cup of coffee."

"Coffee?" The soldier jerked a thumb in Isaac's direction. "This here darky wants coffee." His companions laughed. "Move along, boy."

Isaac stood still.

The soldier who spoke looked up again. "You still here? I got a mind to haul your ass over to Shepherdstown and sell you to the first slave trader I see."

"Begging your pardon, sir." Isaac bowed. "Where's the road to Philadelphia?"

"Yonder." The soldier pointed behind him. "Now get."

* * *

The deserted road led past Union encampments and along fields untouched by battle. Isaac searched the cloud-filled sky. No stars to guide him, but this was his road north. He walked briskly, rubbing his arms to ward off the night chill. He'd walked roads at night before and he'd run from slavery before, but he'd never been free before. Tonight, Isaac wasn't a runaway. Tonight Isaac walked this road a free man, as free as Henry McConnell, and he'd be walking this freedom road all the way to Raleigh's door.

The pounding of hoofs announced a rider from the direction of the battlefield. Isaac dove behind a low fence and rolled into a tangle of briars. The soldier in Union blue raced past without giving Isaac a glance. No pattyrollers, just army business. Isaac laughed to himself. The closer he got to that Promised Land, the more skittery he'd become. He searched the road as he pulled himself out of the brambles. Maryland was still a slave state. He'd best be alert.

Clouds parted, revealing a scattering of stars to the east. Isaac pushed on. He'd walk at night. He was free, but Maryland slave owners might not see it that way. Would Raleigh be glad to see him? It had been what, a year since he'd seen her? What if she'd found another man? Lord, what if she'd married?

Dawn approached. It was time to hide. Isaac scrambled over a rail fence, slipped through a cornfield, and ducked into the forest beyond. He settled against an old tree and piled leaves around his legs. Maybe he was free, but it was still cold. Soon, he'd be in Philadelphia, a free man, same as Henry . . . He closed his eyes.

Chapter Forty-four
September 1862

Leaves rustled in the underbrush. Squirrel? Isaac opened his eyes. Sunlight filtered through a tapestry of autumn colors. He sat still, straining to hear. Nothing. He closed his eyes again and leaned against the tree. Just critters. He'd stay put 'til nightfall.

A twig snapped.

Isaac twisted, peering around the trunk of the old maple. Was there something behind those bushes? Isaac sprang to his feet, hefting a fallen limb as a club. "Y-you come on out. Don't make me come get you." He crouched, his heart pounding, as he peered into the tangled undergrowth.

"Don't shoot," a meek voice answered. An arm appeared above the bushes, then another. Slowly, a soldier in blue stepped into the clearing.

Just a boy—and scared to beat all. Isaac lowered his club. "I ain't got no gun. I ain't gonna hurt you none."

The soldier trembled, his hands still in the air.

"Come on over here." Isaac waved the soldier toward him. "I ain't gonna hurt you."

Hesitantly, the young soldier lowered his hands and took a step toward Isaac. "Y-you're a Negro . . ."

"It appears that surprises a lot of you Yankees."

"But you're wearing the rebel gray."

Isaac tugged at his gray jacket. "I ain't no Johnny Reb—was a slave though." He settled against the tree and pulled a piece of hardtack from his coat pocket, breaking it in half. "You hungry?"

The boy took the offering, then brushed off some leaves and sat beside him.

Isaac handed him a canteen. "What's you doing out here, so far from the army?"

The boy peered nervously at Isaac, then returned to chewing the hardtack.

Isaac stared into the morning sky. "Me, I's heading to Philadelphia. I has a woman waiting there."

The boy stood and brushed himself off. "T-thanks for the food and the water."

"You can't set a spell? Where's you headed?"

The boy searched left and right, then settled his gaze on Isaac. "I'm from New York."

"You running?"

"Ain't running." He backed away. "It ain't like that." A tear streaked his cheek.

"None of my business." Isaac waved his hands in front of him. "Ain't none of my never mind."

The boy turned and slipped through the brush toward the road.

Isaac pulled his cap down on his forehead and closed his eyes. That boy was running, sure enough. Sunlight filtered through the treetops warming the September morning. Isaac drifted . . .

* * *

Pounding hoofs and the clatter of sabers on the road above wrested Isaac from his nap. He opened one eye. The young Union soldier stood before him again, glancing cautiously over his shoulder.

"Best to move at night," Isaac said. "Patrols don't see so good then."

The soldier pointed to the ground next to Isaac. "Mind if I sit?"

Isaac shrugged.

The Yankee pointed toward the road as he leaned against the tree. "Mess of folks moving around up there—couriers, patrols, and such. Reckon I'll just sit a spell." He settled beside Isaac. "You running, I mean, you being a slave and all?"

"Massa Henry," Isaac said, "he's the man what owned me. He got his self wounded, so now them Yankee doctors is looking out for him. I reckoned it was time for me to mosey on up north and find my freedom."

"I'm heading north too." The soldier nodded. "I'm done with soldiering." He poked the leaves with a stick. "You seen all the fighting back yonder?"

"Sure enough," Isaac replied. "Me and Henry was down on this farm lane with some boys from Mississippi. The fighting was something awful—bodies all piled atop one another, bleeding and dying."

The soldier traced a line in the dirt with his stick. "Me, I was in this here cornfield. Lost most of my company. We pushed them Rebs out, but they come back, hollering and screaming that rebel yell. It liked to curl the hair on my neck. The corn was taller'n a man when we first went in, but them Texacans opened with their cannon and muskets and mowed that field flat." He paused, then looked at Isaac. "I seen men cut in half. My cousin, Johnny Marshall's his name, he got shot clear through his eyeball. His brains splattered all over me." The soldier brushed his jacket. "There weren't no place to hide."

Isaac scanned the woods. "We's safe enough down here. We'll head north, come nightfall. Best get some rest." He lowered his cap over his eyes and propped his chin on his chest.

"I ain't no coward," The Yankee snuffled.

Isaac lifted the brim of his cap and looked at the soldier. "Come night, you can help me find us some food. For now, get some sleep."

* * *

"Sh-h-h. Stay low. Ain't you never stole no chickens up there in New York?" Isaac waved the young soldier toward the shadows. "Wait here. If'n you sees anybody, make like a whippoorwill."

He wiggled through the rail fence and snuck around the corner of the barn. A row of nesting boxes sat under a shed roof, surrounded by a fence of woven twigs. Sleeping birds cooed quietly as Isaac lifted the gate and slipped inside. He cupped his hand over the head of a nesting hen, clamping down on her beak, and snapped her neck. He held the hen close, covering it with his arms, muffling the flapping wings. The hen house returned to the soft rhythm of sleeping birds. Isaac crept back to his accomplice.

"Come morning, we'll cook up this here pullet, but for now, we has to put some miles between us and them armies." Isaac hooked the bird's head under his rope belt and clambered through the hedgerow. "Dark as it is, we'll be safe on the road. You got a name?

What does they call you?"

The soldier fell in step beside Isaac. "William, William Richardson Brown, but folks up home just calls me Billy."

"Good to meet you, Billy. Folks down home just calls me Isaac." He smiled.

"You ain't gonna tell nobody I'm running, is you?" Billy asked.

Isaac glanced at the boy. "Nobody never said you was running, so how can I tells what I doesn't know?"

Billy nodded. He took several steps before he spoke again. "Your master, he wounded bad?"

"Took a bayonet through his shoulder, but it missed his vitals. Miss Hannah, she's doctoring him, she said he might could live, if'n he gets tended to good."

Billy blew into his hands, then rubbed them together. "I heard tales about them prisons. He ain't gonna find doctoring there."

"What's you saying?"

Billy shoved his hands in his pockets. "Just saying I hears stories; short on food, short on doctoring, wounded don't get better, they just dies."

"Them Yankees ain't gonna doctor Massa Henry?" Isaac asked.

"Maybe exchange him, if he's lucky."

Isaac cocked his head. "Exchange him?"

"Trade him for Union soldiers that were captured by your rebs. I seen them exchanging prisoners the day after the battle, up by that Dunker church on the road to Hagerstown, 'cept I reckon they're finished exchanging for now, since your whole reb army hightailed it back across the Potomac."

"Maybe he'll still get his self exchanged. Could be Miss Hannah is setting to work on that right now."

"Maybe, but it don't sound like his chances are good."

"We got a rider coming." Isaac pointed up the road at a figure in the distance silhouetted against the night sky. "Best hop that fence and lay low 'til he's past."

They slipped between the fence rails and hid behind a sheaf of corn stalks. The rider approached from the east and passed at an easy gait. "Yankee," Isaac whispered as he peered from behind the cover. "Appears to be an officer."

"Weren't no provost patrol. Most likely a courier." Billy dusted off his britches with his cap.

Isaac studied the stars. "We got us two, maybe three hours before daylight. We'd best be moving, then find us a place to hide."

* * *

Sunlight caught the tops of the trees as Isaac slid down a leaf-strewn embankment with his canteen. Billy might be waking soon. Isaac would get a fire started and cook up their bird.

He knelt by the creek. Icy water floated leaves over glistening stones. He uncorked the canteen and held it under. Was Henry going to that prison camp? Billy said it was a bad place . . .

"You, halt!"

Isaac spun around, crouching as he peered through the trees. The voice seemed to come from where he'd left Billy.

"Hands in the air, now!"

Isaac crawled up the bank until he overlooked the small clearing where he and Billy had slept.

Three Yankees surrounded Billy, their muskets at the ready. One soldier wore the chevrons of a sergeant. "A deserter, eh?" He shoved Billy with his musket.

"N-no sir. I ain't deserting, I just got separated from my unit during the fighting."

"And what unit would that be?" The sergeant smiled and glanced at his comrades.

"Twenty-first New York, Patrick's brigade, sir." Billy inched away from the sergeant.

"Now, let me see if I got this right. You fought in that cornfield over yonder—kilt you a passel of Johnny Rebs too, I'll wager—then you just happened to find yourself wandering 'round miles away from the army on this here road to New York? Is that what you's saying?"

Billy wiped his mouth with his sleeve. His gaze darted from one soldier to another. He retreated. "It ain't like that, I ain't deserting, I just got separated . . ."

The sergeant smashed Billy in the stomach with the butt of his musket. "Hog tie this yellow-bellied coward. The Colonel's got a special place for your kind—in front of a firing squad."

The other soldiers grabbed Billy's arms. He tried to pull away. "No, it ain't like that. Please, mister . . ."

"Gag the coward so's I don't have to hear his bellyaching," the sergeant commanded.

One of the soldiers stuffed a rag in Billy's mouth.

"Come on, men. We got more of these yellow bastards that need catching." The sergeant turned and walked toward the road. The two privates grabbed Billy and dragged him along.

Isaac remained hidden behind a tree until the footfalls faded through the dry leaves and the forest settled once again into the quiet of an autumn morning. He dug into the dirt with his heel. There wasn't anything he could have done. That boy was going off to be shot dead, all because he was scared of getting shot dead. It made no sense. Isaac had been plenty scared too. That sunken road was no place for folks who didn't like getting shot at—and Henry'd be scared too, if he knew about that prison . . .

"Tarnation." Isaac scrambled to his feet. "Ain't no sense being free if I can't do my own deciding." He followed the upturned leaves that marked the path taken by the provost patrol and their young prisoner.

* * *

"'Tis a surprise to see thee again. Henry will be pleased."

"How's he doing, ma'am?" Isaac stared at the still form under the blanket.

"I am concerned. In the days since thy departure he has worsened. I fear the prison camp will be his undoing."

Isaac knelt and lifted Henry's blanket. "He ain't looking none too good. Maybe, if'n he's ill, he won't have to go to that prison?"

Hannah dipped a rag in a bucket and dabbed Henry's brow. She shook her head. "The guards gathered a group yesterday, some much worse than Henry. They sent them off in wagons. It is only a question of time." She dropped the rag in the bucket and closed her eyes. Sunlight danced on freckles dotting the bridge of her nose. She sighed. "What became of your dreams of Philadelphia and, what was her name, Raleigh? I thought thee would be in Pennsylvania by now."

Isaac gazed across the field of wounded. "When's they coming for the prisoners again?"

She shook her head. "I have no knowledge of their intentions. What is thee thinking?"

"Can he travel?" Isaac stood.

"No." Hannah stammered, "he is weak. He does not have the strength. I would be afraid . . ."

"His chances better traveling north to prison or traveling south?"

Hannah stared at Isaac. "The direction matters not . . ."

"He'll be dead if'n he goes to that prison," Isaac said. "Maybe he'll live if'n he gets back with his own kind."

"Yes, Fort Delaware would certainly be fatal, but how . . . ?"

"Will you take care of him?" Isaac pointed at Henry. "If'n we's traveling, that is?"

"I . . . my place is here, with the wounded, with all the wounded. I could not . . ."

"One, maybe two days, then you comes back."

"But what of the guards?" She gestured toward the few sentries guarding the prison hospital.

"Might be tonight, maybe morning." Isaac stood. "You be ready."

Hannah began to speak, then simply looked at Isaac and nodded.

* * *

The mule twitched his ear as Isaac snapped the reins. The army supply wagon lurched forward, rumbling up the dirt road past rows of white canvas tents. He glanced at the long box in the wagon bed. Pa would have pulled it apart and made him build it over, but there wasn't time—it would have to do.

Union soldiers moved aside as the wagon passed. Isaac held the mule to a walk. Occasionally, a soldier might see the passing wagon and seem to notice the black teamster in a soiled linen shirt tipping his blue kepi and smiling. "Morning sir. Top o' the morning, sir."

He crossed Antietam Creek, then took a long route around the Union camps, coming into the prison area from the east.

A sentry stepped in front of the wagon, his musket at high port. "Halt. State your business."

Isaac touched the brim of his cap, then pointed toward the back of the wagon. "I's fetching one of them dead rebel boys for the long ride home."

The sentry glanced at the coffin, nodded, and stepped aside.

Isaac tipped his hat as the mule sidestepped, found his footing, and pulled. The wagon rolled through the gate and into the field of Confederate wounded. Isaac guided the mule past a shallow trench where rebel prisoners were burying their fallen comrades. A short distance beyond, doctors working over a makeshift table sawed at the leg of another unfortunate victim. The morning's collection of amputated limbs was already knee high. Isaac covered his nose with his bandana and twitched the reins. The mule quickened his step.

Henry lay in the shade, his head propped on a rolled blanket. He stared as Isaac climbed down from the wagon. "Thought you lit out for that freedom land."

Ignoring Henry, Isaac turned to Hannah. "He seems a mite better this morning."

She nodded. "I pray that is so."

"Isaac . . ." Henry called in a weak voice. He rolled to his side and coughed, then laid back on his makeshift pillow. "I figured you'd be in Philadelphia by now."

"I come back."

"No . . ." Henry grabbed Isaac's trouser. "You was supposed to be marrying up with that Raleigh girl and starting your carpenter's shop."

Isaac knelt beside Henry. "Got business here needs tending to first."

Henry struggled to one elbow. "You don't owe me that. You done enough. Go . . ."

Isaac turned to Hannah. "Reckon he'll be able to travel?"

"Damn it, What about Raleigh?" Henry grabbed Isaac's arm. "How long do you expect her to wait?"

Isaac turned away. Would she wait? What if she was already spoken for?

"Isaac, you remember that night down by the creek when you told me how you was just property? I've been thinking on that. You were right."

Isaac stared at Henry.

"Go north. Your place is in Philadelphia. I'm giving you your freedom, go . . ."

Isaac smiled. "It ain't yours to give, Henry McConnell."

"I . . . I don't understand." Henry's gaze darted from Isaac to

Hannah. "What . . . ?"

Isaac held up his hand. "You McConnells owned my body, but y'all never owned my soul. I found my freedom on that road to Philadelphia," he said, pointing toward the low hills to the east. "I ain't no slave crawling back to his massa; I's a free man, making a free choice. Now, when you and me gets back to Virginia, folks there might be believing I's your slave, and maybe we'd best be letting 'em think that, but you and me, we'll be knowing the truth, ain't that right, Henry McConnell?"

Henry let go of Isaac's arm and lay his head back. He sighed. "Damn it, you was a pain in the ass slave anyway. Can't be any worse if you're free. But I'd still rather you was heading north . . ."

"That boy weren't never real quick on the learning." Isaac smiled at Hannah. "This here be taking him some time to get used to."

* * *

Isaac poked the small fire with a stick. "Miss Hanna, you understands, you gots to act like you's his sister. Won't nobody raise no questions. Once we's in Virginia, them rebs will tend to Henry and you'll be back here before you's missed. Then I'll be on that road north again."

Hannah wrapped her arms around her knees and rocked back. "Thee really thinks this will work?"

"Has to. I ain't got no better idea. Besides, the good Lord made stealing that mule and wagon too easy—like it was his plan all along."

"Borrow. Thee *borrowed* the mule and wagon. I know thee will arrange to have both returned to their rightful owners in due course."

"Borrowed. Yes ma'am." Isaac smiled. "We'd best get him loaded." Isaac stood and walked to Henry. "You ready?" He slid his arms under Henry and lifted. "Climb on up. I'll pass him on to you." Isaac lowered Henry to the wagon bed. Hannah supported him while Isaac climbed up.

"Gentle now, Miss Hannah. You see to it I doesn't bang his head or nothing." Isaac lifted Henry again and lowered him into the rough pine box.

"You sure about those breathing holes?" Henry stared wide-

291

eyed from the makeshift coffin.

"No, I ain't real sure," Isaac said. "Couldn't make no holes what'd be noticeable, but if'n you stops breathing, just knock twice." He began setting the lid in place.

Henry held up his hand, stopping the lid. "Maybe this isn't such a good idea."

"Maybe you'd rather take your chances with them Yankees at Fort Delaware? Hush, you's supposed to be dead." Isaac nailed down the lid.

Chapter Forty-five
September 1862

"Morning ma'am." The sentry tipped his cap. "Where would ya be heading at such an early hour?"

Hannah seemed unsure of what to say. The mule snorted, then nuzzled a clump of grass. Finally, Isaac jerked his thumb toward the back of the wagon. "It's her brother, sir. We's taking him home. The poor woman's grieving something awful, him being dead and all . . ."

The sentry peered in the back of the wagon. "Coffin, huh? Must be an officer. Sorry about your loss, ma'am." He touched the brim of his hat and stepped aside.

"Thank you, sir. We has many a mile to travel and the captain's already getting ripe, so we's in a mite of a hurry." Isaac touched his own cap in a return salute, then flicked the reins. "Tch, tch. Get on there, mule." The wagon rolled onto a farm lane headed toward Sharpsburg. Soldiers stepped aside, giving no attention to the wagon or its passengers.

"Ripening? Honestly, Isaac, how does thee think of such horrid things?"

"Just giving that good soldier one more reason to hurry us on. If'n he's like most folks around here, I expect he's seen all the dying he cares to see."

"Thee never ceases to come up with a surprise. So, where did thee find that coffin?"

"Barn over yonder." Isaac nodded toward the fields behind them. "I borrowed a few planks from the back of a stall and made use of their tools. You best wipe that smile off your face—you's supposed to be mourning."

Hannah blushed, covering her mouth with her hanky. "Thee is

so convincing. I must do better at playing my role."

Isaac reached behind and banged his fist on the coffin. A muted knock came in response. "Reckon maybe I'll be leaving him in there a spell. Least trouble he's been since I can't remember when."

Hannah giggled, then quickly covered her mouth and peeked from under her bonnet with a look of apology.

Broken wagons, abandoned muskets, clothing, and military equipment of every description littered the road from Sharpsburg to Shepherdstown. A dozen riders approached from the south, an officer in blue riding in the lead. The soldier riding beside him carried a guidon snapping in the breeze. The officer raised his hand, halting the patrol in front of the wagon. "Morning, ma'am." The lieutenant saluted, then pointed to the back of the wagon. "A relative?"

"My brother." Hannah held her hanky to her mouth.

"Sorry for your loss ma'am," the lieutenant said. "Rebel?"

She nodded.

"What outfit?"

A panicked look came over her.

"Nineteenth Mississippi," Isaac replied. "He done met his maker on that sunken road on the far side of Sharpsburg."

The lieutenant gave Hannah a suspicious glance, then addressed Isaac. "You do all her talking, boy? Maybe we'd best take a look . . ."

"He was only trying to spare me the grief of having to talk about my poor, departed Henry. Look if you must, but I fear he has become a mite ripe." Tears streamed down Hannah's cheeks.

"No need, ma'am." The lieutenant waved his hand. "I've been impertinent. Please accept my apologies. It's a long road to Mississippi and the September sun is warm." He backed his horse away the wagon. "I trust you will not have too unpleasant a journey." He touched the brim of his cap. "Good day to you, ma'am." The lieutenant spurred his horse and galloped off at the front of his patrol.

"Ripe?" Isaac pointed to her face. "And where'd them tears come from?"

"If thee were to hide thy smallest finger in a kerchief," Hannah held up her little finger wrapped in a hanky, "then bite down on thy fingernail, tears would be closer than thee thinks."

Isaac banged on the coffin. "Henry, you ripen any more, Isaac's fetching his shovel and burying your carcass right here."

A muffled knock came in reply.

* * *

Union troops crowded the fields north of Shepherdstown. Isaac turned the wagon off the main road. "We come up this way from Harper's Ferry a few days back. The bridge into town is out, but there's a ford about a mile downstream." He pointed to the bluffs rising above the Potomac River. "We'll cross there." Isaac flicked the reins.

Union artillery guarded the ford behind a thin line of pickets. Shell craters and shattered trees bore evidence of a recent battle. Henry moaned as the wagon bounced along a rutted farm lane toward the crossing. Rebel pickets watched from the bluffs above the south bank of the river.

"Begging your pardon, ma'am." A soldier in blue stepped out to the road and held up his hand. "Wouldn't recommend going no further." He nodded toward the bluffs. "There's rebel sharpshooters up yonder. They've been keeping our heads down during the daylight."

"But we are southern," Hannah said. "Surely they will not fire on their own kind." She fanned herself, putting on airs as she must have supposed were befitting a fine Southern lady.

The soldier pointed at Isaac. "They's partial to shooting them what wears the blue."

Isaac glanced up at his kepi, then snatched the cap off his head and tossed it in the back of the wagon. He reached under the seat and retrieved his wide-brimmed black felt slouch hat.

"They's still a mite quick on the trigger, boy. You'd best wait for dark . . ." The soldier wiped his brow.

"That branch, the long one," Hannah said, pointing to a broken limb on the side of the road, "Please pass it here."

The soldier handed Hannah the thin branch. She reached beneath her skirts and ripped a swatch from her petticoats, then tied the tattered rag to the branch and hoisted her makeshift flag. "No son of Virginia would dare fire upon a grieving widow under the protection of a flag of truce. Drive on, Isaac."

The mule pulled them around a bend and onto an open stretch

of road under the direct observation of the rebel pickets. Isaac leaned toward Hannah and whispered, "Sister . . ."

"I beg thy pardon?"

"You's his sister, not his widow . . ."

Hannah blushed.

Above, a handful of rebel soldiers stood in their rifle pits, some with their caps held over their hearts, as the wagon forded the shallow river.

* * *

"Ain't home, but least ways you's in Virginia." Isaac eased Henry onto a blanket beside the campfire. He climbed into the wagon and tossed the casket to the ground. "Firewood."

"Good." Henry coughed and rubbed his shoulder. "I don't ever want to see that thing again."

"How is thee feeling?" Hannah sat on a stump, holding a small skillet over the fire.

"Like I've been kicked by a mule." Henry's voice barely rose above the crackle of the fire.

"Thee needs rest." She turned to Isaac. "Is hardtack all thee has?"

"Be thankful for that, ma'am. Weren't for the Yankees, we wouldn't have nothing." Isaac spread his blanket next to Henry's and sat down. "Come morning, I'll take him over to the Confederate hospital, then you and me best be heading back north."

"Isaac, it is wonderful what thee has done for thy friend."

Isaac shrugged.

"What I mean to say is, thee has given up so much, taken such a risk, and for a man that, for all of thy life, has held thee in bondage."

"Weren't none of his doing." Isaac glanced at the sleeping form beside him. "Henry can't help what he was born to no more'n I can." He removed his hat and rolled the brim. "Him and me, we been watching after one another since before we was in long britches. I weren't gonna let him go off and die in that prison."

"Then tomorrow we must get him to the hospital. I am concerned that his wound will not heal without proper care."

* * *

Abandoned wagons cluttered the streets. Houses, churches, and hotels—the makeshift hospitals of war—spilled their tenants onto lawns and porches. The cries of men under the surgeon's knife and the stench of rotting flesh filled the air. Gaunt specters in tattered gray stared vacantly at the passing wagon. Isaac flicked the reins, coaxing the mule through the tangled remnants of the beaten army.

"His chances was better at that Yankee prison," Isaac said.

"Thee must not lose hope. There, beyond that oak, the large stone building, does thee see the yellow flag?" Hannah pointed ahead. "That must be the hospital headquarters. There we will find answers."

Isaac guided the wagon around a rut, nudging a horse tied to the hitching rail in front of a shop. The horse snorted, kicked up his hoofs, and danced aside.

"Here. Pull over here." Hannah motioned. "I will enquire within." She climbed down, brushed herself off, and approached a young soldier who wore the double bars of a first lieutenant. Her back was to the wagon as she appeared to speak.

The officer came toward the wagon. "I'll have the orderlies unload him, ma'am, but I can't say when a doctor might be available."

She placed her hands on her hips and leaned toward the officer. "He is my own flesh and blood. Thee is mistaken if thee thinks I shall abide such neglect." Hannah turned on her heel and stormed toward the large stone building. The lieutenant stared at Isaac and shrugged, then walked away.

Isaac held the brake with his foot and relaxed the reins. The mule bowed his head, appearing to doze. The day promised to be warm. Isaac wiped his brow.

"Where . . . where are we?" Henry spoke in a feeble voice from the back of the wagon. He squinted, holding up a hand to block the midday sun.

"Shepherdstown. Miss Hannah's getting you admitted to this here Confederate hospital, then me and her, we'll be heading back north."

Henry slumped, rubbing his wounded shoulder. "You reckon she'd stay? I mean, to tend to my wound and all?"

Isaac shook his head. There was some things about that boy that never changed . . . . "How's you doing?"

"Hungry," Henry replied.

"Miss Hannah says that's a good sign."

"You got anything?"

"Hardtack." Isaac reached in his pocket, pulling out a dark cracker.

Henry took the offering, then dropped onto his bed and closed his eyes. He took a deep breath and exhaled. When he opened his eyes again he held the cracker in front of him. "You sure you ain't trying to kill me? These here'll tear up a man's insides."

"You gotta die of something," Isaac said. "It might as well be Yankee food as Yankee bullets—or bayonets. How's that shoulder?"

"Hurting some. When you get to Philadelphia and find your lady friend, write me, you hear?"

"I expect I will," Isaac replied. "Now, you'd best lay back and take it easy. You's looking a mite peaked. Here comes Miss Hannah."

Hannah rushed down the steps, brushing past a cluster of soldiers huddled on the walk. She held her skirts as she hurried across the lawn. "We will not abide such incompetence. Let us be gone." She climbed up beside Isaac, folded her arms across her chest, and stared at the road ahead.

"Begging your pardon, ma'am, but where's we headed?" Isaac pointed at Henry. "And what about him?"

"The doctor—chief surgeon for the division, mind thee—he said they have all they can do to keep up with the amputations. Said if Henry needed something cut off, they'd be most happy to oblige, however he did not anticipate being able to provide ongoing care of the quality I would expect—no, I would demand."

Isaac rubbed the back of his neck. "Sharpsburg?"

Hannah closed her eyes and clutched the wooden seat with both hands. "He will surely die without proper care."

Isaac flicked the reins. As the mule awoke, Isaac turned the wagon. They rode in silence until the bustle of Shepherdstown faded, replaced by the solitude of a quiet country road.

At the next crossroads, Isaac halted the wagon and scanned the sky, then studied the shadows on the ground. "Miss Hannah. Your Yankees is up yonder." He pointed. "If'n no wagon comes along to give you a ride, well, it ain't no more'n twenty miles to Sharpsburg. You'll most likely make it on foot by nightfall."

She stared. "And thee?"

"We's heading south." Isaac nodded toward the road to the right. "I's taking Henry home."

"But . . . Philadelphia, Raleigh?"

"Time enough after," Isaac said. "Henry's my worry now. I needs to get him home to South Boston."

"If thee goes back, they will place thee in chains. Thee will lose thy freedom."

Isaac nodded toward Henry. "Not if he stays alive."

"Which he won't." She adjusted her bonnet. "Not without someone skilled in providing proper care."

Isaac raised an eyebrow.

"If thee is to sit here all the morning, we shall never see South Boston. Will thee turn the wagon, or shall I take the reins?"

Chapter Forty-six
October 1862

Isaac covered Henry with the tarpaulin, tucking in the corners to hold it against the squall. "I done the best I can," he said. "But I reckon you'll be getting wet."

Henry moaned.

Wind-driven rain splashed against the canvas and danced across Isaac's back. His woolen shell jacket and the rough linen shirt beneath were soaked, pressing cold against his skin.

"Thee must find us shelter or he will be taken with fever." Hannah huddled on the wagon seat, shivering under Isaac's poncho.

"We passed through Staunton town early this morning," Isaac said. "Is you thinking we should head on back?"

"That would be too far," Hannah replied. "Perhaps thee can find a farm, possibly a barn to cover us from the storm?"

"We passed a farmhouse a mile back," Isaac said. "You want I should turn around?"

"Please do." Hannah pulled the poncho around her face. "Henry is sick and I fear I am not dressed for this weather."

Isaac turned the mule and headed north. The storm brought an early nightfall to the Shenandoah Valley. He twitched the mule's rump with the reins. The animal flattened his ears, gummed the metal bit, and picked up the pace. Only the splash of hoofs and the creak of wagon axles intruded on the monotony of the rain.

"There." Isaac pointed. "The house is down yonder." He guided the mule onto the narrow path. After a quarter mile, the tree-lined lane opened into a barnyard surrounding a wooden two-story house. Light from a downstairs window cast a warm glow across the narrow front porch.

"Wait here. I shall ask for traveling mercies." Hannah climbed down and ran to the door. In a moment, the light moved and then the door opened, revealing a stooped old man with flowing gray hair and a shaggy beard. Hannah and the man talked. She pointed to the wagon. He nodded, then stepped inside and closed the door. Hannah walked back, pulling her slicker tightly around her head.

"He appears to be a good Christian, though afflicted with a suspicious nature. He will permit us the use of his barn for the night."

"Better'n nothing," Isaac said. "But it ain't no hearth and fire." He drove to the barn, then jumped down and swung open the double doors. Taking the mule by the halter, he led him into the darkened building. "See if there be a match in that cup beside the lantern yonder."

Hannah struck a match and lit the lantern. A golden hue filled the small building, revealing three stalls, two with horses, a loft filled with hay and an assortment of riding tack, farm implements, and hand tools hanging from hooks and rafters.

Isaac lifted Henry from the wagon.

"Wait, his blanket is soaked." She pulled a saddle blanket from the top rail of a stall. "This is dry. Lay him here."

Isaac laid Henry down.

"Cold . . ." Henry opened his eyes and shivered.

"He's chilled something awful, Miss Hannah." As Isaac held him, Henry shivered uncontrollably. "You reckon that farmer has some hot soup?"

Hannah blew into her hands, then rubbed them together. She pushed a wisp of wet hair from her eyes and glanced toward the door. "He seemed quite strict. He said we should not leave the barn this evening for any reason, and we should be on the road by first light. The man appeared to be quite concerned that anyone would be out and about."

"See if'n you can warm him some. There's another saddle blanket yonder." Isaac pointed to the back wall.

"And what will thee do?"

"Ain't certain," Isaac replied. "But Henry needs more'n we can give him here." He opened the barn door and studied the farmhouse for a moment, then stepped out, closing the door behind him. He dashed across the small barnyard through the driving rain and jumped onto the porch. Lamplight flickered through a window. Isaac knocked on the door. From within came the scurrying of feet, then the clop of boots across a bare wooden floor. The door opened a crack, exposing the chiseled face of the old farmer. He looked Isaac up and down.

"What do you want?"

Isaac removed his hat, clutching it in front of him. "We has a wounded soldier," Isaac said, nodding toward the barn. "He's coming down with the chills. Wondering if'n you has hot soup or tea to spare, and maybe a blanket?"

"Ain't enough I lets you sleep in the dag-blamed barn? Now you bothers me to cook your vittles? Go, and be glad you has that barn for the night." The farmer shooed him from the door.

"A friend of a friend sent me," Isaac said, pointing to the monkey wrench patterned quilt hanging on the porch rail. "Mighty poor weather to be airing your bedding."

The farmer glanced at the soaked quilt. "What's it to ya?"

"We ain't no danger, mister," Isaac said. "I shepherded some of them travelers a time or two myself. I just wants something warm for a sick man so's he don't die."

"I don't cotton to no slave-holding Confederates," the man said. "Let 'em all die."

"Please, mister. He's my friend."

The door opened wider. The farmer looked Isaac up and down. "You his slave?"

"No sir. I's free, just taking a wounded boy back to his mother, then I'll be heading north."

"What about that woman?"

"Miss Hannah?" Isaac smiled and glanced toward the barn. "She's one of them Quaker abolitionist ladies, best I can figure." Isaac chuckled. "It don't make no sense, her taking up with a Johnny Reb."

"Taking in a wounded Confederate soldier and his slave?" The farmer stroked his beard. "I'll be durned if that don't make for a real good story. Might come in handy if there was patrols here about. Go on then, fetch that rebel and bring him in here by the fire before he up and dies—and don't you be letting on none about what you think you know—the best secret's them that's kept."

* * *

Isaac laid Henry in front of the hearth, covering him with a blanket. He then held his hands to the fire as the farmer added another log. Sparks swirled up the chimney.

The stone fireplace stood out from the wall, surrounded by whitewashed wooden panels outlined in decorative molding. One panel appeared to be pulled away from the wall by almost an inch, its edge smeared by a dirty handprint. The style of the mantle was familiar—a passable copy of Thomas Day's craftsmanship.

Hannah set a steaming cup on the floor next to Henry, then sat and eased his head into her lap. She lifted the cup to his lips. "Slowly—thee mustn't scald thyself."

"Miss Hannah," the farmer said, settling into his rocker. "What brings a nice Philadelphia girl down here to tend wounded rebels?" He adjusted the blanket on his lap. His rocker creaked against the pinewood floor.

"I posted with the U.S. Sanitary Commission so I could serve the wounded—all the wounded—it matters not their uniform."

"Noble, and foolish" the farmer replied.

"Why does thee say that?"

The farmer struck a match against the edge of his chair. Several quick drags on his briar pipe sucked the flame into the bowl. He rocked back and blew out a cloud of smoke. "Folks here about don't take kindly to abolitionists. If word was to get out, folks might choose to pay me a visit, and haul you back north on a rail."

Hannah's eyes flashed panic. "I don't recall mentioning my politics. I am only tending to an unfortunate soul on his wearisome journey home. A simple act of Christian charity."

"Some folks might believe that."

Henry coughed and opened his eyes. He glanced around. "Throat hurts," he whispered. "Where are we?"

"A friend has taken thee in." Hannah held the tea to his mouth. "Sip this, it will soothe thy throat." She stroked his forehead.

The farmer rose from his rocker and climbed the stairs. Moments later he returned, his arms filled with blankets that he tossed on the sofa. "I'd best be turning in. Y'all should be warm enough with these. Holler if you need anything." He started up the stairway, then froze when an urgent knock came at the door.

The farmer's face turned ashen. He hobbled down the steps.

Isaac sidestepped to the hearth and planted his foot on the

loose panel. As he pushed, the panel snapped into place.

The farmer raised the latch and opened the front door a crack. "It's late. What do you want?"

The door flew open, knocking the farmer back. Two bearded men in wide brimmed hats and floor length dusters pushed into the room. The shorter of the two held a double-barreled shotgun in the crook of his arm. The taller man snatched off his hat and made a slight bow when he noticed Hannah. "Begging your pardon ma'am."

He turned to the farmer. "Sam, there's runaways here about and folks is saying you's had some mighty curious visitations. What's you knowing about that?"

The farmer rubbed his beard and scowled. "You tell old lady Crutchfield to keep her guldurned nose out of my business. The only visitations up here's been this here Confederate boy." He pointed to Henry. "He was wounded at Sharpsburg he was, and on his way home to his mother. This here good woman's been caring for him, and he'll be mending a mite quicker without you holding that durned door wide open and chilling his bones."

"Sorry, ma'am." The leader of the patrol nodded toward Hannah and closed the door. "What about him, Sam?" He pointed to Isaac. "You ain't got no slaves. Where'd the nigger come from?"

"He belongs to me." Hannah spoke up. "Isaac is my houseboy, and he is helping me take my brother home, that is if he survives. As if his wound was not enough, he is now down with the fever."

"Sorry ma'am. I . . . I didn't know. We's just on the lookout for runaways. Didn't mean to cause you no concern."

"And I appreciate that," Hannah said. "Now, if you will excuse me, my brother is weak, he needs his sleep."

"Yes ma'am." The man bowed and retreated to the door.

The farmer reached for the latch. "You tell that busybody old hag we'll all be sleeping better if'n she'd tend to her own affairs and leave us loyal, God-fearing southern folks alone."

"Sorry, Sam. Don't take it personal. We didn't mean you no harm." The intruder pulled the door closed behind him.

"I don't trust 'em none at all." The farmer bolted the door. Outside, the pounding of horse's hoofs trailed away.

"Why would they be looking here for runaway slaves?" Hannah raised her eyebrows and stared at the farmer.

"I's just a durned farmer minding my own business. Some old busybody thinks she can cause me trouble by getting them patrols riled up. Damn 'em anyway." The farmer stomped up the stairs.

Hannah turned to Isaac with a questioning look.

"You takes the sofa, Miss Hannah. I'll put my blanket here, next to Henry."

* * *

"Looks to be a good day. The sun'll bake out that cough," Isaac said. "You'll be mending good and proper, now that we's dry." Isaac tucked the blanket under Henry and placed two loaves of warm bread and a side of ham in the back of the wagon. "You's mighty generous. We thanks you kindly, sir." He waved to the old farmer on the porch.

The farmer pointed toward the rising sun. "Follow that road due east. You'll be over the Blue Ridge by nightfall, then turn south. The patrols shouldn't give you no trouble."

"Yes, thee has been kind to share thy hearth and thy food," Hannah said. "We are most thankful." She smiled as she settled onto the wagon seat.

Isaac finished making Henry as comfortable as he could, then he jumped from the wagon and walked to the porch. "Massa Sam," he whispered. "You's a good man. I hopes we didn't bring no trouble down on you or your flock." He nodded toward the house.

"Best thing could of happened, you being here," the farmer replied. "Folks was getting ideas. Ol' man Tillman there, the fella what done all the talking last night, he'd a tore up this place if'n that reb of yours hadn't a been here. You bought me some time, but I reckon I'd best take that quilt down for now, let things settle."

"Thank you again, sir." Isaac held out his hand.

The farmer stared at the hand. "A white man ought not be seen shaking hands with no nigra. Can't say who might be watching." He turned and walked to the door.

Isaac brushed his hand across his britches and started down the steps.

The farmer opened the door to go in the house, then turned toward Isaac. "God go with you, son."

Chapter Forty-seven
October 1862

"Ho! Ho there, mule." Isaac stomped on the long handled brake. "We'll be headed down that road soon enough. Grab a mouthful o' sweet grass while Isaac sets here a spell." He doffed his hat, using it to shield his eyes from the glare of the setting sun. Shadows stretched across the dry Virginia fields in the valley below. To the west, remnants of a split rail fence tumbled along the edge of an overgrown field of summer wheat.

The mule continued pulling against his harness. Isaac held the reins, wiping sweat from his brow with the worn sleeve of his gray shell jacket.

A breeze lifted a hint of wood smoke up from the valley. To the southeast, tall oaks reached over the dark waters of Bennett's Creek where he and Henry had splashed away the summers of their youth. On a rise a half-mile further south, the weathered old cookhouse nestled behind the green roofs of the big house.

"Thee is remembering?"

Isaac set his hat on his head and nodded. "And considering. I ain't had much time to learn about being free, but down yonder, I'll be right back into them shackles."

"Thee has done more for Henry than any man should ask of another. Thy mission is finished, and honorably so." Hannah squeezed Isaac's hand. "Henry is healing nicely and thee has brought us within sight of his home. I can handle the wagon this final mile."

"Pa used to say, 'There be the easy path and there be the right path.' This'n ain't easy, but I reckon I knows what I needs to do." He flicked the reins.

* * *

The sound of hoofs brought Florence to the parlor window. As she drew the curtain, a mule plodded into the barnyard pulling a large wagon. Silhouetted in the fading light were two riders, one small, perhaps a child or a woman, and the other a man wearing a broad brimmed hat. He sat erect, his posture and mannerisms strangely familiar.

"Miss Polly. Miss Polly, we has visitors." Florence released the curtain and stepped behind the wheelchair.

Polly bounded down the front stairs, brushing back her hair and straightening her dress. A muffled knock sounded at the front door. She looked at Florence.

Florence turned Morgan's chair toward the doorway and nodded.

Polly lifted the latch and opened the door.

A tall man entered cradling another man in his arms. His dark face was partially hidden by his slouch hat as he looked down at his burden. A woman in a plain dress followed quietly.

Florence gasped "Lordy, can it be?" Her hand came slowly to her mouth. "Isaac? Is that really you?"

Isaac laid Henry on the sofa, then straightened and removed his hat. "Evening, Mama."

Florence trembled. Tears streaked her cheeks. "You's hurt . . ." She touched the scar on the side of his head.

"Ain't nothing, Mama." He placed his hands on her shoulders.

Florence gazed up at him, then threw her arms around his waist and buried her face in his chest. "Dear Lord, you did hear my prayers thank you, thank you . . ."

Thwack!

Florence turned quickly.

Morgan held his hand above the arm of his wheelchair and brought it down again. Thwack!

"Massa McConnell?" Florence wiped her eyes.

He waved her closer and whispered. "What of Henry?"

"Took a bayonet at Sharpsburg," Isaac said. "But he's mending good. This here's Miss Hannah." He motioned toward Hannah. "She's been tending to him."

"Good evening." Hannah said with a smile.

"Hello, Hannah. My name is Polly. I'm the lady of the house, at least while my mother is in Richmond." She curtsied. "It is a pleasure to meet you."

"Henry!" The raspy voice seemed insistent.

Florence pushed the wheelchair next to the sofa and Polly placed Henry's hand in Morgan's.

"Hello, Papa," Henry said.

Tears welled in Morgan's eyes. He looked at Isaac. "Thank you," he mouthed.

"Hannah, will you stay with us awhile?" Polly took Hannah by the arm and escorted her into the parlor. "Mother's in Richmond, don't know when she's ever coming home, and I do so wish for the company of another woman."

"If thee does not mind. I had hoped to see Henry through his convalescence."

"Thee?" Polly cocked her head.

"Quaker—and a right good doctor." Henry winked.

"I declare, I can't tell which of you sounds worse." Florence placed her hand on Henry's as it rested in Morgan's grasp. "Ain't neither one of you talking above a cat's whisper." She smiled at Hannah. "It'll be good having another body around to help with the nursing."

"Where's Joseph?" Isaac glanced about the room.

Florence shook her head and smiled. "That boy spends most of his evenings down by the quarters these days."

"And Tempie?" Isaac asked. "She had that baby yet?"

She swallowed hard. Of course she'd have to tell him, but couldn't it have waited? Florence lowered her voice. "Miss Polly, Miss Hannah, will you two tend these here sick ones?" She pointed toward Henry and Morgan.

Hannah quickly nodded.

"Come," Florence said, taking Isaac by the arm. "Walk with me."

* * *

"But Mama, she was just a child. It weren't her time." Isaac wiped his eyes as they strolled down the lane toward the quarters. The waning moon cast a silver glow over the harvested fields. It couldn't be true, not his sister, not Tempie . . .

"The Lord said it was her time. She went peaceable; didn't feel no pain."

"The baby?"

"Weren't meant to be," Florence said. "The Lord took that child so's Tempie could have an angel with her in heaven."

"That damned Cato—this is his fault . . ." Isaac turned toward Florence.

"Hush." She grabbed Isaac's arm. "Ain't no child of mine gonna be cussing like no Yankee peddler."

"But Mama, he kilt my sister." Isaac punched his fist into the palm of his hand. "I'll whup him so's he won't never forget the evil he done."

"Whupping ain't bringing your sister back." Florence patted his arm. "Leave it be."

Isaac pulled away. "Weren't no call for what he done to her. I'll cut him good." He wielded an imaginary knife.

"Isaac. Listen." Florence grabbed both of his arms. "It weren't Cato."

He drew back. "How you know?"

She took his hands and slowly raised her head, starring into Isaac's eyes. "The baby was white."

Isaac stammered as he began to speak.

Florence put a finger to his lips. "I reckon we won't never know the daddy. I prays it weren't nobody on this farm, and I prays he didn't hurt her much."

Isaac let out a breath. His shoulders sagged. "She knew. She knew and she didn't tell nobody?"

"I expect she had her reasons. It be in the Lord's hands now."

Isaac wrapped his arms around Florence and pulled her close. "I wish Pa was here."

* * *

"Morning Miss Hannah." Isaac set a cup of sassafras tea on the table beside the chair in the front parlor. "This here's all we got. Coffee's been hard to come by since the war begun."

"Tea will be fine." She seemed to hesitate, then turned toward him. "Polly told me of thy sister. I prayed for thee last night—and thy mother too."

Isaac lowered his head. "It don't seem right. I goes off to war—Manassas, Harpers Ferry, Sharpsburg—and I comes home in one piece, but Tempie . . ."

"Thee mustn't think of it that way. It was God's will. The Lord knows best."

"That's what Mama was saying."

Polly skipped down the stairs, grabbing a shawl from the hall tree. She draped it over her shoulders. "Ready?"

Hannah placed a hand on Isaac's shoulder. "Polly promised to show me around the farm this morning. We might visit Tempie's grave. Would thee like to join us?"

Isaac shook his head. "I ain't ready for that. I reckon I'd best stay put and tend to Henry." He pulled the chair next to the sofa.

"Henry will appreciate that," Hannah said as Polly took her by the arm. Together, they headed out the door, their voices trailing into the distance.

Isaac turned to the lump curled under a blanket on the sofa. "You hungry?"

Henry opened one eye. "You ain't near as pretty as my other nurse."

"Hardtack's what you be needing, but all I gots is eggs and bacon. I throwed in a couple of Mama's biscuits too."

Henry struggled to a sitting position and took the plate. "You think she is?"

"Who?" Isaac stared at him. "What?"

"Hannah. You think she's sweet on me?"

"If'n that poor girl's got a lick of sense, she'll be hopping the next train north."

The crash of a glass against pinewood floors echoed from the back parlor, followed by Florence's voice. "If'n you throws it, I'll just be getting another. Now, you drinks these here medicinals before I gets upset."

"Your mama's a hard woman," Henry said with a laugh. "Mother sure never talked to him like that."

"I reckon she is." Isaac chuckled. "Just ask Pa."

Henry's face grew somber. "Wish I could. You got to know that . . ."

Isaac squeezed Henry's good shoulder as he stood. He walked to the window. The fields were harvested, but the barns were in need of whitewash. It was all so familiar, yet somehow distant, as though it had only existed in a dream. Somewhere to the south, Pa worked the cotton, ignorant of all that had happened; not knowing about Tempie . . .

Pounding hoofs pulled Isaac from his reverie. The front door flew open and Patrick stormed in, slapping his riding crop against the side of his brown frock coat. Suddenly, he halted and stared. "Well, I'll be . . . Little brother's home from the war again."

"Nice to see you too." Henry waved his fork in Patrick's direction.

"Boy," Patrick said, motioning to Isaac, "unsaddle my horse and rub her down good. If she gets chilled, it'll be your ass."

Isaac didn't move.

"You hard of hearing, boy?"

"Isaac's a free man," Henry said. "He ain't yours to boss around." He set his plate on the end table.

"Free? Says who?" Patrick swung at Isaac with his crop.

Isaac caught Patrick's wrist in mid-arc, glaring as he twisted his arm. "The last man what took a swing at me met his maker on the battlefield."

Patrick's face flushed. His gaze darted from Isaac to Henry, and then back to Isaac, his eyes growing wide as the riding crop slipped from his hand and rattled to the floor.

Isaac released his grip.

"Are you going to let your nigger get away with this?" Patrick stepped toward Henry, wagging his finger. "Did you see what he did? I've a mind to gather a few folks and have an old fashioned lynching."

"The man's free," Henry said. "You touch him, it's murder."

"You don't have the authority to set him free," Patrick replied. "He belongs to this farm, and I've got papers right here." He reached in his coat pocket. "Judge Ellis over at South Boston signed them this morning. I've been assigned conservator of Father's estate. Everything on this farm, including the slaves, belongs to me."

"You can't get away with that," Henry said. "Papa'd never agree . . ."

"He doesn't have to. The judge signed the papers. Father has no say." Reaching under his coat, Patrick withdrew a Navy Colt. He pointed the pistol at Isaac. "I sold your pa and I reckon you'll bring even more. Get over there." He motioned toward Henry with the pistol.

"You're stealing from Papa? I won't let you." Henry struggled to stand, but collapsed onto the sofa, knocking a lamp off the side table. "Damn you to hell."

"There, there little brother. Save your strength, "Patrick said. "You'll need it to rejoin your outfit because you sure aren't staying here. As of today, this farm is mine."

"Like hell . . ." Henry tried to get up again.

Patrick rolled back the hammer and aimed. "Maybe I should finish what the Yankees started . . ."

Isaac dove in front of Henry as the pistol discharged. Searing pain, like a red hot poker, coursed through his shoulder as he crashed to the floor. He tried to push himself up with his one good arm when the deafening roar of a shotgun filled the room and plaster cascaded from a gaping hole in the ceiling above Patrick. Isaac turned toward the second shot.

Morgan sat in his wheelchair in the doorway between the two parlors. Smoke curled from a double-barreled fowling piece resting on his lap.

Florence stood behind him. "Patrick, your papa says drop that pistol, else he gives you the second barrel."

Patrick raised his pistol. "No nigger talks to me like that . . ."

Morgan shouldered the shotgun.

"Your papa, he can't talk so good, but there ain't never been nothing wrong with his hearing." She bent over as Morgan whispered in her ear. "He says, you drops that pistol or you die."

"He's not in charge now. I have papers that say so . . ." Patrick waved his arms like a frustrated barrister pleading his case.

"On the table. Now!" Morgan ordered in a raspy whisper.

Florence bent over again, leaning toward Morgan. She nodded and straightened. "He says you ain't his son no more and you's to set them papers and that pistol on the table, then you's to get on your horse and ride—and if'n you ever sets foot on this farm again, you'll be the one tied to that old oak and I'll be the one giving the lashes."

Morgan cocked the hammer on the second barrel.

"You'll pay for this." Patrick dropped the pistol on the table.

Henry snatched the papers from his hand.

"You bring shame to the McConnell name," Morgan said. He motioned with the barrel of his shotgun. "Go."

Patrick glared at Henry, then turned on his heel and marched out the door.

Morgan lowered the shotgun and took a deep breath, then glanced at Florence. "Lashes?"

She pursed her lips. "I figured it was what you'd say, if'n you was in your proper voice."

* * *

"Been a week," Isaac said. "He ain't coming back." He put his arm under Henry and helped him from the sofa.

"Don't bet on it. I hear he's riding with the irregulars now; they're a bad lot." Henry grimaced as he stood. "And the day's coming when he'll kill me, or I him."

"It won't be today," Isaac said. "So I'd best get you fed."

Together, they walked to the dining room. Morgan, Polly, and Hannah were all seated around the table. Florence stood in the doorway as Isaac eased Henry into his chair.

Staring at Isaac, Morgan pointed to a vacant chair.

Isaac searched his mother's face, then Henry's. What should he do? He couldn't sit there—it wouldn't be proper.

"Papa says sit. You'd best sit." Henry raised his eyebrows and smiled.

Isaac pulled out the chair next to Henry, then hesitated.

"How are you ever going to survive as a free man in Philadelphia if all you do is cower like you just got caught stealing pies off the window sill?" Henry patted the chair seat.

Isaac sat.

"I told Papa how you were heading to Philadelphia when you came back for me," Henry said. "I also told him how you said you were free to choose, and it was your choice to save me. Well, Papa, he's not much on words these days," He smiled and patted Morgan's hand, "but he wants you to have this." Henry laid a paper on the table.

Isaac unfolded the document and stared at it, then shook his head. "I don't reckon I understands all them big words."

Leaning forward, Morgan whispered, "You've been paid for, boy."

Isaac shuddered. "Been sold . . . ?" He glanced quickly at Henry.

"Manumission." Henry tapped his finger on the document. "Freedom papers. Your daddy paid for you, and even if he hadn't, you'd be free anyway for what you done for me, but that alone

314

won't get you back north. These here papers prove you're free, and if anybody questions them, they can write the McConnells of South Boston and we'll vouch for you."

Isaac studied the papers again. A name was written in the center of the page in block letters in dark blue ink:

Isaac McConnell

"Keep them safe." Morgan's hand trembled as he pointed at Isaac. "Where's your pocket?"

Isaac patted the sides of his shell jacket, then shook his head.

"Damn . . ." Morgan's voice rattled from his chest.

"Massa, you'd best be watching that mouth," Florence said. "I has the lye soap and I ain't afraid to use it."

Morgan smiled and pointed to Polly. "Coat," he whispered.

Reaching behind her chair, Polly retrieved a dark blue frock coat. She stood and held it up.

Morgan waved excitedly. "Try it . . ."

Isaac slipped into the coat. The velvet lapels were smooth as a sow's belly. He brushed the sides, slipping his hands into deep, lined pockets.

Henry pulled back the lapel and pointed. Inside, within the satin lining, was another pocket.

Isaac folded his freedom papers and placed them in the inner pocket. "Thank you, Massa McConnell. This here is the nicest coat Isaac ever knowed."

"Patrick won't be needing it anymore," Henry said. "And it's a proper frock for a Philadelphia man." He nodded approvingly, then turned to Florence and held up more papers. "Papa says you and Joseph are free to go too."

Florence stared at Isaac, then turned to Morgan. "Begging your pardon, Massa, but this here be my home and Lord willing, one day my Abraham, he'll be coming back here looking for me. You just put them papers someplace safe 'cause Florence gotta stay right here and wait for her man."

"Good." Morgan smiled. "My Polly . . . that girl can't cook worth a . . ." he winked at Florence. "Hoot."

Chapter Forty-eight
October 1862

"The wagon'll hold me to the roads," Isaac said, brushing his brown wool trousers, another gift from Patrick's wardrobe. "That's where them pattyrollers is."

"But you'll make better time, and that Yankee wagon and the mule, they're yours." Henry rubbed his wounded shoulder as he sat in the parlor. "You have your freedom papers, so the patrols shouldn't give you any trouble."

"I likes traveling light, keeping to the woods. Isaac knows them woods."

"Sure you don't want to wait? Banjo can take you over to South Boston. We'll buy you a train ticket up to Richmond."

Isaac shook his head.

Henry set his tea down and pulled the lap robe over his legs. "You figure you'll really find Raleigh?"

"I won't know less'n I tries."

"Isaac, I . . ." Henry took a deep breath, then looked up. "Write when you get to Philadelphia, you hear?"

"When I gets there, I'll send word," Isaac said. "You get your own self mended—and don't be going back to no army."

Henry laughed. "There you go, trying to take care of me again."

"Too big a job for me," Isaac said. "I reckon I'll leave Miss Hannah to worry on that."

Henry's face reddened.

"I'd best be going. Don't you worry none, I'll be fine." Isaac pulled on his new blue coat.

Henry struggled to his feet and held out his hand. "Friend?"

Isaac grasped the hand and smiled. "I ain't your property."

* * *

The golden hues of evening lingered in the treetops as Isaac strolled to the slave quarters. He'd said his farewells before as a runaway, and again as a slave following his master to war. This was different. Mr. Jones' words came back to him: "Ain't nobody gonna pay no mind to no nigger what's dressed like what he is."

Isaac tugged the lapels of his new coat. He was dressed like what he was—a free man. He smiled as he shoved his hands into the soft, deep pockets. Something in there? He pulled out an envelope someone must have tucked in the pocket when he wasn't looking. Inside, folded within a piece of paper, were two ten-dollar bills, U.S. currency. Isaac placed the bills back in his pocket. He had a new coat, and now, folding money—freedom was feeling mighty good.

He paused at the entrance to the quarters. Several slaves were already gathered around the fire.

Mama Rose looked up from the pot she was tending and waved. "Isaac, get on over here."

"'Evening, Mama Rose. 'Evening, folks," Isaac said as he entered the glow of the fireside.

Banjo came forward. With seeming reverence, he touched the lapels of Isaac's coat. "Ou-wee. Would ya feel that?" Banjo whistled through the gaps in his teeth. "We got us one of them rich northern nigras here. Boy, you'd best be remembering where you come from when you gets up there to Philadelphia, you hear?"

"Sure enough, Banjo," Isaac said. "I'll be thinking on y'all, praying for you too."

Mama Rose gave him a hug. "And we be praying for you, boy. There's a mess of danger between South Boston and that Promised Land. Lord be with you."

Lilly held out a sack. "Some vittles for your journey."

He opened the bag and took a deep whiff of the delicious aroma. "M-m-m. Corn doggers. Thank you Aunt Lilly." Isaac kissed her cheek. "I'll be missing you."

A tear moistened Lilly's eye. She clutched his hand. "We'll be looking after your mama, little Joseph too. Now, you get on. Go find that Promised Land. We'll all be seeing you again one day—over yonder, 'crost that Jordan."

* * *

The path skirted empty fields as it wound through the desolate winter forest and climbed a low rise overlooking a turn in Bennett's Creek. Oaks and poplars reached bare limbs toward the twilight sky around a small clearing. A lone figure stood in the glade. Isaac approached quietly.

"Cato, that you?"

Cato nodded and pointed to the fresh grave. "I comes here as often as I can. I don't understand nothing about what happened, but I know she loved me." He wiped his eyes. "We was fixing to jump the broom."

"You's the man she wanted," Isaac said. He rested his hand on Cato's shoulder.

Cato bowed his head, then took a deep breath and looked up. "I'd best be moving on. Wind's from the south tonight."

"Pattyrollers?"

Cato nodded. "If'n I gets caught over this way again, be another hard whupping. You heading north?"

"Reckon so."

"Then I leaves you to say your good-byes to Tempie. You be safe, Isaac."

"And you." Isaac held out his hand.

Cato looked into Isaac's eyes and smiled. "Lord be with you, friend." He shook hands, then slipped into the darkening forest.

Isaac surveyed the small cemetery. His gaze fell upon a yellow wildflower in bloom next to the path. "Ain't you in the wrong season?" He carefully dug the flower out and replanted it on the mound in front of him.

"I'll be thinking on you, little sister. You tell ol' July that Isaac's been asking about him." He picked up a fistful of dirt. "Good bye, sis. You's in a better place now. Ain't no overseers on your side of the river." The dirt sifted through his fingers, falling silently on the grave.

* * *

As he approached the old post road, Isaac paused and touched his breast pocket. Would his papers work at night? McConnell land ended yonder. He'd best keep to the woods.

A crescent moon hung in the southern sky, casting shadows on the road. He'd head for the small bridge over the stream that ran past the post road and into the woods beyond. It was there he'd last seen his pa. He crawled through the rails of a wooden fence. At least it wasn't raining this time.

"Well, looky here," a gruff voice called from the shadows. "Must be one of them McConnell niggers sneaking off again."

Isaac recoiled as a large horse appeared from the shadows. The rider rose in his stirrups. "Get out here where I can see you, boy."

Isaac stepped away from the fence.

Moonlight caught Clancy's haggard face. "You?" He leaned forward in the saddle. "I thought you got yourself killed in that war."

"Ain't dead yet," Isaac replied, "and you's on McConnell land."

"Don't sass me, boy." Clancy shook a coiled whip. "What's a slave doing out here at night?"

"I ain't no slave."

The whip cracked, slicing Isaac's cheek. "I said don't sass me."

"Ain't no sass." Isaac dabbed at a trickle of blood. "Massa McConnell done gave me my papers."

"Is that so?" Clancy said. "Let's see."

Isaac patted his breast pocket. "They's right here."

"A likely story." Clancy held out his hand. "If you got 'em, give 'em here."

"I ain't giving you my freedom papers."

The whip caught Isaac's shoulder. "A nigger out and about at this hour without papers just might get his self hung."

Isaac darted to the left, but Clancy's horse jumped in the same direction, blocking his path. The whip smacked against Isaac's arm.

"Show me them papers, boy." Clancy snapped his fingers. "If you's really free, show me the proof."

Isaac hesitated, then reached in his pocket. "You look, then you gives 'em back . . ."

Squinting, Clancy held the papers close to his face. He struck a match on the leg of his trousers and held the flame in front of the document as he began to read, "I do hereby emancipate my slave, Isaac, hereafter known as Isaac McConnell . . ." Clancy smiled. "Damned nice of the old man, but I wonder what Patrick thinks about that?" He touched the match to the papers.

Isaac lunged, grabbing the flaming document. Clancy's boot caught him square in the chest and drove him hard to the ground. He rolled onto the paper, extinguishing the flame.

"Damn, is they all burnt?" Clancy snickered. "Guess you ain't free no more. I knows a constable down Yanceyville way who'll pay three hundred dollars for your black hide."

Isaac sprang to his feet and dove at Clancy. The butt of Clancy's whip smashed against the side of his head.

"You ain't learning so good, boy. You's as dumb as that pickaninny sister of yours."

"You?" Isaac balled his fists. "It was you that took her?"

Clancy laughed. "Didn't require a whole lot of taking. I don't reckon she'd ever had the pleasure of a real man before."

Isaac glared. "You son-of-a-bitch . . ."

When the whip cracked again Isaac blocked the blow, wrapping the leather strap around his forearm. He grabbed hold and yanked with all his might. Clancy tumbled from the saddle, crashing hard to the ground.

"I'm through talking," Clancy said, as he sprang to his feet and drew a long knife from his belt. "I'll have those black ears of yours hanging on a cord 'round my neck."

Isaac sidestepped as the blade nicked his ribs. He grabbed Clancy's arm and twisted. The knife fell from Clancy's grip.

"She weren't no good," Clancy said. "Was like humping a cold sack of potatoes." He pulled away from Isaac. "Now it's your time to die, nigger." He drew his pistol.

In a single motion, Isaac scooped a handful of dirt and flung it in Clancy's face as he dove for the pistol. They both hit the ground, struggling for control of the weapon. Clancy rolled on top of Isaac and shoved the pistol in his face. He sneered as Isaac's grip weakened. "You're done now, boy . . ."

Isaac shoved the barrel aside as the weapon fired. Flames seared his cheek. A metallic ringing echoed in his ears, but he held on tightly as they tumbled into the creek. Isaac smashed his fist into Clancy's face, then wrenched the gun away and heaved it out of reach.

Breaking free, Clancy staggered to his feet. "You got lucky, boy. Guess I gotta kill you with my bare hands . . ." He lowered his head and charged.

Isaac sidestepped the attack and caught Clancy in the crotch with his boot. Clancy let out a scream and collapsed to the rocky creek bed.

"You done raped my sister, you whips my family, and you sets my papers on fire," Isaac yelled, standing ankle deep in the water. "Maybe you's the one needs to be dying tonight."

Clancy pushed himself to his knees and glared. "You ain't got the grit . . ."

With a splash, Isaac's foot crashed into Clancy's chin, smashing teeth against teeth. Blood spurted from Clancy's mouth as he collapsed. Isaac pounced, his fist raised, but Clancy swung first, smashing a rock against Isaac's head. The world went dark and then icy water splashed across his face. His vision cleared to reveal Clancy looming over him, a large rock raised above his head.

With a twisting kick, Isaac caught the side of Clancy's knee, cracking bones. As the larger man collapsed, Isaac jumped on him and grabbed his beard with both hands. He shoved Clancy's head beneath the water and pinned it there with his full weight. "This is for Tempie . . ."

Moonlight danced on the submerged, contorted face. Clancy's eyes rolled back. The desperate flailing ended. Isaac relaxed his grip. Killing was the last thing on his mind as he left the McConnell farm earlier that evening, but now he knew—if Clancy had lived, Isaac's family would have always been in peril.

Suddenly the water erupted and Clancy lurched, wild-eyed and sputtering, from the icy stream. His gaze locked onto Isaac. "Damn your black hide . . ."

Isaac pounded the leering face back beneath the water. "Lord, forgive me." He glanced skyward, then grabbed Clancy's beard in both hands. "If'n one verse does for the chicken, best give two for the snake." Using all his weight to hold Clancy under, he began to sing, "Swing low, sweet chariot . . ."

* * *

Had it been two verses or three? Exhausted, Isaac struggled to his feet and took a deep breath. He prodded the corpse with his foot. "Lord, You knows Isaac ain't partial to killing, but that man didn't give me no choice." He splashed cold water on his bruised face.

Behind him, Clancy's horse whinnied. Isaac spun around. A giant of a man stood silhouetted against the night sky.

"He dead?" The deep voice rumbled like an old bullfrog.

"Big Jim, that you? He come at me . . ."

Big Jim waded into the creek and studied Clancy. "They hangs nigras what kills a white man."

"I ain't gonna face that." Isaac balled his fists and crouched, bracing for the fight he was sure would come. "He brung misery down on all of us, Big Jim. He raped my sister and burned my freedom papers. He was pure evil. That man needed killing."

Big Jim nudged the dead body with his foot. "And now he needs burying."

"Wh-what's you saying?" Isaac slowly straightened.

"I's saying the man needs burying." He pointed at the body. "Big Jim knows where the wild hogs won't find them bones." He smiled. "It ain't murder if'n nobody knows he's dead."

Isaac stared at the hulking overseer. "You ain't taking me in?"

"I ain't no hard man, Isaac, least ways, not like you thinks." Big Jim lowered his head. "Big Jim, he just wanted him some of them comforts, so when Massa Patrick says, 'Big Jim you use that whip,' Big Jim, he was scared to say no." He looked at Isaac. "I ain't got the spine to stand up to them white folks, not like you or your pa, but I got spine enough to bury this varmint."

"I'll give you a hand . . ." Isaac grabbed Clancy's feet.

Big Jim waved him away. "You get on up there to that Philadelphia city. There ain't nothing here Big Jim can't handle."

"For sure?"

"Go on, get." Big Jim shooed him with the back of his hand.

"You's a good man, Jim. I's beholding to you." Isaac started across the stream.

"Wait. These yours?" Big Jim passed him the papers.

Isaac smoothed the crumpled document. Morgan's signature still showed next to a seared corner. "Freedom papers." He tucked the document into his pocket. "Reckon they's still legal enough to get me to that Promised Land."

"Lord," Big Jim said. "I prays I can get me some of them papers someday."

"It ain't papers what makes you free," Isaac said. "You's only free when you chooses to be free. It don't matter none what the white man says."

Big Jim nodded. "I prays Big Jim can find the grit to make that choice one of these days." He bent down and took something from around Clancy's neck. "I remembers when you was wearing this." He tossed it to Isaac.

Isaac snatched the object from the air, then opened his hand to reveal a small pinewood pendant threaded on a rawhide cord. His thumb found the raised wooden star as he slipped the lanyard over his head. Clutching his medallion, he sensed his father's arm resting on his shoulders as he searched the heavens. Directly overhead, the drinking gourd sparkled against an ebony sky, its pointer stars showing the way.

ABOUT THE AUTHOR

Jeff Andrews was born in 1947 in Mt. Holly, New Jersey and grew up in neighboring Moorestown, New Jersey. He has an undergraduate degree in Business Administration from Baldwin-Wallace College and a Master of Science in Administration from George Washington University. Jeff served twenty years in the U.S. Marine Corps, including service in Vietnam and Beirut, Lebanon. After retiring from the military Jeff worked in financial services and taught college (part-time) before turning to writing. He now divides his time between writing, church, volunteer work, and family.

Jeff and his wife, Mary Lou, live in Virginia Beach, Virginia.

Coming soon:

The Gandy Dancer

His career is on the rocks. His ex-wife is demanding more money. A woman he can't even remember accuses him of fathering her child. Newspaper reporter Mitch Corsini shrugs and takes another drink. But when his estranged daughter mysteriously disappears, his life finally has a purpose: find the child he's neglected for too long and rekindle the love they once shared.

Mitch's quest takes him to the Virginia mountains and his ancestral home. There, seventy-year-old family secrets and the fate of a long-forgotten railroad worker shatter the foundations of his world, forcing Mitch to confront his true identity as he becomes locked in a life or death struggle to save his daughter.

The Gandy Dancer weaves parallel story lines, one modern, one set in the 1930s. Readers familiar with *The Freedom Star* might appreciate the appearance of Isaac's descendants and his star medallion in this 80,000-word novel.

Learn more about Jeff Andrews' books at:
www.jeff-andrews.com

Made in the USA
Lexington, KY
01 September 2012